PEPPERCORN WOMAN

*'Throw it to the dogs. Do as I say or by Christ
I'll do it myself and throw you in after it!'*
Tyler Cadell's cruel order spells heartbreak
for his wife Garnet and their new-born
baby. She flees to save herself, but cannot
save her child and is taken in by a band of
Black Country Romanies. Although loved
by their leader, Judah Kane, Garnet moves
on once she has regained her strength.
Meanwhile Tyler, hoping to ally his fortune
with that of Lady Olivia Denton, learns of
Garnet's whereabouts and determines to be
rid of her once and for all.

PEPPERCORN WOMAN

PEPPERCORN WOMAN

by

Meg Hutchinson

Magna Large Print Books
Long Preston, North Yorkshire,
BD23 4ND, England.

British Library Cataloguing in Publication Data.

Hutchinson, Meg
 Peppercorn woman.

  A catalogue record of this book is
  available from the British Library

  ISBN   0-7505-1915-0

First published in Great Britain in 2002 by Hodder & Stoughton
A division of Hodder Headline

Published in Large Print 2002 by arrangement with
Hodder & Stoughton Ltd.

Magna Large Print is an imprint of Library Magna Books Ltd.

Printed and bound in Great Britain by
T.J. (International) Ltd., Cornwall, PL28 8RW

Chapter One

'Throw it to the dogs!'

Drained of colour, Tyler Cadell stared at the woman watching him, horror etched deep on her face.

Livid with rage he struck out with a booted foot sending a small ebony table crashing against the wall, a crazed shout echoing after it.

'Do it ... do it now!'

'You can't mean that...'

His eyes hard as blue granite, he lowered his voice to a menacing whisper. 'I mean every word. You feed that monstrosity to the dogs! Do as I say or by Christ I'll do it myself and throw you in after it!'

Huddled beneath a hedge, shawl drawn tight against the lancing rain, Garnet Cadell sobbed as memories trod relentlessly through her mind.

The letter had said Tyler would be home in one week's time. His business in India now finished he had a few things to settle in London and then he would be home.

Tall, fair haired and blue eyed he had swept her off her feet the night they had met at the Commissioner's Ball in Mariwhal. For a year he had paid court to her, calling at her parents' bungalow on the hill that overlooked the bustling Indian town, ever polite, ever the gentleman. There had been no hint at all at that time, no pointer to the cruelty that was the very core of Tyler Cadell. They had been married there in India and a few months later her parents were dead of typhus.

Her loving gentle parents. A long-drawn sob rattling through her chest drowned the sound of a snapping twig.

She had not been allowed to return to Mariwhal to bury the two people she had loved most in the world, to see where they would lie together, to whisper them a last goodbye. *'I cannot allow you to take the risk, my love, perhaps in a year or so, once I can be certain all danger of infection is passed.'*

Why couldn't he have let her return to that town while the infection was rife? That way would have been easier, that way he could have taken what he really wanted from her much sooner and she...? She would have been at peace with her beloved parents.

A sudden flurry of wind caught at the hurrying drops of rain flinging them needle sharp against her face, but deep in the misery of her thoughts she did not feel them, nor did she hear the soft tread of a boot.

Three days! Three days was all it had taken for Tyler to put her on a boat for England. He would follow as soon as he could, meantime Raschid would take care of her.

And he had taken care of her. A sob she could not hold back spilled into the dark silence, and once more the soft tread of feet was masked. Raschid, Tyler's Indian man-servant, had cared for her as a father might, seeing to her every comfort on that long voyage back to England, then on to the Midlands and her father's childhood home. The home where her own child had been born, her beautiful dark-eyed child.

'You'll get nothing but the influenza sitting there in this weather.'

A foot hitting sharp against her thigh brought terror flooding back.

'No!' A scream piercing the rain-swept night. Garnet was on her feet, her thin frame hurling itself forwards. 'I won't let you ... I won't let you kill my baby!'

'Tyler, my dear, you must try to forget, you cannot go on grieving this way, you are making yourself ill.'

'Mrs Benson is right, Cadell.' Arthur Benson nodded agreement with his plump wife. 'All the fretting in the world won't make no difference. The past be over and done with, heed what I says and let it go.'

'You are both very kind and I know you

mean well...'

Rising quickly from his chair, Tyler Cadell strode to the window, his back turned to the industrialist and his wife, his shoulders holding just the right amount of tension.

'We knows what you 'ave been through, it was an ordeal would 'ave killed a lesser man, but you survived it and now 'ard as it is you must get on wi' life.'

'I have my business–'

'Oh ar, lad, you has that,' the older man interrupted, 'but you know what they say about all work and no play, they makes dull companions.'

His head lowering slightly, the taut shoulders dropping a little, Tyler smiled to himself as he caught the woman's sympathetic murmur.

'I apologise.' The huskiness in his voice reached that perfect level, just clear of heart-break. 'My company is not fitting for kindness such as yourself and Mrs Benson have shown since–'

Breaking off, a dramatic half-stifled sob finishing the act, he was hard pressed to keep the smile hidden as Winifred Benson bustled to his side.

'You have no need of apology my dear, Mr Benson meant only that too much of one and too little of another don't be good for a man; work and grief be right, they have their place, but they needs be balanced if a body is to keep his right mind. It has been two years, though to you it must seem forever since your wife and little one was took. But like Mr Benson says that be in the past and hard though it be you must pick up your life again.'

'I have no life without my loved ones...'

If the strangled swallow caught in his throat, Tyler Cadell congratulated himself. Each performance got better, he was as good an actor as Sir David Garrett.

Tears rolling down her ample cheeks Winifred sniffed loudly, fumbling in her pocket for a handkerchief.

This was the opportunity he had waited for, a God-given chance, but he must play it carefully.

Brows drawn together, a look of abject apology on his face, Tyler turned quickly taking the podgy hands between his own long-fingered ones.

'Forgive me, I didn't mean for my grief to touch you. I would not give unhappiness to so caring a person, to ... to one who has been like my own dear mother. How can I tell you–' he raised the hands to his lips, kissing each one in turn, '–how can I show you the remorse I feel?'

'We ain't asking for no apology,' Arthur Benson's florid features broke into a smile as he watched his wife's hands being kissed. 'All we asks is that you picks yourself up and gets yourself out once in a while.'

Eyes glittering with a forced film of moisture, Tyler looked deep into the woman's eyes. She was a fool like her husband, but she could be a useful fool! Still holding one hand he lowered the other, releasing it against her skirts. Then, the faintest trace of a smile touching his mouth, he brushed a tear with his forefinger as he whispered, 'I will enter the world again … if you will guide my path.'

The evening had been a triumph. The exact amount of pathos. His smile broad and open, Tyler Cadell slipped the shirt free of his body, throwing it carelessly across the bed. Nothing worked so well with a woman as a man fighting to suppress his tears, to hide his emotions. Winifred Benson had reacted as he knew she would, she had fallen for his lies … and she would go on falling for them for just as long as it suited him! She would dance to his fiddle as others would, as his housekeeper must dance.

Undershirt following shirt across the bed he stared at himself in the long cheval mirror, at the tall lean body, muscles rippling in the fine shoulders and taut legs. He had cut a dashing figure in the regiment and on the polo field, there were times he almost wished he had not given up his commission, but retiring on the pittance of an Army pension, where every penny would

14

need to do the work of two was not to the taste of Tyler Cadell. So when he had been introduced to the Wintons and their quite pretty daughter he had seen the chance of a vastly more acceptable way of life and had grabbed it with both hands. Garnet had been so easy to woo. Left in England at a school for young ladies, then joining her parents in Mariwhal and being introduced to a handsome Guards officer resplendent in scarlet and gold uniform who paid her the kind of attention she had never been paid before, she had been only too happy to accept his proposal of marriage. Her parents had gladly given their consent. But that was not all the Wintons had given. This house, their tea plantation, together with a thriving spice importing business and of course the lucrative business of supplying metal goods to the Armed Forces of the Crown.

Smiling at the reflection in the mirror he bowed slightly.

'Congratulations, Mr Cadell,' he said aloud, 'you have done well, you have done very well.'

But he was not finished. There were fresh fields to conquer, fresh games to play; and the playing was about to begin.

Taking the freshly laundered night-shirt laid ready for him he slipped it over his head then touched a hand to the face that had months ago lost the last traces of the heat of the Indian sun. No, it showed no trace. He leaned nearer, peering closely in the mirror. A few lines at the corners of the eyes caused by the glare ... but that could happen in any country, it was the colour of his skin, the deep tanning effect of constant sunlight he did not want; but it was gone ... all gone and with it any fears.

But had the fears gone ... truly gone? Throwing back the covers and slipping into bed he reached for the lamp stood on his night table turning the flame down until its dull gleam lit only the immediate area of his pillows, hesitated as he saw the shadows rush forward, their incandescent shapes hovering like dark phantoms. If the fears had gone why the nightly reluctance to extinguish the lamp completely, why this dread of what those circling shadows might hold?

They held nothing!

Annoyed with his thoughts he blew out the tiny flame killing the last of its light, but the thoughts clinging to the edges of consciousness were not so easily got rid of.

It had had to be done!

The child had had to die!

With his eyes shut hard against the menacing shadows he dismissed the threads of guilt trying to weave together in his mind.

To allow it to live would have meant the end of everything he hoped to have, no ...

16

everything he *intended* to have. It would have been a blight on his life, a drawback to all he had gained, to that which was yet to be gained. He had done the right thing, the child was better dead; that way it brought him sympathy, the kind that would open many doors.

Nobody knew, except for Florrie Wilkes and she would not tell, not unless she wanted to end her days on the gallows and that is how it would be by the time Tyler Cadell told the courts his story. A woman who had harboured her mistress in a love affair with her Indian manservant then deliberately destroyed the fruit of their union, had cold-bloodedly thrown the body of a child to the dogs.

There would be no question in the minds of the jurors, those twelve good men and true. Tyler's mouth curved in a cynical smile. They would not doubt the word of a man so devastated he could not bring himself to mingle in society, a man who despite the heart-break could not bring himself to have his wife's name blackened or the memory of an innocent child ostracised, but instead had lived with the misery of the knowledge of what she had done to him, lived in silence and in pain.

Yes, with the child dead his way was clear.

Gritting his teeth against the tortured scream echoing in his memory he turned his face into the pillows.

The child was gone, his wife had not been seen for two years. Tomorrow he would consult a lawyer. It was time for Tyler Cadell to take a new wife.

'You shouldna' 'ave fetched 'er to the camp, the bringing trawls naught but trouble in its wake...!'

Loud and condemning the words carried on the damp night air reaching inside the gypsy caravan. Setting a blanket over the girl she had sponged then dressed in a rough calico night-gown, Hepzibah Kane rose to her feet, her black skirts rustling as she flung open the door. Standing on the uppermost of three steps that reached to the rain-sodden ground she stared at the men sitting around a blazing fire set between the grouped caravans, its dancing flames flickering over their wooden bodies giving life to painted roses, movement to carved leaves and branches.

'We welcomes no gaujo to our midst, to let one lay its head in a gypsy camp, an' that one a juval, be askin' for misfortune. We all be of the same mind.' The man cast a quick glance at the faces of the men listening in silence. 'Tek the woman to where you found 'er, tek 'er now afore the mornin' sun finds 'er 'ere.'

'I teks no warning from you, Lorcan Nash,

if warning be the meaning of your words.'

Hepzibah listened to the answer come from her son, heard the quiet iron of his will and was proud.

'I was elected leader by the Kris, and while I be first man it will be done according to what I say and I say that woman or any other being, whether Romany or gaujo, that be in need of help will find it here in this camp.'

'Then it might be as you should no longer be first man!' Ringlets of dark hair highlighted by the leaping flames, Lorcan Nash stepped forward, a swagger in every line of his lean frame.

Chapter Two

From her place on the steps of the caravan built with her son's own hands, Hepzibah Kane drew her shawl tight about her. This was not the first time Lorcan Nash had spoken those words but tonight her inner sense warned the final challenge was close, a challenge that her son must accept and defeat or he must leave the camp for good, for he would not live with the shame that losing to Nash would bring to him.

From the night-shrouded caravans a host

19

of people drifted closer to the circle of firelight, women grouped behind the men, heads close together as they whispered.

The shadows no hindrance to her keen eyes, Hepzibah scanned the faces of the Kris, the heads of each family who together formed the council of elders responsible for the everyday running of this small community and who had elected her son their leader. But each face was impassive, showing no sign of interest or favour.

'Could be the time 'as come when you should step aside, give way to a better man,' Lorcan Nash sneered, 'that better man bein' me, unless o' course there be another wishin' to mek the challenge, in which case I'll be glad to tek 'im on in due course.'

'Every last man in this camp be a better man than you and a snake would prove a finer first man. But make your challenge Nash, and let the fates decide the outcome, as for myself this is what I give for your chances.'

At the murmur of voices, Hepzibah watched her son spit into the fire, and saw the look of fury that crossed the other man's face.

'Wait!'

Her voice rang clear bringing a silence that gave no ease to the tension that bound the two men in a ring of steel.

'Once made the challenge must be

20

followed through, that be Romany law; who emerges as victor be as it may, but first man can only be elected by the Kris, that too be Romany law.'

Coming down the last of the steps to stand in the circle of light she stared into the sneering face.

'So then, Lorcan Nash, before the words are said, remember, a barking dog meks no kill.'

Amid the murmurs of the women and the nods of the men, Lorcan Nash grinned.

'If it be that by delay you thinks to save your son from dishonour, Hepzibah Kane, then I pities you for it be a bitter cup of shame you'll drink from.'

Throwing the black shawl back from her head, Hepzibah stood proud, the light of the fire lending a coronet of blue to hair still the colour of a raven's wing, flames turning the jet of her eyes to gleaming crimson.

Sharp and clear as the notes of a ringing bell her words reached every ear. 'I will never know shame from my son, and you will never bring content nor pride to this camp.'

His grin became a derisive laugh, Lorcan Nash threw a look to the listening men.

'How like a juval ... how like a woman! So let the son prove whether the words of the mother hold any worth for I says her lies!'

Grasping her son's arm, restraining him as he lunged at the laughing face, Hepzibah stared for a moment into the fire and when she again looked at Nash her eyes glowed like the logs themselves.

'You doubt the words of my tongue...'

Every other voice suddenly stilled, the shadows seeming to press closer as if they also would listen.

'...you query the truth wrapped in them, then listen again, Lorcan Nash, and this time you need hold no doubts. Before the third night of the second rising of the full moon the wagon of Lorcan Nash will be given to the flames!'

'No!' Skirts and hair flying a young woman thrust her way through the ring of people, dropping to her knees before Hepzibah. 'Take back the words,' she screamed, 'take them back!'

'The words fly on the wind,' Hepzibah shook her head, 'they cannot be called back.'

'Get back to your mother!' Lorcan Nash's face had lost its sneering grin, a pallor visible as he hauled the young woman to her feet. 'I need no wench to plead for me an' I sets no store by the ramblings of a woman.'

'Then you be a fool!' A second, older woman stepped from the assembled group, light from the camp fire glinting on strands of silver spread through her dark hair.

'You should set store for everyone here knows the words of Hepzibah Kane be ones we all should mark.'

Pushing the girl aside she faced Hepzibah and this time her words were accompanied by a look of pleading.

'Take back the words, lift your curse from the last o' my chavvies, the only one of my children left to me, take back that which ye 'ave laid upon my son.'

Flickering and dancing the flames darted fingers of light over Hepzibah's face, playing off eyelids closed for a moment and when they opened showed eyes that shone with a light that owed nothing to the fire. Her gaze travelling beyond the shadows her body trembled slightly then she was speaking again, her voice strangely flat and calm.

'The way o' man's life be written upon 'is forehead at the second of 'is entering into the world and the time of 'is leaving be set alongside. As it be marked so will it be done. For Lorcan Nash it be written, before the third night of the second rising of the full moon...'

'No!' The girl screamed again throwing herself forward beside Nash's mother; her face was twisted with anger but it was fear held the uppermost note as she shrieked. 'Tis not true, tis said only to protect her own, her knows Lorcan will defeat him in the challenge, her knows Judah Kane be no match, for that reason her lays that curse, to keep–'

The screams of the girl being dragged away by two older women broke the silence that had settled over the group as Hepzibah had spoken. Now, muttering between themselves they watched the women stood within the circle of firelight.

The wild cries of the girl floating back from the shadows penetrated the dream-like trance and once more Hepzibah spoke, this time with her usual penetrating look, the flat monotony of her tone completely gone.

'Hepzibah Kane lays no curse.' Her words were for the woman who moments before had pleaded with her, but a shiver of breeze carried them to every ear. 'Tis the hand of fate guides the way of Lorcan Nash, there be none here has the changing of that.'

A sob broke from the lips of the other woman stood by the fire and her head dropped forward on to her chest. Pulling her shawl over her head she turned away, speaking not a word as she climbed into her caravan.

Glaring at the man who had as good as branded him a coward Judah handed his mother to the stool kept beside their wagon, before stepping back to the rim of the blazing fire, the reflection of the flames ringing his head with a gleaming halo as he faced the man who challenged him.

'So, Nash…' Clear and firm as those of his mother his words reached every corner of

24

the listening camp. '…you wish to be called first man, then make your challenge now, speak the words, for such be the right of every man here. Say it now, as for the others they will do as all true Romanys do, honour the victor and follow his lead.'

'There'll be another night, Judah Kane!' His mouth twisting, Lorcan Nash spat out the words as though each one was poison on his tongue. 'A night when no fire nor light of moon shows what might be waiting.'

'What might show *you.*' Judah's voice rang with contempt. 'That be your way, the way of a snake; but then I knows your way well as does every man here, as does the widow Korjyck. Wait in the dark, strike from behind, that be the choosing of Lorcan Nash. Then wait for me as you waited for Korjyck, but be sure you've paid your tributes to the god you follow before you try your hand, for that will be the last night you will strike any man.'

His glance travelling over the faces of the watchers, Judah's voice rose.

'The acceptance of the challenge will be met from any who cares to make it. Tonight it was not offered, but should it be you of the Kris desire Lorcan Nash be leader then I will step aside now. Let each man make his sign.'

It took only a moment for the first man to answer. Rising to his feet he lifted one hand in a slow deliberate movement then slashed it horizontally through the air, his voice loud as he answered. 'This be the choosing of Clee Tuckett.'

One by one the rest followed, each denying Nash, each choosing the leadership of Judah. Only Lorcan Nash made no reply. Hate swirling like a cloak about him he stormed away, merging into the night shadows.

They had made their choice. Hepzibah took her smoke-blackened kettle, filling it from the leather water jack hung on the side of the wagon. Her son would remain as first man but how long would it be before Lorcan Nash tried again, how long before he carried out the threat he had made this night? She could find the answer in the cards, consult the crystal, but her powers had been given to serve others, she must not use them for herself.

Hooking the kettle over the glowing embers as the last of the men drifted away to sleep she fetched her son's blanket from the caravan. While the gaujo woman slept inside he could not make his bed beneath it, he would rest with old Ned Sproat.

Taking the blanket, Judah watched his mother brew a can of tea. Had he done the wrong thing in bringing that woman here, would it bring discord to the camp? But in bringing her he had followed the Romany way: *refuse not your hand to any man or creature that be in need.* Was that not the age-old rule, had it not been followed from time beyond memory?

'Your conscience be troubled.' Hepzibah handed him a tin mug filled with hot tea.

Squatting on his haunches, Judah stared at the remnants of the fire.

'Should I have forgotten the teaching?' he asked quietly. 'Should I have left the woman where I found her?'

Looking at him, the gleam of firelight touching his strong handsome face, Hepzibah was suddenly seeing a night more than thirty years ago; the night her man had been named first man. He had been strong and handsome as her son was now. He had known that to be leader of his people needed more than the strength of his arm, it needed strength of heart. Wisdom would come with the years but without knowledge that came from the heart and the strength of will to carry it through then leadership was not his right. The father had always weighed the wisdom of the head with the mercy of the heart, would his son do the same?

'The day will be born soon,' she answered softly, 'if it be you thinks you was mistook in your action then return the woman to the place you found 'er afore the cock crows.'

Sipping her own warming drink Hepzibah sensed the hesitation in the figure hunched

27

at her feet. She had answered as she should, the decision must be his alone.

'P'raps it be I was wrong, could be that bringing a gaujo woman here will bring dissension...'

Taking a long-stemmed clay pipe and small leather pouch from the pocket of her voluminous black skirts, Hepzibah pressed tobacco into the bowl drawing a burning stick from the fire to light it.

'...p'raps I should have talked with the Kris first, asked the elders what they thought...'

Puffing at her pipe, watching the smoke from it rise towards the moon-silvered sky, Hapzibah Kane listened to her son wrestle with his doubts. Wisdom of the mind, mercy of the heart, strength of will... Judah must find the way alone.

'...but asking would have altered nothing...'

Teeth clamping on the pipe stem, Hepzibah felt the blood freeze in her veins. Being leader of his people, the head of the camp counted for naught with her, listening to the song of his heart was what she desired for her son.

'...nor will I alter that which is done. The woman stays till she be well, and if because of it my wagon must travel alone then that is how it will be, I will not break with the law of the Romany even though the woman be not of our kind.'

Rising to his feet he drew a knife from the sash bound about his middle passing the blade across the heel of one palm, his voice brushing the shadows.

'Bound in blood Romany to Romany,
bound in blood brother to brother,
bound in blood to Romany law.'

The time-worn words drifted into the night. Watching the tiny drops fall into the flames, blending crimson with crimson at the fire's glowing heart, Hepzibah breathed her thanks to the powers she felt were watching. They had guided her son as, God willing, they would always guide him. Judah Kane had made his decision and sealed the same in blood, he would follow the true path people had followed since the birth of time; the food and shelter of his camp fire would be offered to all who needed it, he would uphold the ancient way, the way of the true Romany, the way of right.

The pipe still held between her teeth she remembered what had been shown to her as she led that girl into the wagon. It had happened as it always did. Her mind, her very body had seemed to empty of all that was Hepzibah Kane, and in the place of lungs and stomach only a great all-filling breathlessness; but the heart remained, beating with a truth she felt throb in her soul, pulsing with the words, soundless yet clear as any bell, words that were none of her own. But there, in the dim light of the wagon's lantern there had been no words, only the vision that floated before her inner eyes, a vision she should share with her son.

Tapping the remains of precious tobacco from her pipe back into the tin she returned both to her pocket. Rising from the stool she glanced at Judah.

'There be another blanket in the wagon, come fetch it.'

Watching her step towards the caravan he frowned. 'You knows I shouldn't be stepping inside the wagon so long as the woman be there.'

Already at the steps his mother turned. 'I be at your side, think you one o' they would say that Hepzibah Kane allowed aught that be unclean?'

'All in this camp knows that be not so, as I myself knows. But to enter a wagon holding any unmarried raklie, save the girl be his own sister, be forbidden, that too is part of our law and I will not break it.'

Having watched him walk away, taking his one blanket to the wagon of Ned Sproat, Hepzibah poured the last of the tea from the kettle, nursing her tin mug between her hands. The father and the son, they were of one blood, one heart. The honour of the first was bred deep in the bone of the other. Judah Kane would not dishonour the ways of the Romany, not even for his mother.

He was worthy to be called first man.

Chapter Three

'No … please, please not the child, don't kill my baby, no … o … o!'

Eyes wide, senses flaring with terror, Garnet sat up sharply. The nightmare again, the nightmare of remembering the same horror that lay with her at night and walked with her by day, the horror that would never stop.

'But I didn't do anything,' she whispered, the pain of her dream still tingling on every nerve. 'I did not deceive you with Raschid…'

'So you be wakened.'

Eyes that had been seeing only the past swivelled towards the broad shaft of daylight that danced about a black figure. Amah? But it couldn't be, the woman who had been both nurse and servant during her time in India never dressed in black. 'Tyler!' A sob breaking from her, Garnet shrank back.

'I be not named as you call.' Hepzibah

31

stepped into the narrow confined space that served as living and sleeping quarters. Nor be I the one as terrifies the soul inside ye.' The last only in her thoughts she closed the door behind her. Pricked ears and watching eyes would wait a while longer before satisfying their curiosity.

Blinking in the pale light that dribbled in through the one small window set above the bed she had been sleeping in, Garnet looked fearfully at the black shape.

'Please, I have done no wrong, I have taken nothing but a few berries from the hedge...'

'Quiet yourself, wench.' Hepzibah stepped further into the light. 'There be none here accuses ye.'

'Where is here?' Nervousness throbbing in her voice Garnet glanced quickly around the cramped space then back to the woman watching her.

'Here be the home of a Romany.'

Pushing off the blanket, Garnet swung her legs to the floor, blood rushing to her head so she swayed on her feet.

'Ye best be not tryin' to walk, not for a while. As it be ye'll find that bed be kinder to ye than the underside of a hedge.'

'Romany?' Her sight as yet still unclear, Garnet watched the black shape move, stand beside the tiny boxed-in stove, then Hepzibah fed wood into its red mouth.

'Them as don't follow the travellin' ways knows us as gypsies.'

'Gypsies?'

'Ar, wench, gypsies!' Hepzibah turned, rubbing her hands on a cloth taken from beside the stove. 'Robbers, cut purses, thieves, rogues and vagabonds, ye tek your pick for each be names given by them as knows no better; but whichever ye chooses to name us by there'll be no hurt come to ye in this camp nor any to hold ye should ye choose to go. Bide or stay it all be one to Hepzibah Kane.'

'Please, I meant no disrespect. It was just I had ... have no idea...' Trying to stand, to follow the shape she now recognised as a woman dressed in wide black skirts, a shawl fastened about her shoulders as she clambered out of the wagon, Garnet's senses reeled again forcing her to drop back to the bed.

'It were Judah.' Once more closing the door left open behind her as she had entered the dimly lit room, Hepzibah held out the tin mug in her hand. 'He found ye near unconscious an' soaked through wi' rain. Under a hedge ye were a'moaning and a'sobbin', an' all to do wi' throwin' summat to the dogs.' That was enough for now. Hepzibah offered the mug again. She would not speak of the cries in the night or of the names she had heard as the girl had tossed

33

and turned, a terror of the mind haunting the sleep.

Murmuring her thanks, Garnet took the drink, relishing the wonderful taste of hot tea. After so many days and nights of nothing but berries from the hedgerows and water from brooks and streams the comfort of it brought tears stinging against her eyelids.

'There be a dish of oatmeal over the fire and a sup o' warm milk to crown it. It be nothing grand but ye be welcome to partake o' it should ye care.'

Hot porridge! The very thought of eating something warm was like a blessing from heaven. But it was a blessing she could not accept. Whoever this woman and the man she named as Judah were, she could not reward their kindness by taking their food.

'The tea is most welcome and I thank you kindly for it,' she said, tears thick in her throat, 'it is more than enough for me, I have no need of food.'

'If that be *your* thinkin' then ye be sore in need o' brains!' Hepzibah snapped. 'It teks no more'n half of one eye to see ye be near starved.'

Laying the tin mug on a chest of drawers which doubled as a table, Garnet's hand shook as much as her voice.

'I ... I cannot accept what I cannot pay for either with money or with labour...'

'The offer of Romany comfort, a place beside his fire and a share of his meal comes wi'out price tag!' The old woman's rebuttal was swift and sharp. 'It be given free and of the heart. Take it or leave it as ye will but to balance it against payment comes of ill breeding!'

'No, I did not mean it as such ... please, I–'

Pushing to her feet, her hand stretching towards the woman, Garnet took one step then crumpled, falling and twisting down into endless darkness.

Not too quickly. Tyler Cadell sat astride a snorting stallion, his glance roving over the land brought to him by marriage. He must not re-enter society too rapidly. He had done very nicely from that little venture, it wouldn't do to risk spoiling his image of soul-destroyed husband. Isaac Winton had only one child and to her had come his money and various businesses. Yes, Garnet Winton had brought the wealth he needed but not the wealth he wanted. He deserved more than a house in a town black with the soot of iron foundries, its horizon pock-marked with the stacks of chimneys and the winding wheels of coal pits. He deserved it and he would get it, and the Winton money was his stepping stone.

They had had no idea, so happy to give

their only child to a man who would love and care for her; and he had done that ... for a month. He smiled, taking in the cornfields and meadowland that as yet still girdled Bentley, the morning sun darting beams of gold-white light on the canal that ran across them. It had been one of the money-spinning ideas of his late father-in-law to allowing the construction of a waterway that gave him not only part ownership of it but free passage for his narrow boats carrying coal from his mines as well as iron and steel from his foundries.

What had prompted the man to go to India? His tea interests there were being well managed. Perhaps it was simply a desire to see more of the world than the so descriptively named Black Country. But going to India had not been one of Isaac Winton's better moves, not for him or his family ... but for Tyler Cadell it had been a master stroke.

Eyes travelling over recently harvested fields towards the nearby Bentley Mill they rested momentarily on the small gypsy camp nestled in a hollow. He could have Raschid call the constabulary and have them run off his land; or he could do it himself with a shotgun, have himself a bit of fun. That was the only thing he missed after resigning his commission, the sport of the chase, and it hadn't much mattered whether the hunted were animals or members of the indigenous population, it was one and the same to him, both species were vermin! Yes, he might well return later, pot himself a few gypos.

Turning the horse about, setting it to a steady trot he rode back towards the house, his thoughts already turned to the conversation of last night. He had played the part of the broken-hearted husband and father to perfection, in fact he had enjoyed it so much he just might let it go on a while longer, let the foolish Winifred Benson carry on with an idea she thought to be hers alone but in reality was one that had long dwelt in the mind of Tyler Cadell.

A second marriage. Yes, he had harboured the thought, but a second wife would be no daughter of a small-town industrialist, Tyler Cadell would marry into gentry; his new bride must bring him position as well as money.

'Rub him down well, and have the bay ready for this afternoon, I fancy doing a spot of shooting.'

In the stable yard of Bentley House he swung from the saddle, throwing the reins into the face of the manservant who ran to meet him.

'There are visitors...'

Tyler turned away. 'I don't want to be bothered. Tell whoever it is to leave their card.'

Blinking against the sting of leather around his eye the man answered. 'It is Mrs Winifred Benson...'

'Tcha!'

He was not interested. Raschid's glance followed the tall figure striding towards the gracious old building. Would he be the same once he had read that other visiting card?

The gaujo had not left the camp, in fact she had not set foot out of that wagon. Packing a willow basket with clothes pegs cut from beech twigs and sprigs of dried heather picked from the northern moors, Marisa Lakin let her anger show. Her being brought here had created the perfect opportunity for Lorcan to make the challenge, to fight Judah Kane for the right to be called first man, but the words had not been said; Lorcan had backed off, and all because of Hepzibah Kane. Covering the basket with a blue and white chequered cloth, Marisa swung it on to her hip, cradling it with one arm. That woman's way of speaking had the rest of their folks in awe of her, but not so Marisa Lakin. She was not feared of the old crone or of her prophecies. They could all prophesise, they could all tell of things yet to be and if they didn't come to pass then that was the changing whims of fate! But the tellings of Hepzibah Kane had always come to pass! She kicked angrily at the dog come hopefully to lie at her feet, cursing it as it slunk away. But there was one thing the all-knowing Hepzibah didn't know, and wouldn't until it were too late. Glaring at the prettily painted caravan Marisa smiled, hate in every nuance of it. No, the woman would not know and by the time she did Lorcan Nash would be first man.

'I'll walk a 'ways wi' ye, there be herbs and plants I be a wantin'.'

Marisa turned to see the widow Korjyck watching her. Despite herself Marisa shivered as she met those piercing brown eyes. This woman did not simply look into another's face, she peered into their very soul. And what had been seen in hers? She glanced down at the basket, fussing unnecessarily with the cover. Had the wife of Tonio Korjyck seen the truth of what had happened a year ago, the truth which was only hinted at, which none in the camp could prove? But what if she had, what if she knew! There was nothing she could do, nothing any of them could do.

'You be welcome to walk along o' me.' Pulling her shawl over her head Marisa forced a smile. 'I be thinking to try the big house over past yonder meadow, could be the mistress might like her palm read.'

'Could also be as they sets the dogs on ye, t'ain't everybody welcomes a gypsy past their gate. Might be ye'll find better pickings

39

in the town.' Setting her own basket on her hip the older woman set off, following the line of the hollow to crest it at the further end.

Walking beside her Marisa cursed inwardly. It had been set for her to meet with Lorcan, they had few chances to be alone together and this was one she had lain awake thinking of, this was to have been the chance to tell her plans to him; but he would see her and the widow walking together and the heath would swallow him like a mist wraith in the morning sun. Her chance was gone thanks to the woman hobbling beside her; it was a pity she hadn't met the same fate as her man! Bitterness coating her tongue like acid, Marisa walked in silence. Maybe one night soon she would!

A distance away Bentley House stood square and solid, its double rows of bow-top windows reflecting the sun like precious gems, the lawns and neatly kept fields adding a further beauty to its setting. Reaching their boundary, Marisa paused to stare. The gaujo house was very fine but she had seen grander and had often been allowed into a kitchen and given a silver sixpence for telling a fortune.

'I'll risk the dogs.' She looked at the other woman. 'Good fortune in the town.'

Watching her walk away towards the house, skirts flouncing with every step, head

40

high beneath its covering of black shawl the older woman's eyes glowed with their own hatred. That wench and the son of Beshlie Nash together were responsible, they had killed her man, killed and robbed him; there was no proving of it but she knew, deep in her heart she knew. 'Good fortune go with ye,' she whispered beneath her breath, 'but the days of its walking beside ye be numbered.'

'There be heaviness in your soul...'

A sprig of dried lavender in her hand, Marisa shook her head slowly, a look of sympathy on her handsome face as she spoke to the woman standing squarely in a doorway set in the rear of the house. The barking of dogs locked away somewhere had the woman open the door before she reached it. But she hadn't called for the animals to be let loose.

'...and a great sorrow in your heart...'

The woman was already hooked. Marisa forbade the smile of triumph rising inside her. This one would be good for sixpence, maybe more.

'...a sorrow you hide from the world, but it be there in your eyes. Buy a sprig o' lavender from a poor gypsy, let the luck it carries lighten your burden.'

'I don't want no lavender!' Florrie Wilkes took a step backwards, the door already

41

closing. 'An' you be off afore the master sees you, he don't tek kindly to gypsies, he be like to set the dogs on you!'

'Lavender don't be all I carries.'

Marisa stood her ground. The door would not close completely.

'I wants no ribbons nor lace neither!' The door closed a little more.

'What be in my basket don't be all I has to offer, I can tell you the answers to questions that have long tormented you, I know the secrets you hold in your heart.'

Slowly the door opened wide as before. Marisa remained still, the lavender in her hand.

'You reads the palm, you tells the future?'

'Clear as your mistress reads her book.'

'Ain't no mistress to this house.'

That was the first of her information. Marisa tucked the sprig of dried herb beneath the cover of her basket. Years of learning from her mother and grandmother had taught her how to lead the gaujo women into disclosing things, information that could be twisted and woven like threads in a tapestry and then produced, seeming as if by some mystic power she already knew their past; to predict future events from that was child's play.

'But that don't be the way it 'as always been.'

Marisa could have laughed at the surprised

look her answer brought to the woman's face. It was only common sense, a house of this age must once have had a mistress, more like several, but the woman was obviously thinking of its last one, that was her second item of information.

'There were times this house was happy,' she risked her chances of hitting a third nail on the head, 'times when a child's voice was heard in its rooms.'

'Hardly a child.' Unwittingly Florrie added to the gypsy girl's knowledge. 'No more than a babby, not yet reached its first half year poor little mite and dead of its father's fury.'

'And it's mother's heart broken.' Marisa's face the picture of innocent sympathy she followed Florrie into the scullery. Not the kitchen this time but good enough. Laying her basket on the floor she settled on the well-scrubbed chair the woman pointed to and, as she too sat down, took both hands between her own.

'You 'ave long served in this house,' she began after seeming to scrutinise both palms, 'you 'ave seen it go through good times and bad.'

'Ar,' Florrie nodded, 'I worked for them as was parents to the young mistress.'

Was ... young ... both words registered in Marisa's mind.

'They were good people, and kind to the

43

folk that worked for them, especially to you,' she said softly.

Florrie nodded again. 'Ar, that be so. Kind hearted was the Wintons, and trustin'; it was to Florrie Wilkes they left the carin' of their daughter whenever her come 'ome from her school.'

'They saw their child in safe hands while they was in foreign places.'

Tracing a line of the woman's palm with one finger, Marisa held her breath. Would the woman follow the path being so carefully laid for her?

'I doubts any place be more foreign…'

Marisa breathed again keeping her glance on the hands of the woman clucking like a hen.

'…India, I asks what be more foreign than that, an' what place more dangerous wi' all them brown folk, not white like a good Christian, they most like follows after the devil an' I told Garnet so when her set her mind to followin' after her parents; you be settin' foot in a land that be no place for a good livin' innocent young wench, I told 'er, but Florrie Wilkes would 'ave fared as well 'olding her breath.'

'I see a young woman,' Marisa spoke quietly moving her finger over the palm as if the other woman's words had not been heard, 'a pretty girl of tender years. She be laughing … telling you of something it be in

44

her mind to do, but you ... you are not happy, you think there be unhappiness waiting, waiting in a land far from this one. There!' She pointed a forefinger, jabbing it at a spot in the woman's hand where two lines joined. 'There is the parting, there the heartbreak. Two lives ended, a man and a woman.'

'Ar.' Florrie sniffed. 'They ended afore knowing another had begun.'

Pretending not to have heard, making it seem she was in the throes of a power beyond herself, Marisa droned on, her finger moving over the lines etched deep into the older woman's palm.

'The girl is weeping but there is one beside her who does not ... a man who does not weep.'

'No, that one 'ad no cause to weep. The Wintons dying and leavin' all to their only child were the savin' o' Tyler Cadell...'

Marisa kept the smile from her voice. 'They died before another had begun', that was what this foolish gaujo had told her, that was enough to see her safely over the next hurdle.

'She weeps for her parents, for their not knowing she carried their grandchild in her womb, but there be no sorrow in the heart of the man she took for husband. He sees only his own good fortune in their passing, and now the girl given to him to cherish as they had...'

45

'Be God knows where!' Shaking on a sob the words burst from Florrie. 'The child 'er bore here in this 'ouse be dead an' her–'

The sound of a door closing shut off the rest.

Marisa's glance lifted as the woman turned. Stood framed in the doorway of the scullery a brown-faced man dressed in baggy white trousers, a white cloth bound about his head, stared at them with impassive brown eyes.

Relief plain in her gasp Florrie Wilkes waved a hand abruptly. 'Get out of my kitchen. I've told you afore I'll 'ave none of your 'eathen prying in 'ere!'

His glance travelling over Marisa, resting briefly on her own eyes, the man turned away.

'I thought for a moment it were the master.' Florrie rose, fumbling in the pocket of her skirts for a coin she pressed into Marisa's hand. 'But it were only the Indian, though chance be the master be close behind, where one be the other ain't far, so you takes your payment and go. His temper wouldn't be helped by findin' such as you in his 'ouse.'

Several fields between her and Bentley House, Marisa paused. It had been a rewarding half hour. She tossed the shilling, watching it turn and tumble throwing off darts of light as the sun's rays danced on its silver body. Catching the coin as it fell to her hand she curled her fingers tightly over it. A very rewarding half hour; but somehow she felt the full reward had not yet been paid.

Chapter Four

The Lady Olivia Denton.

Tyler Cadell tapped the small gold-edged visiting card against his fingers.

Lady Olivia. Wealthy? Maybe. Old? Perhaps. Social position? A calling card sporting a coronet would say yes, and definitely one of some importance. Maybe the lady had an unmarried female relative! Slipping the card into the pocket of his riding coat he made for his room at the same time calling loudly for Raschid. His afternoon of hunting could wait, he would pay a call on Mrs Winifred Benson.

Flinging off his clothes, letting them lie where they fell, he padded into the bathroom.

'Nothing too heavy.' He glanced at the bottle of perfumed bath oil the manservant held over the bath of hot water. 'I don't want to go in that house smelling sweeter than its owner, though God knows that wouldn't take a lot of doing.'

47

Nodding acceptance of oil of magnolia he stepped into the bath, sliding down into the scented water.

This could well prove to be what he wanted. But what if there were difficulties concerning his former marriage? But that was a stupid question. What difficulty could there be! He had not seen his wife for two years, everyone he knew, or at least everyone that mattered thought her dead with her child...

The child! Thank God it was dead. He had seen with his own eyes, seen Raschid throw it to the dogs, watched as they tore it apart devouring every last trace; and Garnet...? When he returned to that room she was gone. It had all turned out well for him. He smiled to himself as brown hands soaped his back. It had left the way clear, clear to realise his prospects; Tyler Cadell would no longer be an unknown, a small-town man with small-town acquaintances, he would be a man of consequence with friends of con-sequence!

Dressed and seated again astride his favourite stallion he kicked away the figure stood holding the animal's head, not bothering to look behind as the manservant fell back against the wall of the stable. He had refused the carriage, this visit must appear unrehearsed, informal, made on the spur of the moment with no intention of any visit to Bentley House.

'Buy a posy for your lady, sir?'

His attention dulled by his thoughts. Tyler was not ready for the voice that seemed to rise from the bracken. Instinctively his whip hand rose.

'I meant no harm, sir. I offered naught but a posy.'

Smiling, teeth white against skin honeyed by the sun, black hair falling like heavy rain clouds about her shoulders, Marisa rose to her feet. It had been a long wait but some inner force had held her there, a force which said that in that home and its owner could be found rich rewards – reward enough to set up a gypsy girl for life.

'I could have trampled you!' Tyler checked the startled horse. 'Have you no more sense than to come up behind a man?'

'You wouldn't have trampled me,' Marisa's eyes sparkled like black diamonds. 'I saw you coming long afore you reached me, nor did I come from behind.'

Staring into those glittering eyes Tyler felt a familiar twitch on his groin. The wench was attractive, a shilling might be well spent.

'Nor did you have the sense to move away.'

Watching the hand holding the whip lower to his side, Marisa drew aside her shawl displaying high taut breasts and tiny waist.

'No, sir,' she smiled, 'I had the sense to stay.'

'Sleep, my precious one, sleep. I won't let him hurt you, Mother won't ever let him hurt you; I love you, my darling, my baby...'

A bowl of rabbit broth in hand, Hepzibah Kane listened to the ramblings of the girl sleeping in her bed. Most of the day had gone in sleep, but it were troubled sleep that would bring no refreshment of mind or body.

Setting the broth on the stove she opened a drawer of the chest, taking out a cloth of fine white cotton. The woman her son had fetched to the camp had suffered, that were seen from the thinness of her body and the ragged state of her clothes though they had been kept clean; only the remnants of last night's storm had clung to the edge of skirts and petticoats. A woman of quality! Hepzibah nodded to herself as she shook open the cloth. The woman Judah had found huddled beneath the hedge was poorer than a church mouse, but her was a woman of quality.

'No ... don't take her ... no ... o ... o!'

'Shh ... it be well, it be well.' Speaking softly as the younger woman woke, Hepzibah closed the door. There were listening ears close by, but the time were not yet they should be satisfied.

'You were dreamin' tis all, naught to be a' feared on.'

Pretending not to notice the look of heart-break cross the drawn face as the woman put aside the blanket she had nursed against her breast, Hepzibah spread the cloth over her knees then handed her the broth.

Had it been this day, or of a day past? Frowning, Garnet tried to remember. The woman had offered her oatmeal then taken umbrage at her saying she could not pay for it either with money or yet with labour. But this bed, the care that had obviously been taken of her, this woman need not have given it, need not have accepted her into her home; but she had and she had been repaid with rudeness.

'I'm sorry...'

The thought turning into words she looked at the woman fetching a spoon from a tin box kept beside the stove.

'...I meant no harm when I spoke of payment, I–'

'Then there be none took.'

Handing over the spoon, Hepzibah cut the explanation short.

'All deeds be the same, good or bad they be seen by the Lord and tis Him will make payment.'

'*All deeds be seen by the Lord.*' Left alone, Garnet heard the words ring in her mind. Had He seen the deed done by her husband, had He seen her baby killed? Tears rolling down her cheeks she stared at the bowl on her lap. Had the Lord made payment for that?

How long had it been, how long had she searched for a child she knew to be dead, how long had she been blind to the truth? Too long! She stabbed the spoon into the broth. She had given way to fantasy too long, now *she* would do the work of the Lord, somehow she would exact vengeance, somehow she would make Tyler Cadell pay for the murder of his child!

Her meal finished she climbed from the bed, dressing in the clothes set on a frame about the arm stove, clothes that smelled of fresh heather and had been patched with neat stitches.

With steps still a little uncertain she left the caravan, pausing as the faces of several women turned her way.

'I'll tek that, you sit yourself down on your stool afore ye sits on the ground, them legs ye be on don't be strong enough yet to 'old ye though ye be no further through than a fish atween the eyes!' Grumbling loudly, Hepzibah took the empty bowl and spoon, seeing Garnet safe on the three-legged stool before taking them to wash in a bowl of water.

'Be ye feelin' better, wench?'

'Much better, thank you,' Garnet answered the newcomer.

''Tis the widow Korjyck's potions be the doin' o' that, tis them give ye the sleep ye needed.' Hepzibah returned a nod to her visitor.

'T'were only herbs brewed in a drop o' water.' The woman who had enquired of her health answered as Hepzibah indicated her. 'They grows on the 'eath an' be free to all.'

'Free they be an' cost naught 'cept the pickin' o' 'em, but without the knowledge they be good as useless.' Hepzibah laid the freshly washed bowl and spoon on an up-ended log to dry.

'How long have I been here?' Garnet had waited until the other woman moved away before asking her question, then waited again while Hepzibah filled her clay pipe and settled with it on an upturned bucket.

'A night an' a day.' The old woman puffed. 'An' afore ye says as ye must be gone think ye on this. Health of the body be quickly recovered but the sickness of the heart be not so quick to fade. Biding here among the folk of this camp ye'll find comfort though it be of no great measure, but most of all ye'll find a place where ye can face that which plagues ye.'

'It think that has happened already,' Garnet answered quietly. 'I know what it is I want to do, what it is I must do if I am ever to know peace.'

Squinting through the tobacco smoke curling back to wreathe her face, Hepzibah watched the troubled face. Would she choose to go or to stay, the choice must be of her making, hers and no other.

'It was kind of your son to bring me here, and kind of all of you to help me.' Garnet smiled at the widow Korjyck settling herself at the fire and lighting her own pipe with a stick drawn from its flames. 'But the bed I slept in belongs to another and I cannot keep it from them a second night.'

''T' were the wagon of Hepzibah Kane ye slept in, one ye can rest in til ye be well,' Hepzibah answered.

Across the fire the widow Korjyck removed the pipe from between yellowed teeth.

'The wagon of Hepzibah Kane houses a son. While ye bide in it it be barred to 'im, neither can he make his bed beneath it. But the wagon of Alcina Korjyck 'ouses no man; if it be the putting of Judah Kane from his wagon has ye a' worryin' then tis welcome ye be to rest a night wi' me.'

They were all so kind. Garnet felt her throat thicken. They had asked no questions, simply accepted her. In how many villages had she found that, in how many of the houses she had been turned from? Yet here in a gypsy caravan, among the very people she had been taught to mistrust she had found only civility and kindness.

No longer able to control the tears rising

inside her, Garnet whispered her thanks. Another day among these people would give her back her strength, the strength to search for Tyler Cadell.

The gypsy wench was handsome and she would have been willing but he had declined the invitation in those sultry eyes. He wanted no smell of her on his body when he paid his call on Winifred Benson. There must be no taint to his clothing. Tyler Cadell smiled. As for that on his soul, no one would ever know of that.

'Tyler, my dear boy...'

Taking a lace-mittened hand, touching it to his lips, Tyler hid the contempt that shone in his eyes as he was welcomed into Winifred Benson's sitting room. Plump and overdressed the woman was laughable, but at the moment useful.

'...how wonderful you have brought yourself to venture from that 'ouse. I was just telling Lady Olivia how we were feared you never would again.'

'Lady Olivia?' Releasing the plump fingers, Tyler straightened, letting his glance travel to a slighter figure sat beneath a tall velvet-draped window then immediately back to Winifred. 'Forgive me, I was not told you were entertaining. I must not intrude, perhaps some other time.'

'Nonsense. You are not intruding and we

55

will not hear of your leaving. My dear,' she held a hand towards the girl who smiled as she rose and came to join them, 'my dear, allow me to present Mr Tyler Cadell.'

'Mr Cadell.' Her soft eyes dancing the girl dropped the merest of curtsies.

'Mr Cadell is but a short time home from India.'

'Oh, how interesting...' The girl smiled again.

It could have been said out of politeness but glancing again into that moss-green softness of her eyes, Tyler caught a glimpse of something deeper; interest in the travel or the traveller?

'You really must tell me all about it. It must be so wonderful to travel, to experience different cultures; I long to do so, Mr Cadell, but my uncle will not allow it; so you see you simply *have* to tell me of your adventures.'

'They all seem long ago, I would not call two years a short time, Lady Olivia.'

'But not long enough to forget.'

'No.' Letting his theatrical grief flood into his face, Tyler swallowed hard. 'Not long enough to forget!'

That was enough, reel in the line too quickly and it was apt to snap and then the fish was lost. Turning to the older woman his voice reached the depth of huskiness he had practised diligently. 'Forgive my

56

thoughtless intrusion, it ... it will not happen again.'

Leaving the house he brought his horse to a halt on the crest of a ring of low hills cuddling a small valley, and looked down on the tiny gypsy encampment. His timing had been perfect, he had left the Benson house at just the right moment ... one moment before heart-break. He laughed, the sound of it sending a pair of startled blackbirds rising from a nearby cover of trees. He had more talent than he'd given himself credit for; if things ever got bad for him then perhaps he might turn to the boards. But life was not going to turn bad on him. He had the Winton money and the Winton house and soon he would have a titled wife; meantime ... he watched the smoke of the camp fire rise in a slender column of grey to the clear afternoon sky ... meantime the gypsy girl would provide entertainment.

The man had not answered her invitation. Marisa Lakin ignored her mother's call. He had been interested. He had liked what he'd seen. She threw aside the basket, its few remaining pegs scattering on the ground beside the caravan. But he hadn't stayed; he'd stared, letting his eyes take in more than the wares she carried but then he'd ridden on.

'There be wood needs getting for the fire,

or mebbe ye wants your father back an' 'is meal not cooked!' Pilar Lakin looked up from the potatoes she was scrubbing. 'A nice temper that would see 'im in.'

'Why didn't you gather the wood?' Marisa's own temper flared. 'No doubt cos you've seen off the afternoon wi' a pipe an' gabbin' to the rest who sit on their arses while the young 'uns does the work of bringin' in a livin'!'

Her mouth tightening, Pilar remained seated on her low stool. A pup that bit the teat was no good to bitch or pack.

'What was done wi' my afternoon be business to do wi' nobody 'cept me. Ye've long tried mekin' it yourn, now I tells ye, get Lorcan Nash to sleep beneath this wagon, get 'im to take ye as ye tried to get Judah Kane, but he spurned ye as Nash will spurn ye, ye'll 'ave no wagon to sit beside, none to call ye're own an' now this one be denied yea; ye've set foot inside it for the last time! Get yeself away–' she rose to her feet '–an' tek this of a memory.' Lifting the bowl she threw the contents, covering the gaping Marisa with water and potato peelings.

Individual cooking fires dying slowly in the inky darkness ringed the camp in a circle of living gems. Sat with Hepzibah on the steps of the wagon, Garnet watched the Kris, the group of men gathered about the larger

58

central fire.

Outlined by the light of dancing flames she saw Judah rise to his feet. Tall and broad shouldered he had a natural grace of movement. Watching him now she could understand his mother's pride in him, the love that rang in her voice when she spoke of him, the kind of love she would have felt for her own child, the child that had been snatched from her, that had been torn to pieces...

'It is a practice we have long lived by...'

Judah's voice rang clear and loud on darkness that could almost be touched, but it did not hide the sob of the girl sat beside Hepzibah. This one had suffered a good few hardships but the gifts of fate were not yet all delivered. Hepzibah watched her son as she tried to ignore that which would not be ignored, that churning low in her stomach that told her the fates had not yet aimed their last blow at the gaujo wench, and somehow her son would feel its sting.

'...Romany women see to the chavvies, their hand has always ruled the children until boys become of an age when they can be taught the business of making a living, at that time they come under the father's hand; girls remain under the guidance of the mother til marriage...'

It was not so different from the practice of non-Romanys. Garnet listened to the acknowledging ums and ahs of the seated men and the softer confirmation of their wives stood behind. Children of her own world were cherished, guided and taught with love and understanding by both parents in turn; at least those had been her thoughts, her hopes. Tyler would love their child as she loved her, but Tyler had killed her!

'...but Marisa Lakin be not married...'

Judah's words breaking again on her thoughts, Garnet caught the faint flurry of movement at the edge of shadow, then the girl called Marisa was pushed into the light.

'...yet the authority of the mother be flouted by her. Any raklie refusing to abide by the hand of her mother be refusing to abide by Romany law. Be ye all agreed on this?'

What would happen to the girl? Garnet watched the figure shoved further into the ring of light, her head thrown back in defiance. Surely whatever it was these people decided to do would have to be seen to be done, just as the accusation being made against the girl was a form of public trial.

The chorus of ayes dying away, Judah spoke on. 'With her mother's wagon denied her, Marisa Lakin stands in need of a home. Be there any man will take her in marriage?'

In the following silence Marisa turned slowly, her eyes finding each man's and before each she spat contemptuously on the ground. Then for a moment her gaze lifted, crossing the flickering shadows to find those of Hepzibah.

'There be none of your whelps I would bed with,' she sneered, 'none I would tie my life to; but ask your question again in three days, ask it of Lorcan Nash when he returns and hear the answer he'll give.'

'The question will be asked the third evening from this,' Judah nodded to the girl and as she was pulled from the ring he turned his gaze again on the seated men. 'But until that time Marisa Lakin needs be given shelter.'

'That be the concern of the women,' a man answered.

'Be that the voice of the Kris?'

'It be.'

The answer flitted from man to man and as the last one repeated it a woman's voice broke from the shadows.

'A bitch that snaps at the 'and that fed it finds no place at my fire!'

'Nor mine!' Travelling as rapidly as the answer given by the men the women's refusals winged through the darkness.

'And the law of our people, the law that says no being in need shall be turned from a Romany camp?'

'And what of custom, Judah Kane?' Stepping forward, the glow of fire lighting her face, one of the older women glared, her

61

hands on her hips. 'What of the unspoken rule that be old as time, the rule that 'as kept our families in harmony for as long as man 'as trod the earth, the rule that says an unmarried raklie that turns her back on her mother's authority be driven from the camp? I says to let her bide be to bring trouble.'

From the shadows, Marisa's scornful laugh rang out. 'An' would that be more or less than the trouble the fetching of a gaujo woman will bring?'

The question flung from the darkness brought a sudden silence. As part of the hushed group, Hepzibah watched her son. Last night he had drawn the blade across his palm, sealed his word with his own blood; but that had been done with no eyes watching other than her own. For a long moment he stood staring into the fire, his head bent, then it lifted and in the movement Hepzibah saw the strength of the father.

'The decision to allow the gaujo woman to stay was mine and this one also be mine.' Judah spoke clearly. 'Marisa Lakin will not be turned away. I have no place to offer her but as first man I say she can sleep beside the fire and no tongue may plague her nor any hand be raised against her.'

'Be there a place for the words of Alcina Korjyck?'

Hepzibah's glance snapped to the woman

coming to face her son.

'There is a place for the words of all in this camp, whether man or woman.'

'Then I speak.' The woman answered Judah's quiet words in a tone that reached beyond the firelight. 'This day I offered a sleeping place to the gaujo to the woman brought here by Judah Kane. I offered it so he could tek back 'is rightful place beneath 'is mother's wagon. The offer was thanked for by Hepzibah Kane but refused; the action of her son was for her to deal with, the carin' o' the woman was for them alone. Now I makes the offer to Marisa Lakin, there be a bed place on the floor o' my wagon, an' a blanket to cover ye, tek it if ye will.'

Beside her in the deep greyness of night, Garnet heard the swift intake of Hepzibah's breath, a sound echoed by the shadow-robed women, and above it all that same scornful laugh.

Chapter Five

'Why does no one speak to her? They all turn their back at her approach, even the children.'

Garnet dried the bowls washed by

Hepzibah then stacked them away in a box constructed on the rear of the painted caravan.

'They follows the custom of our people.' Hepzibah glanced covertly at the figure eating her meal beside a tiny fire lit at the very edge of the encampment. 'From the earliest o' times it 'as been the way of punishment for any Romany who flouts the rules. The wench will meet with no hurt to the body but neither will her meet with smile or word, and that rule will be 'eld fast by any other Romany met wi' on the road.'

'But how will they know?'

The morning chores done the older woman took down a basket hooked on to the side of the caravan and proceeded to fill it with clothes pegs Judah had whittled the night before.

'There be ways, as ye'll see for yourself should ye choose to stay.'

Should she choose to stay! Lifting the blackened leather water bottle from its place next to several more willow baskets, Garnet filled the large kettle. The offer of a home with them could be no more explicit but it was an offer she would not accept ... had it been made two years ago ... or was it longer even than that?...

With the water container back on its hook it took both hands to lift the kettle on to the cast-iron cooking prop fixed firmly into the ground close to the fire.

...more than two years, the thought ran on, she would have remained with these kind people and blessed her lucky stars for the chance. Two years. She stared at the glowing sticks, their edges coated with grey ash. She hadn't known where she had been, where she went next, her one driving thought being to find her baby, to hold her in her arms; she had refused to believe the nightmare of truth, refused to face what she knew had been done. But now she must face it for no matter how far she travelled she would never again know the sweet swelling of the heart, feel that great surge of love sing through the whole of her body as she looked into the face of her child. Tyler Cadell had robbed her of that, he had killed the joy in her, destroyed all pleasure life had held.

'*Throw it to the dogs...*'

The words that had so many times brought her screaming into wakefulness screeched now in her brain and the spectre of Tyler Cadell's tall figure, its face twisted with fury, a whip raised above its head, formed in the smoke of the fire.

'*...feed that obscenity to the dogs...*'

Caught as ever in the horror of it, Garnet could not throw off the thoughts. Helpless in the mesh of terror she stared at the phantom only her eyes could see.

'*...do as I say or by Christ I'll do it myself...*'

'Wench ... wench what ails ye, what be wrong?'

Surprisingly strong, Hepzibah's arms closed about her, holding her as sobs tumbled one over the other.

'He killed her...!'

The cry carrying on the still air, Marisa Lakin looked up.

'...Tyler killed my baby!'

Pressing the girl's face close against her breast, Hepzibah cut off the cries. Whatever had passed in the gaujo's life was not for the ears of Marisa Lakin. Gently guiding their steps she ushered her inside the caravan.

'Ye needs to rest.'

Sat on the bed the other woman lowered her to, Garnet shook her head.

'No, I need to talk.'

At the open doorway the black skirts rustled. 'Hepzibah Kane asks naught of ye, yer business be yer own.'

'Please, I feel that to talk would help, I ... I have no one else I can ask to listen, and no one I would trust more to hold my secret.'

The girl's words were genuine. Hepzibah's hand rested on the door. She had travelled the roads too many years, spoken to too many gaujos to be deceived by them. Turning, she looked across at the thin figure, light from the window of the bed space sparking a myriad darts among the thick folds of auburn hair, and felt again that strange feeling she had experienced the night she had helped the girl to bed, a churning low in the stomach, as if somebody long-yearned-for had at last arrived.

'Speak if ye wish, only remember, there be no pressure put upon ye.'

Waiting until Hepzibah had settled on a stool before the unlit stove that had been polished to black silver, her wide skirts spread like some huge fan about her legs, Garnet struggled to find words with which to begin.

Outside, the last of the women were disappearing over the gentle swell of ground towards the town, babies slung in a shawl passed over one shoulder and tied beneath their breast, toddlers clutching at their skirts whilst older ones raced and tumbled ahead. From her seat on the ground, Marisa Lakin watched the last one swallowed by the horizon then rose and silent as any cat moved to the offside of the Kane wagon. The gaujo woman had a story to tell and Marisa Lakin wanted to hear.

'I ... I was married in India...'

Her ears sharp, Marisa strained to catch the words floating quietly from the open doorway.

'...I had gone out there to be with my parents...'

Slowly, punctuated with sobs, the words

fell into the silence, the whole of her story told in pain.

'...I thought Tyler would love her as I loved her, but when he saw her...'

Crouched against the caravan, Marisa catching her breath as the last words came in a bevy of wild sobs.

'...he ... he killed her ... he ... threw her to the dogs.'

'And ye?' Hepzibah's first intervention was gentle.

'I... I tried to follow, to take back my baby but Mrs Wilkes held me back, she said Tyler would kill me too unless I left Bentley House at once before he returned to the bedroom.'

Bentley House! Marisa pushed silently to her feet.

'...*It was to Florrie Wilkes they left the carin' of their daughter...*'

The words of the woman sat in that scullery flashed back to her mind.

'...*India, what be more foreign than that?... Not yet reached its first half year ... dead of its father's fury...*'

A slow smile crossing her face Marisa turned, running with wide swift strides for the screening thicket of trees.

The wench had cried herself to sleep. Hepzibah added sticks to the fire glowing beneath her cooking pot. There had been talk of her leavin', of fendin' for 'erself, but what was hidden behind the words? Their real meaning was revenge. The wench wanted to find the man who 'ad murdered 'er babe an' do the same for 'im. That were wild talk, the talk of a heart blisterin' beneath its pain. Find 'im no doubt her would given time, but kill? Flames rising new from the fire held Hepzibah's stare. There be more depth to a woman than be often realised, and a woman in agony be deeper than most; could be it would 'appen, the love of a mother be a force to move mountains ... or to plunge a knife into a man's chest!

'Be the girl well?'

Hepzibah glanced up at her son, his frame broad and strong against the glow of the new moon. A force to move mountains!

'Well enough.' Pushing up from her haunches she received his kiss of greeting. ''Er be sleepin'.' Pouring water into the bowl used only for washing the body she watched him strip away neck cloth and shirt, soaping himself well as he did every night before taking his meal. He had refused Marisa Lakin, that one 'eld no attraction for 'im as did not other of the juvals in this camp or any other they met with on the road; it 'ad seemed there was no woman would take the 'eart of Judah Kane, until now.

Ladling broth into a basin she set it among the hot ashes. There was a warmth in his voice when he spoke of the gaujo woman that weren't there when speakin' of any other, an' a look that rested on 'er when he thought no other eye watched. But his mother's eye 'ad seen, and her heart knowed what stirred in his.

But that were a longing could not be given room to grow. Judah Kane must choose from among his own, to love outside be to enquire after heart-break.

Coming to the fire, Judah took his meal on his knee, glancing as he did so around the camp and noting each family grouped about its own fire.

'Has all been well?'

Squatting on her stool, Hepzibah nodded. He asked the question while looking at each man's family in turn but what he truly asked was of the woman, how had her fared this day?

'It's been as you ask–' she deflected the question leading it sidewards on to a different path '–nobody 'as raised a hand agen Marisa Lakin but neither, 'as a body spoken to 'er save the gaujo.'

'She spoke to Marisa?' Judah's eyes flashed to the wagon.

'Ar.' Free of its shawl her dark head caught the brilliant light of the full moon as his mother nodded. ''Er spoke, but then

70

Romany rules applies only to Romany an' that one don't be Romany!'

His eyes once again on the bowl balanced on his knees, Judah recognised the deeper, unspoken meaning of those few words. They were a warning, a warning against looking where he should not, of loving where he should not.

'I 'eard talk of a sale while I were in the town.' Judah's meal done, Hepzibah took the bowl and spoon, washing them immediately in a blue enamelled bowl kept widely separate from those used for laundry and washing the body. 'I heard it from two women as I called at the door to sell pegs. Talked on as though I weren't there they did, it was only an old gypsy woman at their door, a woman of no account. But even an old gypsy has ears an' those of Hepzibah Kane be sharp. T'were a sale o' horses. The master along o' Victoria 'ouse be sellin' off a pair an' seemingly the husband o' one of the women 'ad been asked to apprise 'em. Hmmph!' She stacked the bowl and spoon noisily in the box on the rear of the wagon. 'What do gaujos know about 'orses? No more'n ye can balance on the 'ead of a pin!'

That was as maybe. Judah watched his mother pack her clay pipe with tobacco then light it with a stick from the fire. But some of them kept fine animals and a pair from a house such as that! He watched smoke from

71

the pipe curl upwards, drifting a spiral of grey gauze across the golden face of the moon. He had seen that house when they had made camp in the neighbouring town of Wednesbury. Square-built and gracious it stood tall in its setting of well-cared-for grounds, a reflection of the wealth of its owner; judging by the pride obvious in the building it seemed safe to assume that same pride and care would be given to the choosing and rearing of horse flesh; the kind of horse flesh that would give good returns at the Stow fair.

'Did the women speak of when the sale was to be made?'

Hepzibah chewed on the long slender stem, taking her time in answering. 'They said!' She blew a stream of smoke to mingle with sparks darting to hide among the shadows. 'Seems it be day after tomorrow. One o' them spoke of being able to buy a fine dinner on that afternoon.'

'If the animals be of the blood I expects then they be set to fetch a fine price; who be the buyer I wonder?'

'Be you thinkin' o' offering?'

Shuffling one foot, Judah kicked a fallen stick back into the fire. 'Think you I should?'

Beneath the covering shadows, Hepzibah's mouth curved in a smile. 'I think what it be I've always thought, ye 'as the same judgement as the man that fathered ye, an' the same good sense, follow what it tells ye now.'

A sudden noise from the mouth of the small valley that housed the encampment had Judah on his feet. Joined in an instant by the rest of the men all with stout branches in their hands, he walked toward the disturbance.

Judah Kane had it in mind to bid for a pair of fine horses! Hidden in the rough grass bordering the Kane wagon, Marisa had listened to every word. Now, taking advantage of the stir caused by that noise from beyond the fringes of the camp she rose, gliding silently towards the wagon of Alcina Korjyck. Knowing she could not enter until the other woman did she squatted on the ground well clear of the widow's fire. Buying horses from the stables of a fine house would take money, lots of money; enough to ruin any man should he lose it!

Judah Kane had spurned her. Marisa stared at the line of men, her eyes seeking one among the rest. He had refused what she had offered, turned his back on her; and worse ... the whole camp knew it, knew it and smirked. But they would smirk differently when Judah Kane were made to look a fool, the pride knocked from him; and she, Marisa Lakin would do it. He would regret refusing to take her for his wife and when she were married to Lorcan Nash, then Hepzibah Kane would regret it too.

Drawing her patterned shawl about her, Marisa watched the figure stood staring after the men. The woman of the first man were looked to, be it wife or mother, her word was accepted by the other women. Soon now, Lorcan would be first man and Marisa Lakin would be his wife; when that time came Hepzibah Kane would no longer be a woman of consequence.

The conversation of the men returning to their fires, the branches carried low against the thighs, carried across the firelit shadows to where Marisa sat. The sound they had heard had been the wheels not of a dreaded police cart but of a gypsy wagon, Lorcan's wagon. The time of revenge was nearer than she had hoped.

Sitting still in that same place Marisa watched the huge melon orb of the moon attended by fleeting wisps of cloud.

'...*before the third night of the second rising of the full moon...*'

From somewhere deep inside the words rose, bringing in their wake a coldness that gripped her heart. This was the first full moon since they had been spoken. In twenty days it would have waned completely, given way to another ... *the second rising of a full moon.*

But the words of Hepzibah Kane would never come to fruition. Marisa glanced about her at the dying deserted fires, the darkened windows of the wagons. Rising silently, taking special care where each footstep was placed she crossed the darkened space to the wagon of Lorcan Nash.

'Day after tomorrow you say?'

Awake even before her hand had touched his sleeve, Lorcan Nash had rolled out from beneath the wagon.

'I heard it clear,' Marisa answered softly. 'The sale be being made from Victoria House over in Wednesbury.'

'I knows the place,' Lorcan nodded, 'an' I knows any horse from that stable won't be sold for pennies. Judah Kane will need a pocket o' guineas to buy the kind o' breed they have there.'

'And a pocket of guineas he'll have, unless o' course he should lose them atwixt here and that house.'

'Judah Kane don't be careless.'

'No!' Marisa glanced at the moon, paler now as the sky gave birth to the day. 'Judah Kane don't be that careless, but then he don't expect it to be taken from him except in exchange for a horse.'

Watching the face lit by the coming dawn, Lorcan felt a twist in his stomach. Wide and deeply brown the eyes gleamed in a skin of dark honey, the mouth full and wide smiled

75

over teeth white and even, while hair black as a raven's wings tumbled to her waist. Marisa Lakin was attractive, he might almost say beautiful. But a viper skin held beauty ... yet its mouth held poison! Beautiful yet dangerous. His stomach twisted again. That was Marisa Lakin.

'What be that to mean?' He spoke quietly though the thought was still loud in his mind.

Brown eyes gleamed but a moment later were hooded, the answer contemptuous.

'It means Judah Kane won't be expecting a body to be lyin' in wait for him; why should he? T'were only his mother heard what them women spoke of, at least that be what they both believe. You could be that body waiting, you can take that money an' leave him dead as you left Tonio Korjyck.'

'Quiet, you fool!' Harsh as a whiplash the word snapped out, his hand closing painfully over her arm.

'There be none awake to hear.' Marisa tore her arm free.

'That be your good fortune,' Lorcan snarled. 'Speak of it no more within this camp less it be you wants to finish up in a ditch, your throat cut as Korjyck's was cut!'

'There be two can threaten, Lorcan Nash!' Her head tossed back on her neck, Marisa glared at the man she would have take her for a wife, a man who aroused no feeling of love in her. 'I needs only to scream to bring the men rushing from their beds, I needs only to tell what I knows to the Kris…'

'That would be the ending of you.'

'True!' Marisa met the threat with defiance. 'But it would also be the ending of you. Think of this as you lie in your bed. One can destroy the other, or one can help raise the other. With me you can become first man, without me you can become a corpse!'

As the last word drifted into the receding darkness, Lorcan laughed softly. 'If you believes Hepzibah Kane I be as good as one o' them now. How many more days to the rising of the second moon … how many more days of life be left to Lorcan Nash?'

'But I don't believe and neither should you,' Marisa snapped. 'To dwell on that woman's ravings be to drive yourself mad. So kill her son, kill Judah Kane and drive his mother from the camp. Take your place as first man…'

'And take you as wife, then whose words are turned to prophecies, the words o' Marisa Lakin?'

The swiftly spoken words were acid in their contempt. Rising from her haunches, making no impression on the silence that draped the camp, Marisa turned back to Alcina Korkyck's caravan. There was no love in Lorcan Nash for her, they were even in that. But where love could be strong, hate could be stronger ... and Marisa Lakin had always been capable of strong feelings!

Chapter Six

'I... I beg your pardon, I thought your meal finished or I would not have disturbed you.'

Colour rising to her pale cheeks, Garnet hesitated on the steps of the caravan.

'You cause me no disturbance.' The quick answer was a lie, but only he knew it, only he felt the quickening of his pulse as he looked at the gaujo woman. Judah laid aside the bowl he had eaten from.

'Your mother has gone with the others to the town, I offered to go...'

'You don't be strong enough yet for calling.'

'Calling? I had no idea your mother was to visit anyone.'

'Visit!' Judah smiled. 'Calling don't be visiting as you would have it mean; calling, for Romany women, be selling their wares doorstep to doorstep, that means a lot of walking and that be too much for you just yet.'

'I assure you I feel quite well, thanks to the kindness of your mother.'

'Hepzibah Kane knows the ways of healing,' Judah nodded, 'and the widow Korjyck be versed in the use of plants and herbs; you could have had no finer nursing in—'

In my own home! Garnet finished his words in silence. But she had no home, Tyler Cadell had seen to that.

Seeing the look that flitted across the colourless face, Judah cursed himself for a fool. It was obvious no one cared a tuppenny damn for this woman, nor had done for a fair length of time, she had nobody to nurse her, fine or otherwise, nobody to care if she lived or died.

Sensing his thoughts, Garnet turned back towards the door of the caravan. She would wait for him to leave then wash the bowl he had used.

'It is usual to drink a dish o' tea after a meal.'

He had not intended to say that, he had not meant to speak again but the words had come of their own volition. Judah stared into the fire, low and red beneath the cooking pot. In fact he had not meant to return to the camp at all. So why had he broken with his usual practice, why return at midday when he had never done so before? He was hungry, he needed to eat? No that too was lies, hunger could be satisfied elsewhere; unless it was the hunger that chewed his stomach in the long night hours and did not ease during the day: the hunger to look upon the face of the woman he had pulled from a hedge.

She had watched the women serve their men with food when they came home, always following it with a large mug of fresh brewed tea. Hepzibah had shown her where things were kept and with his reminder she reached for the gaudily painted tin box that held the strong-smelling tea.

'I'll do that.'

Grasping the kettle as she struggled to lift it from the curved hook of the iron prop hammered into the ground beside the fire, Judah felt her fingers brush against his own and the touch brought a rush of blood surging through his veins. He had touched many a woman's hand, danced with girls after the days trading at the horse fairs but none had touched him with fire as this one did. Hardly able to keep his hand from shaking he poured boiling water on the tea leaves, his eyes avoiding her as he returned to his seat.

She could not do the work of the women of the camp, he had made that obvious. Garnet felt the warmth of embarrassment creep to her cheeks as the kettle was taken from her. Maybe given time ... but during that time she would be taking food she had played no part in earning, she would be

80

adding to the burden of people who had already been more than kind.

'Mr Kane,' she handed the mug to him then stood with hands folded across her skirts, 'everyone has been most kind since you brought me here, especially yourself and your mother; my only regret is that I have no other way of showing my gratitude than with words.'

'Has any way been asked?'

Seeing his fingers stiffen about the mug, Garnet paused awkwardly. She had not phrased her feelings in the best way. Judah Kane carried the same pride as his mother.

'N-no.' She stammered, searching for the way to state what was inside her, to say what she must without giving injury or slight to that pride. 'Nothing has been asked but...'

'Then nothing more is needed. Words are the music of the soul, and spoken with a sweet tongue they play sweet in the heart of the listener for as long as he breathes.' Laying aside the unfinished tea he rose, looking for one moment deep into her eyes and when he spoke his voice was strong with emotion. 'Never underestimate the power of words, they can sing in the heart or they can burn in the brain, either way they can never be withdrawn nor never forgotten; and my words to you be these, so long as you need a home you will find it here in this camp.'

Atop the rise of land, Marisa squinted

81

against the glare of sunlight. The gaujo woman and Judah Kane! Jealousy sharp as the knife of Satan stabbed through her. He had refused her, he showed no interest in any Romany raklie, yet this woman had him trailing back at midday like a dog after a bitch! But then let him have his day of pleasure. She lowered her hand and as it touched her side a cold venomous smile curved her mouth. For Judah Kane a day was all that was left!

She had not told him. She had not said what she had meant to say, that tomorrow she was leaving. Sponging bowl and spoon in water taken from the kettle, Garnet watched the tall figure already reaching the crest of gently rising ground. She had nowhere to go and not a penny to go with but she would not abuse that man's charity any longer.

'Be Hepzibah ailing?'

Surprise stealing her breath, Garnet spun round, her elbow sending basin and dishes clattering to the ground.

'What...?' she gasped.

'I asked, be Hepzibah ailing?' Marisa kicked out at the dog come to lick her hand.

Relief flooding her face, Garnet bent to pick up the fallen crockery. 'No, no, Hepzibah is not ill, why should you think that?'

'No reason.' Marisa watched the figure fall away beyond the swell of ground. 'Except it be unlike Judah Kane to be at his wagon during the day unless some thing be amiss.'

'There is nothing amiss that I know of.'

But there be something I knows of. The same knife-thrust stabbing at her stomach, Marisa watched the utensils of Judah's meal being put away.

'That be well.' She hitched her basket higher on her hip.

'I'm sorry I cannot offer you tea, but it is not mine to give.'

'And Hepzibah Kane would sooner give me death than a sup of her tea.' Marisa laughed acidly. 'But that be no fault o' yours and will form no obstacle between us; you 'ave a kindness you shows in speaking with me when no other body in this camp will.'

'I... I asked Hepzibah first.' A faint flush of pink followed the confession. 'I did not wish to offend, but she told me an outsider was not bound by Romany custom and that I was free to talk where I would.'

Anger rising as fast as a flood tide, Marisa hid it by straightening the cloth covering her basket. An outsider! Yes, this woman was all of that; but that wouldn't be the way of it for long, not if Judah Kane had his way ... but then Judah Kane would not live long enough to have his way.

'How long will it go on, refusing to speak to you I mean?'

The wild surge of anger under control,

Marisa looked up but her eyes were brown circles of ice.

'My mother will hold to it til her be dead, and likewise a few more, as for the rest they will chirp pretty enough when I be wife to the first man.'

'You are to marry Mr Kane?'

'Judah Kane!' Black hair swirled as Marisa's head tossed contemptuously. 'I will never be wife to Judah Kane!'

As she took the leather water jack in her hands, Garnet's frown was puzzled. 'But you said you were to be the wife of the first man, is that not what Mr Kane is?'

The coldness in those brown eyes intensified and in their arctic depths, Garnet could see the traces of something that chilled her more than any winter frosts.

'Oh he be first man ... now, but soon that will be changed, it will be Lorcan Nash will be first man and then we'll see what happens to Hep–'

Ending abruptly, Marisa allowed a smile to touch her mouth but beneath it the iciness remained.

'You would not know of the meeting of the Kris a few nights back, you were sleeping. Words passed between Kane and Lorcan and they will pass again tonight; tonight Lorcan Nash will give the challenge, he will call upon his right to bid for the place of first man, but first he will acknowledge before all that I be his chosen wife.'

Hitching the empty water jack in her arms, Garnet tried to smile but the tiny perplexed frown remained between her brows. She had heard the bitterness but where was the pleasure? Surely a woman on the brink of marriage to the man of her choice should be happy, and Marisa did not give the impression she would let anyone force her into marriage; so why the feeling that there was no happiness in the girl who watched her with frozen eyes?

'Allow me to wish you joy in your marriage.' It was said sincerely but somehow the words sounded flat and lifeless, Garnet's mind dwelling on what had been said of the challenge. What form did it take? Was there a danger to Judah Kane?

A fear she could find no basis for trickled along her nerves. She had not seen the man Marisa spoke of, but deep inside she felt a mistrust of him ... of them both. Guilty at the thought yet unable to shake free of it she excused herself, walking to the brook that ran along the foot of the low-lying hill.

Why had Hepzibah not spoken of a forthcoming challenge ... did she also fear a possible danger to her son?

With the water jack filled she lifted it into her arms, holding the weight clumsily against her chest. She was being silly allowing herself to think that way, this was

England, and in 1898 people no longer went around issuing challenges that meant duels, settling arguments with swords or pistols. Hepzibah had said nothing because the whole affair was commonplace. Walking back to the wagon, hooking the water jack in place, Garnet knew that was the least true thought of all.

Tonight the camp would know. On the edge of the encampment, the nearest spot she had dared to light her own cooking fire, Marisa stared across the wide stretches of open heath. They would hear Lorcan say of his intent to take her for his wife, that would settle that old woman's hash! Let Hepzibah Kane utter her threats after that, nobody would take any notice and Marisa Lakin would be accepted back. But not into her mother's wagon! Anger surged afresh. Her mother had never had any time for her, she had only ever seen her as somebody to fetch and carry, she had resented her birth, hating her as if the denial of a living son were the fault of the living daughter. But once that daughter were wife to the first man, then Pilar Lakin, like Hepzibah Kane, would be turned away, it would be those women would find no place in this camp to light their fires! Yes, tonight when the meal was finished, Lorcan would call a meeting of the Kris and Marisa Lakin would come into her own.

The sudden barking of the dogs catching her attention she started into the shadows gathered beyond the touch of firelight. The men were returning. A smile of satisfaction curved her mouth as she dropped to the tree stump that provided her with a seat. One more hour. One more hour was all Marisa Lakin would serve as outcast.

They had talked long. Marisa shifted impatiently on the tree stump. The Kris has gathered at Lorcan's request but he had yet to call her, to name her his chosen wife before them.

Across the open space ringed by caravans she watched the men, seated figures etched black against the deepening night, their conversation lost in the shadows before it could reach her. Now ... it would be now! Triumph flaring hot and burning every nerve she watched the figure of Lorcan Nash rise, the turn of his head as he looked to where Judah Kane sat. This was the moment she had waited for, the time to take her place as wife of the first man.

Thought of the pleasure of seeing Hepzibah Kane's face drop when Lorcan challenged for leadership chased away the irritation of moments ago. Rising slowly she threw aside the encompassing shawl. Black hair rippling over her shoulders, eyes shining as if to challenge the high-riding moon, head held high she walked towards the gathering.

'I claim the right to challenge for leadership...'

On the fringe of the group Marisa ignored the women who grumblingly moved to stand away from her. In a very few minutes now they would trip a different jig.

'...and I also claim the right to choose the time of its making...'

Loud and strong, Lorcan's voice spread into the night. Marisa smiled. That was how he would be heard from this night on, his words strong and firm, and no man with the rashness to defy him – or her!

'...that time don't be now...'

What was he saying! Marisa caught her breath. What did he mean *the time don't be now?*

'...tomorrow my wagon leaves for Brough.'

'Brough!' One of the listeners voiced surprise. 'But it be the fair at Stowe we goin' to.'

'That be your privilege,' Lorcan answered, 'but the wagon o' Lorcan Nash will be drawn up at Brough.'

'And what of your aiming to make first man?'

From her place beyond the seated men, Marisa's lungs ached for release but breath remained imprisoned as she waited for the answer to Judah's question.

'I said I would 'ave the choosing of the time an' that choice be the twentieth day from this. On that day will my wagon return to this spot. Tis here the words be spoken and custom says it be the same place the outcome must be decided. Judah Kane...'

Shadows cast by flames dancing over his lithe muscular frame and lending it extra fluidity, Judah rose, seeming to move with them, becoming almost one with the night.

At the edge of the watching group, Marisa felt the breath rush from her.

'...Judah Kane.' Repeated, the words rang over the hushed camp. 'As be the right of a Romany of full blood I speak the words. I challenge for leadership, answer now, be the words accepted?'

Sat on the steps of her wagon, Hepzibah Kane's eyes rested not on the tall proud figure of her son or that of the man facing him, but on the figure of a woman. Marisa Lakin figured large in all of this, of that there was little doubt; hers was the hand that brewed the potion of hate, her jealousy the tool that could rip this camp apart.

A flurry of voices buzzing like bees on the wing caught her ears and Hepzibah switched her glance to her son. He had faced the claim as she had known he would, acknowledged the obligation placed upon him. In twenty days he would honour the pledge taken at his appointing. Any man contesting the right to lead would be met in honest competition; but how much of honesty dwelled in the body of Lorcan Nash, and how much malevolence in the heart of the woman thinking to become his wife?

'And what of the rest of it?'

High pitched, Marisa's voice silenced the hum of conversation.

'What of your words to me, Lorcan Nash?'

Stepping through the circle of seated figures she strode forward, the same flame-thrown shadows playing over tight breasts and uptilted head.

Suddenly the very darkness seemed to throb with the tension of the moment.

From her wagon, Hepzibah saw Lorcan stiffen. He wouldn't take kindly to being forced to speak, no matter what promise had been given privately; no man cared to be taken to task publicly, and no Romany man suffered a woman to have the doing of it.

'Twenty days, Judah Kane!'

He hadn't even looked at the girl stood beside him. He'd made no sign of recognising her presence or her claims, only those final words to Judah then he'd gone from the firelight, walking away into the blackness.

Chapter Seven

'Not that, you stupid fool!'

Tyler Cadell slapped at the hand holding out a slim velvet-covered box.

'You asked for the topaz.'

His anger like a razor's edge slicing deep, his mouth thinning to a slit, Tyler stared at the brown face.

'I've told you this before,' deadly as a serpent the words hissed into the room, 'when you speak to me you say sahib, do you hear ... you say sahib? Say it!' One hand flashing out grabbed the front of the tunic of the silent manservant. 'Say it, you bastard!'

Several inches shorter than his master, the man stared back, the look in his eyes fanning the rage that swept so quickly over Tyler Cadell.

'Don't stare at me–'

A blow to the face jerked the turbanned head but the look in those brown eyes remained unchanged.

'I said don't stare at me...'

Fingers curled into a half fist slammed against the man's cheek. Released at the same moment the servant staggered backwards but still his eyes remained fastened on those of the man whose animosity glowed from him like a torch.

Turning back to his dressing mirror, adjusting a mauve silk cravat as if the last few moments had never happened, Tyler smiled at his well-dressed reflection but when he spoke his voice held a tightness.

'Take that away and bring the opal pendant, the one set around with blue diamonds.'

Picking up the fallen box the manservant waited.

'Well get on with it.' Tyler's fingers rested warningly on the cravat.

'At once.' The Indian bowed. 'At once ... sahib.'

Fool! Alone in the bedroom Tyler stared at the closed door. The man was a fool needing to be told everything at least a dozen times, but then what could a man expect of a bloody wog! He ought never to have brought him to England, he should be sent back to Mariwhal. Taking a silk handkerchief carefully matched to the colour of his cravat, Tyler glanced at the figure re-entering the bedroom. Get himself wed to the Lady Olivia Denton and the Indian could go... Mariwhal or the canal? Smiling, he took the small box offered to him. He would decide that later.

He had given no answer. Huddled in her

92

shawl, Marisa ignored the sharp bite of dawn. There had been no mention of his taking her for wife, no promise given. She had been brushed aside, of less importance than any mongrels that followed at his heels. But she was no dog ... she would not be used then left to fend alone, she deserved her place. Without her he would not have known of the money Tonio Korjyck had carried that night, money enough to buy the wagon he drove. Without her to back his lies it might be Lorcan Nash would be dead. Yet he had refused to acknowledge her. Rising slowly she stared about the sleeping camp at the tiny black mounds that were dead cooking fires, at the assortment of wagons etched dark against the deep grey sky, at the wagon of Lorcan Nash. He could have taken her in marriage along with the buying of that, taken her from her mother's caravan and given her a place among the women, the position of a woman with a wagon and man to care for, but there were reasons to wait he had told her, he must become first man before taking a wife.

And tonight he could have taken that step, tonight he could have defeated Judah Kane, he could have spoken of the promises made to her but the words had been left unsaid before the Kris. Lorcan Nash had walked away, passed her by without so much as a look.

For that there could be no lie, no words to pluck the sting from her flesh. Taking the slender iron spike that held her kettle she fingered its long pointed end. The wagon of Lorcan Nash would not be going to Brough fair.

'I've waited of you comin'.'

The spike raised over the figure wrapped in its blanket, Marisa gasped as her wrist was caught in a fierce grip.

'I knowed what was in your heart, that you would want the life of Lorcan Nash, that be why it be naught but pillows lie in that blanket.'

Twisting the spike from her fingers Lorcan threw it to the ground but still held her wrist in a vicious grip.

'What did you think to gain by calling me out in front of the whole camp?'

'I thought to gain the keepin' of a promise!' Marisa's fury blazed. 'I thought to hear you say to the Kris what you said to me the night...'

'I said never to speak of that!' Both hands streaking to her shoulders he shook hard before sending her sprawling to the ground. 'I should kill you now, still those threats o' your'n for ever.'

Above her, Marisa saw the glint of dawn on the slim steel blade he snatched from the cloth bound about his waist. He would not hesitate to use it; man, woman or animal he would kill any that got in his way.

'Kill me then!' Forcing a soft defiant laugh she stared up at him. 'Kill me and you'll never know what Marisa Lakin knows, you'll never learn what I heard of the gaujo woman.'

Dropping to his knees astride her he lowered the knife, touching its tip to the base of her throat.

'What do I care for the gaujo, her be nothing to me.'

'He be nothing lyin' there in Hepzibah Kane's wagon but handed over to the right folk her could bring much more than you intends to take from Hepzibah's son.'

'What be you meanin', 'ow could the gaujo be worth money?'

Swallowing hard, Marisa felt she sharp prick against her skin. One press of that knife and she would be dead, but she would rather be dead than spend the rest of her life as the butt of the women's snide remarks. Lifting a hand she fastened her fingers over the ones holding the knife, pressing the tip more firmly against her throat.

'Kill me,' her eyes glittered beneath him, 'kill me and throw away your chances, the chance of pickin' up a bigger sum than ever you'll get trading horse flesh.'

'Take care, woman.' Withdrawing his hand Lorcan returned the knife to his waistband. 'Tell me wrong and next time the spike you carried with you tonight will find its mark, right through your heart.'

Pushing free of him, Marisa stood up, shaking the dust from her skirts before answering.

'You've heard her speak, heard the way o' her tongue. It says her be no common gaujo scrapin' a living where her can.'

'Tcha!' Lorcan snorted contemptuously. 'An' that be what I 'ave to think on as being worth money?'

He was a fool. Marisa hid her own contempt. Why should a woman be forced to stay in the shadow of the brainless idiots many men were. But that was the way of the world. A woman's light must shine dimly, but even beneath a bushel there were some burned brightly.

'The eye don't see all.' Marisa spoke softly, masking her scorn. 'Clothes don't always speak the language o' the tongue. The gaujo woman be beggered now but that ain't always been so; I says her 'as seen a better way o' life than be hers now.'

'Then why don't her be livin' it?'

From the shadows a soft growl answered the question but was quieted by a whisper from Lorcan.

Her own words sharp as his, Marisa spat each one slowly. 'It don't only be a Romany turns his back on a woman! Kaulo ratti, the dark blood, it don't be peculiar to the gypsy, it runs in veins other than our own; the

96

gaujo too can forsake his word, he also can cheat and lie.'

'You think the juval be one had a man's back turned on her?'

Lifting her shawl to her head, Marisa's nerves tingled. The next minute would decide her fate. Lorcan Nash would either agree her terms or drive his knife blade deep into her throat.

'I know it.' She stared deep into eyes every bit as piercing as her own. 'I know the woman sleeping in the wagon of Hepzibah Kane be from a family that has money, and I knows the way a deal o' that money can be yours.'

He had gone as he told the Kris he would be. Marisa packed her basket with lyng picked from the heath, its tiny purple flowers resting between glossy green leaves. It looked pretty enough but for how long could she make a living selling it? The women of the town would not go on buying heather no matter how beguiling her promise of reading the future from their palm, and with no man to fashion pegs she had nothing more to trade for a penny or a loaf of bread.

But last night she had traded more than heather or pegs, last night she had traded her word. Lorcan Nash had fumed. She laid the chequered cloth over the basket. Though he had drawn the knife threatening her afresh she had told him no more, saying only that when he returned from Brough she would tell him all, but not until they were made man and wife before the Kris.

And Lorcan Nash had agreed. The basket balanced on her hip she set off towards the town. His brain had absorbed the fact she would not play with her life; that what she had told him held if not all then at least the kernel of truth and it was that truth that would bring him money.

And if what she thought were wrong, if the two and two she had put together didn't count to four?

'But it don't be wrong!' The words laughed quietly into the morning. 'I heard what I heard, an' I know what I know.'

'And what might that be?'

Holding his horse stationary, Tyler Cadell watched the figure crest the small rise.

'What is it you heard, and what do you know?'

She had forgotten how clearly words carried on the heath, even words spoken as quietly as the ones she had uttered.

'Buy a posy, sir?' Gathering her wits quickly she smiled, taking a bunch of purple blossomed lyng from her basket and holding it out to him.

'That doesn't answer my question.'

'Be it needing answer?'

Nervous at the approach of a stranger, the

horse shied but Tyler held it firm.

'I never ask a question without expecting it to be answered, and I rarely ask the same one twice, not even from someone as pretty as you.'

'Nor do I.' Marisa widened her smile. 'No matter it be asked by a stranger 'andsome as you.'

'*Touché.*' Tyler laughed, fishing a coin from the pocket of his waistcoat and tossing it to her. 'You deserve your pay though I have no use for a posy.'

The posy in her hand she allowed the coin to fall to the ground without looking at it. Her eyes still on his she kept the smile on her mouth. 'I thanks you for your intent, but I needs no man's charity. Take your coin and I'll keep my posy.'

'Damn you!' He raised the whip above his head at the same time wrestling with the horse frightened by the sudden movement of its rider.

'I wish the same for you, sir!' Hair spreading like black mist Marisa ran on down the slope. He was the gaujo she had seen before, and the same gleam of interest lay deep in his eyes. Like as not he were unused to being answered in his own vein, like as not he would not let it pass. The sound of hooves bearing down on her bore out her belief, in a moment now she would know if her answer had been taken badly.

'Do you people have no sense!' Reining the horse so sharply it reared as it drew in front of her, Tyler again raised the short-handled whip, his face white with anger. 'I could take the skin off you for that!'

Head thrown back, brown eyes gleaming, Marisa stared at the man who could so easily injure her; any other woman would apologise, beg his forgiveness. But Marisa Lakin was not any woman and she wasn't interested in forgiveness, his or anybody else's.

'A woman's skin be easy took.' Her smile fading, Marisa stared boldly into that handsome face. 'But the pleasure that affords don't last long. Once done it be over for good, whereas there be other ways o' ventin' your anger ... or of takin' your pleasure ... pleasure that can be taken many times over.'

Dropping the basket to the ground she unfastened her shawl, letting it slide from her shoulders to display taut breasts thrusting against a gaily embroidered blouse.

As the whip lowered slowly she watched the anger in his stare give way to a different desire. He was like other men she had seen look at her that way, he felt the same smouldering in his groin, an ache he would pay well to satisfy. No, this man with his fancy clothes and fine horse was no different ... except he had money!

So why shouldn't some of that money be hers ... and why share what was to be got with Lorcan Nash? He'd made promises afore, given them in plenty and broken them as easy; who was to say he would keep that given with this day's dawn, who was to say he would marry her on his return from Brough fair? And if it be he went back on his word once more, if he didn't make her his wife then Marisa Lakin would be left to follow after the others on foot for there was no woman in the camp would let her, a raklie that defied her mother, ride their wagon. She was already without family, disowned and ignored by all save the outsider fetched back by Judah Kane, and a woman on her own must needs take any man who offered or remain as she was now. That meant taking the lowest, and that Marisa Lakin would never do! but with money of her own she could have her own horse and wagon, feed herself; and a woman with money were no blight nor obligation, with money she would find a place in any camp.

Provocation in every line of her, invitation heavy in her eyes she let the shawl slide slowly to the ground. 'Well, sir,' she asked, her voice smoky with promise, 'which way be your pleasure to take?'

'Not here.' Thick with desire the words seemed to stick on his tongue. Leaning forward he grabbed her arm, hauling her up behind him.

He had tasted women before. Lying in the perfumed water of his bath, Tyler Cadell closed his eyes. He had often taken a native woman while in India, so had most of the officers of Her Majesty's Army, that was one of the perks; and then of course there was the odd *affaire d'amour*. Men sent off to quell an uprising or to put a troublesome Maharaja in his place left behind wives who were not averse to the attentions of a good-looking young captain, especially when those attentions were given in bed. But that gypsy had been like no other woman he'd ever had. The native women had been deferential, accepting anything it took his fancy to do, afraid to refuse; and the others, they had been sickeningly coy, pretending a shyness, a reserve it wasn't in any of them to have, and when they were in bed their lovemaking had been mediocre, unvaried to the point of monotony as no doubt the Lady Olivia's would prove. But not so the gypsy wench, she had writhed and twisted beneath him in that barn, matched his desire with her own, played his body as he had thought to play hers, draining him of his senses; but though she had matched him he realised she had not given her all, there was more yet to be had … and he would have it.

Perhaps he ought not to have paid her such a sum; half a sovereign to tumble a gypsy, he'd have been the laughing stock of the regiment. But refusing to match her price would have meant an end to pleasure the like of which he had not experienced before. She would have been gone without trace. Beside which it had been worth every penny. Half a sovereign had bought him an hour in paradise, and an opal pendant set about with blue diamonds? That had paid for no more than a smile.

Olivia Denton had taken the gift, taken it with a smile that said nothing.

Against closed lids he saw the mouth smile at him but the moss-green eyes were cold as winter seas. The Lady Olivia Denton! She had elegance, charm, even beauty in a plain sort of way, but her real beauty lay in the fortune she would bring to the man that married her and he intended to be that man. And excitement in his bed? He slid lower into the caressing warmth of the water. There was a certain gypsy wench would provide that.

Chapter Eight

'I think we should go back.'

Garnet glanced at the sky. It had been clear when they had set out, the blue of it startling against banks of white fluffy clouds. But as the day grew older the clouds had raced together, the purity of their colour becoming stained with grey; now they hung threateningly still barely a touch above the horizon.

The girl walking beside her followed her anxious glance at the sky and smiled. 'There be time yet, no storm will break this side o' nightfall and we'll be back long afore the first raindrop falls.'

Perhaps the girl was right, perhaps the storm would not break for some hours yet. But even so Garnet quickened her step.

The girl, Talaitha, had offered to take her calling, to show her the way of making her living. It could prove useful, Garnet had seen that at once; when she left these people she would have to find a way to feed herself and the gypsy way was better than none. She meant to leave this morning but Talaitha's offer had been one she knew she could not afford to turn down. Hepzibah too had been in favour, encouraging her to go with the girl. 'Watch and listen,' she had said, 'learn all ye can for learnin' stands a body in good stead and Romany lore be worth the learnin' for ye never knows when the day might be ye'll stand in need o' it.'

And it had been worth all of the walking, though she would never have the courage to say the things Talaitha had said to the women answering her knock, not even if she practised them for ever.

But she could remember them, they danced on the surface of memory.

'*...you 'as a lucky face, lady ... buy a posy an' it will bring fortune to your door ... you've known sorrow, that be true don't it my rawnie? But that be passed, soon the sun of prosperity will shine on this 'ouse ... take a few pegs, lady, an' the smile of 'eaven will bring all you desires...*'

Fast and unrehearsed the words tripped from Talaitha's tongue, varying little from door to door unless the door were opened by a younger woman who wore no ring on her left hand. Then Talaitha would smile and lower her voice to a whisper to share some confidence not for the ears of any other.

'*...there be a man,*' she would murmur, '*one who will love you dearly...*' Then as the girl shook her head or blushingly denied any such man, Talaitha would nod all knowingly. '*...you don't know of 'im yet but he be there a'waitin' in the shadows, but he be no common man...*'

That would be when Talaitha would smile and wish the girl a good day but inevitably she would be quietly called back and a sale of pegs or lace concluded before the girl heard any more, and always it would end with '*...you knows my meanin', my rawnie,*' or '*...it be God's own truth I be a'tellin' you ain't*

105

I now?' And safe out of hearing Talaitha would laugh with delight.

'There be no 'arm in what I tells folk,' she had answered when Garnet had questioned the morality of it, 'they either buys what I 'ave to sell or they don't, I don't 'ardly beat 'em over the 'ead 'til they does.'

Maybe not physically. Garnet found it difficult to suppress the niggle of doubt that still played in the back of her mind. But what impressionable young girl, or a woman tied to a life little better than drudgery, could resist the promise contained in Talaitha's words? Could she offer the same hopes in exchange for a few coppers? Yes, it had been worth all of the day's walking; and yes, she had learned, learned that not for all the security and comfort that had once been hers could she fill a woman's heart with lies, learned she could never replace longing with falsehood.

Longing! What could replace her own longing, what could fill the gap left by the killing of her child, what salve could heal the wound left where the heart should be?

Ebony. That had been her first whispered word when her new-born daughter had been placed in her arms. Ebony. It suited the dark hair already covering the tiny head and although the child could not be baptised until her father returned from India the name had remained waiting for

Tyler to love and accept it.

Lost among the silence of her mind, Garnet seemed to feel the warmth of that tiny body held close against her own, to feel the suck of a small mouth at her nipple, the touch of fingers each so small, so perfect against her breast.

But Tyler had not accepted it. Neither had he accepted the child. Why? Oh, she knew why. A sob shuddering on her lips, Garnet made no answer to Talaitha's anxious enquiry as to her well-being. She knew the reason for the rage that had engulfed her husband as he'd looked at the child; hadn't he told her, hadn't he screamed it as he struck out at the helpless infant? But none of his accusations held any truth, she had not taken Raschid as her lover, the daughter born to her had not been the bastard child of Tyler Cadell's manservant.

She had tried to tell him so, tried to protect her baby but she had no strength against the rage that blazed in him, no strength to save her daughter from being thrown to her father's dogs!

'I... I think we best do as you says...'

A sharp persistent tug at her sleeve dragged Garnet from the past.

'...we best be getting ba–'

A gasp of pain cutting off her words the girl clutched a hand to her stomach.

Her senses dulled by remembered pain,

Garnet did not at once comprehend the reason for Talaitha's sinking to the ground.

'It be the child—' the girl clutched again at her swollen stomach, '—I thinks it be comin'.'

But it couldn't be the child! Her mind clearing, Garnet stared at the girl, the contents of her fallen basket strewn across the ground beside her. She was heavily pregnant but the child was not due. She had laughed when Garnet had questioned the wisdom of her going calling, saying she had a month before the birth was due.

But Talaitha was breathless with pain. Kneeling beside her, Garnet felt a flicker of unease. They had seen virtually no one since leaving the camp except the women who answered at the odd cottage or farmhouse. The heath had stretched all around them, empty of life except for birds and rabbits which scampered at their approach. It had not been the best of choices taking the widespread dwellings but the girl had insisted. With the rest of the women calling in the town it would be more beneficial for them to take the outlying places. But they had gone too far, the last house they had called at was half an hour behind them, too far for the girl to walk, but she herself could go for help and if she ran…

Breathing hard as a fresh spasm left her pale cheeked the girl caught at Garnet's arm.

'We ... we've got to get on, it do be the child.'

It was still a long walk to the camp. Garnet looked at the heath, empty and desolate beneath clouds so low they seemed to touch it. What if the girl could not manage such a distance, what if the birth was even more imminent than it seemed? They needed help, and soon.

'It's all right.' She loosed the hand from, her arm. 'You rest here and I will go back to that last farm, they will have a cart...'

'No!' Talaitha struggled to her feet. 'I has to go back, the ... the child must be born in my own wagon.'

Garnet gathered the strewn pegs and posies, pushing them into the basket. She could not drag the girl back to that farm but to let her try walking seemed like courting trouble. The weight of the girl heavy against her, making each step the work of three, Garnet prayed silently. Let us meet with someone, please God let us meet someone who can help.

How far had they come? Stopping now every few yards as fresh spasms of pain had Talaitha fighting for breath, Garnet felt that first touch of unease turn to fear. The sky was almost black, clouds gathered into one dense mass blotted out the last feeble rays of light and the heath held no sign of life.

'I... I has to rest ... just for a minute.'

The muscles of her arm jerking as it was relieved of its burden, Garnet forced herself to think. They would get no further than a few yards like this, the girl was already near exhaustion, and they couldn't go back now. She must make her as comfortable as possible and then go for help alone.

'No.' Grey with pain Talaitha shook her head when hearing the plan. 'Please, don't leave me by myself … please, I be frightened.'

'There is no need, there is nothing on the heath will harm you,' Garnet soothed, 'the clouds will go soon and it will be light enough to see.'

'It don't be the dark I be feared of, it be–' She stiffened, clenching her teeth as another lance of pain stabbed her. Watching her, Garnet too seemed to feel it. She had been afraid. Given the comfort of a doctor and Mrs Wilkes, in her own bedroom with everything laid ready, she had still been afraid, so how much more this girl? Out on the heath with only a virtual stranger to turn to.

'I won't leave you.' Kneeling beside Talaitha she folded both arms about her. The warmth of her own body and her whispered words were the only comfort she could give but they would be there for as long as they were needed. She knew precious little of childbirth and nothing at all of how a delivery was carried out. Like the girl in her arms she knew only the pain. But there was a worse pain, a pain so excruciating it burned its mark deep into the soul, so deep no balm could reach it; the pain of losing the child you had carried for nine months, the child you suffered torment to bring into the world.

There was no telling how long she knelt there holding the girl as she cried out from her own world of torment, but each cry of agony added to the fear clutching Garnet's heart in an icy grip. Maybe there was something wrong, maybe the child could not be born in the normal way! No ... she pushed the thought away ... she must not even think such a thing.

Most births took a long time, so Mrs Wilkes had told her when she had voiced that very fear, and a first child usually took longest. This was Talaitha's first child, this birth would be no different.

Suddenly pushing free the girl arched like a bow, her scream sliding into a moan.

'Help me,' she breathed, 'dear God in heaven, help me!'

Out of the darkness a clap of thunder rolled and great drops of rain splashed down on the upturned face.

Was that heaven's answer? The fear that for hours had haunted Garnet turned instantly to anger, settling like a stone in her chest. Were this girl's prayers to be answered as hers had been, was this new life to be snatched away as her daughter's had been?

There was a worse pain... The thought returned, blinding in its clarity. She would not let that happen, with or without the help of heaven she would not let that happen.

Removing her shawl she spread it on the ground then helped the sweating girl on to it, talking softly as she loosened her clothing.

'We can do it if we help each other.' She smoothed back strands of wet hair from Talaitha's brow. 'Will you help me?'

Drawing a long breath, her mouth opening wide on the grinding pain the girl could only nod.

What should she do next? Rain lancing her face, Garnet tried to remember. Mrs Wilkes had brought in kettles of hot water, but she had no water, hot or cold. The doctor had a Gladstone bag filled with instruments and potions that would numb a little of the pain. The only instruments she had were her own two hands and the only potion her words of encouragement and assurance.

But how could she assure? She who did not know what to do.

Think! Blinking the rain from her eyes she winced as a great flash of lightning streaked across the black sky. First she must stay calm, panic and the girl would panic; somehow she must seem as though, apart from the storm, none of this was new to her. Talaitha knew Judah Kane had found her beneath a hedge, her clothes testifying to the fact she had lived rough, so why should she not believe she had helped deliver babies while on the road?

'Breathe deeply.' The words of the doctor returned, releasing her tongue from the anxiety that had it dry in her mouth. 'Try to relax between each spasm.'

How idiotic that had sounded to her as she had writhed in pain, and how futile as wave followed on red-hot wave.

'I have to remove your underwear.'

Did the girl feel the same hopeless fear she was feeling? Did she resent an outsider touching her in so intimate a fashion? But there was no one else. Sliding away the large cotton drawers, Garnet pushed them beneath the cover of the basket; it would not keep them dry but at least the wind would not carry them away.

Had she been told to push? The memory was vague, dancing elusively away into the shadows of half-conscious memory. If she had, then at what stage had that been … was this girl ready to push?

Overhead, thunder rolled grabbing the girl's scream, folding it away into itself, smothering it in darkness.

Now, it had to be now. Talaitha was at the end of her tether, she could suffer no more pain.

'Push.' Whether it was time or not, Garnet shouted the word as thunder crashed again. 'Push ... push!'

But the girl did not move and as lightning streaked white across the sky, Garnet saw her eyes were closed.

'No... o ...o! I won't let you, I won't let you!'

Her own scream grabbed by thunder she threw the girl's skirts above her waist, fumbling in the darkness for the child that lay half in, half out of its mother's body. Lifting it she held it in her hands but there was no whimper, no cry of a tiny creature taking its first breath.

Aware only of her own pain, of that terrible searing pain of loss all over again, Garnet struck out at the fates that had played their game of death.

'I won't let you, not again ... not again...!'

In the madness of pain one hand held the child while the other flailed at the rain-filled night; then as she sobbed her hand struck against the tiny body and a weak answering cry mixed with her own.

It was alive! Crying with relief she hugged the tiny body, the child was alive! But it must be kept warm, and the mother...

But Talaitha lay unmoving. The new-born

child still clutched against her. Garnet bent over the girl. 'I'm sorry,' she wept, 'I am so sorry...'

'Be it alive?' No more than a whisper the words rang in Garnet's heart like a great bell.

'Yes.' Laughter and tears mixed into one she held the tiny figure for the girl to see.

In the brilliant flash that lit the sky, Garnet saw the weak smile cross the tired face.

'The cord,' the girl whispered again, 'it must be cut, you must separate the child from the cord.'

Cut! Elation draining from her, Garnet frowned. How was she to do that? There was nothing in the basket but pegs and heather.

'You must bite through it.' Intuition telling her the problem, the girl rallied her strength. 'It be done like that often among women on the road, you must bite it clean through ... quickly afore the cold strikes too deep.'

She couldn't do it, she could not take that thing in her mouth. Garnet felt her stomach heave.

'Please!' In the darkness Talaitha felt for her hand squeezing it gently. 'You 'as to do it. The child must be kept from the night air, it be too cold for it and it can't be wrapped while it be still joined to me.'

It was more than she could do; more than should be asked of any woman. 'I can't,' the

115

whisper was for herself, 'I can't, I can't...'

'Then it will die, my child will be taken from me.'

'*Taken from me.*'

Louder than any clap of thunder the words hammered in Garnet's mind. Taken, as her own child had been taken.

The tiny figure lay still in her hands, its body cold against her fingers.

'*...quickly afore the cold strikes too deep...*'

Was it already too late, had the flame of life fluttered out while she had hesitated? No, please ... please not that! It must not be dead, she would not let it be dead.

Sobs bursting deep inside she bent over the tiny child, her teeth closing on the spongy cord.

It was cold, so cold. Touched against her face the body of the child was still ... lifeless. Rain lashing into her eyes, into her mouth, she clutched it fiercely to her. 'Don't die,' she whispered, 'don't die ... don't die!'

'Wrap the child, keep it from the cold.'

As if coming from a great distance the words seeped quietly into her brain.

The baby must be kept warm, protected from the rain. But with what? Once more in control of her emotions, Garnet rubbed the tiny body vigorously and as she did so another brilliant flash illuminated the sky and heath and in its light she saw the girl push her skirts over her ankles.

116

Unaware of anything save the scrap of humanity held in her hands Garnet did not hear her own murmured prayer of thanks. Laying the child on its mother's knees she stepped out of her petticoat then wrapped the little form in it. But that alone would not hold life in the fragile body, it could be hours before the storm ended and the sky lighten enough so they could see their way. Quickly removing her patched skirt she shook it, freeing it of what rain she could. It was damp but not yet soaked through, and though far from ideal it was all she had.

Wrapping that over the cotton petticoat, folding it over so every scrap of it protected the baby she handed the precious bundle to Talaitha, setting it beneath her shawl.

'Hold your son...' she breathed, 'keep him safe.'

Then, clad only in blouse and drawers she lay across her, shielding them both with her body.

Chapter Nine

'He be sheltering in some barn,' the men had told her. 'Judah don't be daft enough to cross the 'eath in a storm.' But a storm wouldn't keep 'im from his home. Hepzibah stared from the doorway of her wagon. If they believed their own words why then go to search for him, if he were simply sheltering in some barn why had they gone out in such weather?

Because they didn't believe their own words! Her eyes watched silver-tipped clouds race away to the horizon. They knowed what she knowed, that Judah Kane lay out there somewhere in the dark of night, that her son might well be dead.

The men had been on the brink of leaving the camp. Carrying candles protected in jam jars from the wind and rain they were setting off to look for the Tuckett wench and the gaujo woman gone calling with her, but they waited as her had called to them. They had tried to reassure her but as her anxiety persisted they had separated into two teams, one going in the direction of the town, the rest following the opposite way ... the way the two women had taken.

Judah had gone to Wednesbury. She listened to the rain drumming on the roof of the wagon. He had taken much o' the money kept in the cupboard beneath her bed 'oping to buy the horses her had told him of. But Judah 'adn't never reached that town. Instinct that had spoken in her heart since midday spoke again now and Hepzibah listened. Something had 'appened, something bad.

118

Her stare, returned to the shadows, rested on the dark squat shape of Alcina Korjyck's wagon. That Lakin racklie lay in there, the wench that 'oped to wed with Lorcan Nash. Wed! She snorted into the darkness, he would do better tying himself to a bitch! The wench was no good, it had been in her from being a child; do what she would was the whole of her creed and it was one would bring evil in its wake.

Her had watched the wench as the sun lowered to its bed. Watched the tilt of her head, the flounce of her skirts as she had sauntered into the camp and crossed to the place of her fire, skirts that had been lifted for more than a piddle on the 'eath! And the money in her pocket ... oh yes, there was money, the look on her arrogant face told as much ... that 'adn't all been got in exchange for what lay in her basket; more like she had sold what lay between her legs! Lorcan Nash were a fool to believe he would be first man, either to lead this camp or to enter Marisa Lakin's body. The wench was a trollop and her worshipped the god of a trollop: money! The power of money and the authority it could bring over others. Marisa Lakin was greedy for both but of the two it was her lust for authority gleamed brightest, and her would sell more than her body to get it. And hope of authority for her lay in the getting of Lorcan Nash. The two of them together ... did they be in some way responsible for her son's absence?

But Nash 'ad left soon after first light, the journey to Brough were long. Brough! Hepzibah chewed on the stem of her unlit pipe. Why go there when the rest of the wagons would follow the road to Stowe? Did he 'ave more to trade than were seen to leave with 'im, more than he wanted the other men to see; and might that something be the horses Judah 'ad set off to buy, bought from their stable with money taken from Judah's pocket?

But none except herself knowed of the selling, and her tongue had told of it to no one but Judah. The gaujo woman had been sleeping in the wagon and none other were nigh enough to 'ear. None that could be seen! The fear that held Hepzibah's heart tightened its hold still further. Or none that wanted to be seen! 'Ad ears listened from the shadows ... the same ears that 'eard Tonio Korjyck would be returning to his wagon wi' money in his pocket ... 'ad the same thing 'appened to Judah as had 'appened to him?

The swift leavin' o' Lorcan Nash were not natural, and the swagger o' that wench were more than before...

Slipping the pipe into her pocket she gazed at the moon, pale and slivery in the clearing sky, conviction growing inside her.

120

Whatever 'ad befallen her son were it the work o' the hands o' Lorcan Nash, and the guiding of 'em, were that the jealousy o' Marisa Lakin?

The crystal would tell 'er, it would answer both fear and suspicion. But there 'ad been a promise given when the ball 'ad passed to her from her mother, a promise to use it only as a 'elp to others.

'Abuse its powers and they'll be gone from ye.' That had been her mother's caution and it remained with her every time a request were made to read the crystal.

'It be used only to 'elp a body sore in need.' She whispered to the moon. 'Now it be me be sore of 'eart, it be me needs to know, do my son be dead?'

'T'were no use, it were too late, 'e were already dead afore we found...'

The words seemed to ride a black veil that lifted from her eyes only to descend again, letting her see and hear vaguely before blotting out the world once more.

'...seemed 'e 'ad been dead some time...'

Dead! Garnet struggled with the dark mist that threatened to retake her senses. The baby was dead, Tyler had thrown her child to the dogs.

'No... o ...o!'

Pushed by a great fountain of grief the words stretched into a long moan.

121

'Wench ... wench, quiet yerself, it be all right...'

Somewhere in the darkness a strong force was pressing on her, trying to pull her away, trying to take her child.

'No, I won't let you take her, I won't let you have her...'

Fighting with all her strength Garnet tried to fight off the strong hands that held her, but they were too much. Forcing her downwards they held her.

'Please, Tyler!' Her strength almost spent, Garnet could only sob. 'Please don't do it, don't kill my child!'

'Quiet yerself!'

Sharp yet edged with pity the voice penetrated the mist still shrouding her mind. Opening her eyes, Garnet blinked as a face swam inches from her own.

'Tyler, please...!'

'I don't be Tyler!'

Sharp as before the voice answered and the face of Hepzibah Kane came into focus.

'Quiet yerself!' Hepzibah repeated. 'There be others close by and one among 'em ye wouldn't want to be knowin' yer business.'

Like a wave washing over sand the memory of the past hours rushed in on Garnet, clearing her mind, washing it free of unreality. It had not been Tyler ... it had not been her own child ... but a child was dead, she had heard those words, they were not illusion. The child was dead ... it had to be the one she had helped deliver on the heath!

'I'm so sorry ... I'm so very sorry...' Eyes swimming with tears she looked at the woman still holding her wrists. 'I tried to save the baby ... I tried but I didn't know what else to do... Oh God, I didn't know what else to do!'

'Ye did all were to be done.' Releasing her hands the older woman smiled. 'There be naught of blame ye can set agen yeself.'

'I know what it is to lose your baby, I know the heart-break that poor girl is suffering...'

'Heart-break!' Hepzibah chuckled. 'The wife o' Clee Tuckett don't be suffering no 'eart-break, 'er be pleased as a cock wi' two tails.'

Pleased ... how could Talaitha be pleased? Her baby was dead!

'What gives ye to think the wench be 'eart-broken?'

'Wouldn't any mother be...?' Sitting up, Garnet watched as Hepzibah moved to where a kettle and mug stood on an upturned chest. 'Losing a child is like losing part of your own heart.'

'Who said the child be lost?'

The chuckle gone from her voice, Hepzibah whipped round.

'I heard what was said.'

'So ye 'eard ... and just what did it be that ye 'eard?'

Meeting those piercing eyes, Garnet faltered. Had she really heard those words, or had they been part of a nightmare?

'Well, what was it ye 'eard?'

There was nothing to be gained by pretending. This kind woman wanted to protect her, to keep the truth from causing yet more pain, but the pain of truth left a clean wound, a wound that would heal and leave no scar.

'I heard someone say it was of no use. That it was too late, he was dead before he was found, that he had been dead some time. I'm sorry ... I tried...'

'So you 'eard tell 'e were dead!'

'Yes.' Eyes heavy with tears watched the kettle being lifted from the chest.

'And you 'eard the word *child?*'

'No, but it had to be the baby that was spoken of.'

'Why?' Hepzibah slammed the kettle down hard. 'Cos ye says so? Ye be like all gaujos, ye sees the flames where no fire be lit. Ar, the talk were of a death, but that death were not of a chavvie, it were no child were taken but a jukel!'

'A jukel?' Garnet frowned, the word telling her nothing.

'A dog!' Hepzibah's sharpness erupted in the stirring of the tea she had brewed. 'It were Judah's dog they found dead!'

124

Her eyes on the stick of elder wood she was working into a flower, Marisa was aware of the dark-skirted figure climbing from Alcina Korjyck's wagon. She had been turned out, put into the night to make way for a gaujo!

Sliding the knife along the body of the stick she teased a sliver of bark back upon itself 'til it resembled the curled petal of a chrysanthemum.

Her place in that wagon was given to the woman Judah Kane had dragged from a hedge! Marisa Lakin was of no consequence...! She sliced the knife along the stick ... of no importance, an outcast among her own. But that was not how it would always be. Her mother would regret the day she had turned her back, and the woman climbing now into her own wagon would also know regret ... and the sorrow she had now would be multiplied a thousandfold!

Lorcan had made a mess of things, but it were no mess could not be straightened. The carving finished, she placed the pretty artificial flower on the ground beside her. He must have waited over by Bescot as they'd planned. Left the wagon concealed from the track and waited for Judah Kane to pass on his way to Wednesbury; then, as with Tonio Korjyck, attacked him. But unlike Korjyck, Judah Kane was not dead, he was alive in that wagon!

Had he seen his attacker? Marisa had to

force her fingers to carry on working. Did Judah Kane know who it were had left him for dead? And Lorcan Nash? Had that dog bitten him before he clubbed it to death? That it were Lorcan's work she had no doubts, but were he also dead or dying from the wounds that dog could have inflicted?

Lorcan Nash dead! The thought echoed in her mind. If so then the place she hoped to occupy in this camp would never be hers; and neither would the place her cherished, unless steps be took.

Yet if he weren't dead but still did not return, if once again his word to her were no more than spit in the wind?

Taking another stick of elder she sliced into it, watching the thin narrow strip curve delicately back on itself.

Wagons travelled every road and track of the country with the habit of pulling into the same sites. But it were not only wagons that travelled, news came with every one. Should Lorcan Nash not come to her, she would go to him; she would find him … and her knife would find his heart!

They had carried Judah Kane into camp just at the moment the gaujo woman had been brought in along of the Tuckett wench and her whelp. Marisa gouged the stick savagely. Now she were being fussed over by his mother. It were a brave thing the gaujo had done, the whole camp had said as

126

much. A cold smile creeping into her eyes she sliced the stick with a slower, more precise movement. Bravery should be rewarded and that woman would get hers, every last bit of it!

'I have not spoken to Mr Kane, but his mother has told me he will recover, only it will take time.'

The girl she had helped at the birth of her child smiled at Garnet. 'I be told the same.'

'Then it must be so.'

'Ar.' Talaitha nodded. 'You'll see for yourself in a week or so; Judah Kane don't be one as takes easy to his bed, but should ye be so soon from your own?'

'I could not have you leave without wishing you and your son well. I am so glad neither of you came to any harm.'

'Takes more than a thunderstorm on the 'eath to bring 'arm to a gypsy, but as for the little 'un,' she glanced to where the child lay tucked in a drawer set beside the bed, 'I reckon he wouldn't be 'ere right now if it weren't for you. You remained there wi' me when many another would 'ave run, you stripped off your own clothes to wrap my babby against the night; me and mine won't never forget that, and as long as you needs a place to lay your 'ead and a family to welcome you then you'll find a place at the Tuckett fire.'

Crossing to where the drawer rested on the floor, Garnet knelt, touching a finger to the satiny cheek. Ebony had had skin like satin and hair as dark as the fluffy down covering this child's head, her fingers had been perfect as the ones curling now about her own, her child also had been loved and wanted as this one was. Only not by her father! Tyler Cadell had neither loved nor wanted his daughter, Tyler Cadell had thrown her tiny body to the dogs!

''E won't break...'

The laugh from behind bringing Garnet from her thoughts she turned.

'You can take 'im up, hold 'im if you wants, 'e be little but 'e won't break.'

It had been so long. She had searched so very many long months, each day praying to find the child, unable to face the horrendous truth that she would never see her baby again, that the daughter she loved was dead.

Feeling a pain so strong in her heart she wanted to scream from the stab of it she lifted the tiny bundle, holding it close to her breast, brushing the sleeping eyes with her lips.

'I loved you so much,' she whispered, 'you were the idol of my heart, the jewel of my soul, my miracle of love; but he killed you ... he killed you...'

'Mother says 'e be a fair weight, considerin'.'

Touching her face to that of the sleeping infant, Garnet hid the heart-break beneath a smile.

'He is beautiful, a real little Khan.'

'A what?'

Rising to her feet, Garnet faced the girl, the baby still held in her arms.

'I lived for a time with my parents in India. In that country some rulers are called Khan. They are honourable, proud and fiercely protective of their land and people. That, I am sure, is the way your son will grow, proud and honourable, protective towards his people.'

'What did you say them rulers be called?'

'Khan.'

Taking the child into her own arms the girl smiled. 'Then that be 'ow he will be called, his name will be Khan.'

Judah had not been killed. About to use the crystal, to use the power it held to reveal the whereabouts of Judah, she had been stopped by the shouts of the returning men.

Adding salt to the pot simmering over the fire, Hepzibah thought over the happenings of those night hours.

She had felt no worry at first, Judah could 'ave been sat at some other fire, it were the Romany way to talk with those camped along your way, but as the hours lengthened the bands about her heart had tightened;

129

and not only for 'er son but for the gaujo along wi' the wife o' young Clee Tuckett an' the child in 'er womb.

Judah an' the Tuckett wench, it could be understood why there were worry for them, they were of 'er blood, of 'er kind. But the gaujo ... why 'ad worry for 'er been of the kind to cause a sickness o' the heart? Why did the woman affect her so?

After tasting from the pot she laid the ladle aside, settling herself on the stool beside the blazing log.

The feeling 'ad rose in her the night of 'elping the wench to bed in the wagon and it rose again while watching for sign of her returning that night. A strange fluttering it had been, deep inside, a ferment in the stomach like a hope that something long awaited were come at last.

That were of no sense! Hepzibah silently repeated the words she had already told herself several times in the last few days. But repeat them as she would, the feeling stayed.

And the girl had chosen to stay. 'I will not leave.' It had been said with a firmness not 'eard in the wench afore. 'You cannot go calling and be here to care for Mr Kane at the same time, I shall go calling.'

'An' sleep where? Ye knows the Romany way, no man rests in the same wagon as a raklie 'cept the girl be his own sister.'

Taking a knife from a box slung on the

side of the wagon, Hepzibah settled on her stool to begin the task of whittling pegs. She had expected the curt response to put an end to talk of staying but the wench had smiled, that same soft tone answering: 'I have slept beneath hedges before, I can do so again.'

But her would sleep under no hedge. Before the camp had broke up and the wagons set out on the road the men had shown their respect for the actions of the gaujo. The younger boys had been set to making a half circle of holes in the ground behind Hepzibah's wagon using the pointed end of a kettle prop while older lads cut branches of hazel from the nearby copse. It had taken the men less than an hour to strip the branches and smooth them into rods, settling one end in the small post holes and the other in holes cut into a stouter central ridge pole, covering the whole with a length of canvas secured to the ground with wooden skewers, furnished inside with bedding of bracken covered with blankets.

Glancing at the bender tent, Hepzibah smiled. The wench would sleep warm and dry.

An' that 'ad been that! But why? The question she knew so well gnawed her once more. Why 'ad 'er not sent the wench on her way, or made her travel with the others to Stowe?

'Ye mind an' keep close to the roads, the 'eath don't be kind to them as be little used to their secrets.'

She looked up, watching Garnet lift the basket to her hip. It could be easy seen the wench 'ad no true Romany for kin, that skin were too pale even though wind an' rain 'ad lashed it, then there were the hair, red an' glowing it shone about her head like dark fire.

'Mind ye be back afore the sun lowers!' She could not help but add the further caution.

Looking at the figure, wide skirts swathing the stool so it looked as if it sat floating on air, Garnet smiled. Given yellow clothing instead of black it might look like the statue she had once seen of a smiling Buddha.

'Ye mind me now, back afore sunset.'

'I will.' A sudden constriction in her throat, Garnet walked quickly away. There had been more than concern in that voice, more than consideration or even kindness … it had sounded more like love. No one had spoken to her in such a tone since … but she must not think of that, her parents were dead, that part of her life was gone; all that was left to her was bitterness and the nightmare horror of what her husband had done … that and her own promise to avenge the death of her child.

Chapter Ten

The gypsy wench would come to the barn...

Tyler Cadell eased his arms into the riding coat held for him by his brown-skinned manservant.

...she had come every afternoon, and why not, where else in this benighted place would she earn half a sovereign for an hour's roll in the hay? He had told himself the price was too high, that he would not pay it next time, but next time had become the next and the next and still he paid.

Slapping away gloves held ready for him he tutted irritably, tapping a booted foot as the manservant went to fetch a different pair from a tall chest of drawers.

He should see the wench off, and today he would. He would take what was offered then put a boot to her gypsy arse!

'Trying your patience am I, Raschid?'

His smile a mixture of acid and contempt, his eyes blue-grey ice, he looked at the man holding out several pairs of gloves.

'Then why do you stay, why not take yourself back to India? Why, Raschid ... why?'

Laughing, he chose gloves of soft tan

leather then knocked the rest to the floor, the laugh dying, giving way to a snarl.

'Shall I tell you why, shall I tell everyone why ... that you are unwanted there as you are here, shall I tell them?'

Watching the door close behind the turbanned figure, Tyler's hands clenched into fists, his mouth a straight, hard line.

'Shall I tell them...' he muttered, '...shall I tell them!'

Taking a few minutes in which to allow his outburst to subside he glanced at himself in the mirror, satisfied with the reflection he saw there. The Lady Olivia Denton was satisfied too. Another few weeks and he would propose. He had consulted with a lawyer in Birmingham, it were better to go to the city rather than Wednesbury or Darlaston, those towns were a little too close for his peace of mind; after all, someone other than Florrie Wilkes might know the date of the marriage of Isaac Winton's daughter.

Seven years! Fingers still stiff with anger he smoothed an already perfectly knotted cravat. The law required a seven-year wait before divorce could be granted. There was no definite proof of his wife being dead. The court would not accept...

The bloody court would not accept! Anger erupting in a hot consuming tide he kicked out the dressing mirror, shattering it into a myriad glistening fragments. Then the court would not be asked, it would not know he was marrying illegally; it would not have the opportunity to say that somewhere Garnet Winton-Cadell might still be alive; ... neither would Olivia Denton nor her titled uncle.

'Will I set lunch for you, sir?'

Glancing at the woman stood at the head of the corridor that led on to the kitchen stairs, Tyler's displeasure returned. He would like to get rid of her yet realised she was best kept under his nose ... but an unhappy state of affairs could always be settled ... one way or another.

'No.' He strode on, then halting half-way across the room he looked back. 'There will be guests for dinner tonight, see to it.'

Guests, and he'd left it till now afore sayin'! Swallowing the admonition rising sharply to her tongue, Florrie nodded.

''Ow many places will you want set, sir?'

'I'll let you know when I return,' he answered, relishing the look that crossed his housekeeper's face. Taking one more step towards the door he paused then added as if in afterthought, 'Oh, and let's not have another of your dreary unpalatable dishes, do give some thought to those unfortunate enough to be eating it. Should we perhaps leave your tedious lamb behind for one night and try ... *try...*' he emphasised the

135

word, 'something a little more ambitious?'

A little more ambitious! Florrie stared after her departing master. There were only one ambition knowed to her, an' that were the plunging of a knife in his gizzard! He were the one should 'ave been killed, it should have been him with his sly ways and lying tongue, he should have been given to the dogs, not a helpless babe who'd never done no hurt to nobody.

But since when had life been fair? She turned, walking slowly back to the kitchen. It had taken a master and a mistress who knowed how to treat a body with respect; taken a young woman scarce out of her girl years and throwed her into God alone knowed what. And in their place had set a jumped-up nobody, a man who cared for naught but himself. True, he could assume the air of a gentleman, but air blowed many ways; gentlemen needed breeding as well as manners, and Tyler Cadell showed precious little of either, the like of that one could never be any man's superior, not even that 'eathen Indian he kept as manservant.

There were something between them two! Stood by the gleaming range that dominated the kitchen she let the thought play in her mind. Why would any man, white, black or brown suffer the sort of treatment that foreigner took from Cadell? A boot or a fist meeting almost every word. Why not make away? There had to be others would give him a position, for much as she disliked him it had to be admitted the man had more respect for others and more refinement of character in his little finger than the other had in his whole body. Cadell had a hold over her, lies would drip like honey from his tongue to see her strung up on the gallows, but what hold did he have over the Indian?

'I think we might both find better pickings if we separates.'

She had waited beyond the crest of the hill, out of sight of Hepzibah Kane's keen eyes. Marisa smiled at the woman walking beside her. She had suggested they stay together for the first few hours, and the offer had been gladly accepted but now she needed to be rid of the encumbrance. Mid afternoon, she reckoned, glancing at the sun; she would lose her chance of a half sovereign unless a move were made quickly.

'That way leads to the town,' she indicated to where the path branched to the left, 'you take that way. There'll be women aplenty shopping for food and they'll mostly 'ave a penny for a strip o' lace or sixpence to 'ear what the future be 'olding for them.'

'I could not pretend to read a woman's palm, it would be a deceit!'

'It would be a sixpence,' Marisa tossed her head, 'but then if you says you can't do it then I supposes as you can't; you'll like get enough from the pegs to buy a neck o' mutton for to make a meal.'

'Hepzibah had me give my word to be back before the sun goes down.' Garnet glanced skyward. 'How far to the town?'

'It be close enough, you 'ave time aplenty if you cuts across the 'eath.'

Her eyes following the direction the other girl pointed, Garnet felt a twinge of concern. There was no road, no clearly marked path led across the rough bracken.

'I was told to keep close to the road.'

'In that case you might as well go back to the wagons now. It be a waste o' effort two callin' at the cottages, I'll go an' we'll share whatever coppers I makes.'

She could not do that, she could not leave Marisa to do the work alone. Smiling her refusal, at the same time assuring the girl she would manage perfectly well on her own, Garnet set off across the wide empty stretch of the heath.

That hadn't been too difficult. Lost to sight in the opposite direction, Marisa pulled the shawl from her head and pushed it into her basket, then gathering the hem of her brown skirt she tucked a corner of it into the waistband exposing a glimpse of white cotton petticoat. One day her would wear skirts of red, of blue, of any colour her desired, a froth of petticoats bordered round with layer on layer of lace, an' all would be of silk, and Marisa Lakin would dress like the finest o' the town an' the gaujo her was meeting with would pay for it. What her would ask today would be only the start ... she ran her fingers through the sable folds of her hair, the breeze carrying it away in a veil of black ... what he wanted her would give, but it would be at her price!

Reaching the barn set on the furthest edge of a hay field where it met the heath she glanced all around before slipping inside. Used to house winter feed for cattle it was unlikely any farm worker would be close by this time of the year, but making sure took little time and could save a lot of trouble. Gypsies were tolerated camping on the heath, but no farmer would stand for having one of them near his barns, even one holding nothing but hay.

He had not come. Marisa blinked, the interior of the barn gloomy and dark after clear sunlight. But then she had arrived each day before him, this would be no different.

Retrieving the shawl from her basket she spread it on a mound of soft dry hay then kicking off her boots she lay down, stretching her arms to each side.

'That is a picture would make any man feel welcome.'

Recognising the voice, she lay still for a

moment, then widening her legs just a little answered in a thick smoky tone, 'I could make him feel more than welcome.'

Throwing down the short riding whip, Tyler Cadell's face creased in a satisfied smile as he removed his jacket. The afternoon would be a pleasant one.

Rolling away as he lowered himself beside her, Marisa laughed softly. 'You can do better than that, let me show you how.'

Standing in a shaft of light finding its way through the roof she released the button of her skirt, letting it slide slowly to her ankles, petticoat following. Her eyes never leaving his face she toyed with the fastening of long cotton drawers, hearing the gasp of his breath as she left them tight about her shapely waist, her fingers slowly ... slowly loosening the ribbon that held the blouse across her breasts.

'Do you need me to teach you more?'

'Yes.' Tyler swallowed loudly. 'Teach me more.'

The ribbon lying between her fingers, Marisa laughed again, a husky promise filled laugh.

'Lessons cost money.'

A twitch of the stomach stronger than the trace of anger the girl's words arose in him he answered.

'You'll get your half sovereign.'

She would get more than that, or this

stallion would go without his oats! Letting the ribbon drop from her hands she lifted the blouse over her head holding it a few seconds, arms lifted high revealing taut thrusting breasts.

Pushed up on his elbows, Tyler Cadell drew a quick breath. The gypsy bitch was greedy, but she was exciting.

'More?'

'Yes!' His breath tight he answered the teasing query.

The blouse falling away behind, Marisa lowered her arms bringing her hands slowly, caressingly over her full breasts. Then, every movement a skilled act of seduction, she loosened the drawers letting them slide slowly down her bare legs.

Her smile pure invitation, Marisa heard the answer in the loud gasp as she lifted her hair, spreading it like a halo of ebony.

Watching her, Tyler felt the twitch become a jerk.

Standing there, her skirts a dusky cloud about her feet, her hair a sable mantle spreading behind, she was a dark Venus rising from the waters. This was what he wanted, what he knew he would never get from the so properly brought up women like Olivia; this gypsy would give him all that a wife might not, new experiences, new delights. A wife with a title, and a mistress with no bedroom inhibitions, what more could a man ask?

His arms reaching for her, Marisa let the heavy folds of hair fall about her breasts. Leaning forward, brushing both nipples against his fingertips she laughed again, softly, teasingly.

'Not yet ... you don't be ready.'

Not ready! Tyler swallowed hard. Christ it was almost choking him!

'It be better my way.'

Grasping his hands, her eyes gleaming coals that burned into his, she drew him to his feet. Stretched on tiptoe she pressed her lips to his, her fingers releasing buttons, pushing the shirt free of his body, unfastening until her hands lingered on bare flesh.

'Now!'

His gasp stopped by her tongue exploring his mouth, a shudder rocked him as fingers brushed against his groin. Lord he wanted this woman, wanted everything she could give him!

Her hands riding slowly back across his stomach to his chest, Marisa released his mouth. Lowering to her knees, fingers following the same torturing sensuous trail to his groin, she smiled up into a face passion had drawn tight and hard as his manhood.

Yes, he were ready. Hidden in her heart the smile widened to one of triumph. But first things first; her business and only then his pleasure.

Touching her mouth to a spot below the navel she traced her tongue across the warm flesh then leaning nearer took the throbbing organ, holding it between her breasts.

'I can't be stayin'.' Releasing him abruptly she was on her feet, her skirts in her hands before the realisation of what she said broke in on his fevered mind.

'What?' He stared, confusion settling in a frown between his eyebrows.

'I says as I 'ave to be goin', I don't be able to stay 'ere any longer.'

Denial never easy to come to terms with, Tyler's mood changed instantly. Grabbing her he snatched her close into him. 'Why?' he ground out. 'Why do you have to be going, why now?'

'I wants to stay, I likes pleasurin' with you, but the wagons be pullin' out, if I don't be with them I'll be wi'out a home, I'll 'ave no place to sleep except for the hedges, so you see I 'ave to go.'

Was she telling the truth, or was it simply a ruse, a gypsy lie spoken in the hope of getting more money for her services? But would she risk half a sovereign against a lie? Holding her tight to him, Tyler let thought argue against thought. Would she risk his walking away now? The softness of that body pressed close into him, the scent of lavender-washed hair in his nostrils, Tyler felt the searing heat of passion flare along his veins and knew it didn't matter, lie or truth it didn't matter! It was already too late to care, his desire for her was too strong, it was a fever in his blood, a madness he did not want to cure.

'You have to stay,' he pressed his mouth against her throat, 'I won't let you leave.'

Whimpering softly as he pulled her savagely against the hardness of him Marisa made pretence of pushing free, hearing the jagged intake of breath as her hands slid along his back and stroked over his naked buttocks, smiling inwardly as her touch jerked him like a puppet.

'But I 'ave to go,' she breathed against his kisses, 'don't you see, without a wagon of my own I 'as to go along wi' the others, I can't stay 'ere to live on the open heath. But p'raps this one last time, if we makes it quick...'

Touching her mouth to his, holding it with her own she drew one hand voluptuously over his hip, trailing it into the curve of his groin to brush against the taut mounds of flesh.

'No!' Drawing his mouth free, Tyler grasped the hand that tormented him. 'We won't make it quick and you won't leave. You'll have your wagon.'

Closing her eyes, hiding the gleam of

exultation, Marisa let herself be lowered to the ground.

It was already sunset, another few minutes and the sun would be lost over the horizon. Dread rising like an unwanted tide, Garnet looked around her at the deserted stretches of heath. She had seen no one since leaving Marisa, nor had she found the town the girl had spoken of. She must have been walking in circles. She looked again at the skyline, crimson now with the rays of the setting sun. It was beautiful but soon that soft red gold would give way to black and the heath would be enveloped in darkness.

A sob catching at her breath she forced herself to walk on. She must not be caught that way again, she could not spend another night in the middle of nowhere ... and this one alone!

She had tried to get her bearings, tried to remember the way she and Marisa had come, but no matter which direction she followed there had been only the emptiness of the heath. Why had she not paid more attention to their route, taken note of some building or landmark? But what building, what landmark? Apart from the odd cluster of trees or mound of grey rock there had been none.

Stumbling in her haste to beat the lengthening shadows she tripped, falling heavily to her knees. It was no good! She knelt where she had fallen, her head drooped on her chest. She was lost!

'Be something wrong ... be you hurt or ill?'

Almost sick with relief at hearing a voice, Garnet lifted her head, looking through tears at the man stood a few yards from her.

'No, no I am not hurt.' Glad that at last there was someone who could possibly set her on the right path, she scrambled to her feet, retrieving the basket that had rolled a little away.

'I seen you tumble, I feared when you didn't get up straight off that you'd injured yourself.'

The comfort of assistance after the worry of perhaps spending the night alone on the heath shone in Garnet's smile. 'No,' she brushed at her skirts, 'I am not injured though I am lost, could you possibly tell me where the gypsy camp is?'

'Gypsy camp?' The man's voice held a quiet laugh. 'There be p'raps a dozen spread around these parts, whereabouts was you wanting to be?'

Only with the question did Garnet realise she could not answer. She did not know where the wagons rested; she had not thought to ask and no one had told her. The town, was all Marisa had called the place to which she had pointed, but she had given it no name.

'I … I don't know.' Her confusion returning she stared into the swiftly gathering dark. 'My friend went one way and I went the other.'

'So where was you making for?'

Garnet shook her head. 'I only know it was a town, but the camp, perhaps you might have heard of its leader … Judah … Judah Kane?'

'Can't say as I 'ave.' The man swung his head slowly. 'The name don't ring no bell with me, but there be a gypsy camp about half a mile yonder. It might not be the one you be seeking but like as not they'll know where it is and see you safe to it. I can take you along there if you wishes.'

'Yes … yes, please. That's very kind of you.'

'Then you best not be going that way.' The man laughed as, hoisting the basket more comfortably on her hip, Garnet made to walk on. 'You go that way and you'll end up in the cut … the gypsy camp be t'other way.'

Half a mile he had said. Falling into step beside him, Garnet felt the tension of minutes ago ease from her mind. She would arrive after sunset but perhaps Hepzibah would understand.

'I thought p'raps you was from another village or some such, ain't often you come across a gypsy 'avin' lost her way.'

They had walked some minutes in silence, the man speaking again was a welcome sound in the darkness of the new night.

Garnet smiled. With the basket balanced on her hip she must look like Marisa or any other of the women in the group.

'I am not a gypsy,' she answered, 'they were kind enough to offer me shelter for a few nights.'

'Shelter ... then you be on the road?'

It was sharp, incisive and with it Garnet's nerves tingled.

'I ... I lost my way, the gypsies...'

'Seems you does that often, lose your way.'

He stopped suddenly and in the light of the rising moon Garnet caught the flash of a grin and again the trill of warning sang along her veins. Clutching the basket she tried to keep her nervousness from her voice.

'Thank you for showing me the way. I ... I can manage alone from here.'

'Not so fast!' He stepped in front of her. 'I don't do nothin' for charity, I gets paid for what I does for folk.'

The day had been a poor one. Her mind raced over the past hours. She had seen no one, sold nothing.

The tremble that rocked her nerves now rocked her voice as she answered.

'I'm sorry, I have sold nothing, I have no money...'

'Now ain't that a shame!' He stepped closer, one hand fastening on the basket. 'But there be other ways of payin' for a good deed, a service for a service you might call it.'

'Please, if you will come to the camp I am certain Mr Kane will reimburse you for your time.'

'Oh, I be sure he will.' The man laughed gratingly. 'With a stick about the 'ead. I weren't born yesterday, I be up to gypsy tricks; I'll take my payment now.'

Chapter Eleven

In the silver wash of moonlight the man's eyes gleamed. She had heard of his kind but, carefully hiding herself away every evening at nightfall, had never come face to face with a man of that sort until now. Bracken tangling about her feet Garnet stepped away. If she ran he would catch her in seconds, she could strike him, kick out at him but what effect would that have, he was far stronger than she.

Perhaps if she talked, kept up a conversation, after a little while he might go away. Desperately afraid, Garnet tried to keep her thoughts logical.

'My friends will be looking for me,' she tried again, 'they will be along soon I am sure of it...'

'Soon!' He laughed again, the sound of it hard against the velvet softness of the night. 'But soon ain't now, I don't hear no voices; them gypsies might well be looking for you but they won't find you just yet, there be time yet to pay your dues.'

With the last word he snatched the basket, throwing it into the shadows. A scream silent on her lips, Garnet turned to run but the bracken twined about her feet bringing her heavily to the ground.

'Now that be what I calls right sensible of you.' Standing over her the man unbuckled his belt. 'Paying up like a sensible wench.'

In the uncertain light, Garnet saw the trousers fall revealing the pale tint of flesh.

'No...!' Fallen on to her back she scrambled crab-like over the rough ground, afraid to take her eyes from the grinning face. 'No, please, I ... I will pay you...'

'Too bloody sure you'll pay me! You'll pay me now.'

Dropping to his knees, straddled across her, he fastened one hand in her hair, the other snatching her blouse and ripping it to the waist.

'I be going to enjoy this, this be a bonus I 'adn't thought to get.'

Tearing away her cotton chemise he

150

fastened a coarse hand over her breast, his laugh joining the cry that at last found its way from her throat.

'Cry out all you wants,' he lowered himself bringing his face inches above her own, 'I likes a woman to cry out, it adds a little bit o' spice to the entertainment.'

Grabbing at the ground each side of her, frantically trying to pull herself from beneath him, Garnet moaned as a vicious tug pulled her face to his.

'A little kiss…'

His breath, hot and reeking of stale food, filling her nostrils Garnet tried to turn away but each movement seemed to add to the man's perverted pleasure.

'… a kiss or two afore I gives you what you be waiting for.'

One hand touching against something solid, Garnet held back the scream bubbling in her mouth. If she could manage to grasp it… Shuddering as his mouth locked on to hers she worked her fingers around the cold hard object, it was a stone …. A hand-sized piece of stone.

'That be better.' Releasing her mouth, he grinned as he squeezed the tender flesh of her breast. 'I be right, don't I? You likes it same as me.'

'Yes.' Garnet's fingers gripped the stone. 'I will enjoy this very much!'

The first snigger half-way from his mouth,

Garnet brought the stone smashing against his head. Not waiting until the blow rolled him from her she kicked herself clear. Scrambling to her feet she began to run.

'No you don't, you bloody bitch!'

The blow had not knocked him senseless, it had not even dazed him!

Panic engulfing her, holding her in a blind drowning wave she ran, but fast as her feet drummed on the earth those of her attacker drummed louder.

'No woman strikes this man and gets away with it...'

From close behind the furious words ripped savagely into the night.

'... I be going to take what I intended then I'll beat your bloody brains out!'

Let Judah come now, please God let–

Her silent prayer unfinished, Garnet screamed as a violent push to her back sent her stumbling forwards, the man's harsh laugh adding to her terror as she toppled, falling down into the yawning blackness of an open pit shaft.

The wench 'ad not returned. Hepzibah looked at the moon-filled sky. The promise to be back before the sun slept 'ad not been kept. Glancing across the space left by the departed wagons she watched the figure sat close to a small fire. Marisa Lakin 'ad come back alone to where the Kane wagon stood.

The gaujo 'ad gone to work the town, she'd said, answering all questions with a toss of her dark head; 'I told 'er *stay close* but 'er went 'er own way.'

Told 'er stay close! Hepzibah spat derisively into the flames of her own fire. More like to 'ave sent the wench off on 'er own, and that along the wrong path. But with the men gone and Judah laid up in his bed there were naught to be done. The 'eath were treacherous, riddled with 'oles big enough to swallow a body an' some big enough to take a wagon an' leave no trace.

The wench were used with being on the road, with sleepin' 'neath a hedge. Hepzibah comforted herself with the thought. That be what her would do tonight, come the dawn her would turn up safe and sound.

A stifled moan caught only by her own sharp ears, Hepzibah pushed wearily to her feet. It had been long years since her 'ad known the nursing of a sick man and it were tiring. The widow Korjyck had offered to stay behind to 'elp with the carin' o' Judah, and Lord knowed it were a kindness but the caring of a man be for the wife or a mother, and Judah 'ad no wife.

But for 'ow long? The question never far from her brain rose again as Hepzibah poured boiling water from the kettle into a small metal basin in which she had earlier placed a handful of marigold petals.

153

He'd asked no wench to be wife to 'im, shown no interest in any juval whether of his own community or any met with on the road or at the horse fairs they visited several times every year.

Taking a sliver of juniper wood kept solely for the purpose she stirred the mixture, a sweet-smelling steam rising to her nose.

No, Judah had shown no interest in any woman ... until now. Several times in waking moments he'd asked after the gaujo.

The basin in her hands, Hepzibah clambered up the steps of her wagon.

But the gaujo woman 'ad a husband, and though there were men who'd pay little mind to that, Judah didn't be one of them.

'There'll be no sign this side o' mornin'.'

Turning up the lamp that swung from a hook driven into the wooden canopy of the wagon she answered the query before it was put, catching the look of anxiety mixed with pain as Judah sat up.

"Old ye still or ye'll go 'opening that wound afresh.' Her words sharp, Hepzibah set the basin on the chest that served as a table.

'Did nobody see her, see where she went?'

'The Lakin wench tells as 'ow it were toward the town.'

'Then her should be back by this time.'

Her should if Marisa Lakin 'ad told the true way! Immersing a piece of freshly boiled cloth in the basin then squeezing the liquid from it she laid it gently over the angry-looking gash to the side of Judah's neck. A few more inches and whoever 'ad struck that blow would 'ave left behind a dead man, his skull crushed.

'The wench were caught by the night.' She bathed the wound gently. 'Be thankful 'er 'ad the wisdom to rest somewheres an' not face the 'eath in darkness.'

His mother was right. Garnet would be doing the wisest thing, she would find a barn or a shelter somewhere and wait out the night there. If only the camp had not broken up today ... if only he could stand on his feet.

'The wound be clean, the marigold 'ave avoided it turnin' bad.'

Leaving the cloth in place, Hepzibah reached a small jar from the cupboard. Untying the string that held its waxed cloth cover in place she spread a fresh wad of cloth with ointment which she had made from clove to deaden pain and marigold to keep away infection. Alcina Korjyck were not the only woman to know the secrets of woods and 'eath!

Removing the cloth she had used to bathe the wound she inspected it closely before applying the pad of ointment and tying it in lace with a strip of the clean cloth.

Judah's broken flesh her could heal, but

what if the heart be broken.

Returning the jar to the cupboard she gathered bowl and cloth, carrying them outside.

Her son 'ad a giant share o' good sense ... but good sense didn't always prevail against the power of a man's love!

Putting the strips of soiled cloth into the laundry bowl that already held flowers of camomile for disinfectant she covered it with boiling water before emptying the small basin at the furthest edge of the encampment.

He had wanted to leave his bed and go search when sunset had come and the woman had not returned, and he might yet try again, but that couldn't be: much as 'er liked the quiet-spoken gaujo the welfare o' Judah must come first. Dipping into her pocket, Hepzibah withdrew a tiny bottle, the green of its glass sparkling in the light of the fire.

Judah must come first! Uncorking the bottle she tipped several drops of fluid into the meal set aside for her son.

Juice of the poppy would keep him asleep 'til well after a new dawn blessed the earth with light.

Why did her body hurt so much?

Trying to move, Garnet moaned and lay still. Why all this pain? Her whole body

156

throbbed as if she had fallen...!

But she had fallen! Memory pushing through the mists clouding her mind, her eyes flew open. Something had struck her between the shoulder blades ... she had been running ... that man! She caught her breath, holding it, afraid to let go in case it should be heard. That man had offered to help, to see her safely to a gypsy camp, but then...

She stared upwards, seeing a small circle, a patch of dark sky dotted with stars.

Why so little sky ... why a small patch when the sky was so wide and vast? With breath stinging her lungs she tried to release it without making a sound as the whole awful picture rushed in on her.

That man had asked for payment and that payment had been her, he had meant to rape her. Was he here somewhere looking for her, still bent on satisfying his lust?

Trying to move again she gasped at the pain ripping along arm and shoulder. Clamping her lips together she stared at the star-dotted patch above her head. If she lay still and didn't make a sound perhaps he would not find her, perhaps the darkness and the long bracken would hide her.

Every nerve at breaking point she strained to catch the slightest sound. If he came near could she make a run for it, disappear into the blackness before he was aware of her?

Wincing with every breath, she knew that was a futile hope, her only chance lay in her silence and absolute stillness.

How long would he search ... how long before he found her?

So near it seemed it must touch her, a scuffling rustled the bracken. It was him, he was there beside her.

Magnified by the fear that rocked her, the sound grew, swelled, expanding into a great balloon of noise holding her within itself, carrying her with it as it floated into a black silent world.

'No ... o ...o!' Moaning softly at being pulled from the oblivion of that dark silent place back into one filled with fear and pain, Garnet opened her eyes. The circle above her head had been inky, dark as soot-blackened water but now it was iron-grey tinged with silver pearl. The night was passed, surely she was safe now, that man must have gone. But she would wait a while longer, listen for any movement that might tell her otherwise.

Easing her legs, stretching their length, she winced as a sharpness like the tips of a dozen knives found its way through her thin skirts. She had lain in bracken many times but never found it so coarse as to prick her skin.

Gritting her teeth against the bite of every movement she forced herself to sit upright. There had been no sound other than the

158

call of a fox in the distance, and the light overhead was stronger. Focusing on the shadows still surrounding her, Garnet felt a newer, more terrible fear grip her heart; it was not the bracken-covered heath she had lain in, it was a pit, a deep rock-jutting hole in the earth!

He must have seen where she had fallen, he had been so close as to touch her, yet she had lain in this hole all through the night. Why had that man not pulled her out ... had he thought her dead ... that falling on to such sharp rock had killed her ... or was it that he had left her there deliberately, left her to die?

She had walked for hours on the heath meeting no one until he came along, that could be so again. There had been no cottage or farm, no building of any sort, no sign of human habitation anywhere. Terror beating a pulse in her throat she stared at the circle of sky rapidly taking on the light of day. That could mean no person might come this way for hours ... if at all!

Fear lending power to her cries she called for help, cry after cry echoing into the silence only to be absorbed by it, dying away without answer.

He had left her to die!

Realisation stark and sharp as the rock that pricked her flesh, Garnet recognised the truth.

Left in a hole on a deserted part of the heath he had thought to hide his assault of her. She might never be found and that way he would be safe.

How could he do that! Garnet caught the sob trembling in her throat. How could any man treat a woman that way? To rape her was cruel enough but to deliberately leave her to die slowly in an open pit was evil.

Fear turning to panic that masked the pain of clawing at bare rock she dragged herself to her feet. She must get out! She had to get out.

Sobbing openly as panic mounted within her, she reached for a large jaggedly pointed stone protruding from the shaft above her head. Hauling herself upwards, her feet scrambling for a hold, she screamed as the rock broke free and threw her down, striking the side of her head as it fell.

Rising from her bed on the floor of the wagon, Hepzibah looked at her son. He was sleeping yet; the juice of the poppy had done its work well. Turning off the lamp she had kept burning low through the night, she went quietly from the wagon.

The woman had not returned. Pulling her shawl close against the cool breath of dawn, she placed several sticks in the smouldering ash of last night's fire then set the kettle on the hook of the cooking rod, leaving it to

160

boil while she washed herself in cold water.

She had lain long into the night listening for a sound that would tell of the woman's return, but the night had come and gone without sign.

Taking a mug of fresh-brewed tea she sat herself on her stool.

But the night hours had not been empty. She sipped the tea. They had been peopled with thoughts, with hopes long held by many gypsies but believed by few; hopes that there would come one who would fight their cause, see them not as rogues and vagabonds, a blight that must be swept away, but as people with a right to live, a right to the countryside that was forever being closed to them.

And with the coming of Garnet Cadell she had felt in some strange inexplicable way that hope was one step nearer.

But that were a daft thought! Hepzibah stared into the new-born flames. Any champion of the Romany would needs be born of Romany blood, who else would stand for them!

Yet the feeling had been strong, and the wench had stood by the side of young Clee Tuckett's wife through the birthing of their son. But helping a girl give birth were a different kettle of fish. It were no midwife the Romany nation needed, it were a miracle.

Refilling her mug, Hepzibah held it between her gnarled hands, savouring its warmth. Miracles never happened, as for a champion who would bring justice for the Romany, hoping for that was like reaching for the moon on water!

Her tea finished she gathered the utensils for bathing and dressing her son's wound. Judah had been lucky the dog had been close enough to save him. But who had it saved him from ... her son had made no mention ... did he know his attacker ... had he seen who struck that blow to his neck?

Glancing across to where a mound of ash smouldered she looked at the blanket-wrapped figure lying close beside it. The Lakin wench knowed of it, if naught else were certain that were. Nash and her would lend their 'ands to anything that would make him first man; rob and kill as everybody believed Tonio Korjyck had been robbed and killed. Striking a man from behind bore Lorcan Nash's stamp all over it, like the coward he was he took a man from the back; but Nash struck in the dark and Judah had been attacked in daylight, besides which Nash had left hours before, taking his wagon to Brough.

Picking up the basin of boiled water, Hepzibah gripped it with tightened fingers. In daylight or in darkness a snake would still strike! In a few days Nash would return and the answer would be written in his eyes.

Carrying the basin into the wagon she set it on the chest.

The answer would be written and Hepzibah Kane would have the reading of it!

Chapter Twelve

Well satisfied with his performance, Tyler Cadell gave the horse a pat before handing the rein to a waiting groom. The rest of the hunt, he knew, had watched him, waiting to see him unseated at the first fence. But he had ridden well, up in front with the leaders all of the way. Touching short whip to riding cap in salute, he turned away from his fellow huntsman as his host walked across to him.

'It was a good ride.' He answered the other man's enquiry. 'Most exhilarating, I must congratulate you on your horses, you have a fine stable.'

'Yes,' the Viscount Riverton ran his own hand over the animal's glossy flank. 'They give a man a run for his money.'

Watching the groom lead the animal away, Tyler nodded, 'I can well believe it, sir, I certainly would not wager against any one of them.'

'Smart man.' The viscount laughed. 'You

obviously know your horses.'

'I rode regularly whilst in India.'

'I didn't think the army ran horses like these.'

'They didn't.' Tyler heard the surprise in the other man's tone. 'At least not in my regiment, but the local Nawab owned a good stable and he would often invite myself and fellow officers to partake in a game of polo.'

Tapping his left leg with a cane, James Riverton turned towards a gracious brick-built house. Square-set surrounded by well-kept gardens and bordered by farmland it breathed elegance and wealth.

'Polo,' he smiled ruefully, 'that's how I got this, a good game for all that.'

Had he been in India? Tyler felt a cold touch against his spine. Olivia had not mentioned anything of that when she had talked of her uncle. Christ! What if the man knew ... what if he'd heard? Gossip was cherished out there, passed among the British like life-preserving medicine; savoured and repeated and never forgotten!

'Were you in India?' He tried not to sound tentative.

'Not with the regiments. My father would not allow it, had I been killed it would have seen the earldom die out; I was the only son and my father looked to me to have children ... to safeguard the title. But alas that can't

164

be, I am the last of a long illustrious line and when I go the title goes with me.'

He had not been with the army, but even so the grapevine out there slithered faster than a cobra. Wanting to know the reason for the man being in India, but not pressing the question for fear of arousing any curiosity, Tyler kept his silence.

'No, my father would not countenance the Queen's colours,' James Riverton went on. 'My few weeks in India were part of the grand tour. That was one thing my father insisted I do, give me a wider view of the world, broaden my education. Well it did that all right,' he laughed cynically, 'it taught me an appreciation of many things and not all of them art. The exotic East held many temptations several of which no young man should have submitted to; but if you promise never to tell the earl then I will admit to you I did, and what is more I enjoyed the submission.'

Joining the laughter, Tyler relaxed. Had this man been told what had happened all those years ago then he would not be so friendly.

'Ah yes, India!' Reaching the house, James dismissed the dogs following at their heels. 'Fascinating place, I enjoyed the few weeks I spent there. Damned hot, though, can't say I'd want to live in a climate like that, melting the eyes in your head one month and washing your brain away the next; thank God England doesn't have monsoons.'

'Did I hear you mention monsoons?'

Elegant in palest green moiré silk, sherry-coloured hair coiled high on her head, Olivia Denton smiled as both men strode into the gracious oak-panelled hall of Victoria House.

'You did, my dear. Cadell here was just saying he played polo in India ... dreadful climate, give a man nothing but the gout or a gammy leg playing that blasted game.'

'Now, now,' she shook her head in pretend reprimand, 'we must remember it also gives us tea and yours, my dear uncle, has been waiting fully half an hour.'

'What? Oh yes, tea. Sorry, my dear.'

Tucking her arm through his, Olivia Denton smiled into the distinguished face of the man some years her senior, a face, Tyler noted, that had by no means lost its handsome looks.

Following to a sitting room conveniently located off the hall he flicked a more concentrated glance over the man who had invited him to his house. Left with a limp it seemed caused him pain he had not taken part in the afternoon sport but had politely been at the stable to greet his guests' return. Watching him now, settled in a velvet-covered wing chair, smiling fondly as he accepted tea from his niece, Tyler saw the closeness between them. How much older was this man than the daughter of a dead brother, ten ... twenty years? Not that it made a deal of difference apart from the inconvenience of him having that many more years left of life, years before his niece would inherit.

'I am the last of a long illustrious line and when I go the title goes with me.'

A pity a woman could not inherit the earldom! Accepting cup and plate, he smiled at Olivia Denton. That title would fall into extinction with the death of James Riverton, while he would so relish one for himself; but the money the niece would bring would provide a soothing balm for the affliction of being plain Tyler Cadell .. at least until a more lasting cure were found!

'I'm sorry, Lister, it is entirely out of the question, I promised my uncle I would spend the whole of the year with him and I will not renege on my promise.'

Across the room Olivia Denton was shaking her head at the wry face being pulled by another of the guests, a young man who had been paying her a great deal of attention, one he guessed was hoping to make the Lady Olivia Denton his bride.

Sipping his tea, Tyler watched the play between the two. The fellow was young, one of several he had met since forming a friendship with Olivia. He had teased her with the idea of marrying one of them but she had quickly dismissed it. What they wanted and what she wanted were two very different things.

She had touched a hand to his arm as she had said it, lowering her lashes as a touch of colour rose to her cheeks, the next words being said more swiftly. Her darling uncle would never attempt to persuade her to marry where she had no wish to.

But would 'darling uncle' allow his niece to marry a common soldier?

Replacing cup and plate on the elegant afternoon-tea trolley, the thought lingered in his mind. In this day and age money could conveniently be counted upon to overcome many obstacles, and with a considerable amount of Riverton's fortune at his disposal and the ability of the likes of the people he was meeting to open influential doors, then who could tell? A title might just find its way to being his.

'So, you liked my stable did you?'

The viscount's question driving the reflection into the background, Tyler switched on an attentive smile.

'I did indeed. They must be of great pleasure to you.'

'I don't ride as often as I did, gammy leg an' all, but breeding a good horse and seeing it run is a pleasure in itself. Trouble is I hate to part with them. I sold a pair a day or so back then regretted it almost at once, but as Olivia tells me I either have to sell some or must sell Victoria House for the place will soon be too small to stable them all.'

'You are too possessive, uncle...'

Tyler caught the smile that passed between the two as the girl came to stand beside the older man's chair.

'...you would like to keep everything the same but you have to change things sooner or later, is that not so, Mr Cadell?'

Catching her cool green look, Tyler had a quick mental vision of those hot brown ones laughing up at him from a mound of hay. There were things he would change if he could.

'I fear it is,' he answered, allowing the merest hint of a smile to find his mouth. 'Though were I your uncle there are two things I would hope never to part with.'

'And those are?'

Cool as before those eyes rested on his and again he visualised the smouldering look of a gypsy wench lying naked, her arms lifting to him.

'Were I the viscount,' he answered, his thoughts well hidden, 'I would hope never to have to part with my niece.'

'Well said!' The viscount laughed, watching his blushing relative rejoin those others of his guests. 'However, the girl will go one day, that I'm resigned to. But Olivia was only one of the things you said you would be unwilling to part with; tell me man, what was the other you had in mind?'

'The Arab stallion. You must pardon my frankness, sir, but I cannot put this any other way; you would be a fool to sell so fine a horse. Put him to covering the best of your mares and you could have a string of horses to match any Maharaja in India.'

Seated across from him, James Riverton nodded, his glance going to the elegant figure of his niece. 'You are very observant, Cadell,' he said quietly, 'you have lighted upon the two most valuable assets to my life.'

And one most valuable to mine! Tyler kept the smile tucked away. James Riverton could keep his Arab stallion but Tyler Cadell would take his niece.

Huddled in the bottom of the pit, Garnet moaned softly while, as if from a million miles away, the sound of a dog barking seeped into her mind. But it was only a dream, another part of the nightmare that refused to let her go, a terrible darkness that pulled her back into its depths each time she tried to wake. But now she did not want to wake, in this world of darkness the pain of remembering was dulled, soon she would sleep again and feel the sting of it no more.

'Ebony.' It trickled in a whisper as her

arms clutched an imaginary figure to her breast. 'I have found you my own darling...'

'Hey!'

The call from overhead was almost lost beneath the furious bark of a dog but, sliding out of reach of it, Garnet made no answer.

'What's old Ben found this time?'

Coming to stand beside his son, Enoch Babb stared down into the overgrown pit shaft. 'Strewth! It looks to be a woman!'

'Ow do ya reckon her come to be down there, do you reckon it be her was murdered?'

All the excitement of a ten-year-old shining in his eyes the boy looked up at his father.

'I reckons ya best put rein on that imagination o' your'n or one day it'll run off wi' ya!' Enoch put a hand to the lad's shoulder, holding him as he leaned dangerously over the crumbling edge of the gaping hole.

'But 'er could 'ave been,' the boy persisted, ''er could 'ave been murdered an' throwed down the shaft by whoever done it 'oping the body wouldn't never be found.'

'It could also be that a certain somebody I knows on will get a kick to 'is arse if he keeps goin' on about bodies an' murders.'

Enoch hauled his son away, leaving a safer margin of ground between them and the shaft.

171

'Ain't you goin' to do summat, tell the coppers?'

'And get sent to the gallows!' Enoch shook his head.

'It don't do to go gettin' yerself mixed up in wi' the constabulary, they'd like as not pin the 'ole thing to the tail o' my jacket. No, son, I says we leaves well enough alone.'

'But what if 'er don't be dead, what if 'er still be alive?'

'Don't talk so crackpotical!' Enoch snapped sharply. 'O' course 'er be dead or 'er would 'ave called out, 'er would 'ave been bound to 'ear the racket old Ben set up.'

'Not if 'er d'ain't be conscious.'

For all of his wild imagining the boy often made a great deal of sense. Enoch Babb released his hold on his son. It might be the woman lying at the bottom of that pit did still breathe, that she made no sound because she heard none.

'We 'as to find out, don't we, Father? We can't just leave, turn aside like the Levite in Mother's Bible.'

His son was right, they couldn't leave the woman before knowing there was nothing to be done for her. Going to stand again at the edge of the yawning gap in the earth, Enoch Babb stared at the unmoving huddle at its base before turning again to where the boy stood watching.

172

'You go back,' he said, 'tell your mother what it be we've found, 'er will know what to bring an' you fetch Samson and a length o' rope, Ben 'ere will guard the barge.'

He never should have been swayed. Enoch watched the figure of his son race away towards the canal, the brown and white bull terrier keeping pace at his heels. The lad meant well and his heart was in the right place but he had little understanding of the ways of the law. It should be a man was innocent til proved otherwise but for the likes of a barge rat with no money to pay a fancy lawyer it was more like to be the other way around; and if anybody should come by and find him standing over a pit that held a dead woman it would be the gallows, for nobody would believe he had found her there already dead.

With his nerves on edge he jumped at every rustle of grass, every twitter of birds. He couldn't risk being here any longer, he had a wife and part-grown son to provide for.

Glancing once more at the inert huddle below his feet, he turned. If he left now he would meet Clara and the lad, he could turn them back. Less than half a dozen yards from the pit a cry halted him. Coming over the horizon of the heath his son waved a hand.

'We can't go turnin' our backs!' Clara

Babb stared at her husband. 'What sort o' Christian act be that for a body to do? 'Ere I be, Enoch Babb, an' 'ere I stays til I knows beyond guessin' that wench down there be beyond my 'elp.'

'An' what if 'er don't be gone ... what then?' Enoch cast another anxious glance about them. 'We gets the bobbies an' I gets throwed into gaol, they won't never believe it were not me as done that woman in.'

'Then we don't get no bobbies, but I be goin' to know what it be I wants to know afore we moves from 'ere!'

It were not often Clara wore that face; adamant, one iron master had called it when he'd tried cutting the carrying price for the third time; and what an iron master couldn't shift, Enoch Babb stood little chance of moving.

Resigning himself to what he realised must be done if he were to leave this spot quickly, Enoch took the coil of rope from his son.

'Tie the other end to the hame.'

'Best let the lad go down the 'ole,' Clara said as Enoch passed the rope around his own waist, 'Jack don't be so 'eavy. With you an' that woman tied to the rope...'

'Samson can tek that weight easy enough.'

'Ar that 'e can.' Clara nodded. 'But rope can't be counted strong as the 'orse, it could give under a burden such as you be puttin' it to.'

'What Mother says be only sense.' Having secured the rope to the rigid metal side of the horse's collar, the boy turned eagerly to his father. 'It would only be 'alf the weight if it be me goes down.'

'That be as it might.' Enoch shook his head. 'But a mine shaft be no place forra lad, even though it be just a gin pit.'

'There be no cause to go worryin' for our lad.' Clara smiled encouragingly at the eager young face. 'Do ye think I'd let 'im go down that 'ole if I thought for one second there be danger? Ye can see for yerself that pit be no more'n ten feet deep an' the bottom be pure ironstone. Whoever begun it give up when 'e found it be all rock an' no coal. I says lower the lad in, 'e can tie that wench to the rope every bit as secure as you can.'

'I'll be in an' out in two ticks.' Taking the rope from his father the boy knotted it beneath his arms.

'You teks care, lad.' Pride and concern sat deep in Enoch's eyes as he lowered the boy slowly into the gaping hole.

Landed beside the still form the boy removed the rope, fastening it about a form that gave no sound or movement.

'Now you, lad–' Enoch watched from above, his head circled in a ring of blue sky '–tie yerself on.'

'Best tek one at a time,' the lad called back, 'the rope be frayed where it rubs the sides o' the barges as the barge passes beneath. Could be two folk might be too big a strain. Tek the woman then let the rope down for me.'

That lad were getting a mite big for his boots. The thought twitching in his mind, Enoch set the horse moving, slowly taking up the strain, step by step hauling its burden up into the light of day.

Her son was mending, the blow of his attacker had not done the work it was meant to do.

Filling her basket with pegs she had whittled the day before, Hepzibah covered them with a chequered cloth. At the side of the clearing Judah was looking to the horse. In days fewer than the fingers of one hand, Lorcan Nash would return. On that day would her suspicions be answered, on that day she would know.

Judah had given no clue as to whether or not he knew who it was had taken the horses he'd bought from the owner of Victoria House then stolen the rest of his money from his pocket. The money caused him little concern she knew, and the horses he could replace, but the pain of losing the dog he'd had from childhood would long remain in his heart.

'But I knows who it be.' Fastening her shawl about her middle, Hepzibah glared at the figure busy packing a basket beside her own fire. 'An' I knows Marisa Lakin 'ad fingers in the brewin' o' it, same as I knows it don't be no sellin' o' pegs nor no dukkerin takes that one from 'er fire every day, it be no tellin' o' fortunes brings food for 'er cookin' pot!'

Seeing the dark head turn her way, Hepzibah spat her distaste openly on to the ground. That juval were no good, hers were a melalo heart, a kalo heart, filthy and black with lies! But lies had a way of rebounding, turning back on the one that traded in them, demanding their own dues.

Lifting the basket to her hip, she set off across the heath.

For each lie there was a reckoning and for every reckoning a penalty.

Measure for measure, Marisa Lakin would pay in full.

Chapter Thirteen

Stood beside the cabin of the narrow boat, Garnet stared at the vista of fields shorn of their summer crops. It had been three days since these people had pulled her from a slow death in that abandoned pit shaft; tomorrow she would see that place again.

A tremor of apprehension running through her she thought again of what Clara Babb had told her, how for the first hours of her rescue she had lain unconscious. With no way of knowing where to return her and having a deadline that meant they got no pay if they did not meet it, they had had no option but to leave her on that heath or take her with them.

'*But what act would that be for Christian folk, to go leaving a body helpless and alone on the 'eath?*' Clara had asked. '*I wouldn't have slept nights!*'

So they had taken her along with them to Brierley Hill and now they were making the long journey back to Willenhall.

...They '*would be passing Darlaston...*'

Garnet's fingers tensed on the narrow wood rail that ran around the edge of the cabin roof as she remembered the words.

'*...though if you prefers you can wait til we reaches Bentley Heath afore you leaves the* Warrior, *for that were the place we found you.*'

Bentley Heath!

The words had almost stopped the heart in her breast. All the time spent at the gypsies' camp she had been so near the home she had once loved, the home Tyler Cadell's jealous rage had driven her from. Was he still there, did he still live at Bentley House, the place he had murdered his child?

She would soon know, but first she must find the site of the gypsy wagons, thank Hepzibah and Judah for all they had done for her, thank them as she thanked the Babbs.

'T'were no more than Christian!' Clara had waved those thanks aside but each moment of kindness was written deep in Garnet's heart. Maybe one day she would have a chance to repay them all

'It be hereabouts, Ben an' me was rabbitin', t'was him as found you in that shaft.'

'I'm very grateful.' Garnet smiled at the boy come to stand beside her, though her fingers still clutched at the fretwork rail.

'Like I says, it were Ben, without him I would never have spotted you; the shaft were all but closed across with bracken.'

'Then I am grateful to Ben, but he could not have called for help as you did.'

'You be wrong there, miss, beggin' your pardon, you don't want to go selling old Ben short, he has more brains in that head of his than many a human man ... least that be what Mother says and I don't think her be much wrong. Ben would have fetched help all right, he has his own way of making Father or meself take notice.'

Glancing towards the bow he jerked his head, indicating a bridge that hung low over the canal.

'That be Netherton tunnel, there be no

tow path for Samson so we have to leg our way through it.'

His explanation brief the boy jumped from the barge, running the length of the tow rope trailing the water as the horse came to a halt. Quickly unfastening it from the hames circling the collar he slapped the animal's rump.

'Mother will walk him to the far side.' His grin wide as the waterway itself the lad jumped back on board and, as Garnet watched, lay on his back on the roof of the cabin, his head touching that of his father lying stretched on the opposite side.

Letting the boat drift the last few yards to the tunnel entrance he lifted his feet, placing them squarely on the wall.

'This be called legging,' the grin flashed wider, 'we walks the boat through tunnels.'

Fascinated, Garnet watched him pass one foot over the other using the force of his legs to push the boat along. Emerging from the other side he laughed at the surprised look on her face.

'Ain't you never seen a boat legged afore?'

She had not. Garnet watched him attach the rope once more to the patiently waiting horse. Neither her mother nor Mrs Wilkes would ever have countenanced her being anywhere near the canal.

'We'll be coming in to Dudley Port around dusk, we'll moor there for the night.'

Clara Babb took the boy's hand stretched to steady her aboard, then looked with sympathetic eyes at the young woman they had rescued from almost certain death. She had told them how she had come to be in that half-dug gin pit, but that was not all the horror of her young life, that was not the sole cause of the agony that lay in those unhappy eyes. Whatever had happened to this wench had left its mark burned deep into her soul.

'Mrs Babb...'

Touching a hand to the woman's stringy arm, Garnet tried to smile but though it touched her lips it failed to lessen the pain in her eyes.

'...I don't know how to thank you...'

Clara Babb patted the hand touching her arm. 'Thanks don't be due to we, that be the Lord's due. T'were His hand guided our Jack and the dog to findin' you and to Him should you gie thanks.'

'I do that night and day.'

'Then that be all needs be said.'

'No, no it is not,' Garnet answered quickly. 'You cared for me when you need not have done, you took me into your home and shared your food with me when you must have known I could not repay you except with words. But one day, I don't know how or when, but one day I will pay back all you have done for me; I will not forget ... I will never forget.'

Her weather-beaten face reflecting the pleasure of being thanked, Clara Babb tried to hide it by bustling into the tiny living quarters of the narrow boat, taking a dish from the oven, basting the contents with a long-handled spoon.

'There'll be no food to share should this be burned, the lad won't thank neither of we for that for poor man's goose be his favourite meal.'

Poor man's goose. Had Mrs Wilkes ever heard the name the bargee's wife gave to bullock's liver baked with onions, sage and bacon?

'What can I do to help?'

Returning the dish to the oven the woman smoothed her hands over an apron kept surprisingly clean given the circumstances of her life.

'You don't needs do anything, but I suppose you'll feel more at ease with a chore to busy your hands so you can peel a pot of taties; there be a sack of them up top, our Jack will show you where. Take a bowl and knife along with you.'

Sat on deck, the meal over, Garnet stared into the velvet softness of approaching night.

Tomorrow they would reach Bentley Heath. Tomorrow would begin her quest for vengeance.

Lord, the wench could give lessons on pleasuring a man! Tyler Cadell felt the warm naked body slide over him. He had come to this barn every day since first meeting the girl now laughing down at him, and every day brought new passion, new excitement; passion and excitement Olivia Denton would never arouse. The gypsy was everything Olivia was not. Fire and ice. He gasped as the girl straddled him, fitting the warm moistness of her body over his hardened flesh, laughing softly as she rode him like a horse.

Fire and ice! Blood pounding his veins like a flash flood he arched to the sensual rhythm. One so different from the other, both so necessary to his life.

A final surge of flame exploding in his stomach he lay with closed eyes.

'I won't be comin' tomorrow.'

Spent as he was, Tyler's eyes flashed open.

'Why?' he demanded sharply. 'Why will you not be coming?'

Picking up her clothes from where Tyler had flung them on the hay, holding them so they hid none of her nakedness, Marisa smiled.

'I has a livin' to earn.'

Watching the slim nakedness outlined by the stream of light filtering through the decaying roof, the dark hair dropping a sable mantle about her shoulders, Tyler felt the anvil beat of jealousy. He paid her well yet she had to earn a living ... and how would it be earned? Not like this, she would not give any other man what she gave to him!

The languor that had gripped him following their lovemaking vanished on a different tide. Jumping to his feet he caught her to him, holding her viciously tight.

'You earn a good enough living out of me.' The words spat into her face as he snatched her head back on her neck. 'What I pay for no other man shares.'

'Not this they don't.'

Her eyes holding his Marisa dropped the clothes, drawing her hands along his naked thighs, cupping them around the mounds of flesh nestled in his groin, the jerk of fresh arousal telling her what she already knew. The gaujo would pay whatever she asked.

'Then how?' The renewed pleasure of her fingers only adding to the intensity of jealousy, Tyler snatched her head still further.

'As any gypsy do.' Marisa held her stare. 'By calling at 'ouses, selling pegs or tellin' a woman 'er fortune.'

'Then let that be enough!'

'Be this enough for you?' Marisa brushed her fingers the length of his newly awakened flesh. 'It 'as to be, for tomorrow the wagons leave Bentley.'

'Leave!' Holding her at arm's length he glared at her smiling face. 'Then let them. You have your own wagon, you can stay.'

He had given her money to buy a wagon but the wagon of Lorcan Nash would be hers ... when he married her.

Pressing herself close against him she drifted a tongue over his chest, feeling the shudder of pleasure ripple through him.

'I has a place to light my cookin' fire an' a wagon to lay my head in, but a gypsy girl be like any other woman, her needs clothes to cover 'er body, clothes for a man to tear away!'

'You little bitch ... you bloody conniving little bitch–'

Catching his breath as she slid slowly to her knees, her tongue tracing a line the length of him before touching the tip of his agitated manhood, Tyler grasped her head, pressing her face close into his groin.

Shaking free of his hands, Marisa looked up, her lips parting in an invitation he could not refuse.

'You'll get your clothes,' he moaned as the hedonistic pleasure of being taken into her mouth swept over him. 'You'll get your clothes and anything else you want.'

The barn way behind her, Marisa shook her hair free of the patterned shawl. The gaujo had been generous. Smiling, she looked at the pile of sovereigns resting in her palms. Five! She hugged the delight of it to herself. Five gold sovereigns! The gaujo was more than generous, he was a fool! But not Marisa Lakin. These sovereigns and those given for the buying of a wagon would not be parted with so easy as he had parted with them. They were hers and would be shown to nobody, not even to Lorcan Nash.

Hiding them in the pocket of her cotton drawers she walked on towards the hollow that sheltered Hepzibah Kane's wagon and the bender tent behind it.

The men had built that tent to shelter the woman fetched by Judah Kane, a non Romany, but for Marisa Lakin they had built nothing. Balancing her basket on one hip she stared at the wisp of grey smoke curling into the shadowing sky and gave free rein to the bitterness of her thoughts. With the wagon of Alcina Korjyck leaving with the others there had been no shelter, no place but the hedge for her to curl under. The tent with its mattress of heather and covering of warm blankets had remained empty, its comfort barred to her.

'I be of their blood!' The words shot like bullets into the silence of the heath. 'Marisa Lakin be true Romany!'

She walked on towards the distant spiral of smoke, the acid of her thoughts stinging her mind. Marisa Lakin was Romany born and, like any Romany, knew how to take revenge on those that did her wrong. Judah Kane had refused her as a bride, her own mother had turned her back on her ... they had all of them turned their backs yet all had accepted a red-haired gaujo woman!

Cresting the small rise she looked down at the lone caravan nestled at its base.

Yes, they had all accepted the outsider while leaving Marisa Lakin to fend for herself; but her time would soon be here, soon they would all regret turning their backs.

Sat beside her fire, Hepzibah watched the younger woman flounce across the small clearing. There was a badness in that one, a wickedness that was the devil's birth gift. It had been a sickness in her all her life, developing with the years, hardening with the passing of time until it seemed ready to devour them all. As it had almost devoured Judah?

Beneath half-lowered lids Hepzibah followed the movements of the girl stirring the ashes of her fire, feeding it with sticks.

Marisa Lakin's hand might not be the one that had struck Judah down but hers had been the planning of it, on that Hepzibah would wager her life.

Crushing a spring of dried sage she sprinkled it into the pot in which the rabbit snared earlier in the day was almost cooked.

The two of them together, that girl and Lorcan Nash, they it were had almost killed her son; they it were would 'ave the reckoning of it.

In twenty days, Nash had said. She touched her skirt, feeling the twig pocketed with her pipe. She had notched it every sunrise, marked each day since that man's leaving for Brough, two more and the counting would be done.

'I gave no thought to her leaving with no word of the intent.'

Judah stared into flames that lit the heartache in his face. 'It seemed from her manner that would be the last thing dwelt in her mind.'

They had talked long since finishing the evening meal and beneath it all had lain the hurt and longing her son would not speak of.

'We shouldna judge what it don't be given we to know.' Hepzibah's reply was quiet. What Judah really wanted to ask was why had the woman left *him?*

'We know as her never came back!'

'That be true,' she nodded, 'but it could be the time of her leaving were decided by a power other than her own.'

He glanced up quickly, concern etched deep in every line of his strong features.

'You think her met with an accident?'

With the clay pipe held between her teeth Hepzibah watched the dancing colours that were the heart of the fire. She had known many thoughts since the coming of the gaujo woman, and with them many hopes but none of them the hope her son had held in his heart. His was the longing to take the woman for his wife ... but that could not be, fate would not give her to him.

'I makes no pretence o' knowing what keeps that wench from my fire,' she answered, 'but I would be lying were I to say I makes no pretence o' knowing what it be drives the sleep from ye each night; but ye must forget, the desire of the heart be not always granted.'

'Nor be it always denied.'

The stubborn note seemed to ring, bouncing back from the shadows, coming to rest heavily on Hepzibah's heart. If her son was to know any kind of peace from his torment she must tell him now.

'The gaujo woman be married...' Beside her Judah sat unmoving. '...the owner of Bentley 'Ouse be husband to Garnet Cadell.'

Speaking in little more than a whisper aware of Marisa curled in her blanket only yards from them, Hepzibah repeated all she had learned; the cries of those first few nights then the story told by Garnet herself.

'…I thought as you when first her come,' she finished softly, 'that fate 'ad sent her to dwell among the Romany. But my 'opes were different to the ones ye held, mine were that the one our people 'ave long awaited were somehow come; we both be wrong, son, we must both forget.'

'That don't be possible!' He jabbed a foot at a half-burned stick sending a shower of sparks bursting into the darkness.

Removing the pipe from her mouth, Hepzibah tapped the bowl against her palm and threw the remnant of ash into the fire. 'The crystal don't never lie, it will show what be possible an' what be impossible, but it takes courage to look into the unknown; do ye 'ave that courage, the will to see what the crystal tells of ye an' of the woman?'

At his nod she slipped the pipe into her pocket, then carrying a smouldering twig to light the lamp she led the way into the caravan.

'A smidgen o' cloth from the clothes her came in lies in the chest.' Lifting the lamp from its hook she held it over the lid. 'My hand shall not touch it, yours be the question, yours must be the hand that brings the cloth.'

She had snipped away a scrap of worn cloth when mending the woman's chemise, some inner sense telling her the time would come when it would be needed. Cloth that had lain next to the heart gave a truer picture. Watching Judah place it on the lowered lid she set the lamp beside it, then turned to fetch a velvet-wrapped object from a cupboard stood in a corner of the cramped room.

'This be the crystal used by my mother and 'ers. It be the same as was used by 'er mother afore 'er and by 'er mother in turn and so on back to times long gone. Be you satisfied of the truth o' that?'

In the circle of lamp light Judah's head nodded.

'And be you satisfied that what it will show this night be of itself and not the need of Hepzibah Kane?'

'I be satisfied.'

He answered quickly, strong in the knowledge that no Romany would dare tamper with the crystal or put false interpretation upon whatever might be revealed in its depths.

Setting the object she had fetched on to the scrap of cotton cloth she drew away its velvet cover, staring for a moment at the glistening beauty of it.

'Then join your 'ands with mine.'

Drawing a deep breath she took his hands, raising them above the gleaming crystal. For a few seconds it remained clear, light of the lamp reflecting the pure heart of the glass, then as they both stared into it a haze began to form; light and misty as a child's breath it swirled, thickening and darkening until the ball became filled with a grey cloud.

Their fingers still entwined, Hepzibah lowered them, forming a ring about the darkened orb. Almost the same moment it cleared.

'Pay full mind to what ye sees.'

At his mother's caution Judah bent closer over the table, his breath catching sharply as he saw the vague shape of a figure form where the mist had been.

'The crystal answers.' Hepzibah felt the tension in the fingers that gripped her own.

Intent on what he was seeing, Judah made no reply. The figure was clearer now, more sharply defined; the figure of a woman. But that was not all. At her shoulder a second figure formed, a man holding a whip in an upraised hand, his face a mask of fury as he struck at her. Watching the woman scream her silent fear, Judah felt his own heart die as she turned for comfort to the new figure taking shape behind her, the figure of a second man, one who brought a child!

Releasing her hands as the figures faded leaving the crystal clear, Hepzibah replaced the velvet cover then returned it to the cupboard.

'Ye saw … ye looked well at the face?'

Following him from the wagon she read the answer that lay unspoken in Judah's heart. He had seen the image of Garnet Cadell and of the face she had turned to for comfort; the face that was not Judah Kane.

'It was as you said.' They had sat long beside the fire before he spoke. 'The woman is not meant for me.'

That was all her son had seen. Judah had said his goodnight and now she sat alone. Lifting her glance to the sky she stared at the full moon holding the earth in a radiant net of gold. She could not blame him, unhappiness lowered a veil over the vision of the mind.

But she had seen! Hepzibah smiled at moon-gilded clouds. She too had seen images in the crystal, the image of Garnet Cadell taking into her arms the crescent moon.

That had been the hope in her heart, the feeling that had been with her from the beginning, the feeling that one long yearned for was to come at last, one her people would know by the mark of the crescent moon above the heart. It were not Garnet Cadell they waited for but the child!

Lowering her gaze to the fire, Hepzibah felt the joy dull against the pain of truth. The champion they waited on would not be born of a Romany, it would not be a child of Judah Kane, but of a gaujo!

Chapter Fourteen

The flower she was carving now finished, Marisa laid it alongside others in her basket. It was doubtful the women of the town would buy more pegs but the cleverly cut flower head seemed to have taken their fancy, a touch of paint and a pretty vase...

A rumble from beyond the turn of the track catching her attention she looked up. The wagons were returning. Shouts of children and barking of dogs accompanying each one they drove into camp, each positioning in the space it had occupied some twenty days before.

Twenty days! Marisa squinted against the brightness of the day. Lorcan had promised that in twenty days he would make good his challenge for the place of first man; and on that same day he would take her as his wife. The waiting was over. Watching the last of the string of lumbering vehicles pull into place her gaze shot back along the track bordering the rise of ground, then returned to the one space left between the wagons. That of Lorcan Nash had not come!

Turning her back slowly on the women greeting Hepzibah she clenched her teeth, holding in the waves of anger that rose from the lowest depths. Was this one more promise Lorcan Nash be turning from ... would he sooner give up thought of becoming first man than marry with Marisa Lakin? She had dangled the promise of money, much more money than he'd taken from Tonio Korjyck, more than had likely been in the pocket of Judah Kane, more money than he might dream of making, but Lorcan Nash had not returned!

Forcing herself into a calmness that only skimmed the surface she picked up her basket. She would not let the others see her anger, guess at her fears; they would not gloat at her expense.

But tonight they would gloat ... if by supper Lorcan Nash had still not returned then Marisa Lakin would be the butt of every woman's laughter.

Her hair free of her patterned shawl, head held high and skirts flouncing, she walked from sight beyond the small line of hillocks before letting her shoulders sag. If Lorcan did not return, if he did not take her for wife, what then? She had money enough for a small wagon and even for a horse to pull it, but what was a horse and wagon when set against her pride ... what salve would that prove against the gossip and jeers that would go on behind her back? Yes, a wagon of her own and the capability to support herself would afford her a place among many a group of travellers, but news went along with every gypsy, and telling of her being refused by Lorcan Nash would follow wherever she went.

But the day was not over yet. Her glance raked the heath following the expanse of barren horizon. There was still time for him to come.

The soft rumble of a growl deep in a dog's throat brought Judah to his feet. Trained never to bark or growl while rabbiting it could only herald the approach of strangers. Touching a hand to the animal's head, his soft command quieting it instantly, he stared into the distance. Two figures, a man and a woman, coming from the far side of the heath.

Watching them come nearer, Judah felt a sudden flare shoot along his nerves. There! There it was again! He couldn't be imagining things. But he could! It were not unknown for the heart to trick the mind; when a body wanted a thing badly enough it was too easily deceived, the eyes saw what they wanted to see instead of what was really before them.

But there ... again, that flash of deep red caught by the first gold of sunset, the red of a woman's hair. But it was not her, there were other women with hair the colour of a garnet! The one he looked for was gone, she had left days ago, gone for ever from his life.

Beside him the dog's throat rumbled again but the hackles beneath Judah's hand did not rise. Strange, no man got within hailing distance without any of the dogs barking their challenge! Surprised at the animal's behaviour, Judah squinted against the light, his nerves flaring again as the woman's head turned towards him.

'Mr Kane – Judah?'

The call was tentative, uncertain, but the voice was hers. Hope locking his throat, Judah made no answer.

'Be you Judah Kane?'

The stronger, more authoritative voice of the man releasing his tongue, Judah nodded. 'I be Judah Kane ... who be asking?'

Quieting the dog a second time, Judah watched the two approach.

'I be Enoch Babb, I be bargee of the *Warrior*. I works the cut atwixt Willenhall an' Brierley Hill.'

Was this the husband his mother had spoken of? Momentary confusion had Judah stare at the rough clothing of the man holding out his hand. But the husband, Hepzibah Kane had told, was the owner of Bentley House not a bargee. The second man! Memory stirred, retrieving the second figure that had formed in the crystal. Was this man that figure ... had Garnet left the camp to go to him?

'Judah, I'm so sorry...'

'There be no need... You were free to leave the moment you pleased...'

Politeness overcoming a sadness he still could not wholly face, Judah shook the proffered hand and kept his glance on the weather-beaten features of the man.

'If it be her things you be going to collect it be Hepzibah Kane's wagon you should ask for, though I should tell you the clothes this woman stands up in be all her had the night I found her beneath a hedge.'

The curtness of Judah's words, his refusal to look at her, why... What had she done? Glancing at Enoch, Garnet's eyes held the question.

'Me an' my lad were out on this stretch, o' heath a few days gone,' he spoke sharply, the words bringing a warning growl from the dog but Enoch didn't stop, ''e were doing what you be doing now, but it were no rabbit the dog found, it were this woman, 'er were ten foot down a 'alf-dug gin pit! 'Er were unconscious when me an' my lad hauled 'er out and 'er stayed that way while my wife seen to the carin' of 'er. We hoped to be able to return 'er to wherever it were 'er wanted to be but when by mornin' 'er were still mekin' no sense we 'ad to sail. If a bargee don't get cargo to its place o' unloading on time then a bargee don't get paid and me and mine can't live on fresh air, mister.'

He had found her in a half-dug pit shaft! Then she had not left purposely, not left without a word.

'This be where 'er asked to be brought when we come back, said 'er had to find some gypsy camp, be you from there?'

'Judah,' Garnet turned to him as Enoch finished speaking. 'I wanted to see Hepzibah, to see you ... I wanted to tell you myself the reason I did not return.'

Looking into the summer-green eyes he saw every time he closed his own, Judah's heart twisted with love and longing. I belong there, he thought, but you do not. The thought a brand in his heart he nodded to Enoch. 'I be from there. You have my thanks for what you've done.'

Enoch's smile chasing the shadows of apprehension he answered quickly. 'Like the missis would say were 'er here, a kindly deed be all folk like we 'ave to give and we needs naught for doing it save a smile from the Lord.'

'That is yours without question, Enoch.' Garnet touched a calloused hand. 'I will never forget your kindness to me.'

'He says he found you in a mine shaft.' Stood beside her watching the bargee walk away, Judah curled his fingers against his palms, fighting the urge to take her in his arms.

'Jack, his son, found me.'

'But didn't you 'ave sense enough to know the heath be pitted with old shafts!'

Longing finding an essence of relief in anger, Judah's voice was hard.

'I … I didn't think … I am not familiar with the heath.'

'All the more reason to avoid it, especially when you be alone! And the canal, why be that side when it were the town you were going to?'

'I lost my way. Each time I thought I had found the path it was a track that led nowhere. I must have been walking in a circle, there was no landmark I could recognise.'

He could see the truth of that. Judah's glance travelled the expanse of flat heathland. Anyone not used to such could easily be trapped by its emptiness. He glanced at the woman walking beside him. '*…I am not familiar with the heath…*' Her words returned quietly to his mind. How could she have been; the wife of the owner of Bentley House was hardly likely to have spent her time traipsing the heath.

'Marisa said the town was but half an hour's walk, that if I kept close to the path I could not fail to get there.'

Anger that a moment ago had been mollified by common sense reared again in Judah.

'Marisa ... you were with Marisa Lakin?'

The dog's nose cold and damp against her fingers, Garnet patted the rough head. 'She was kind enough to say I could go calling with her.'

Marisa Lakin had said naught of being with this woman, naught of taking her calling. True, his mother ignored the girl but when a woman be gone without word or trace! Marisa Lakin could have spoken ... fetched folk from the town to help search.

'She pointed out the way to me, she said it would be pointless both of us calling at the cottages or farmhouses, there would not be enough women willing to buy, that it would be more sensible for one of us to go into the town.'

'And that were the way pointed?'

Glancing the way they had come, Judah felt the heat of anger cool then settle like a cold hard stone in his chest. That way led away from Darlaston, anyone not familiar with it and walking in darkness could find themselves in the canal ... or down a pit shaft! Marisa Lakin had pointed that way!

Holding the dawning truth to himself he went on. 'You were lucky not to have broken your neck when you pitched yourself into that hole.'

'I did not fall, Judah.'

The quiet whisper of it almost stopping

his heart, Judah listened to the full story and when it ended he knew what it was he had to do.

'That is the last of them ... sahib.'

Tyler Cadell caught the tiny hesitation and smiled to himself. It went against the grain to afford him that address, but why should he worry about the finer feelings of a servant, and a bloody Indian to boot? Sahib! He smiled again; not too far into the future, Tyler Cadell would be addressed by a far grander title than that.

Draping the string of square-cut sapphires over his fingers he watched the play of lamp light reflect in their depths. Blue as ice and just as passionless. Every bit a match for those eyes. Still, it was not passion he wanted from Olivia Denton, he had that in plenty from his little gypsy love; no, the jewels he was lavishing on the viscount's niece were being spent in the procurement of a wife. And that must be achieved soon, his pocket was not bottomless and the coal mines that were part of Garnet's inheritance had already been sold.

Garnet ... she had been such a fool ... but tonight was not to be given to thinking of fools, tonight he would ask the question.

Placing the lovely necklace in its box he slipped it into the pocket of a perfectly tailored cashmere jacket. An attractive passionate gypsy lover and a titled wife ... the better of both worlds would be his ... yet better could always be improved upon.

Hearing a tap at his door he caught up chamois gloves as the turbanned man-servant entered the bedroom.

'There is a visitor wishes to see you, sahib.'

'Visitor!' Tyler checked his immaculate appearance once again. 'Who?'

'No name was given.'

'Card ... you can read the bloody card, can't you?'

'No card was presented.'

Irritated by his calmness, Tyler glared at the softly spoken servant.

'Then get rid of whoever it is, I am not at home to visitors, especially the sort too ignorant to present a card.'

'I think perhaps visiting cards are not a part of this woman's social graces.'

'Woman?' Tyler frowned. 'I'm not expecting any woman, tell her I can't see her.'

'Mrs Wilkes told her that...'

'Then you bloody well tell her! What the hell do I keep you for?'

'I spoke to the woman, she said you would see her or very soon see something you might relish far less.'

A threat? The gloves gripped in one hand slapped hard into the palm of the other. But what woman could make threats against him?

'Mrs Wilkes said to ask you should she send for a constable to see the gypsy off?'

Gypsy! Tyler's hands became still. He had left the wench less than two hours before and she had behaved as usual; if the woman downstairs were her what could she want ... more money? Ask for that and she would feel a whip about her back.

'I'll be down in a few minutes, I'll ring when I'm ready to see her.'

Waiting until he was alone, Tyler threw the gloves savagely across the room. The last thing he wanted was a rumpus with a gypsy... Gypsies travelled and so did any gossip they might leave on a doorstep.

Seated in the study, displeasure heavy between his brows, he waved a dismissive hand as the manservant ushered his visitor in.

'What brings you here?' he barked before the door was properly closed.

'Something you might be pleased to find out afore the law comes bangin' on your door.'

'Law! What lies are you dreaming up now?'

Beyond the still partly open door, Raschid heard an answering anger in the girl's reply.

'Marisa Lakin be bringin' no lie. I seen 'er. I seen the woman that be wife to you, I seen Garnet Cadell...'

'Quiet!'

As the word whipped out the Indian pressed flat against the wall of a deeply shadowed alcove, holding his breath as he heard his master step into the hall to check no one was there.

''Er was brought into camp days ago...'

Back at the study door the servant listened.

'...for some time 'er were addled in the 'ead, makin' no sense. But later 'er told me ... 'er told me summat you might be willing to pay to have me forget.'

The bitch was greedy, too greedy. Perhaps the time had come to end their relationship, time for her to meet with a small accident, a small but deadly accident!

'This woman you claim to have seen, if she does in fact exist, what makes you think she is telling the truth?'

'Truth or lie it be of no matter to me, but should what I were told be spread about the town then I doubts not it'll matter to you.'

'I know of no such woman.'

Watching the eyes, cold and glittering as a serpent's, Marisa knew otherwise. On the surface his handsome face and blond hair feathered back from a perfectly shaped brow gave the impression of honesty, of a man possessed of all the moral virtues, but behind that fact, deep inside, his heart held a blackness, an evil moulded of the devil.

'Then Marisa Lakin be wastin' 'er time.'

'Wait!'

The call halting her as she turned to leave, Marisa hid her smile of triumph. He knew Garnet Cadell, and he would want to know her whereabouts. But for information such as that he would pay more than five sovereigns.

'What is it this woman appears to have told you?'

She must not say it was told not to her but to Hepzibah Kane; to let him hear the fact that the story was known to others would be to kiss her reward goodbye.

'Enough to see you on the gallows, but we both knows that needn't be the outcome.'

'Money!' His lip curled. 'You want money, how like a gypsy slut!'

'It be a gypsy slut can see to it that neck o' yourn be stretched by a rope!'

Tyler caught the flash of black eyes as she flung the words at him. She had to be speaking the truth, she would never dare come to this house, making such accusations were it any other way. She would get her payment … but not all of it in gold.

'Twenty sovereigns.' He rose, crossing the room to a bureau on the other side.

'Keepin' the telling of a babby thrown to the dogs a secret will take more than the payin' o' twenty sovereigns.'

She did know! His fingers clutching a box, he allowed a smile of cold derision to play openly on his mouth.

'Greedy as ever, my little gypsy whore!'

Her own smile icy, Marisa stared back at him. 'And you'll pay the gypsy whore's price ... as ever!'

Emptying the box on the desk he watched her eyes follow the glittering trail. 'That is all there is in the house. Tell me the rest of what you know and it's yours.'

It had been so easy. The sovereigns deep in her pocket, Marisa smiled as she ran from the house. And what had been easy this time would be easier with the next ... and the next. Cadell would pay the gypsy whore, pay her many times over, but it would not be for his satisfaction, his naked body would ride hers no more, from this night on the satisfaction of their meetings would be all hers.

It had been fate had turned her footsteps, turned her from making a last call at a cottage, turned her homeward. Slowing to a walk she laughed softly, her face lifting to the moon full and low against the horizon. They had not seen her as they walked close together; Judah Kane bringing the gaujo woman back to camp ... Judah Kane who had refused the offer of Marisa Lakin. Well let him enjoy the sight of her pretty face and red hair, he would not know the joy of it for long.

She was alive! Left alone in the study Tyler stared at the empty box. His wife was alive and living with a group of gypsies! This could put an end to all his aspirations. True, he could have her committed to an insane asylum but, once thrown, mud had a way of sticking. She might not be believed were she to claim he had killed the child, but then what of the tale he had told ... of his wife's death along with that of her daughter ... how would society view that?

It could not be allowed! He swept a hand across the desk, sending the box crashing to the floor. The gypsy bitch could not be the only one to meet with a fatal accident, Garnet too must be got rid of and this time it must be for good.

But how? One of the gypsies, perhaps? No, that wasn't the way.

'Will you still be wanting the carriage ... sahib?'

They were both watching him, the Indian and the housekeeper, their eyes glued to him as he walked from the study. They must not see the anger that burned in him ... the anger or the fear.

'Of course.' He shrugged into the coat held ready for him. 'You need not wait up, I shall stay the night at Victoria House.'

Beyond the tall iron gates he turned the carriage towards Wednesbury. He would be away the whole night, but it would not be the cool charm of Lady Olivia Denton that detained him, or the gracious out-of-town house kept by her uncle that would provide him with a bed. The asking of the lady's hand must wait a little longer. Tonight Tyler Cadell had business of a different kind.

Chapter Fifteen

'...*Before the third night of the second rising of the full moon...*'

Lorcan Nash ate the meal his mother had cooked. The full moon had made its second rising two nights since. Despite himself he felt a touch of cold against his spine. Since being a child he had listened to his mother and the other women talk in hushed voices of words Hepzibah Kane had spoken. But they were naught but words, empty and useless as a barren womb, spoken simply to frighten.

The meal finished he put the bowl aside, lighting his pipe while his mother washed the dishes in silence. This was the way she had been the whole time they had been on the road, the words of Hepzibah Kane holding her with old fears. But no words frightened Lorcan Nash; tonight the woman's words would be shown for the claptrap they were … and the son would no longer be first man.

'There be no need of ye standing there, ye be like to be the wife o' my son afore dawnbreak so ye might as well sit ye beside the fire now.'

Hearing his mother speak he looked beyond her to the fringe of shadow surrounding the wagon. Marisa Lakin! The cool touch against his spine vanished in a blaze of hot anger. She had called him out in front of the Kris, demanded he speak the words of promise before them and now she stood at his wagon, but that one would never ride in it, she would never be wife to him!

'I feared you not comin' back.'

'Why should you 'ave fears o' that?' He watched her step into the ring of light shed by the fire, the boldness in her step, the arrogant tilt of her dark head aggravating the anger already hot inside him. The girl acted above herself, paying no mind to custom; since when did an unwed racklie sit herself beside any man's fire save that of her father? But custom and Marisa Lakin made uneasy bed-fellows.

'Your wagon were not among the others return.'

'Be that any wonder,' he laughed, 'the road from Brough and the road from Stowe don't follow the same direction.'

She had heard the sneer beneath the laugh, but she would ignore it. She smiled back at him. Man and wife were for life and life stretched a long path, Lorcan Nash would travel but few miles along it before he learned she was a woman not to be sneered at.

'Ye'll take a meal o' rabbit stew; family must needs 'ave no bad blood atwixt them, an' ye'll be family afore the night be done.'

Surprise stealing her answer, Marisa took the bowl and spoon. Had Lorcan spoken to his mother, told her of his promise, told her what tonight he would tell the Kris? He must have done, why else would the woman break the rule and speak to her, why serve her a meal beside her own fire, if it wasn't to show acceptance of her?

'It was you waylaid Judah Kane?'

'Softly...' Lorcan's glance snapped quickly to where his mother stood washing the bowl Marisa had emptied, '...we'll talk o' that later.'

'But it were you?'

Banging the long-stemmed clay pipe against his palm, Lorcan's irritation broiled. 'Yes!' he hissed. 'It were me struck 'im down and took the last pennies from his pocket along wi' the 'orses he bought from Victoria House; they showed a nice profit at Brough Fair.'

'T'would 'ave been of greater profit 'ad

you made sure and killed 'im, as it be he could name you.'

Lorcan shook his head, his glance wary as his mother stacked bowls and spoons into a box fixed to the rear of the wagon. 'No,' he said as the older woman climbed into the wagon, 'Kane were unconscious afore he had chance to look behind 'im. Had it not been for that dog o' his'n...'

'There be a chance Hepzibah guesses who it were.'

'Chance be a fine thing but it 'olds no value lessen proof rides its back an' there be none o' that.' He paused, black eyes a menacing glitter. 'Try tellin' that which we talked of beside this wagon the night before it left for Brough an' I'll cut the tongue from your mouth.'

Skirts rustling she rose to her feet, her own contempt twisting her face. 'You were always a brave man, Lorcan Nash, quick to raise your 'and against any woman or any man with his back turned to you, but let's see 'ow brave you be in front o' them, let's see you raise your 'and to Judah Kane's face!'

They were gathering. Paying no mind to the figure flouncing away, Lorcan replaced the pipe in his pocket, watching instead the men of the Kris coming one by one to seat themselves in the centre of the clearing.

Let them talk awhile, let Judah Kane enjoy

his last moments as first man. Perhaps it were as well that blow to the 'ead and the knife slash to his neck 'adn't killed him, it would look better in front of the others if he be beaten in fair fight. But those injuries would have weakened him, he wouldn't be over them yet … and Lorcan Nash were not one to bother whether a fight be fair!

'Be it time?'

Glancing at his mother come to stand on the steps of the wagon Lorcan shook his head. 'There be time yet, let them chew the cud awhile, talk whets the appetite for entertainment an' they'll 'ave that a plenty afore the moon be gone from the sky.'

'…*Before the third night of the second rising of the full moon*…'

Looking up at the huge golden orb, its luminescence painting the few clouds with silver, she felt the words echo like a song of death in her heart.

'That be settled then,' Judah's voice reached Garnet sat beside Hepzibah on the steps of the wagon, 'tomorrow we take to the road, but the business of the night be not finished yet, first I must ask does Lorcan Nash repeat the challenge, does he claim the right to compete for first man?'

'That don't be the way.' A lone voice spoke from the circle of men. 'Leaders be *elected*, it be the choosin' o' the Kris says who gets to

213

be first man.'

Catching the nod of Judah's head a spark of hope rose in Garnet. Maybe the men would not agree to the fight. Hepzibah had told her of the challenge made that first night while she had slept and now she prayed it would not be allowed, Judah was not yet fully recovered from being attacked.

'That be so, but it be a time-honoured right of any true-born Romany to challenge for first man and I won't be first to deny it. You all showed your choosing twenty nights ago, now I show mine; I call upon Lorcan Nash to put substance to his words; face me now or take his wagon from this camp.'

Seeing a figure step into the circle of seated men, the flicker of hope died in Garnet. Judah had said no word of still being injured when bringing her back here. She had seen the mark on his neck yet had thought it merely that tussocks of grass catching at his feet had him stumble once or twice. But it must be that he was still weak from the wound, it must be worse than she had thought. Nevertheless he had gone searching for her, Hepzibah had said, because there had to be some reason for her leaving without a word, and Judah would not rest until that reason were known.

Would any of this have happened had she not stayed here? An outsider was not lightly welcomed to stay in gypsy camps, that much she had learned. But this was not an argument that involved her, it was not an argument involving any woman; this was something else, something that lurked deep in the soul of many men, a remnant of that primordial urge for supremacy, an urge that showed itself now in the stance of the man facing Judah.

'Hold yerself!' Hepzibah's hand caught her as she went to rise. 'As Judah said, the business of the night be not yet finished.'

'But it is not right I should be here, this is not for outsiders to share.'

'The woman my son allowed to bide in this camp, the woman who seen to the birthing o' Clee Tuckett's son, be no outsider.'

There could 'ave been more added to that whispering, it could 'ave been said the woman who 'ave the carryin' o' the one who would fight the Romany cause could never be an outsider, but that would tek explanations that were not in accord with this night. Resting her hand on Garnet's arm Hepzibah kept that to herself.

'I speak the words.' Throwing off his jacket Lorcan blinked, the flames of the fire suddenly merging into a red mist. 'Lorcan...' he swayed, one hand going to his brow.

'Wait!' From the shadows his mother stepped forward. 'There will be no challenge...'

Hepzibah's hand moved to her lap, fingers gripping tightly together as the other woman continued to speak.

'...I begs leave to speak before the Kris.'

Murmurs of enquiry flitting rapidly from mouth to mouth turned into silence as Judah raised his hand.

'All be entitled to speak in this camp, woman as well as man. Say what it be you wish the Kris to hear.'

Stepping further into the light the woman glanced at the figure brushing at his eyes and swaying uncertainly on his feet. When she spoke her tone was pitying.

'Lorcan Nash be a fool led by a woman.'

Ringed about her gasps of surprise rustled the shadows, quieting as she went on.

'He were led by Marisa Lakin!'

Pointing a finger into the darkness the woman's eyes glowed and her voice lost all trace of pity.

'That racklie were the voice o' Satan in his ear, the poison o' her tongue quickened desire in him. But it were not desire for 'er, my son 'ad no desire to wed with a whore, for 'er be no less than that. The desire o' Lorcan Nash were for money ... money that were not his. I 'eard them both. Twenty nights gone they talked 'neath my wagon ... tongues be louder in the silence o' dawn ... I 'eard Marisa Lakin tell of a sellin' o' horses over at Victoria House, 'eard them plot together to kill Judah Kane the same way they killed Tonio Korjyck. I 'eard and now I tells ye, no man here will judge my son or the viper that curled 'erself about 'im. See for yerselves,' she waved a hand towards the swaying figure, 'judgement already be made.'

What did she mean? Garnet stared at the scene being played out before her, but her question was stayed by Hepzibah's whisper to stay quiet.

'I be the one that bore 'im.' The woman's voice faltered then went on, 'I be the one to judge 'im. Before the moon leaves the night sky the words o' Hepzibah Kane will be fulfilled. The wagon o' Lorcan Nash will be given to the flames.'

'What 'ave ye done?'

It was a scream that rent the silence as Marisa flung herself into the circle.

'What ye be saying?'

Looking at her, Lorcan's mother laughed.

'I be saying it were my body gave 'im life an' it be my hand teks that life away. I said no man among ye will 'ave the judgin' o' Lorcan Nash, the life o' my son be already over.'

'What have you done?'

Judah stepped forward as Lorcan fell, but the woman held him off then slid to the ground, cradling her son in her arms.

'What 'ad to be done.' She answered quietly. 'Beshlie Nash would not lie peaceful in the grave knowin' his son be a killer. Wrong doin' 'as to be punished ... a life for a life ... don't that be what the good book tells? Well I've followed the teachin' o' the lord, I teks a life to pay for a life; but the Lord be more merciful than me. He would be satisfied wi' one but I teks two; where my son goes, Marisa Lakin follows.'

'No!' Her cry resounding from the wagons Marisa turned to run but her legs buckled and she fell, her hair spreading a veil of darkness over her shoulders.

'See!' The woman's voice became softer, almost fading into the night. 'See, her already wears the black pall! Soon 'er evil will be finished for the poison 'er shared at my fire sits in 'er stomach.' Raising her head she looked towards the shadows, giving one wild burst of laughter. 'It don't only be you, Alcina Korjyck. I knows the ways o' the hedgerows same as you, I knows the power o' wolfbane, 'ow swift it kills. It were wolfbane I put in the stew I cooked then fed it to my son and the serpent that snared 'im, and my life will answer for the doin' of it.'

Her breath catching in her throat she coughed a little, her head drooping. Then, gasping, she turned her gaze to Judah stood close to her.

'Vengeance, it ... it can't be denied the Lord, it be His due ... that be why my stomach 'olds that same poison.'

All three of them dead! Horror holding her to the spot, Garnet stared at the great blaze of fire dimming the light of the moon. Cooking rods and pots, every possession of the dead that would not burn had been buried by the men while Hepzibah and the other women dressed each of the bodies in their finest clothing. Now Lorcan's wagon had been given to the flames.

'That be the way o' the gypsies.' Hepzibah ushered the trembling girl away from the scene. 'A dead man's wagon be burned but it be usual for any money left be shared atwixt family an' if it be he don't 'ave family then it be given to them most in need. That be the way o' stayin' free o' the mullos. But folk in this camp would sooner face them ghosts than take money earned from murder.'

Still shaking from what she had witnessed, Garnet glanced through the window of Hepzibah's wagon.

'The police,' she said, 'what will the police make of all this?'

'There'll be no fetchin' o' constables. Whatever were done this night 'as been atoned for, the bringin' o' the law will add naught but sorrow an' pain for Pilar Lakin.'

She could understand that, but not to report those deaths! Not to tell the truth of what had happened. But had Tyler Cadell told the truth, told what had really happened to his infant daughter? Lorcan Nash's mother had taken the law into her own hands but she had not thrown her son to the dogs.

'I sees from yer face ye think our ways be wrong.'

'No.' Garnet shook her head. 'I … I was thinking.'

Taking the clay pipe from her pocket and lighting it from a match, Hepzibah sat herself beside the open door.

'Rememberin', ye was rememberin'.' She blew a stream of tobacco smoke into the night. 'We all 'as a deal o' that to do afore our lives be finished. Sometimes it can be so heavy as to crush the heart of ye, but sendin' it deep inside, so deep it can be touched by none but ye brings no relief, that way lies bitterness, a canker that eats away the soul. Take yer memories, Garnet Cadell, cherish the bright ones and let the sadness surface when it will, that way pain gets less an', though it never fades completely, it lets ye live yer life.'

'My baby did not live her life…' Tears that had been held back spilled hot and fast.

'That be so,' the older woman answered softly, 'but the child only be really gone when it be banished from the 'eart, keep 'er there an' ye have her so long as ye walks this earth.'

Keep her daughter in her heart. It would never be otherwise. The child had been rejected by her father but she would love and remember so long as she breathed. The child was her heart.

Forcing back her tears she glanced through the wagon's one window. The fierce light of the burning wagon seemed to have pushed away the night, but like in her own life the darkness would soon return.

'I knows the way o' yer thoughts, that for all the pain it brings it be only right the law be told what 'appened 'ere this night, but the Romany sees to his own, wrongs done by Romany be righted by Romany, crimes committed by them be punished by them, naught goes unseen and naught passes but what reckoning don't be made...'

She sucked hard on the stem of the pipe, blowing a curl of smoke that vanished into the shadows.

'...Romanys 'ave their laws same as house folk and they bides well to them. What good can come o' bringing outsider's law? They 'as one for the rich an' a different one for the poor, but for the gypsy they 'as only one judgement: guilty! No matter the act done or the proof be found, the gypsy be guilty! That be why we tells nothing of what took place this night.'

There was pride as well as truth in what Hepzibah had said. Gypsies were mistrusted, seen as rogues and thieves, it had been obvious whenever a woman had answered a knock to her door.

'I did not mean to imply anyone would be evading the law.' Garnet apologised. 'I was thinking only of the funerals, will the priest not require to know...'

'There'll be no priest.' Hepzibah puffed quietly on her clay pipe. 'Nor church neither. The mother o' Lorcan Nash would be given burial in no churchyard, no so-called man o' God would read over 'er for 'er death were brought by 'er own hand. As for the two that lies beside 'er they be gypsies an' as such be not gladly accepted into church ground. As with life so with death, the world turns its back on the Romany, so it is we will bury our own. With the dawn light the men will lay them in the earth that has often been their bed. The eyes of the Lord be all seeing. He will find them and stretch His hand to them, and in spite of the hurt he done my son and Tonio Korjyck, I pray the Almighty give forgiveness to Lorcan Nash an' peace to the soul o' his poor dead mother.'

Hepzibah could pray for the forgiveness of a murderer.

Wrapped in a blanket, Garnet listened to the steady breathing of the woman sleeping in the bed she herself would no longer agree to take.

Hepzibah could find it in her heart to forgive, but in hers Garnet Cadell could find only vengeance. She would never pray forgiveness for Tyler Cadell. Her heart held only one prayer. As you have done so let it be done unto you!

It was all arranged. Tyler Cadell guided the small carriage up the broad sweep to Bentley House. His wife was returned. Well much good would it do her and much good would the sovereigns he had paid do to that gypsy trollop. Soon they would both be gone ... for ever.

He had left horse and carriage overnight with the ostler of the Station Hotel in Wednesbury. That would raise no eyebrows, a gentleman in search of 'private entertainment' often did as he had done, caught the evening train for Wolverhampton not returning before morning.

But the services of a woman he had found in a bawdy house there had not been of the sort any ostler would suspect. His money had paid for more than half an hour's use of her body.

He had paid her well and rehearsed her well, but at the same time he had warned her well. Renege on their agreement, fail to carry out his instructions and it would be a simple matter for him to arrange another ending to their business, one she would find unattractive and quite, quite fatal.

Ignoring the turbanned manservant opening the door to him he bounded up the broad oak staircase.

'Bath!' The order was curt as the servant followed. 'Make sure the temperature is as I like it and ... yes, a little of the oil of Attar, I think.'

Fingers brushing against the pocket of his coat he drew out the box that held the necklace. He must write to Olivia Denton ... his apologies, but the sorrow he thought almost forgotten had swept over him...! Fingering the perfectly matched stones he smiled. He had no sorrow and in a few hours he would have no worries. Garnet would be out of his life for ever and these stones would ensure the Lady Olivia Denton and her aristocratic relative were firmly ... very firmly ... in it.

Dropping the box and necklace on to the bed he threw off the rest of his clothes. Turning to face the long dressing mirror his smile deepened. His body was beautiful, white and beautiful.

The years of Indian sun had set no mark upon it.

Chapter Sixteen

It had been done so tenderly, with so much respect. Stood back from the rest, Garnet watched as small tributes of heather and wild flowers were laid on the ground that covered those three bodies.

Had her parents been laid to rest with as much regard and simple faith, had prayers been said for them with the same heartfelt reverence as Judah had spoken a prayer? She would never know, as she would never know the sort of peace the burying of her own child might have brought, the knowledge that she had been laid to rest with love and devotion.

'There be a meal to cook an' then the breakin' o' the camp to see to.'

Hepzibah spoke matter of factly as she returned but the glisten of tears in Garnet's eyes was not unnoticed.

'I... I will not be travelling with you.' The words she had tried throughout the night to formulate in her mind now slipped quietly from Garnet's lips.

'That be yer choice then there be none will say ye should change it.'

'You have been more than kind, I shall

always be grateful.'

'It 'as been said afore, give thanks to the Lord for the due be His; the Romany just be followin' His teachin'.'

Adding oats to the pot of water suspended over the crackling fire of sticks, Hepzibah hid her true feelings. From the first moment of meeting, this woman had felt special to her and the crystal had shown a reason. But not the whole reason. She stirred the pot with a ladle. Garnet Cadell had shown respect as well as gratitude, hers was an approach to the gypsy not often found among gaujo and as a result she had won their esteem.

But with one it was more than esteem. Glancing across to where Judah was grooming the horse, Hepzibah could not dismiss the sadness that touched her. With her son it was love, a love that would know no fulfilment.

They had said their goodbyes. With sadness a weight in her heart Garnet watched the Kane wagon disappear in the opposite direction. Judah had wanted to walk with her into Darlaston but she had refused; he had his own life and the responsibilities of it were heavy enough without her adding to them. She must look to herself, she had said; for all their kindness to her she was grateful, but now she must fend alone.

'*You will always find a home with us,*' he had

said quietly. *'Should you 'ave need, tell it to any gypsy you meet and word will find me no matter where I be. God keep you, the love of Hepzibah Kane bides with you … as does my own.'*

He had turned from her quickly then, gone before she could reply. Now the words whispered softly in her heart: 'As you both have mine, Judah.'

She could not go to Bentley House at once. Her steps slow, she turned along the path that branched like the fingers of a hand, each track leading to colliery, iron foundry or steel works. Her father had known them all. Now Tyler would know them. He was the one who now held the properties that had once been her father's and in turn should have become those of Tyler's own child. But that child no longer lived. If only Mrs Wilkes had not rushed her from that bedroom, if only Tyler had struck her down, anything … anything but live without her child.

'It be a babby…'

'Yes, she was just a baby.'

'Eh! Be you knowin' them then?'

The words she thought only in her mind had been spoken by a woman who eyed her sharply.

Garnet shook her head as several other women turned a glance on her.

'It be the box you was lookin' at, tells the

227

tale straight away do the box, it be a babby and no more'n two years of life by the size of it, ar, just a babby... Lord save its poor mother.'

Following the gaze of the woman now turned towards a small ragged procession, Garnet clutched the basket Hepzibah had insisted she take.

Two years old, the same age her child would have been. It must be even harder for that woman. Her heart filled with pity as she watched a thin woman, a many-patched skirt reaching to shabby boots, threadbare shawl draped low on her forehead, and clinging to her skirts a boy and a girl of less than five years while behind two older children sobbed quietly. It was hard for all of them but most terrible of all for the thin sobbing woman stumbling along beside the man whose face showed his own heart-rent grief.

Looking at the white, drawn face beneath the shawl, Garnet felt pity thicken to tears that filled her throat. How could the woman come to terms with what she had lost? She had held the child to her breast for so long, heard that first tiny laugh, soothed the pain of first teeth, delighted in the first baby words; that was the extra pleasure she herself had never known, but it was also that woman's extra pain, pain that would stay with her through long dark months to come.

'It be a blessin' in its way, one less mouth to feed an' it seems them two has a hard enough job a feedin' of theirselves.'

'You look to be right about that but there be no doubtin' it be hard on 'em poor souls. Lord tek the little mite and love it as its mother do.'

'Amen to that.'

Beside her each of the watching women crossed her breast as she added her own pious words to the prayer then turned away, boots tapping busily as they hurried about their business.

Only Garnet stayed, her heart crying out that she understood what these people were going through, that she too knew the pain and desolation of losing a beloved child, a child she had not been able to bring to a churchyard, not been able to bury. Hers had had no funeral, no coffin.

She looked at the box carried so carefully in the man's arms, plain rough wood, a posy of buttercups its only adornment.

'Please–' the sad little group drawing level she stepped forward, '–please ... may I?'

A loud heart-broken sob breaking from her lips the woman nodded and the man's own thanks trembled on his tongue.

Placing the bunch of heather she had taken from the basket on to the box she looked into the tear-drowned eyes, her own swimming with sorrow.

'The Lord be merciful to your child and to mine.'

It was said quietly and in that brief moment Garnet knew the woman understood, theirs was a bond shared by many.

Watching the group pass into St Lawrence churchyard she turned. She had to find work, a place to live before facing Tyler; for that she too would need the mercy of the Lord!

'That be 'er ... that be the one, I'd know her anywhere, I don't be mistaken.'

More a shriek than a shout the words rang along the street.

'That be her I tells you ... that be the filthy gypsy robbed me, it were her did it, her stole my money!'

Gypsy! Judah ... Hepzibah! Had they turned back?

The shawl slipping from her head, Garnet turned to look back the way she had come.

'There you be!' The shriek rang out again. 'I told you ... I told you her had red hair, I told you ... that be the one, that be the gypsy come to my door. I should 'ave laid a broom about her shoulders, seen her off there and then but I be too pityin' for others. I let her stand with her pegs and heather and what did her do? Her waited til my back were turned and robbed me, me who were set to buy some of her rubbish.'

'They all be thieves ... vagabonds and

230

thieves! We don't want their sort 'ere thievin' whatever they can lay hands to, runnin' off wi' folks' babbies.' A woman's voice, loud and grating, added its own denouncement.

As quickly as the observers of that pathetic funeral had dispersed so a fresh group gathered, eager for entertainment.

'It was 'er took my man's dinner, swiped it from the table, plate an' all, an' my back turned less time than it teks to tell ... bloody thief!'

Picking up a stone the second woman threw it, hitting Garnet on the side of the head.

'Well 'er'll thieve no more in Darlaston nor any other town agen I finishes with her, the filthy gypsy bitch!'

Another stone finding its mark, Garnet tried to answer but like baying hounds the small crowd closed around her.

'Now then, now then, that'll be enough of that! There'll be no tekin' of the law into your own 'ands ... that be what we 'ave magistrates for. Now you women be off an' leave the law to do its work.'

'See that you does!' Swathed in black skirts, a tiny black bonnet perched on her head, a heavily built woman turned on the constable elbowing his way to Garnet. 'We wants no gypsies in this town, mek sure an' tell the magistrate that, tell him it be gettin' so a body don't be safe in 'er own house, stealin' a man's dinner! The Cat be what that one want, a taste o' the Cat an' 'er'll think twice afore stealin' the next time.'

'Ought not to be no next time,' a further woman grumbled, 'give 'em the noose I says, hang the lot o' them, an' be done with 'em! Dirty bloody gypos, they be no good, all they does is rob folk!'

'Well this gypsy be one you don't be like to see again, the magistrate holds no more liking for them than does yourself.'

Closing a strong hand firmly over Garnet's arm, ignoring her attempts to explain that she knew nothing of the woman accusing her, the constable looked at her.

'You be under arrest...' he said loudly, 'you be under arrest for robbery!'

It had gone as he planned. Tyler Cadell watched the woman slip several sovereigns into her bag. She and her accomplice had played their parts well. Garnet had been taken to Wolverhampton and there given over to a true representative of the law. Tried by the magistrate there, an everyday robbery would not make news that would travel back to Darlaston ... or to Wednesbury! The Lady Olivia Denton and her viscount uncle would be no wiser than before.

'Remember what I told you!' Tyler's mouth tightened. 'One word of what has been done and you will find yourself prematurely in hell. It is as easy to get rid of one woman as it is another!'

Waiting for no reply he turned on his heel. That woman he had hired knew he was not a man to be cheated. She had her money, he would hear no more from her ... or from Garnet. His mouth relaxing he climbed into his carriage. A call at Victoria House would prove a pleasant diversion to the day.

'Gone to Birmingham along with Winifred Benson, something about a new gown, but I'll bet a sovereign to a pig's ear nothing will come of the trip, my niece is like any other woman I know, changes her mind with a breath of the wind.'

Damn! Tyler swore softly as he was shown into the sitting room of the gracious house. He had wanted to see Olivia, to settle the date of their wedding; she had agreed to marry him, but not for love of him, it was the sapphires he had presented her with, those and the thought of a non-ending stream of such valuable jewels Olivia Denton was in love with. But the stream had run dry, if he did not marry the woman soon she was bound to suspect.

'Then I should not burden you with my presence, sir.'

'Don't go yet, Cadell.' The viscount waved a hand toward a silk-brocaded chair. 'There's a matter I wish to discuss with you.

My niece tells me you have proposed marriage to her.'

Tyler's senses quickened. He should have asked this man his permission before proposing, if he was too much a stickler for the social proprieties then the match could be off before it was on.

'That was wrong of me, sir,' he apologised quickly, 'I had thoroughly intended speaking with you first but I am afraid the moment rather overcame me!'

'Or was it my niece?' The older man smiled. 'She can be a trifle ... shall we say ... demanding? Which is exactly what I wish to discuss with you. Olivia is a sweet enough girl but she is also one who has never been denied anything she has asked for, and though in the course of time she will receive a bequest from me I hope that will be a long way in the future. As for the rest of my estate it must be left for the upkeep of Riverton.'

She would not receive the whole of his fortune, the house and majority of his money was to be left to keep the home of his ancestors! Stunned, Tyler listened as the other man continued.

'Understandably what I can bequeath to my niece will be a paltry sum that will no doubt quickly be spent on fripperies. Now had she been a man then the lot could have been hers, Riverton, this house, the title...'

Going to a graceful side table he poured

two glasses of wine from an elegant crystal decanter, handing one to Tyler.

'...but the title can be passed only to a man and whilst I have no son and the family is devoid of a male heir yet still I feel it my duty to ensure Riverton will be cared for, at least so long as my money lasts.'

Riverton, the family seat, together with everything barring a paltry few pounds was not to go to Olivia! Tyler stared into his wine. The title could not be his, that he had known and must live with, but the property ... the money ... he had felt that already in his pocket.

'Forgive me for speaking so bluntly–' the viscount looked over the rim of his glass, '–but Olivia is a girl with expensive tastes, you will need deep pockets in order to keep her as she is accustomed.'

He had pockets! Tyler forced himself to smile as he sipped the full-bodied wine. And they were deep, but they were also nigh on empty. He had given her all of Garnet's jewellery, selling off various assets in order to go on giving. He would get nothing but a bed-fellow from this marriage, but without it he would lose too much. Wed to Olivia he could recoup some of his losses, the jewellery at least he could take back.

'Pockets, no matter their depth, have a way of emptying.'

Did he guess? Had he seen the look his

words had produced? Tyler placed the glass beside him. If so then the game was up now.

'I know my own would have been that way long ago had I not invested what I had in diamonds.'

'Diamonds?' Tyler's attention fastened on the one word.

'Years ago.' Riverton nodded. 'Came across a fellow whilst I was in South Africa, place called Kimberley. Turned out he had a mine he wanted to be rid of, needed the money to return to England, missed his sweetheart too much; so I helped the chap by buying his mine. Three months later we hit a vein that has paid off ever since. Diamonds are the market to be in if you need money, and face it, Cadell, we all need that.'

'We do indeed, sir.' Tyler's brain clicked. 'And as you so rightly say, diamonds are the market to be in.'

'Lucrative!' Filling the glasses once more the other man nodded. 'Very lucrative. But making money means spending money. Speculate to accumulate is my father's belief and in this case his words have proved worthy, so much so I would invest further were not my assets tied up with other things.'

'There are still openings then?'

'Not as such. The Boers, you know, they've staked claim to every patch of ground they can put hand to, but an acquaintance of mine writes me he is thinking of selling his own claim, going to live what is left of his life in luxury and idleness, enjoy what he has made, and believe me it is enough for any family he might have. But I must not bore you further with such...'

'I do not find it boring, far from it.' Tyler leaned forward, interest clearly marked in every line of him. 'This acquaintance you speak of, would he sell to me do you think?'

'You?' The viscount's brow ceased. 'Are you sure you want to lay out so much capital? It is an established mine producing a good quality stone, he will not sell for pennies.'

'Then how much will he sell for?'

'Were it myself I would want thousands, and not a few either. But if you are serious, I will contact him, get you an answer as soon as I can.'

As soon as he could! Driving home, Tyler went over the conversation in his mind. Thousands would mean selling off what was left of the holdings Isaac Winton had left to his daughter, including Bentley House. But what was Bentley House and a couple of iron and steel works compared to a diamond mine? He might not get a title but in a year or so he could be living like a lord.

She had robbed no one. The whole thing

237

was a mistake!

Still dazed by the swiftness of it all, Garnet looked at the man sat in a high-backed chair, his hand grasping a wooden hammer placed beside him on the bench.

'You entered the home of this woman...'

No, that was not true, she had never seen the woman he pointed to.

'...you took advantage of her generosity, stealing from her the moment her back was turned...'

It was a lie, she had never stolen!

'...it is the duty of this court to protect the citizens of Wolverhampton from pickpockets and vagrants; therefore I find you guilty as charged and order you pay one hundred pounds in fine or accept deportation to the colonies.'

The crash of the gavel breaking the stupor that held her, Garnet tried to answer, tried to cry out it was wrong, all wrong, that never in her life had she stolen anything. But the heavy-jowled man had already left the bench and she was being hauled from the room.

She heard the sound of keys being turned in the door behind her. Pushed into a dimly lit room, Garnet looked at the wardress who had accompanied her along the black corridors.

'This be called soap.' The woman pointed to a large bar of dull yellow substance sat in a cracked saucer. 'You gypsies don't know what soap is, but you be one that's going to learn. Get them things off and get yourself in that bath. Quick now!'

A shove of the woman's hefty hand sent Garnet crashing against the cast iron bath.

The magistrate had refused to listen. Beneath the hard passionless eyes of the wardress, Garnet removed her clothing, catching her breath as she stepped into the cold water. He had believed the lies, judged her guilty without allowing her to speak in her own defence. One hundred pounds! Picking up the strong smelling soap she rubbed it over her shivering body. It was an impossible sum, was that why it was imposed ... because he knew it was impossible for her to raise it?

'I see you don't take to washing ... you be like the rest of your gypsy scum ...well, we'll 'ave to see to it ourselves won't we!'

Snatching the soap the wardress rubbed it over the bristles of a scrubbing brush. One hand holding Garnet's head pushed to her chest, she dragged the brush up and down her back, bristles like steel nails driving into her skin.

'You'll be clean while you be here!' The woman scrubbed harder. 'Our convicts be clean when we sends them off to the colonies.'

Throwing the scrubbing brush aside she

grabbed a chipped enamel jug, pouring streams of the icy bath water over Garnet's head.

'Wash that well or else I'll do it for you … with the brush! And when you be done you make sure you leaves this bathroom like a new pin, that is if you wishes to be able to walk when they fetches you from here!'

The threat heavy behind her the hard-faced woman banged the door closed. Lather from the coarse soap stinging into the cuts along her back, Garnet rubbed at her hair, misery closing colder about her than the bath water. She was to be sent to the colonies, she would spend the rest of her life banned from her own home.

But where was home? Climbing from the bath she dried herself on the length of trough cloth hung on a nail driven into the bare brick wall. She had known no home for more than two years, the colonies could hold nothing new for her.

'You will be with me, Ebony,' she whispered. 'You will always be with me; what does it matter where they send me or what they do to me? They can never take you from my heart.'

Chapter Seventeen

It had been a smart move of his. Sat in the study of Bentley House Tyler leafed through the deeds of the property he still owned. Where would he have been had he waited? Dependent upon the charity of Isaac Winton, unable to keep up appearances without that man's money, seen as too poor to maintain his position as Captain in the Guards. That had taken money and every penny left by his own parents had just about gone when Garnet Winton had arrived in Mariwhal.

But he had not waited. Unfolding another paper he stared at it with unseeing eyes. Typhus had broken out in the village a few miles from the Winton's bungalow, the stream that was their water supply had become infected, and as any thoughtful son-in-law would have done he had taken them barrels of water drawn from the well serving the barracks.

As any thoughtful son-in-law would have done! He smiled slowly. But how many sons-in-law would be thoughtful enough to add infected water from the local stream before dropping them at the house?

That had been a little pearl of wisdom. The smile gave way to a sharp frown. If only he could have given some of that water to his wife, had her die of typhus like her parents. But how to explain her death when no one else close to the barracks had died? No, it had to be done that way, she had to be sent back to England. The child had been the perfect excuse, the perfect opportunity, yet it had slipped away from him. Garnet had escaped but she would not escape this time.

A hundred pounds! Seated in the back of the gallery of that courtroom he had heard the sentence for himself. One hundred pounds. He laughed softly. It might as well be the moon was asked for. Seven days. There was no way she could come up with that sort of money in as many years. She was no longer a threat to him; Garnet Winton-Cadell was destined for total obscurity.

As the last of the papers lay unfolded, Tyler felt a little of his euphoria slip away. Not a few thousands had been Riverton's answer. So how many was not a few, twenty … twenty-five? He couldn't raise much, not without the Crescent Iron Works and that was already gone, as were the Hopyard and Priestfield Collieries.

'*Speculate to accumulate.*'

It might be he had speculated and lost!

Most of the money from those sales had been spent on impressing Olivia Denton and her viscount uncle, and too many sovereigns had found their way into the pocket of a certain gypsy whore. He had been a fool, he had allowed desire to rule his mind! But the only desire in the plans he was making now was the desire for money and no woman, gypsy or otherwise, would deter him from that.

Having pulled the tapestry cord hung beside the fireplace he looked up as his manservant entered.

'The painting that hangs in the mistress's bedroom, the one signed Constable, I want it taken down, my wife will choose another more to her taste.'

'The mistress ... your wife ... has been found?'

'Garnet!' Tyler laughed, a brief mirthless sound. 'Oh yes, she has been found but she will not be returning here, nor anywhere else for that matter. Mrs Garnet Cadell is to spend the rest of her life in one of Her Majesty's colonies.' Catching the bewilderment in the man's eyes he laughed again. 'I see you don't understand, but it's simple enough. Garnet was arrested and tried in the Wolverhampton Magistrate's Court, she is to be voluntarily deported in seven days' time.'

Voluntarily! Tyler saw the servant's glance

harden. 'Oh, I agree with you, Raschid, she had very little choice in the matter, in fact she had no choice at all ... and neither do you.'

'Of course I do not.' The turbanned head bowed in apology, 'It is just that when you said your wife would choose another painting...'

Collecting the papers together, slipping them into a leather bag, Tyler rose. 'So she will, my new wife that is. I intend to marry the Lady Olivia Denton ... very soon.'

'What did you do to get yourself put in here?'

A spoonful of thin lentil soup half-way to her mouth a grey-haired woman whispered the question, her glance watchful.

'I can't think...'

Swallowing the soup the woman answered quickly. 'Ain't surprising you can't think, neither can any other poor body that bugger gets 'er claws into. A pummelin' from Bertha Coffin leaves you feeling like you be ready for one, I knows for I've had my share.'

'I meant I could not think of any crime I had committed.'

'Having no money be crime enough.' The woman spooned her soup, eating rapidly. 'A vagrant be the label that sets to you and you needs no other to find yourself in gaol.'

'And you needs no more than a loose tongue to get yourself a few minutes with the Cat! The Governess don't like inmates talking about the justices like that, her be like to reward it with a few lashes. You do see what I mean don't you, Jeffs?'

'Yes, Wardress Coffin.' The grey-haired woman scrambled to her feet, plate and spoon in hand.

'Then if you don't want a striped back I suggest you get back to the laundry; I'll be there myself in an hour or so ... that mouth of yours needs a washing out!'

'And you...' The bamboo cane she carried under her arm touching Garnet's plate the wardress pushed it across the table. '... there be work for you to do; you've sat long enough filling your gypsy belly at parish expense, but by the time you've finished you'll be too tired to take advantage of the good nature of the parish ... or of me!'

It had not been an empty threat. Stood in the bathroom, Garnet sponged her aching body with the cold water, wincing as the sting of carbolic soap bit into her lacerated hands. The work the wardress had spoken of had been to scrub every corridor.

You don't get floors clean by looking at 'em!

The cane had come down hard across her back and when she had said the water in the bucket was too hot the woman had grabbed her forearm, forcing her hand into the near-boiling liquid.

She had been at the end of her task, the final yard of the corridors scrubbed almost white when the wardress had returned.

Cupping cold water in her hands Garnet splashed it over her face mingling it with tears of remembered pain.

'I said you don't get floors clean by looking at 'em.'

The words had echoed along the drab corridors, bouncing like bullets off dark-brown painted walls.

'You don't be given to work, like all gypsies you'd rather steal. Well when I tells you to scrub a floor you scrubs it ... clean!'

The woman's boot had come down hard, pinning her fingers to the stone floor. Grinding her foot before removing it she had demanded brush and soap be handed to her.

Reaching for the rough huckaback used as a towel, Garnet held it between fingers stripped of skin. The woman had smiled! She had actually smiled as she ordered her to stand and place both hands palms flat on the wall.

She had smiled! A sob trembling in her throat, Garnet pressed the damp cloth tight to her mouth. Smiled as she had scrubbed viciously, not stopping until blood stood out bright where it dripped on dark paint.

'Get yourself into this.'

A cry breaking from her, Garnet flinched. 'Don't be feared, it be only me.'

Recognising the whispering voice as that of the woman who had spoken to her in the dining hall she lowered the towel, allowing it to be exchanged for an ash-coloured calico night-gown.

'I'll see to things in here, you get yourself into bed afore that sour-faced cow makes her rounds. It'll take nothing at all to rile her and you've had taste enough of her particular form of amusement for one day. Get you into bed and when you hears her clumping great boots you close your eyes, and for God's sake keep 'em closed.'

There had been no time to braid her hair. Her heart thumping, she had barely time enough to slip into the hard narrow bed before the door had opened.

'Not abed yet, Jeffs?'

'Sorry, Wardress Coffin, I be just finished in the bathroom, there were one more to use the bucket.'

'You mean you was the last to wash, you took turn after a dirty gypsy? But then you be no better yourself, you both be slime!'

Her contempt as heavy as her tread, the wardress walked slowly into the bathroom, the cane slapping against skirts as brown as the walls.

'It be well you left that cleaner than your scrawny body. Bed!'

The bark having Jeffs and the rest of the prisoners jumping for their beds, Bertha Coffin walked across to Garnet and touched the cane to her face.

'...*for God's sake keep 'em closed.*'

Feeling the cane like a brand against her skin, her body stiffening beneath the cold twill sheet, she prayed her trembling would not be detected.

'Huh!'

The cane moved, tracing a line across her cheek.

'This one be asleep, that be no surprise for this must be the first bed her's ever known...'

Let the woman leave ... please God, let her leave!

'...but her won't be knowing it many more nights ... this one be bound for the colonies by the end of the week.'

The sudden darkness as the room's solitary candle was blown out, followed by the slam of the closing door released Garnet's breath in a loud quivering sob.

'Do what Coffin say be right, be you sentenced to the colonies?'

Ada Jeffs' whisper was soft as she crept to Garnet's bedside.

'Christ, what did you do to earn that?'

'I can't see as I did anything. One minute I was watching the funeral of a child and the next...'

'You didn't pinch nothing?' Ada perched on the bed.

'I've never stolen anything in my life.'

'Garn, that ain't no truth. Gypsies pinch whatever they can, everybody knows that.'

'I am not a gypsy.'

'But Coffin says you am.'

Using her elbows to prop herself higher in the bed, Grant looked at the thin face, visible now in the faint moonlight filtering through the high-set windows.

'Wardress Coffin is mistaken. It is true I was with a group of gypsies for some time but I am not myself a gypsy; it is also true that gypsies do not steal ... at least the group I knew did not.'

'Then if you ain't robbed nobody what else do there be to get you sent from the country?'

What else indeed? She had asked herself the same question over and over as she had scrubbed those corridors, but she had found no answer.

'Does there have to be a reason?'

It was not really a question but Ada Jeffs answered.

'No wench, there don't have to be no reason for the law to lock you away and put your babbies into the poor house. That were what the parish done for Ada Jeffs, that was the charity they showed me. When my man died 'neath a fall of coal I was left with four little 'uns to feed; then the mine owner had me put from my home 'cos I couldn't pay the rent. I tried every which way to find work that would put food in my children's bellies, but everywhere I was turned away. At last I could stand hearing their hungry cries no more so I stole a loaf and two meat pies from the shop of James Reece along of King Street, that got me two years' hard labour and lost me my babbies.'

'I'm so sorry.' Garnet reached for the woman's hand, the sting of her own forgotten as she clasped it.

'Be sorry for my little 'uns.' The whisper was even quieter and there was a catch in the other woman's throat as she went on. 'In a few month I'll be out of this place of hell, but my babbies ... they won't be free til I finds a home to bring 'em to and a job that feeds 'em.'

'You will find work, I am sure of it.'

It had been meant to comfort but in the hush of the quiet dormitory Garnet heard the sob in the answer.

'Mebbe you be right, wench, p'raps the Lord will smile on both of we, giving me work and sending you back to your family.'

But I have no family. Her eyes wide, Garnet stared at the shadowed ceiling as Ada Jeffs returned to her bed. The Lord was merciful, one day He would surely unite the woman and her children, but even His mercy could not end her own pain, her child was dead and nothing could take away the pain of that.

'I won't let you, I won't let you kill our child... No, Tyler ... no ... o ...o.'

'Wake up ... wake up, wench!'

'No, Tyler, please ... please don't kill my baby...'

'I don't be Tyler ... wake up, wench, wake up afore Coffin comes.'

Hands on her shoulders shaking her hard, Garnet moaned. 'It's not true, Tyler, Ebony is not...'

'Wake up!'

As if a rope were lifting her from some dark pit, Garnet felt herself being pulled to the surface of sleep, a voice constantly urging her to wake. But she did not want to wake, she wanted to stay wherever she was; here she could save her daughter, take Ebony in her arms and...

Then her eyes were open and the hope was gone.

'Lord, wench, I feared Coffin would hear you and bring that cane of hers about your head.'

'Tyler...'

'I told you I don't be Tyler!' Ada Jeffs shook the slight body again. 'You've been dreamin'. I only hope nobody outside of this room heard you cry out.'

251

'I'm sorry if I woke you...'

'Don't matter none about wakin' me.' Ada glanced at the windows set high in the bare walls. 'It be near enough time to rise, best get yourself up and dressed afore Satan's henchman be come to inspect.'

This was to be her last day in this prison, her last day in England. Where were they sending her ... to which colony? She had learned in the first few hours of being here not to ask questions, for the only reply they received was a sharp stroke of a wardress's cane.

With every bone and sinew screaming its own pain she dressed then with meticulous care remade her bed, smoothing every tiny wrinkle from sheet and pillow, each movement of her hands opening the nigh healing of the savage scraping of that scrubbing brush and the vicious weals of a bamboo cane.

'You 'ave had that nightmare afore, ain't that so?'

Spooning thick porridge Garnet nodded. So many times before ... and how many times yet to be endured?

'Who be Ebony?'

Hearing the name raised a picture in her mind of a gurgling contented child, a tiny hand touching her breast as it suckled, raven-dark hair like black silk against honeyed skin, and Garnet could not answer.

'It were a babby weren't it?'

Ada continued to whisper as together they washed breakfast dishes, her sharp eye following the slightest movement of the kitchen wardress.

'It were your babby, and Tyler ... the other name you cried out ... he were your man?'

The approach of the wardress ending the questions, Garnet turned away. She liked Ada Jeffs and was grateful for the woman's help and guidance that had saved her from several beatings by showing the particular way the prison attendants liked things done. For all she knew the questions as to her nightmare were asked of pity and maybe from some thought of driving it away by discussing it, but the pain of remembering was too great and she was relieved when they were separated, Ada being sent to the laundry and herself assigned kitchen duties; here at least she was not under the gaze of the sadistic Bertha Coffin.

Despite her misery, Garnet smiled to herself thinking of the reply Ada had given after lights out two nights ago to the question, was Bertha Coffin married?

'Married!' Ada had laughed. *'Bertha Coffin would 'ave to lift a man out of his grave afore her could get one to marry her.'*

'Dawdling don't be advisable in this place. Keep your dreamin' till you be in your bed.'

The presence of the wardress at her

shoulder sending a tremor of fear through her, Garnet cut into a potato, a string of brown peel dropping into the bowl she had set on the long well-scrubbed work table.

'There be sprouts to be prepared once you finishes that, the Governess is particular fond of sprouts and particular how they be prepared, so make sure you cleans them through.'

'You'll have to find somebody else to do that...'

Bertha Coffin's voice turning the tremor into a positive trembling, Garnet looked across to the open door.

'...this prisoner be wanted.'

Who wanted her, and for what? Why was she being made to change from prison uniform into her own clothing? Knowing she could not ask without receiving a blow in reply she fumbled with the buttons of her blouse, the insistent tapping of the cane adding clumsiness to her throbbing fingers.

'You'll be pleased to know you be leaving.'

Of course! Following behind the heavy figure whose uniform so nearly matched the dark painted walls, Garnet realised what it was she had been sent for. The time had come, she was being deported.

'Through there!' Indicating a door with her cane, the wardress glared.

Wherever she was bound it could be no worse than this. Drawing a deep breath she walked across the room empty except for a plain table and stool. What did it matter to which of the Crown colonies she was sent, without her child life was of no importance. Yet she would have asked one thing of her life: to see Tyler Cadell pay for his crime.

Opening the door she paused.

Men should not seek vengeance, that is the judgement of the Lord.

The saying her mother had often used returned as she blinked at the sharp brightness of the day.

A few yards from her a man turned to face her.

Tyler! She gasped. Tyler had come for her!

Chapter Eighteen

'Do you really think Tyler Cadell will buy that diamond mine?'

Standing at a window that overlooked gardens tapestried with flowers the Viscount Riverton smiled at the question.

'It seems our friend Mr Cadell has spoken of the prospect.'

'He told me ... yes.' Olivia Denton smoothed the skirt of the amber velvet riding habit that fitted close as a glove.

Riverton turned, the smile still evident on

his mouth. 'That is not to be wondered at. I think the man is quite besotted with you my dear, which is what we both would hope, is it not?'

'He would not have asked me to marry him were that not the case.'

'Oh, Olivia, my dear little niece, through the centuries men have married women for many reasons other than that of the heart ... and women likewise. Tell me, what are your feelings for the man who hopes to become your husband?'

Raising a hand to the jaunty feathered cap set an angle on sherry-coloured curls, Olivia's own smile was artful. 'At this moment, uncle, my feelings are of apprehension.'

Opening the door of the elegantly furnished sitting room he waited for her to pass then followed her to the stable yard where two horses were saddled and waiting. Mounted and clear of the listening stable hand he glanced at the attractive face.

'Apprehension,' he asked, 'for what reason?'

Looking straight into his grey eyes, her own cool as grass at dawn, she answered. 'For the reason he might not come up with the purchase price.'

'Ah!' Riverton nodded. 'Now that would be a shame. We all know it takes the profit from a diamond mine to keep you in clothes and diamonds.'

'And to keep you playing the gaming tables, eh uncle!'

'*Touché,* my dear, *touch*é. He smiled again. 'Diamonds are equally necessary to us both.'

'So, do you think Tyler can raise the money needed to buy that mine?'

'You, Olivia, like myself, must wait and see just how much the man comes up with.'

'But do you know the price?'

'Yes, my dear.' Riverton touched his riding crop to the animal's flank. 'I know exactly how much that Kimberley diamond mine is going to cost Mr Tyler Cadell.'

He had sold everything, the last of the Darlaston properties, the tea plantation in India, even the house was mortgaged, all of it turned into cash. But would the amount he had managed to raise be enough?

He had ransacked every room in Bentley House, selling off anything that would bring a shilling, even the Indian's room had not escaped attention. Bloody wog! Tyler's face darkened. He'd had the effrontery to claim those small ivory figurines as belonging to him, a gift from Tyler's mother he had called them. Gift, pah! Stolen when the household was being packed up for that last journey to Simla was more likely!

Simla. Suddenly memories flooded into his mind of the beautiful house set beside the wide lake whose edges were emerald green with reflections of graceful overhanging branches. His mother had loved Simla, spending most of her time in the lush hill country, and that was where she had chosen to be buried, in the gardens she had cherished so much. And his father ... he had spent the remainder of his life grieving, spending money on keeping that house, an expensive useless shrine until on his death barely enough had remained to buy his son a commission in the Army. Why had that house been so important to his father, why spend his life almost revering it ... was it love, or was it a penance? But that was over, finished! With that diamond mine Tyler Cadell would come into his own, he would be a man to reckon with.

Twenty-five thousand pounds! The memories fled, taking the pictures from his mind. He had realised twenty-five thousand pounds. Christ, it was a king's ransom! But Riverton had been sceptical. It might not be sufficient, diamonds were becoming more important every day. Diamonds could form a firmer financial market than gold, he had said. One day they might replace gold altogether as the empire's reserves of wealth, and with a mine producing first-quality stones a man could be secure for life, his status in society firmly entranched; no door, even that of aristocracy, would be closed against someone rich as Croesus, and that is what Kimberley could make him.

Could make him! Tyler reined in his horse, looking over the expanse of barren heathland. And if it didn't, if it failed to be all Riverton had claimed? But it wouldn't, Riverton wasn't a man to dabble in uncertainties. He spurred the animal on. Twenty-five thousand wasn't a sum to play with, Riverton had smiled, but if it was accepted then within six months the same amount would be like chicken feed, an amount to be spent without circumspection.

As he had spent those sovereigns on that gypsy whore! But it had been worth it, her body had pleasured him more than any woman's had done, and her news of Garnet had come in time to avoid any possible embarrassment. At this moment his dear wife was aboard ship, bound for the colonies. Everything was working well; but an hour in the hay with the gypsy woman would have provided an amusing diversion to the afternoon, and the planning of how he would kill her would add pleasure to the entertainment.

Cresting the rise he looked down into the small valley that had held the gypsy wagons. They had been gone for days. His dark-haired beauty had disappeared with the morning mist.

Walking the horse gently down the slope he smiled to himself.

But she would return. The sovereigns that jingled now in her pocket would not last for ever, one day she would come back for more; and she would get more, much much more, but not sovereigns. His little gypsy Venus would be paid in far more lasting coin!

He had gone with the gaujo. Sat beside her wagon, Hepzibah stared out over the wide stretch of empty heath. Her would not 'ave attempted to turn his mind from the doing of it yet her heart feared all the same. The heath were empty but not far away stood the Union Workhouse, the place Walsall town put them folk too poor to keep themselves and 'eld the threat of it over the heads of folk they didn't want near their town, folk like the gypsies.

Half closing one eye she squinted at the sun. An hour and it would be setting, a night in this place were more than was comfortable but Judah were first man and the others had agreed to bide for him.

He had caught up with the wagons a couple of hours after their crossing of Bentley Mill Bridge, that gaujo dressed in a jacket the colour o' baccy, trousers grey and shapeless, baggy as if too big for the body they covered; but it was the hair and skin 'ad caught her eye most, one dark as the wing of a crow, the other the colour of tea the way gaujos took it, drowned with cow's milk. But the creaminess had been darkened by weather as was the skin of a Romany; the man would 'ave no difficulty passing as one.

He'd talked with Judah, none of what was said being overheard but she had seen her son's face pale, whatever the man had said had been enough to see Judah 'ave a few words with the men, telling them to carry on if they wished but each and every one had spoken otherwise.

Taking her pipe from her pocket she set it between her teeth.

Why 'ad every man been willing to stop in this place, so near a house of hell? Her son 'ad simply followed the creed taught by his father and his father's father, help asked for must be given. But that help 'ad been asked only of Judah, yet each family were camped waiting as if for some call.

Chewing on the stem of her empty pipe she watched youngsters help with the horses while others carried wood collected against the lighting of evening fires.

Did they feel what she had felt … did the others feel a longed for birth had happened with the coming o' the red-haired woman, the birth o' Romany freedom?

Nobody knowed o' what the crystal 'ad shown, her tongue nor Judah's 'ad shared it with another. The time was too soon, the woman were hated by the man that was husband to her and the only child born to her was dead of the same hate. Yet the crystal never lied and it 'ad shown a child in her arms, a child marked with the crescent moon.

All of that 'ad been kept deep in her heart, but the action taken today would see the releasin' of it. She nodded to the child sent by its mother to place an armful of firewood beside her cooking rods. Romany blood spoke loud as any tongue, it called to its own and it was calling now, calling for some sign, some attestation that what was hoped for in every man's soul was at last begun.

Tonight Judah would call a meeting of the Kris. Tonight they would be told.

Returning the pipe to her pocket she unhooked the water jack, pouring some of the contents into the tea kettle, then at a call from one of the men she turned to look across the heath. Shading her eyes against the scarlet gold of the sky she watched the tall figure of Judah stride towards them.

'Thank ye, God, thank ye for the keepin'' of ''im.' She whispered softly, knowing no real reason for the relief that trembled in her.

'I were sworn to keep it from anyone and I vowed I would.'

Their evening meal over mother and son

sat side by side. Beyond the circle of light shed by the one central fire the world lay shrouded in darkness.

'Then keep it ye must.' Hepzibah nodded. 'The word of a Romany be fast binding as any wrote on paper.'

'I know that and I be no Romany to break that bond, yet still my heart be sore that I must keep it from my mother.'

'Secrets only be bad when they hides evil and I knows ye will never allow evil into yer heart. Keep yer word lad, hold precious that which be entrusted to ye in faith. The Lord will tell if time be when you must speak out, until then be sure Hepzibah Kane bears no ill will, her bears only pride that her son follows the way of old.'

'I offered that man a place in this camp. Hearing the story he told I offered to let him travel with us, but with his showing me what I were fetched to see I could understand his refusing.'

'Then we will respect the honour he showed ye in asking the help of a Romany before that of one of 'is own kind and speak no more of what it were ye shared today. I asks only it carry the blessing o' the Lord as I asks the same for what must be spoke now before the Kris. Call the men, my son, they must know what I saw in the crystal the night you and I looked into it together.'

'I asks leave to speak.' The men seated in

their customary places, their womenfolk clustered behind, Hepzibah approached the centre.

'It were some days after my son were attacked, days after your wagons left for Stowe. We shared the crystal, looked into it together and what it showed that night I would tell you now. But first I ask for some among you step into the wagon of Hepzibah Kane, to witness along of 'er that which the crystal reveals, they shall testify to the truth of what I tells. Two men and two women of yer choosing.'

The choice made and her story told, Hepzibah led the way into the wagon. A woman reached for the snippet of chemise, a man fetched the crystal to the chest top and, ensuring her hands had the touching of neither, Hepzibah signed for the second woman to remove the velvet cover.

'This be the crystal used from times gone. Be you satisfied o' the truth o' that?'

As she had with her son she followed the ritual of question, nodding as each answer was given until each hand was joined with another, raised in a circle above the gleaming orb. As before it remained a few seconds clear and bright then deep within it a hazy mist formed and rolled, thickening until the whole globe was darkened as if by cloud.

'Let your fingers remain twined.' Instructing them quietly she brought the circle of hands to rest about the glass ball and as they touched the table top it cleared.

'Remember what it were ye heard from the mouth of Hepzibah Kane and pay full heed to what the crystal will show.'

'The haze, it be takin' on shape!'

Hushing the gasp of the woman who spoke, Hepzibah felt the tension mount as figures appeared to take on form in the heart of the glistening glass.

'The crystal speaks,' she said softly, 'watch the truth of it.'

In the silence that followed the haze-formed pictures in the glass showed exactly as before. Transfixed the four people stared at the evidence of Hepzibah's story, the image of the woman Judah Kane had brought into camp, the figure of a red-haired woman taking into her arms a child whose heart was surmounted by the crescent moon.

Tyler! Coming into the daylight from the gloom of that prison she had caught her breath at sight of the figure etched against the sunlight. Tyler himself had come, come to see her safely on her way out of the country.

But it had not been Tyler. True, at first sight she had thought the clothes were his, she had thought she recognised them, then he had turned towards her. The man wearing them had not been her husband but his manservant. It had been Raschid come to see her leave.

Fatigue clawing at her she sank to the ground, her head slumping on her knees. She had been wrong in that too. It was not in order to see her deported he had been there but to see her freed. How? Though she had asked, Raschid had not told her; in fact he had told her practically nothing, no word of whose money had paid her fine, only hurrying her as fast as she could walk away from that gaol. So whose money had it been? With her eyes closed she tried to think. Tyler ... had Tyler paid to have her released and if so why had he not had her brought back to Bentley House? No, it could not have been her husband who rescued her, truth was Tyler would rather see her dead. Yet who other than Tyler Cadell would have one hundred pounds? She would have liked to show her gratitude but Raschid had not divulged the identity of her rescuer, he said only that he was a messenger sent to pay her fine and see her out of that prison. But she must not return to Bentley; he had emphasised the point strongly, taking her hand in his. There was no more money, nothing he could give her to help her on her way except a wish for her safety. He had left her then. Garnet swallowed the tears collected in her throat, tears of emptiness and despair.

'My godmother says to give you this.'

Opening her eyes to the small voice, Garnet gasped. 'Ebony...! Ebony, my darling!'

'I am not Ebony.' The dark-haired child answered solemnly. 'My name is Emily, and Godmother says to give you this.'

A shilling! Garnet stared at the coin lying flat against the small palm then back again to that solemn little face. This might have been her own daughter, her child would have dark curls and bright brown eyes.

'I have to go now. Godmother is waiting.'

Stretching a hand as the coin fell into her lap, Garnet tried to touch the child but she was already walking back to the carriage stood at the road's edge.

'Wait, please.' Holding the coin she pushed to her feet and followed the child already seated in the carriage. Dropping a curtsy she looked at the feather-bonneted woman. 'I thank you for your kindness, ma'am, but I am no beggar.'

The woman's eyebrows rose, her glance running questioningly over the patched skirts and ragged shawl.

'We are not always what we seem, ma'am.' Garnet interpreted the glance. 'Though my clothing indicates the opposite, I have never begged in my life nor will I now; but the charity of your sending your goddaughter to speak with me is an act I will hold in my heart for as long as I might live.'

'You do not accept charity other than the kind word of a child, and your speech is not that of a beggar.'

'No, ma'am.' Placing the coin on the seat beside the woman, Garnet smiled once more at the child then walked away.

She could have been my baby, my little girl. Thoughts sweet yet bitter as gall swirled like falling blossom in her mind. My daughter would have been beautiful as that child is beautiful, she would have been taught to be mindful of others less fortunate.

Less fortunate. She paused, the shout of a carter preventing her stepping into his path. What could be less fortunate than having your own father throw you to his hounds!

But Tyler would be brought to book. Somehow, some day she would see Tyler Cadell pay for the murder of their child.

Resolution lending her strength, she walked on along the busy street trying not to see the women draw their skirts close as she passed or the glares of carters expecting her to steal from their wagons.

Her glance crossing the street she choked back a sob as she read the words painted on a high-sided cart: 'Winton's Tea'. That had been part of her parents' legacy to her, the dowry Tyler had snatched the moment she received it, the bequests that were to help keep her and any children she might have in comfort.

But she must forget all that.

If in the short time they had spent together she had learned anything of the man she had married, if she knew Tyler at all she knew he would never allow her a penny of the money her parents had left.

'...*stay away from Bentley*...'

The partings words of the Indian man-servant was cannon fire in her brain.

'...*never return to Bentley House!*'

It was a warning, the true message of which was stay clear of Tyler Cadell, hide yourself where he will not find you. But where? Where could she hide from a man who had once tried to kill her, and given the chance might do so again?

Hepzibah and Judah, they had offered her a home, they would have hidden her, kept her safe. But she had refused their offer and now they were gone.

'...*Should you 'ave need tell it to any gypsy you meet and word will find me*...'

Where to find a Romany when she didn't even know where she was. But Tyler might soon know where she was! He was sure to enquire which colony she had been sent to if only for his own peace of mind, and when he found she had been released it was equally certain he would search for her.

Breathless from the hurried walk through the busy streets she leaned against the tall stone pillar of a wide gateway. The owner of the house at the head of the drive would not give her shelter but surely would tell her where she was.

'Which town might this be?'

An elderly woman in white frilled cap that covered all but a grey patch of hair drawn back from her brow, an ankle-length matching apron swamping dark navy-blue skirts, stared at the raggedly dressed figure stood on the doorstep.

'It be Priestfield, here! Be you running from the law?' she demanded. 'That's it ain't it, well you be gone from my door, I wants no criminals in my kitchen! The mistress would 'ave forty fits if her knowed a criminal were at her door.'

'I am not a criminal...'

'Then you be in the pudden club, been lying with some man who's throwed you out now the chickens 'ave come home to roost.'

'No, ma'am.' Garnet felt the world suddenly spin about her. 'I ... I'm not with child, it is simply that I have walked a long way.'

'Then you can walk a way further...'

'Mrs Peake, I wish to speak to you regarding my oriental evening. I shall be wanting supper to match.'

'Eh!' The woman turned quickly, Garnet

temporarily forgotten. 'You be wanting oriental supper, you means food such as foreign people eat?'

'That is the idea, Mrs Peake.'

'You means with spices and such, I can't do that, a bit of parsley or a sprig o' thyme be all well and good, but I ain't never 'ad call to do with nothing more.'

'Then you will have to learn, and quickly, my invitations have already gone out.'

'Excuse me, maybe I could help, I have had some experience of cooking with spices.'

'Mrs Peake–' the tall chiffon-draped figure turned toward Garnet, '–I did not know you had a visitor.'

'Be no visitor of mine,' Bessie Peake returned quickly. 'Her be here askin' what town her be in … I was just sending her packin'.'

'What town you are in?'

'Ar, what town.' Answering for her the grey-haired woman looked at Garnet. 'That smells like a week-old kipper to me, it do an' all! I say her be more like to be a criminal, We'll 'ave the constables 'ere in a minute, mark my words if we don't!'

The elegantly dressed woman's smile was kindly as she ran a glance over Garnet's patched skirts.

'We should not judge on appearances, Mrs Peake, a good sword often comes out of a poor scabbard.'

'So it do,' the cook nodded, 'but a rusty sword can cut as deep!'

'Quite so, but one never quite knows what a sword, rusty or otherwise, is capable of doing unless one takes it in hand and tries it.' Her smile still on Garnet she went on. 'You say you are familiar with cooking oriental food?'

'Not oriental, though I am used to cooking with spices. I lived for some time in India, my parents ... my parents had business there.'

If she had caught the slight hesitation the mistress of the house ignored it, her glance sharpened.

'*Had* business, you mean they are retired?'

Behind her the sky was growing darker, soon it would be too dark to find her way.

'My parents are dead,' Garnet answered quickly. 'They died in India. Thank you for telling me the name of this town. Good night, ma'am.' Dropping a curtsy Garnet turned away.

'One moment, a shilling will help you on your way.'

A shilling would buy her a bed and a meal. Garnet turned slowly, her eyes meeting those of the slender, chiffon-gowned woman.

'Thank you, ma'am,' she said quietly, 'but I am no beggar.'

'You do not accept charity other than the

kind word of a child.' The eyes watching her smiled. 'You are the woman in the street, the one who refused the shilling my godchild offered.'

'It was a kind offer and ... and the child was very pretty.'

'Wait!'

Several steps from the door, Garnet halted.

'My oriental supper, what of that? Mrs Peake says she has no idea of how to go about cooking it and if you leave I will have to cancel. Such bad manners so near to the date.'

Her graceful chiffon lifting like gossamer on the evening breeze, the woman's smile touched her mouth.

'You did say maybe you could help, and no matter whether Asian or oriental, those of my guests knowing the difference will not care.'

'I did say it,' Garnet answered, 'and I will willingly, but it would have to be with Mrs Peake's approval, I would not usurp her position in her kitchen.'

There it was again, the pride, the quiet authority. Flora Redmond felt a quick surge of admiration for the ragged figure standing with her head held high. She was no beggar nor woman of the street, that sort did not twice refuse a shilling. There had been an assurance in the girl's speech, an assertion

273

that despite her appearance she knew who she was and from whom she came. Honesty born of good breeding shone in those sad eyes and instinct said the girl would not disappoint or betray a trust.

'So Mrs Peake, it rests with you, does she help or doesn't she?'

'Eh mum, it don't be my place...'

'But you are my cook and my friend. Like this young woman I would not cause disharmony.'

A wide smile crossing her plump face, Bessie Peake nodded to her mistress.

'I ain't knowed you to make a mistake yet an' I don't feels as you be making one now.'

'That is settled then.' Flora Redmond smiled at Garnet. 'A supper such as is served in Asia will do just as well as one served in the Orient. However, seeing as my invitations are already delivered I will ask you to keep that a secret between ourselves.'

Chapter Nineteen

Knelt beside the bed in the small room the cook had shown her to Garnet finished her prayers. Prayer had been all she had to cling to in that prison, all that had kept her going since...

With memories stabbing her heart she climbed into the narrow bed.

They never seemed to fade … at every opportunity those memories filled her mind, the scenes of that terrible night stark and horrifying in their reality. But it was one scene she had not witnessed that brought the true nightmares; the one that had her baby thrown to the dogs, the one that showed teeth tearing at the soft flesh.

Both hands pressed to her mouth could not prevent the anguished sobs leaving it. Why, she asked silently, why let such a dreadful thing happen to an innocent child, why had God allowed it?

Giving way to the searing sorrow inside her she let the tears flow. Her mother had taught that in life every act had a purpose designed and watched over by the Lord, but what purpose could there ever be in the brutal murder of a child or in having an innocent woman condemned to prison?

She had told Flora Redmond of the part that she felt the woman should know. Brushing away tears she stared at the ceiling patterned with moonlight. Bessie Peake had drawn her into the kitchen but before she would take a stool beside the glowing range she had told them both of her times with Hepzibah and of her arrest and imprisonment, but not of Tyler or what he had done.

Why had she told them? Garnet remembered the keen look that had accompanied Flora Redmond's question and the nod given at her quiet response that she would not stay in that woman's house unless she knew of it.

But it had made no difference, the woman had not changed her mind. In fact she had said she had an idea of it all along, where else might the backs of a woman's hands be scrubbed raw?

Bessie had immediately set about bathing them in warm salted water saying the sting of it would soon pass, that it were needed if poison were not to get into them cuts. Touching her hands now to her cheeks, Garnet felt the soothing effect of ointment made from the bark of slippery elm and root of goldenseal. Like Hepzibah, Bessie Peake preferred her own cures to those of a chemist shop; and like the Romany woman she had a roughness that hid a tender heart.

But all through the dressing of her hands, the other woman had watched as if knowing not all of the story had been told. Ought she to have revealed the rest, told of her baby ... would such horror be believed?

Hepzibah had believed. She had listened saying nothing, but in her eyes had been a pity beyond words. They had not discussed it after that one night; perhaps with her experience of life, of the hurt that can be born of hurt, Hepzibah had deemed it best to let sleeping dogs lie; but it was not easy to take that way when every night brought fresh torment, when every night saw you yearn for that evil to be redressed.

The Lord sees all, and all is reckoned in His time.

The words of her mother, soft and soothing against the pain of her heart, Garnet closed her eyes. Maybe tomorrow would bring an answer, maybe tomorrow would bring if not an ending then at least the beginning of an easing of the misery of the past.

'I appreciated what you said to the mistress, that you wouldn't come into this kitchen without I approved of it. Not many women in your position would 'ave said such.'

Drawing white cotton gloves over her sore hands, Garnet took a bowl from a shelf running the length of one wall.

'Being down on one's luck does not give them the right to take advantage.'

'That be summat else not many folk would say.' Bessie Peake laughed. 'I said I'd never knowed the mistress pick a wrong 'un. 'Sides, I noticed when I fetched you inside that you had no collier's mark.'

'Collier's mark?' Garnet frowned.

'Ar, you know, a rim left round the neck when a body has a cat lick instead of a proper all-over wash. Most things I can stand but two I can't be doing with. The first be not knowing what a bar of soap be for and the second be an idle fossack. But I'll take money on the fact you be neither.'

As the laugh pealed out again a bell set with a line of others above the door jangled.

'That be the mistress, her said her would want to see you some time this morning.'

Why would the woman want to see her? Had she changed her mind, was she going to tell her she could not stay in this house after all? Questions racing one after another in her brain, Garnet followed the plump figure to a room on the first floor.

'In you go.'

The smile was meant to be reassuring as Flora Redmond's voice gave permission to enter, but still Garnet was apprehensive. Was it to begin again so soon, the wandering from the village to village, town to town? She knew that being in this house was only a respite, that she could not stay once the preparation of food for the coming evening was finished, but she had not thought that respite to be quite so brief.

'Ah, there you are.'

Garnet's eyes followed the newspaper as it was laid aside. Had there been anything in that relating to her, something to do perhaps with Tyler looking for her?

Flora Redmond smiled. 'First, how would you have me address you? We did not exchange names last evening, you seemed much too tired to answer questions then.'

She could give any name, her maiden name! Garnet glanced again at the newspaper. But where would lies lead, what good would they do in the end?

Her chin lifting, she looked squarely at the woman sat with her back to a tall rectangular window.

'My name is Garnet,' she answered firmly, 'Garnet Winton-Cadell.'

For a moment there was silence between them as a long-fingered hand moved to rest on the newspaper.

Had mention of her name tied in with some report, had some journalist with knowledge of her conviction for theft related it to that of Tyler Cadell?

'Then may I call you Garnet?'

Almost dizzy with relief Garnet could only nod.

'So, Garnet.' Flora Redmond was suddenly brusque. 'What do you suggest I serve at my oriental supper?'

'I er ... I think, ma'am, should your guests be unused to the Indian way of cookery then perhaps something not too hot on the tongue; I suggest a variety of samosas.'

'And they are?'

Suddenly it was like being with her mother again discussing meals for the day with their Indian cook. All her nervousness fading before the wonderfully comforting feeling, Garnet smiled.

'They are triangles of thin pastry stuffed with vegetable or meat and vegetable then the edges are sealed and the whole is fried. They can be eaten hot or cold.'

'Sounds quite delicious.' Flora Redmond nodded. 'Excellent for what I want for a buffet supper. What else can you suggest? And do not worry overmuch if one or two dishes are a little fiery; some of the people I know could do with spicing up ... anyway it will all add to what I hope will be something a little apart from the usual.'

Garnet took a moment to think. 'My mother's favourite was Badam Pursindah, that is lamb with almonds. Ladies might prefer that, it is more gentle on the tongue than say Seek Kabab Massalam.'

'I must confess I have no idea what you are talking about,' the older woman laughed, 'but I am sure you do, though what poor Bessie will make of it all I dread to think. I leave everything to you, what we do not have in the way of spices you have permission to buy. Bessie will go with you.'

'Badman what!' Sitting down hard on her chair, the cook stared as Garnet finished explaining what her mistress required. 'Lord, I can 'ardly say it let alone cook it! It be a good job you come an' no mistake. Tch! I've known Flora Redmond to 'ave

280

some crack-brained ideas in her time but this beats the lot. But if Badmen wotsits be what her wants then that be what her must 'ave. I'll see to the gettin' of lunch then we'd best be off to the market.'

The market! That meant walking those same busy streets she had walked on leaving prison! The streets Tyler was certain to be searching if he knew of her not being dispatched to the colonies.

'Twenty-five thousand pounds ... chicken feed, you hear that, you Indian scum, chicken feed!'

Tyler Cadell struggled drunkenly from his coat, letting it drop to the floor.

'Soon I'll have a house full of servants but they won't be like you, their skins will be white; and you,' he dropped heavily to the bed, staring at his manservant with glazed eyes, 'you can bugger off to the devil!'

Bending to pick up the coat the servant staggered a few steps as a foot slammed into his back.

'You can go to hell ... that 's if they take wogs there, or we can throw you to the dogs ... yes,' he laughed, a half-inebriated laugh, '...there's always the dogs, they eat any meat, white or brown.'

His face impassive the manservant helped remove shoes, shirt and trousers, handing Tyler a perfectly pressed night-shirt before going to hang the clothes in the dressing room.

Why had he stayed with this swine of a man? Closing the wardrobe Raschid looked at himself in the standing mirror. There was no so much different about him and the man in the bedroom, he was as strong, his body as muscular, he was as much a human being! But to some, human beings with brown skin were inferior, subordinate, creations of a minor god, and to Tyler Cadell not even human!'

So why stay? Brown eyes fixed on their own reflection echoed the answer in his mind. You know why you stay.

'Twenty-five thousand.' In the bedroom Tyler laughed again. 'In a year that will be nothing; the Lady Olivia will still live like a lady, we will have a house that will be a match for Riverton, see what her uncle thinks of that. "Can you keep my niece in the standards she is accustomed to…"'

At the door that led back to the bedroom Raschid watched the figure stumble its way into bed.

'…that was what his lordship, the high and mighty Viscount Riverton, was really asking, could I keep his niece in luxury. Well the answer is yes; and her answer tonight was yes.'

Catching sight of his manservant, Tyler roared. 'You hear that, you turbanned offal?

The Lady Olivia Denton is to become my wife.'

Walking slowly to the bed, Raschid looked with contempt at the man already drifting into sleep.

'That cannot be,' he said. 'You already have a wife.'

'*Had!*' Tyler opened bleary eyes. 'I *had* a wife but not any more, the oh so pure little Mrs Cadell be gone ... gone to the colonies, so you see, she is no longer a rope around my neck.'

He had not heard. Raschid continued to tidy the bedroom, each movement followed by heavy snores. As yet he had not found out his wife had been freed, but how long would that state of affairs last, and when it ended what would happen to Garnet Cadell?

He had helped her all he could, telling her never to go near Bentley House, but that was all he had been able to give. He had no money, Tyler Cadell had never dreamed of paying him a penny in wages and now even the ivory figurines that would have sold for a fair sum were gone, swallowed up in the mad race to raise money to buy a diamond mine.

As always, Tyler Cadell had treated him like dust beneath his well-polished shoes, discussing business with his associate the Viscount Riverton as though no one else was in the room. Associate! Looking once more at the sleeping figure he left the room. That was now any man with sense would view that man, never as a friend.

A diamond mine! In his own bedroom Raschid removed the turban, running a hand through thick dark hair. What proof was there such a mine existed or if it did that it was viable; that the stones spoken of so euphorically were what they were claimed to be?

Stripped of his clothes he sluiced cold water over his body. Catching sight of it in a cracked mirror hung above the wash stand he stared for a few moments. So alike yet so different! Tyler Cadell and his Indian manservant, both were men … but not in Tyler's eyes.

'Thank the good Lord that be over.'

Bessie Peake's plump body sagged in the chair set beside the large kitchen range.

'Would it be all right for me to make you a cup of tea?'

'More than all right, Garnet wench, it would be perfect. I don't 'ave enough strength left to take off me bonnet.'

Hanging her shawl in the scullery Garnet moved quickly, setting cup and saucer beside milk jug and sugar basin, then scalding tea leaves in a self-patterned white ironstone teapot.

'Could you set a tray for the mistress while you be about it for I be fair bushed.'

'The market was enough to tire anyone.' Garnet smiled. 'I never saw so many shops.'

'Don't they 'ave shops in India?'

'Not the sort they have here in England. They have what are called bazaars, open-fronted kiosks, long avenues of them sheltered from the sun by cloth draped from one side to the other.'

'Open-fronted, you means they 'ave no door! 'Ow do them shopkeepers stop folk stealin' their goods?'

'There didn't seem to be any stealing, at least not in Mariwhal.'

'Hmmm!' Bessie Peake seemed to mull over Garnet's answer. 'Then the justice in that country 'as to be pretty severe.'

No different to English justice. Garnet reached a tray from a shelf that formed the understay of the dresser, the thought ringing in her mind. But what was justice when it could sentence a woman to deportation for life simply on someone's word?

'There be tray cloths in the drawer and use the china from the dining room.'

With her feet resting on a low stool, Bessie watched the setting out of the tea tray. This was no strange task to them hands, poor as her might be now this wench hadn't always been the same, her had been used to better than field or gutter.

'Mrs Redmond's tray is ready all except for scalding the tea.'

'Ar, so it is.' Taking the cup Garnet handed to her the other woman smiled approvingly. 'But I sees no cup for yourself.'

'I would not presume...'

Adding a spoon of sugar to her cup Bessie stirred vigorously.

'Presume! If that means you don't take it without being invited then I be inviting you now. Sit yourself down and take a cup of tea, that there tray can wait for a couple of minutes.'

Waiting until Garnet was seated with her tea, Bessie Peake shook her head slowly. 'You know, when first you knocked on the door of my kitchen I could 'ave swore you was a criminal, either on the run from a constable or up to no good. But though it be less than a twenty-four hours since, I sees I couldn't 'ave been more wrong no matter how I tried. Seeing you in that market, refusing to take a penny to pay nor a penny in change, letting only my hand touch the money, even telling that woman selling that there spice powder her had reckoned herself short of three farthings... That be a first for the ears of Bessie Peake and for that spice seller by the look that crossed her face. You be no thief, wench; despite of what that there magistrate judged, I says you be no thief.'

'Thank you.' Eyes filling with tears, Garnet looked at the plump face. 'Thank you for believing in me.'

Snuffling against the tears collecting in her own throat, Bessie lifted her cup.

'Best get this drunk and that tray upstairs afore the mistress thinks we've gone to India to buy the stuff for her fancy supper.'

'There were several of the spices we could not get.'

Garnet had carried the tray to the small sitting room as the cook had asked.

'Why was that?'

'It seems there is no call for them, Indian cooking does not appear to be an everyday part of life, many shop keepers had no knowledge of some spices at all.'

'I see.' Flora Redmond ran a critical eye over the tray. 'Does this mean my oriental evening can no longer include a buffet supper?'

'Not at all. It will mean a possible change of dishes.'

'And you can cope with such changes?'

'Yes, ma'am.'

Watching the afternoon light spark ruby glints from the neatly combed hair, the older woman smiled. Poverty was no disgrace to this girl, there were many richer that did not possess her graceful manner nor a fraction of her capabilities. Fine feathers did not always make fine birds.

'Will there be time enough for you to make the dishes you described? They sounded very exotic and two nights is not so very much time.'

'Two nights will be adequate, ma'am.'

Adding milk to the tea she had poured from the elegant silver pot, Flora Redmond leaned back in her chair.

'In that case perhaps I might ask you to do one more thing?'

She had said two nights would be adequate but that had meant working non-stop, she had not reckoned on there being any other call upon her time. But this woman had offered her shelter, albeit until that oriental supper was cooked, she had trusted her enough to have her under her roof. Swallowing her apprehension, Garnet nodded. Let the woman ask; if it were at all possible she would do it.'

Chapter Twenty

'Sign and it's yours.'

Across his desk the Viscount Riverton smiled as he held a pen towards Tyler.

The Halloran diamond mine. Tyler stared at the document lying before him. His offer had been accepted but signing this paper would leave him without a penny.

'Halloran sent these as a token of goodwill and as proof of what the mine is producing.'

Leaving the pen on the desk, Riverton crossed the room to a small safe. Taking out a canvas bag he handed it to Tyler.

'These are not top quality stones,' he said as the bag was tipped on to the desk, 'they are from the uppermost stratum of a new digging. The top layer of ground always bears the lower quality stone, but they are witness of the better stuff just below. Even so–' he fingered the tiny heap of glittering stones '–these are not to be sneezed at, they'll redeem your first few thousand.'

Taking up a few of the stones Tyler turned them on his palm, watching the lancets of light spear in every direction.

'A new digging?' he asked. 'And part of the property being offered for sale?'

'Of course, it would have been mentioned earlier but the new ground hadn't been opened then. Judging by what you have there I would say your twenty-five thousand wouldn't buy a tenth of it in a couple of years' time, but that is simply my opinion. Perhaps you should go out there, see the diggings for yourself, talk to the people there, get a further idea of what is being fetched out of that mine before putting your name to that paper.'

'Will this man Halloran hold that long?'

Scooping the gems into the bag, Riverton held out his hand for those still held by Tyler.

'Really, Cadell, that is something I can't say. Word of that new find getting out can bring buyers from all over, and remember the Boers are there on Halloran's doorstep and they are not short of money; they add a thousand to your offer and he might just let them have it. To be sure of getting the mine you might be best advised to decide now.'

He couldn't afford to go to Africa. Even were there time he couldn't finance a trip there. He'd been so sure yet now the moment of signing was here! As he turned the stones again on his palm the myriad facets of light danced on his face. He had to decide!

'Twenty-five thousand is a lot of money, perhaps you should just forget the whole thing.'

'No!' Dropping the stones into the bag, Tyler picked up the pen and set his signature to the document.

'Congratulations.' Riverton smiled. 'You have just bought your first diamond mine. Let's go share the news with Olivia, tell her she is to be the wife of a very rich man.'

A very rich man. Folding the paper, Tyler slipped it into his pocket. He liked the sound of that. Tyler Cadell, diamond merchant. A little of the pleasure drained.

Rich he would be, dealer in fine diamonds he would be, but still it would be plain *Mr Tyler Cadell.*

The thought still rankled as he rode back across the heath towards Bentley. A title was what he really desired, until he had that he would be nothing more than a shopkeeper, a member of the trading class. The thought a barb in his mind he jerked on the rein, bringing a whinny of protest from his mount.

Riverton had talked of knowing people who knew of ways to open doors. But so far that had been purely talk, how long before words became actions, how long before Riverton made some of those introductions?

Maybe at the ball he was giving to mark the engagement of his niece? Yes, he touched his heels to the animal's flank, what better time! The engagement ball would see the first of those doors opened.

Sat beside Flora Redmond in the first-class train carriage, Garnet kept her smile in her mind. She had been apprehensive when the woman had asked her to do one more thing, dreading what it might be yet knowing were it possible then she would do it.

'*I like to do things well,*' Flora Redmond had said. '*The food served at my supper will be authentic, I would like my costume to be the same.*'

She had smiled at the reply that Garnet

had no such clothing, her own reply holding a depth of understanding.

'*That my dear, is obvious, but as you said, you were in India for some time therefore I presumed you to have knowledge of the garments worn.*'

Garnet had nodded but her eyes must have shown their question for the woman had laughed.

'*It is nothing very dreadful I am about to ask. All I want is a description, if you could manage it a sketch, a drawing my dressmaker can follow in making up a costume.*'

'*A sari!*' It had burst out on a breath of relief that brought another light laugh from the woman watching her. '*A sari was the mode of dress for the women of Mariwhal, though there are I believe different styles of clothing in other areas of India.*'

'*And what does a sari look like?*'

The question had immediately conjured a picture of brilliant colour and flowing cloth, of jewellery and ornaments that glittered from ears and wrists, tiny bells that jingled about the ankles.

'*A sari is a beautiful garment,*' she had replied, still looking at the pictures in her mind, '*it lends an elegance to the figure, a grace to movement, it is an adornment to any woman.*'

'*Then I shall most certainly have a sari. Can you make me a sketch?*'

The mental images fading, Garnet smiled at one that replaced them. Flora Redmond's brow wrinkling into a puzzled frown in answer to Garnet's description. *'A length of cloth! I'm not a parcel to be wrapped like a pound of sausages.'*

It had taken only moments to turn the frown into a smile, the woman listening carefully to the description of the draping of a sari. Now they were on their way to the draper, Flora asking would she help in the choosing of the material.

Of course she had agreed. Garnet glanced through the window at the hurrying landscape, the thought of the partly prepared oriental supper not the sole worry needling her nerves. Once more she was to walk the streets of Wolverhampton town, and even dressed as she was in clothes this woman had given her she would still be recognisable to Tyler.

Leaving the train at Monmore Green station she followed an attentive porter eager to secure a hansom for Flora and a tip for himself.

'Little Moor Street.'

Touching his cap the cabbie set off along streets Garnet did not recognise. Had this been the way they had brought her to that prison?

'Try to forget, my dear.'

Flora Redmond's touch to her scratch-marked hands had been meant to be reassuring, but sat in that cab, Garnet shrank into its depths. Was it always to be like this, frightened to show her face in case her husband caught sight of it?

This was the third draper shop that they had been to and with each successive journey her fear of being spotted increased. Bentley was not so far from Wolverhampton and Tyler was not a man glued to his own doorstep.

'What do you think?'

Flora's question breaking her reverie, Garnet knew she had to reply truthfully though it would mean yet another drive through those streets, another walk into a shop giving the chance of her being seen and recognised.

'The colour is very impressive,' she answered, 'but purple is not the most complimentary to your colouring, and the weight of this,' she took the material between her fingers, 'is too heavy, it would not drape as it should.'

Ignoring the sour expression of the shop-keeper who had just seen her sale disappear, Flora marched from the shop. 'I have no idea where to try next.'

'Beg pardon, ma'am.' The cabbie touched his hat politely, hearing Flora's comments as she left the shop. 'If it be a draper you be lookin' for then I knows of a place. It don't be grand to look at but could be it has what you be wantin'.'

'I think not. My companion and myself are both too tired to shop further. We wish to return to the railway station.'

'We'll pass the place I speaks of as you nears the station 'ma'am. I could easy wait while you looks inside.'

'Just where is this shop you speak of?' Flora looked at the man helping Garnet into the hansom. 'I might tell you that taking us on a goose chase will not result in your receiving a larger fare!'

'This 'ere be Wharf Street, at its end,' he pointed, 'we takes a right turn into Commercial Road and a left turn where it comes into Cleveland Street.'

'Yes, yes!' Flora waved a hand cutting the man short. 'I did not ask for a lesson in geography. I said we were too tired for such a jaunt.'

'Cleveland Street runs straight onto Bank Street and that be next to the station.'

As Garnet settled at her side, Flora smiled. 'And Bank Street is where we no doubt find his draper. He deserves an extra sixpence for perseverance.'

'And somehow I feel it is one he will get.' Garnet returned the smile but almost at once it was gone.'

'My dear,' Flora spoke quietly, 'I cannot ask you to share with me the reason for the sadness I see in your eyes, a sadness I feel has a deeper cause than a wrongful prison sentence; but if I can help...'

'This be Bank Street, ma'am.'

'We will look at your draper shop.' Answering the hopeful call Flora's smile was warm. 'Remember ... if I can help.'

Eyes misted by the woman's words, Garnet stepped from the cab almost colliding with a grey-coated figure in a blue feathered bonnet.

'I beg your pardon, I was not looking where I was going, please forgive me I–' The rest trailed away as she looked into the face of the woman staring back at her, the woman who had demanded her arrest!

The woman had recognised her! Garnet tried to keep her mind on the lovely fabrics being shown to Flora, but every few seconds it returned to the figure on the footpath. There had been shock in those eyes, shock and fear. But that was all she knew of the woman who had accused her; who was she ... and why had she done so terrible a thing? And even worse, would she do the same thing again?

The thought stayed with her the rest of the long hours she worked in the kitchen, draining her until she thought she would scream. Now in the privacy of the tiny bedroom she covered her face with her hands.

'*...if I can help...*'

The words spoken so quietly seemed to taunt. How could Flora Redmond help ...

how could anyone help?

The only way was to leave now, tonight, before the woman could dream up some other excuse to have her arrested, go as far away from Wolverhampton ... from Bentley ... as he could. But she could not leave. Tears squeezed warm and hot between her fingers. Bentley was where her treasured memories lay, the memories of her baby ... and memory was all she had left.

'...*I cannot ask you to share with me the reason for the sadness I see in your eyes...*'

She could not share it with anyone, she could not describe the anguish that filled her night and day. No one could fill the emptiness that was her soul.

'Ebony.' The sob broke on the quiet room. 'Ebony, my baby ... my heart! I miss you so much. Everywhere I look I see children; they have your face, my darling, your beautiful little face; but when I go to them, touch them they are not you and I am alone again. Oh my little one, you will never hear me say how much I love you, never feel my arms rock you to sleep...' Sobs wracking her throat she slid to the floor, folding herself into a tight pain-filled ball, the cries becoming a whisper in her heart.

Oh Lord, take me too ... please God, take me too.

He had signed!

Lady Olivia Denton freed her hair of pins, shaking its luxuriant sherry-coloured folds and watching them cascade over her shoulders.

The money had been paid. Twenty-five thousand pounds and for something the man had never seen!

From the mirror of the dressing table eyes the shade of cool moss stared back at her.

Was he a fool? If so, then how long would the man who had slipped an engagement ring on to her finger be able to hold his lady bride?

Glancing down at her left hand her smile was as cold as the glint that shone from the heart of the square-cut stone.

She would be the wife of a diamond magnate. Her uncle could have chosen less propitiously, but then her uncle was a wise man, he did not make any move without first considering it from every angle.

The wife of a diamond magnate! She twisted her finger, watching the spears of multi-coloured light shoot from the brilliant white stone.

That suited her very well, but Bentley and the house that stood on its empty heath? That would not suit. She would not bury herself in a place whose nearest town existed under daytime sky madc hardly distinguishable from night by the perpetual pall of smoke belched out by factory chimneys and coal dust drifting from its many mines, each pitting the earth like some dreadful pox. The Black Country! She had thought her uncle was simply being amusing when he had spoken of it but she had learned of that mistake within hours of coming to Victoria House.

Lord, how could anyone live here, the bowels of hell must be more inviting! But *she* would not live here, nor would she live at Bentley.

Glancing again into the mirror, the momentary irritation of her thoughts disappearing, she touched a hand to the soft shining curls resting beside her throat.

London ... Paris ... Rome! Diamonds could take her anywhere, and they would. Lady Olivia Denton-Cadell of Bentley.

A laugh as cold as the smile had been rippled over the quiet bedroom.

Not in a thousand years!

'Why the amusement?'

Rising from the delicate gilt chair, Olivia turned towards the figure stretched naked on the bed.

'Just thoughts.'

'You might not like what you hear.'

'I like everything about you, Lady Olivia Denton.'

Walking to the bedside she looked at the man smiling up at her, at the lithe muscled body the handsome, strongly featured face.

'Everything?'

'Mmm.' A long sultry glance rested on her face. 'Though I admit there are some things I like especially.'

'Oh.' Red lips pouted. 'I thought I satisfied you completely.'

'Not yet, my dear...' Reaching a hand to her throat he pulled the slender satin ribbon that held her robe together, then his eyes still holding her own he ran a finger slowly over each breast and down the centre of her body, pausing to touch the navel before coming to rest at the tip of the soft gleaming sherry-coloured mound at the base of her stomach. '...I have that pleasure yet to come, and so do you.'

Tugging a corner of the robe he brought it, tumbling like a blue-green cloud, about her feet.

The pout becoming a taunt she took a small step backwards, making no effort to retrieve the fallen robe. 'Perhaps I shouldn't, my uncle would be most disappointed.'

Spreading his legs a little wider he smiled as the column of hard flesh jerked against his flat stomach. 'And this will be disappointed unless you do.'

'And this?' Stroking both hands up over thighs and hips she cupped both breasts, holding them as he rolled on to one elbow. 'Should I not keep this until I am married?'

The other hand reached for her, pulling

her on to him, his mouth clamping hard on hers as he rolled her beneath him.

'But Tyler…' Olivia laughed softly.

'Tyler? I'm afraid he's going to be a little short-changed!'

His own laugh mingling with hers, Viscount Riverton drove deep into the warm, moist softness beneath him.

'You were correct in your description, Garnet, a sari is indeed a beautiful garment. And oh, the freedom from corsets! I may never wear western dress again.'

Pleased with her own efforts, Garnet watched the other woman pivot and turn before a long dressing mirror. It had taken some time before Flora Redmond had finally settled on pearl silk chiffon patterned with cobweb-fine silver. Teamed now with chased silver bangles and heavy silver necklace and ear-rings gleaming against shining chestnut hair, the whole was a picture of beauty.'

'I feel truly elegant,' Flora smiled her satisfaction, 'and for once in my life I feel like a woman not a fowl trussed up ready for the oven.'

'You look elegant,' Garnet agreed, 'like a true Maharahni.'

'And what would that be?'

'A queen, a queen of an Indian state.'

'I don't think Her Majesty would approve

the title, Victoria is mindful of being the only Empress of India.'

A smile touching her lips Garnet turned to the dressing table strewn with jewellery Flora had chosen from.

'Then we won't tell her! But tonight another regal head should wear a crown.'

Taking up a long rope of pearls she twined them among the coiled hair, looping them across the brow, finally fastening an elaborate emerald ear-ring to hang from its centre.

'There!' She turned to look at the reflection of her work in the mirror.

Flora Redmond regarded herself then lifted her glance to close with that of the girl reflected by her side.

'You have a gift, my dear,' she said quietly, 'a gift of creating beauty, you should use it.'

She had enjoyed helping in the choosing of the sari, of draping it as her Indian maid had taught, of teaming it with accessories that complemented the cloth and its wearer; but tonight was the only time she would do that for once the evening ended her time in this woman's house was also ended.

Seeing the veil drop over her eyes to replace the pleasure with a misery the girl imagined hidden, Flora watched her leave the room, the feeling in her that something terrible lay in the girl's past as strong as it had been on first meeting her.

'Eh, wench, you've done a real good job,

the table in that dining room be a fair picture.' Bessie Peake beamed as Garnet entered the kitchen. 'And the things you've cooked! I tells you I've cooked all me grown days and never used one half of the spices you used, and the other half ... well I ain't never 'eard of them.'

'I hope Mrs Redmond finds the dishes satisfactory.'

'Satisfactory!' Bessie's plump face creased in a wide smile. 'I'll say 'er be satisfied, and many a one will go 'ome tonight wonderin' where it was 'er got that food, to say nothing of that there sari... 'Er looks a picture and no mistake ... though I don't go with leavin' off 'er corsets, ain't good for a woman, it can weaken the bones.'

Collecting the bowl and spoons used in putting the final touches to some of the food, Garnet appeased the older woman's misgivings.

'One evening should do no damage, Mrs Peake. Tomorrow will see everything back to normal.' And see me back on the road, she thought as she carried dishes to the scullery.

'You can leave them to me.' Bessie Peake rose determinedly. 'Them 'ands of your'n don't be ready for the sink yet, I was fretful them gloves wouldn't keep them spice powders you grinded from gettin' to them cuts, so we'll be havin' no washin' up just yet.'

Bowl in hand, Garnet hesitated. She could not leave the woman to wash all of those dishes.

'This be my kitchen and you said as you wouldn't want to go causin' no dis'armony, so you do as you be told an' don't give me any argy bargy!'

The words, though said sharply, held a touch of concern not lost on Garnet whose answer was tinged with feeling.

'I would not dream of arguing with you Mrs Peake.'

Tying her apron strings about her ample midriff the woman sniffed loudly, her retort as sharp as before. 'I should 'ope not neither, you don't be so old you can't catch a cuff about the ear. Now, carry them crocks to the sink and leave me see to them while you brews a nice cup of tea, I reckon we've both earned it.'

The ticking of clocks the only sound in the now quiet house, Garnet carried the last of the supper dishes into the scullery. Bessie Peake had long since consented to her pleas and gone to her bed, as had her mistress.

Glancing at a window admitting the first pale streaks of dawn, she peeled off the cotton gloves. She would not go to bed, she would wash the crockery and then leave the house, it would be better that way less painful than saying goodbye to two women she had come to regard as friends.

The last dish having been returned to its place she slipped silently to the tiny bedroom. Changing the clothes Flora had given for her use while in this house, she donned her patched skirts.

'...*you have a gift, my dear...*'

Looking at the face staring from the mirror above the small wash stand, Garnet felt pain strike her heart as the features appeared to change to those of a smiling dark-haired infant who reached her tiny arms towards her.

'Ebony!' she choked. 'You were my gift, the most cherished gift of my life, one I dreamed was a gift of love.'

Fists pressed against her mouth stopped the sobbing words but could not stem the thoughts ripping her like swords.

A gift of love ... sacrificed to a man's pride.

Chapter Twenty-One

The money were tainted, it were taken in return for wickedness and as such will be accepted by no Romany.

Walking alongside the wagon, Judah let his thoughts drift.

He had wanted to throw the lot down a pit shaft or into the canal where it could lie for ever, taking its evil with it.

But the man who had caught up to the wagons as they crossed over Bentley Mill Bridge had caused him to abandon the idea.

'*He gave me to think again, gave me to think it might be better used than throwing it into the bowels of the earth or beneath the water.*'

Across a table that held nothing but a crucifix the black-garbed nun had listened in silence.

'*I had no wish to come,*' he had gone on, '*to my thinking it be insulting to the Lord, offering that which was wanted by none of your own, but my mother said that not offering it was a wrong in itself ... who were we to decide what the Lord might or might not want, were her words; if it were His will the money have a use then He would accept what were offered, if it were refused then that were the time to cast it away.*'

Sitting with hands folded into wide black sleeves the woman had made no move to touch the pouch drawn at the neck with a string, leaving it where he placed it beside the plain wood crucifix.

'*Perhaps you might tell me of the wickedness attached to the money you offer,*' she had said quietly.

He had balked at that. What had taken place in that hollow were for the knowing of none but those that had witnessed it, yet he had told that man, the man whose face he knew.

'*The Lord values the gift of a man's trust more than a gift of money but His Love is not dependent upon either.*' Beneath her cowl the nun had smiled, a gentle smile that seemed to understand that not all of the sadness in his face was caused by the evil he attributed to that money.

'*Will you not avail yourself of that love, speak of that which troubles you? If you wish I can send for a priest.*'

Touching a hand to the horse patiently pulling the wagon, Judah remembered his answer and the shake of the head it had brought.

'*Man or woman I'll speak of it to none save only to say it has caused enough sorrow. I speak with the Lord in the silence of my heart, there is no need for a go-between, kind though the offer was meant. He knows how it was come by as He knows it cannot be kept. It was given into my keeping as first man; as leader of my people it is my hand must direct where it lies.*'

'*I think it is the Lord's direction has brought you to this orphanage.*' The nun had smiled that gentle smile again. '*I feel it His will the money be used to help the children in our care and while it can be only His hand wipes clean the taint of sin I will pray for His blessing on the work we do with it.*'

The Kris had listened that night as the flames of the camp fire had leapt into the blackness of the sky. Listened and agreed with the action he had taken.

Leading the horse on to the heath that bordered each side of the winding road, he patted the soft neck as he released it from the shafts.

The fruit of that wickedness done by Lorcan Nash and Marisa Lakin had been taken into the Lord's hand. May the accepting of it by that nun be a sign of His forgiveness.

In the quiet setting of the sun Judah prayed silently.

Give peace to their souls, Lord, and peace to the soul of the woman who took their lives and her own.

She had stayed later than intended. Garnet glanced at the strong light coming in at the window of the small bedroom. The tidying of the dining room then the kitchen had taken longer than she thought. Glancing about her she checked she had left nothing out of place. On the stripped-down bed were the skirts and blouse loaned by Flora Redmond, the coat hung in the room's one cupboard. There was no more to be done. Brushing a hand across a cheek still damp from the bout of weeping she took the towel from the rail of the wash stand, then gathering the bed linen she let herself quickly out of the room.

Would Bessie Peake and her mistress see her leaving this way as a thankless act of bad manners, or would they understand? Yet how could they ... how could they know she could not take any more sadness, that her cup of sorrow was full to the brim?

Carrying the linen to the laundry room she set it with the rest of the laundry awaiting the wash.

Yet this way felt wrong, it was not in her nature to leave any kindness unrecognised. She glanced at the door leading back into the scullery and the kitchen. Mrs Peake would surely have pencil and paper with which to note items that needed replacement. If she could find them it would take only moments to write a note of thanks.

'I thought as it were you I 'eard.'

Bessie Peake swung the kettle over a fire coaxed into new life.

'I also sees what I 'oped I wouldn't.'

'I ... I'm sorry to have woken you, I tried—'

'I can see full well what you tried!' Bessie Peake interrupted the stumbling apology. 'An' I thought better of you, I truly did. I hadn't got you down as one to go moonlighting, to leave a body who 'as shown you the kindness which Flora Redmond 'as without so much as a kiss me arse or bugger you!'

She was right to be angry. Garnet felt shame rise hot and fast to her face. Slipping away while the house was sleeping, stealing away like a thief was an insult to these people.

'It don't be worthy of you!'

'Oh Mrs Peake, please ... I can't face any more ... I can't ... I can't...!'

'Eh, wench!' The plump woman was across the kitchen taking a sobbing Garnet in her arms. 'I d'ain't mean to go on at you ... me and my big mouth. Hush, girl, hush. You 'as every right to up and leave whenever you wants and I've got none at all to say otherwise.'

'I did not want to leave this way,' muffled against the woman's chest the words tumbled out, 'but I couldn't bring myself to say any more goodbyes.'

Holding the sobbing figure, Bessie Peake stroked the silken hair. *Couldn't bring herself to say any more goodbyes.* There was heartbreak and grief in those words, more than any young wench should be called upon to bear.

'Sit you there alongside the fire,' she said gently as the sobs subsided. 'A cup of tea will 'elp us both see things in their proper light.'

'I was going to write ... to explain...'

'You needn't explain anything to me, wench.' Teapot in hand, Bessie glanced at

310

the pale tired face. 'It be no business of nobody's what you does. It were wrong of me to go on at you the way I did and I 'pologises for doin' it. Best we says no more about it, I'll explain to the mistress.'

'No, Mrs Peake.' Accepting the cup offered her, Garnet looked with drenched eyes at the older woman. 'I will explain to Mrs Redmond.'

'Bessie Peake was right to apologise.' Flora Redmond watched the girl who had carried her breakfast into the dining room.

'Neither she nor myself can claim any jurisdiction over your actions, how and when you leave this house rests entirely with you; though were I to have that privilege then I would ask you to stay for another few minutes at least, to tell you of last evening. It was a huge success.' Flora sipped her hot tea. 'And that is another reason I would have you stay.'

'Mrs Redmond, I don't understand.'

'You will.' Flora smiled at the frown settling over Garnet's brow. 'Sit down while I explain. Every woman at my little get-together last evening demanded to know who it was had prepared so delicious a buffet, and every one of them asked the name of my dressmaker.'

'I'm pleased the evening went well for you.'

'Not only for me, Garnet, for you too if

311

you let it.'

Seeing the frown settle further over Garnet's brow the other woman went on.

'I told you that you had a skill and that you should use it. Well this is your opportunity.'

Garnet was puzzled. The woman's supper party had been a success, her dress had been admired but how could that be of opportunity to her?

'Forgive me for appearing vague,' she said, 'but I fail to follow your reasoning.'

'Girl, do I have to spell it out!' Flora Redmond laughed. 'Those women asked the identity of last evening's cook and costumier for one reason and one reason only, they too want to host an oriental evening and you are the one they want to organise and prepare it.'

Do the whole thing again, it was impossible!

'Why?' Flora demanded as Garnet said as much. 'Why is it impossible, what you have done once you can do again.'

'What I did for you was done in your kitchen with your utensils and your money to buy the necessary foods and spices, I have none of those things myself and without them...'

'You would not be without them. Listen to me, girl, and think well and carefully before you make your decision, for opportunities of the sort you have now rarely make a second appearance. I took the liberty of telling a friend I would ask for you to meet with her to discuss the possibility of your arranging to undertake a supper party of the kind you did for me. If you agree to see her then the whole thing must be carried out on a strict business basis. She will provide kitchen, the assistance of staff where required, all ingredients and of course will pay your fee at the end.'

'Fee…?'

'Of course.' Flora cut short the exclamation. 'All business, if satisfactory, charges its fee and you my dear, cannot afford to work for none. This is the chance for you to regain something of what you have lost. Maybe you once did not need to earn a living but now you do and this can provide you with more, it can provide you with a purpose in life.'

A purpose in life! Garnet stared at the table. She had a purpose, to see the man who had caused the death of her child pay for his crime. But to do that she needed to live … and not on the charity of others.

'My parents were in business,' she said slowly, 'but I was not taught the rudiments, they thought me never to need that knowledge, they thought my husband…'

'Your parents could not have foreseen what was to happen,' Flora answered solemnly, 'we are not given to seeing into

313

the future. But the present proves sufficient to deal with at the moment. The path leads in two directions ... you must choose which you will take.'

Having put the ultimatum, Flora Redmond watched the nuances of thought flick over the pale face. The girl was beautiful, given the clothes she would shine among the best of society and her manners and bearing made it obvious she once had. So how had she come to this, was the husband she had mentioned dead, had he left her with nothing?

'I would find the cooking no great problem,' Garnet answered at last, 'as for the costumes, I loved designing dresses and perhaps could help in those were my help called for...'

'But?'

'But I would need more than a kitchen, I would need a place in which to live.'

Rising from the table Flora Redmond smiled. 'I have thought of that. You have a place here but it is one I felt from the beginning you would not accept. You have an independence I admire, and a courage I admire more. Come with me, I think I know a way to solve your problem, but first you must get rid of those clothes.'

'The marriage is to take place on the twenty-fourth of December. A Christmas

314

wedding, oh how lovely, and how romantic, my dear.'

Winifred Benson's ample face blossomed as she smiled at Lady Olivia Denton seated beside Tyler in the drawing room of Bentley House.

'Dear Tyler deserves the happiness you will bring him after all the suffering he's borne so bravely.'

'Let's not talk of that.' Tyler smiled his practised smile of a self-control close to breaking.

'The lad be right, this be a time for celebration not for maudlin' over the past; not that I means to diminish it, I didn't mean to imply as it no longer 'as a place in your 'eart!' Arthur Benson added the last quickly, a flush of embarrassment colouring his heavy-jowled face.

'I saw no such implication.' Tyler re-assured the man. 'Of course the past cannot be forgotten; a corner of my heart will for ever hold my first wife and my … my darling child.' The smile became a tremble on his lips, bringing a sob from Winifred as he half turned his face away.

'I never want Tyler to forget.' The gaze that seemed never to hold real warmth touched coolly on the Bensons as Olivia Denton touched a hand to Tyler's. 'But I pray I can take a little of the sadness from his life and replace it with happiness.'

'There be no doubt you can do that, no doubt at all, eh Tyler?'

Sandwiching the hand that touched him between his own, feeling the hardness of the stone in the ring he had given, Tyler smiled into moss-green eyes. 'No, there can be no doubt of that.'

'An advent wedding! What a perfectly splendid choice.' Winifred dabbed plump cheeks with a lace-edged handkerchief.

'Not mine.' Olivia lowered her lashes shyly. 'Nor Tyler's, I think.'

Tyler nodded. 'The viscount, Olivia's uncle, asked if we would hold the ceremony on Christmas Eve, we both agreed but with some reluctance.'

'Understandable, lad, understandable. Why wait for...'

'Arthur!' Winifred Benson glared at the man sitting across from her.

'Beg pardon.' His jowled face looking sheepish, Arthur Benson apologised. 'What I meant to stay was—'

'Best left unsaid,' Winifred interposed firmly. Then with a smile directed at the couple she sailed on. 'What we both really came to ask is ... well...' She hesitated, drawing a breath that swelled her large breasts to balloons, then rushed on, 'What we wants to ask be this, could we have the honour of hosting a pre-wedding party? That be if it don't be looked on as impinging on the rights of your uncle, my dear.'

'Oh Mrs Benson, how wonderfully kind, is it not, Tyler?' Pulling her hand free, Olivia crossed to the couch to sit beside the older woman. 'But there is one thing I would change and I know my uncle will agree to my request, would you do us all the honour of being hostess not at a pre-wedding party but at the marriage supper itself?'

'What say you, Tyler … you think the viscount will agree?'

'I think Viscount Tiverton could not deny his niece anything, as I cannot. But host our wedding or not I am asking you, will you stand as my best man?'

His heavy face beaming his pleasure the industrialist stood up, taking Tyler's hand in a firm grip. 'Ar, lad I'll be that an' proud to do it.'

Olivia's smile a pale shadow against that of the man stood beside Tyler, she turned to the woman sniffing into the handkerchief. 'If I might ask more of your kindness, Mrs Benson, will you help me with my trousseau?'

Head nodding like a thistle in the wind Winifred Benson sobbed louder.

'Then there remains only one more thing we wants to ask,' Arthur's rotund face reflected the delight surging through his wife. 'We asks if it be agreeable to the viscount that Winnie and me hosts this

317

wedding, then would he allow it be paid for by us? I would take it more than kind if the answer were yes for it would be for us like the marriage of a child we ain't never had.'

Will he allow? Tyler Cadell watched the older woman envelop the younger in fat arms. Probably the man would jump for joy.

'See that!' Tyler laughed, playing two small stones beneath the light of the branched gasolier that lit the elegant sitting room. 'See that ... those and the ones to come are my passport into high society, what do you think of that, you Indian pig?'

Picking up the several newspapers strewn across couch and chairs the manservant made no reply.

'This is only the second level.' Tyler tipped his palm, tumbling the stones and watching the lancets of colour dart from them. 'The best is still yet to come.'

'Yes... sahib.' The man's answer was quiet. 'I am sure the best is yet to come.'

A slight undertone catching his ear, Tyler glanced sharply at his servant. 'What do you mean by that, you scum?'

Picking up the last of the papers the manservant's fingers tightened imperceptibly.

'I mean what the sahib says, the best is yet to come.'

'Yes, these are what will bring everything I want.' As he held it between forefinger and

318

thumb, Tyler gazed into the heart of the larger stone. 'Wait a few more months, wait for the larger ones to be polished and set in fine gold, a necklace fit for a queen.'

'The Lady Olivia will like that.'

'Olivia?' Flicking the stone into the air, Tyler watched the iridescent play of colours, the lovely opalescent rainbow sparkling and glinting as it fell back into his palm. 'Who said anything about Olivia? Those stones I speak of will be a present for a real queen, but one she will not wear.'

Folding the last of the newspapers the manservant turned to the smiling Tyler.

'You don't understand, do you?' Cold now, and filled with contempt, Tyler's smile rested on the other man. 'Then I'll explain. The Royal Family appreciate assistance given to the needy, especially when theirs is not the purse paying for it. The necklace I speak of will be auctioned and the money raised will build alms houses, the Royal Albert homes for the poor and needy. The Viscount Riverton assures me the Queen will give her most gracious consent, but that is not all she will give. As Riverton tells me it is the practice to mark Her Majesty's birthday by conferring honours and the building of those homes, dedicating them as a monument to her beloved husband's name, can hardly fail to secure one of those honours for myself.'

'Will one necklace raise enough?'

Returning the stones to their velvet bag Tyler dropped it into the pocket of his waistcoat. 'Auctioned it will make more than enough, after all what man would wish to be seen unwilling to part with his money when it is for such a cause? Her Majesty has keen vision and a cold heart if she deems the memory of her late consort slighted. No, Riverton knows what he is doing suggesting a well-publicised auction instead of a private sale.'

Two for a pair! The Viscount Riverton and Tyler Cadell were both of the same mould; one he knew to be a liar, a man who had not hesitated at murder to achieve what he wanted; the other? He had watched the man's face, seen the apostasy lurk beneath the smile, the eyes that had shown corruption when he thought himself unobserved. Tyler Cadell wanted a title, recognition by and entry into the upper realms of society, but the Viscount Riverton … just what was it that man wanted? Or his niece for that matter.

The newspapers held against his chest he watched the smile spread as Tyler touched a hand to the pocket holding the glittering stones.

'Does the Lady Olivia approve of the plan?'

'Approve!' Tyler's smile faded with a dangerous swiftness. 'What the hell difference does it make whether she approves or disapproves? It will be enough for her that she will be not only the niece of a peer of the realm but the wife of another, she will be the wife of the baron ... or who knows ... maybe the Marquis Cadell of Bentley.'

'The Lady Olivia ... you are planning to marry the Lady Olivia? But that is not possible, you already have a wife.'

'Shut your mouth, you Indian dog!' Tyler's eyes narrowed, his mouth becoming a slit. 'Mention that again and I'll spill your filthy guts all over the floor. Nobody knows about Garnet, everyone who matters thinks her dead...'

'I do not think her dead.' Raschid's brown eyes held those filled with a blazing hate. 'And until there is proof that she is I will not allow this marriage with...'

'*You* will not allow!' Tyler was on his feet. 'You, a bloody wog ... you think you can dictate to me! I'll...'

'This bloody wog speaks perfect English ... sahib...' Raschid held his ground, '...and he knows what happened to your daughter.'

He was threatening him. Tyler stared at the door as his manservant left the room. That bloody Indian pig was threatening him! Well, others had tried that game and lost ... but he must take care, wait his chance and not rush his fences; there was time yet, time to plan how to kill.

Chapter Twenty-Two

It had been a wonderful idea of Flora's. Garnet glanced about the tiny kitchen. It wasn't big enough to swing a cat around in but it was hers and all thanks to Flora Redmond.

'...*first you must get rid of those clothes...*'

Remembering Flora's words she smiled. That had not been the only change in her life. The woman had gone with her that day to 'conduct business with her client'. Garnet smiléd more deeply. It had sounded so terribly pompous and she had been so terribly nervous. But Flora's encouraging nods and almost imperceptible smiles during that meeting had carried her through. 'Remember,' Flora told her the first time she went alone to discuss the organising of a supper party, 'you have good manners bred deep in you, I don't need to speak of that, but you lack confidence. You have something they want, so hold your head high; fair but firm must be the motto you abide by, fair but firm, follow it and you won't go far wrong.'

It had been good advice, the call for her services had rushed ahead like a steam train and the money earned had repaid Flora the money that had bought this house in Bilston. It was one of a row of cottages close beside the small Lunt Colliery. She had not wanted to stay in the large busy town that held the prison, that held fears she might one day be spotted by Tyler. The time would come when she must face him but she was not ready yet. She had told Flora as much, telling her also what she had thought not to share with her; but with Flora, as with Hepzibah, she felt the woman's kindness deserved the truth. Flora had listened, only the tightening of her mouth betraying her anger and disgust at what she heard. That day she had purchased the cottage in Bilston, saying repayment could be made as soon as the business of oriental suppers allowed.

And they had allowed, more quickly than Garnet would have believed possible, one hostess introducing her to another, each wanting something a little more exotic than before. Now this one for Leam House. Delighted with Garnet's choosing of material for a sari the mistress had given her *carte blanche* in the choice of supper menu, saying only it must be foods not previously offered by her friends.

There were many dishes she could serve but no shop she had found in Bilston sold the herbs and spices needed to create them.

This was a problem she had realised would grow, that was why she had gone to the nearby canal to ask for Enoch Babb. She had been lucky, Enoch had been given the letter she had written and Clara had picked up the spices she asked for while the *Warrior* was unloading in Birmingham's Gas Street Basin.

Pots and packets were spread on the well-scrubbed table and she looked at what Clara had brought. Saffron, garlic, pimento, turmeric and cardomons. These would be used to prepare the fish course of Myhee Joguranth, a sole poached in saffron juice, and Lauta Kofta or lobster quenelles, a lamb Biriani, and Teetur Malai which was partridge with lime and almond cream sauce. Dessert had taken some thought. She had hovered between Shahi Tukra or Bakarkhani then settled on the last. A sweet raisin bread sprinkled with slivered almonds and rose water would complement the heavier, more spicy dishes.

Satisfied with her decision she gathered the spices into her basket. The meat and fish would be ready for her at Leam House. Closing the door behind her she was caught by the shout of a young girl. Waiting for her to draw level Garnet looked with startled eyes as a cloth-wrapped object together with basin was shoved into her hands with the words, 'Me mum sent this in payment for the food you give her, says 'er be sorry it couldn't be more but that be all we 'ave, an' me mum says to say 'er scrubbed that basin real well.'

She had wanted to return the object, to say she wanted no payment for that food, that it was left-overs it had seemed shameful to throw away. The woman would never have taken it had she known it was Garnet's own meal.

She walked briskly over the open heathland that formed a border between Bilston and Moxley. It was so different from the large bustling Wolverhampton; the smaller Bilston huddled beneath its horde of smoke-belching chimneys that rose from the medley of enamelling works and the newer Japanning industry slowly taking its place.

The memory of all those weeks and months she had gone hungry, the many days she had begged for a slice of bread or cup of water only to be chased away by dogs or a broom about her shoulders had crowded in on her on seeing that woman carrying a child in her arms, several others clinging to her skirts and each looking as hungry as she once had been. She had given the food gladly. The woman had wept her thanks and from that moment the eldest child had run every errand and sang over every job Garnet could possibly find her.

They had accepted her, the people of Queen Street, taken her among them as had the Romanies.

She looked for sign of those caravans every day she had to cross the heath, searched for the face of Hepzibah among the women she passed in the town but always she was disappointed. Judah and his mother seemed to have left her life for ever. But she never forgot them in her prayers, as she never forgot the Indian manservant. Raschid had been so mindful of her on that voyage back to England, and once at home in Bentley House had been as gentle and caring as a husband ... as caring as Tyler had never been; and it had been Raschid had fetched her from that prison, leaving her as soon as she was clear of the building and never once returning.

Why? Boarding the trolley bus she sat on a slatted wood seat, the basket balanced on her knees. But then she had not known herself the route she had followed on leaving that dreadful place so it was not really to be wondered at that Raschid had not found her.

'Ticket, please.'

Glancing up at the smiling conductor she fumbled in her pocket for the coins.

'No 'urry.' The conductor's broad smile widened. 'You 'ave til you gets off to pay an' if you ain't paid by the time we reaches the terminus, then Amos theer runs you for it.'

Hearing the quip the driver nodded, saying over his shoulder, 'Don't worry mum, I don't run fast enough to catch cold.'

Adding her smile to that of the other passengers, Garnet handed over her sixpence. Taking the four pennies change and the pink ticket she slipped them into her purse, her fingers brushing the small cloth-wrapped gift the young girl had pushed into her hands. Parting the folds of a clean rag she lifted a small wide-bellied cream glazed bowl of thick pottery, its lid enamelled in lovely soft-glowing violets and mauves of delicate irises.

'It's beautiful.'

She had breathed her pleasure aloud and the woman sat beside her nodded. 'Ar wench, it be beautiful. That theer lid be the work of Tommy Holden along of Queen Street or my name ain't Liza Kemp.'

'It was a gift from the Holdens, but how did you know?'

'Well you needn't go to the foot of our stairs!' The woman laughed at Garnet's obvious surprise. 'Ask any of the folk on this trolley an' they'll tell you as I've told you, that lid be the work of Tommy Holden, ain't another in Bilston has the 'and of that man when it comes to paintin', he be a nartist ... a nartist true born; just look at them flowers, all they be missin' be the smell.'

They were beautiful, so lifelike that if you held the lid to your nose you might get a whiff of delicate fragrance.

'Best man with enamels in this whole town...' the woman talked on, but the voice Garnet heard was that of Flora Redmond.

'...*these oriental suppers will be a passing fancy,*' she had warned, '*they will fade when the next amusement catches the attention. Make the most of the opportunity while you can but be watchful for something to replace it with...*'

Re-wrapping the pot in the scrap of rag, Garnet let her thoughts run free. The savoury meat and fish pastes she made in the few free moments she had went down well with the folk of Queen Street.

'*...the gentry don't eat no better...*'

Thomas Holden's appreciation sounded loud among her thoughts.

If she presented her pastes in pots like these ... was that her next opportunity?

'They all think it so exotic!' Tyler Cadell snorted his contempt. 'Dress up like an Indian Maharaja in fancy robes, a jewelled dagger and a turban, your wife got up like a houri and it's so authentic. Authentic!' He kicked out a long-legged table sending an elegant vase swaying on its base. 'Where are the flies and the beggars, where is the God-awful perpetual stink? *That's* authentic!'

Making no answer the manservant

steadied the vase.

'What do they get out of their play acting, besides making fools of themselves? "It is a pleasurable evening!"' he mimicked. 'That is one way of spending an evening I find anything but pleasurable.'

'Then you will not be attending?'

The scowl melting into a cynical smile, Tyler turned it upon the watching servant.

'Of course I will be attending,' he purred, 'and so will you. A Maharaja and his personal body slave, that will create a few envious glances.'

'No!' The handsome mouth set in a straight line. 'I will not go to that house with you to be stared at like some performing monkey!'

'You will not go?' Tyler's voice dropped to a low, menacing snarl. 'You will not go? Oh, but you will … if you know what's good for you and for Florrie Wilkes. You will go and you will perform exactly like a monkey if that should be my wish. Do you understood, you Indian pig?'

He had understood. Raschid laid out the peacock-blue silk and gold-brocaded knee-length coat and plain silk trousers. The woman's life depended upon him accompanying Tyler, and though she had barely ever been more than civil to himself he could not risk Tyler's spite.

It would be an evening of torment. He had

seen that in those vivid blue eyes. There would not be one chance missed of ridiculing him, deriding him before the rest of those guests. And he would suffer it. Not because he was afraid to leave. He had known that ever since coming to England, the truth had stared him in the face then as it stared now. His own welfare meant nothing to him, it was the safety of Garnet … the safety of his master's wife that kept him from going. The two years of never knowing whether she was alive or dead had been hard, wondering every day if his remaining in this house was a hopeless duty. Yet he had not left it in case she returned. But since he had led her from that prison his life had become a living hell. What if Tyler should discover she had not been dispatched to the colonies, that she was somewhere in this country? He wouldn't rest until he had tracked her down.

Maybe he should have asked her to go with him, to make a life together… Turning towards the dressing mirror he looked at the face staring back at him. How could he have done that … how could he have asked her to trust herself to a man with skin the colour of milk-drenched coffee, even one who loved her as much as he did?

He had loved her from the first moment of their meeting and he would love her until the moment he died. But she would never know, never guess at the cruel, biting yet wonderful soul-captured love that burned in him.

'You will never be able to hold her, to speak the words branded deep on your heart.' He watched the reflection mime his whisper. 'You will never say I love you.'

'Be that the way you wanted it, mum?'

Garnet glanced at the fish she had poached in saffron juice and paprika. Set out on a beautiful porcelain dish and poured over with a thick sauce of yoghurt, lovage, pimento and fennel, the aroma would tempt any palate; and the finely chopped chives and coriander leaves the young kitchenmaid had so nervously scattered over it added the last touch of perfection.

'I could not have done better myself.' Garnet smiled her encouragement and as she looked at the faces of the kitchen staff added gratefully, 'Nor could I have done this on my own; thank you all very much for your help.'

'I 'opes them folk upstairs don't eat it...'

'What did you say?' Like an avenging angle the house cook turned on the young girl. 'You 'opes they don't eat it, why you ungrateful little toad, I'll be 'aving summat to say to the mistress come mornin' ... you can 'ave your bundle packed for you'll be on

331

your way...'

'No, please, I d'aint mean it that way...' Quivering beneath the thunderous roll of the cook's anger the girl's frightened eyes pleaded with Garnet. 'I mean only as I 'oped there might be a scrap or two left in them dishes ... it all smells so good and I ain't never 'ad a taste of no oriental cooking; please, mum, I meant no more than that, honest to God I d'ain't!'

'Well you keeps your tongue atwixt your teeth if you be wantin' to bide in this 'ouse!' The scowl sent the girl running for the scullery, but the cook's smile was lenient as she turned to Garnet.

'The wench meant no disrespect, I hopes you sees it that way an' takes no offence.'

'Of course not.' Garnet shook her head. 'At least she did not scrape the bowls with her finger as I did when a child, I remember my mother taking me to task so many times.'

'It be summat all kids do given the chance, strange how a lick from the fingers tasted better than what were given on a plate.'

Laughing at her own memories the woman nodded to the waiting servants to carry the dishes of food to the dining room.

'Oh dear!' Her sigh following them, Garnet watched the last of her efforts disappear from the kitchen.

'That be a big sigh, wench, what be the cause?'

The older woman had already reached the steaming kettle from its hook, scalding tea in a large brown earthenware pot.

'I just hope everything is satisfactory.'

'I would say you need 'ave no qualms about that. I've been cook in this 'ouse for two and twenty years and I knows a well-prepared dish when I sees it. The mistress relies on me to serve her guests with naught but the best, and though tonight I've been only assisting I still wouldn't let a spoonful go into that dining room as what I didn't consider to be the very best; so you sit yourself down and take a sup of tea ... and you–' she called to the scullery maid '–you come take a cup as well then you can see to the washing of these bowls.'

'There be a right tasty smell coming from your kitchen tonight and no mistake, it even has the 'orses cocking their tails up.'

Glancing towards the door that gave on to the rear of the house the cook smiled at the man entering her kitchen.

'Oh ar!' she laughed. 'Well just so long as it don't 'ave yourn doing the same.'

'So what delight have you cooked?'

'You means is there any to spare? The answer to that bein' I won't know till the supper be over an' them dishes carried back 'ere. As for the cooking of it that don't be my doin' but the work of Mrs Garnet.'

'Mrs Garnet be as easy to look at as her

333

cooking be to smell.'

The name she had chosen to be known by seemed to linger on his tongue almost as if he savoured every syllable. Looking at the face with its line of heavy side whiskers curving along a weak chin, the shifty ferret-like eyes and flabby mouth, Garnet felt an instant dislike of the man smiling at her.

'You watch your cheek, me lad, ain't every woman falls for your patter, might one of 'em take exception one of these days.'

The words might have been seriously meant, but the smile widening over the cook's face indicating otherwise the man walked to the table, taking the chair next to Garnet, his glance dropping from her face to her breasts.

'Mrs Garnet knows I mean no 'arm.'

The flabby mouth shone wetly in the yellowy glow of the kitchen's gas lamps and almost instinctively Garnet lifted a hand to the buttons fastening the blouse across her breasts. There was more than the smell of the stables that was unpleasant about the man. Thankful her drink was finished she stood up.

'I will call to see the mistress tomorrow as arranged.' She looked directly at the cook. 'Now I have to go, I have several dishes that must be prepared and left to marinate overnight.'

It was a lie but it would get her away from

334

that man's stare. Packing the last of her own spices into her basket she reached for the coat the young maid fetched from the scullery, trying hard not to shudder as the man took it from her, his hands lingering on her shoulders as he helped her into it.

'You shouldn't go doin' any more tonight, you've worked long enough by the looks of you, you be needin' your bed.'

Stepping away from the man standing so close she could feel the heat of him through the thin coat, Garnet picked up her basket.

'Please thank all of the staff for their help, it has been very pleasant working with you all.'

The woman's face beamed. 'I'll tell it for sure, and I knows they'll be pleased … took a real shine to you they 'ave. Now you let young Kitley 'ere walk you down that drive, it be fair unnerving for a wench to walk that way by 'erself in the dark.'

'No … thank you, that will not be necessary. I …I would not impose upon Mr Kitley.'

'A thing don't be imposing when you be happy doing it…'

His answer almost as quick as her refusal the man pushed back his chair.

'…I be finished over at the stables,' he smiled at the cook, 'so I'll be off 'ome after seeing to Mrs Garnet.'

Outside sulky clouds seemed jealous of

the moon's light throwing themselves across its bright face one after another. Stumbling on the uneven cobbles Garnet felt the man's hand tighten on her arm.

'I meant what I said in there, you be right easy to look at, a man could take a fancy to you.'

'I can find my way alone, there is no need for you to walk with me.'

The hand retained its grip as Garnet tried to pull away and his answer came low and harsh: 'Anybody might think you had summat against Seth Kitley!'

I don't like you, I don't want you touching me! Garnet wanted to scream the words but an inner sense warned against it. Stay calm, try not to let him know he frightens you.

'I have nothing against you. I just do not wish to take your time.'

'You said it was pleasant working with them in the 'ouse.'

'Yes.' Garnet's nerves tingled, her feet scuffling the cobbled yard as he walked her quickly across it.

'I'm glad you liked it but you'll like bein' out 'ere with me much more.'

Wrenching her arm up behind her back he twisted her against him, his free hand covering her mouth. Lifting her off her feet he carried her into the stable, laughing softly against her ear.

'You can moan all you wants, the 'osses

won't mind it and Seth Kitley enjoys it, but scream once and I'll throttle you.'

Landing heavily on her back among a pile of straw, Garnet felt the basket fall from her hand.

'I could see you was my cup of tea soon as I come into that kitchen, all that poncy way of walkin' be a way of leading a bloke on but what you was really after shone in them pretty eyes and Seth Kitley ain't one to refuse a woman what her wants.'

Above her in the gloom the clink of a buckle belt told Garnet what was happening and as he dropped to his knees across her, his hands snatching at her skirts, her terror erupted in the forbidden scream.

'I told you!' A hand smacked viciously across her face, knocking her head sideward. 'I bloody told you! I'll throttle you and throw your scrawny body down the nearest mine shaft ... now, lessen you *wants* to die, you'll open your legs instead of your mouth.'

Sick with fear and revulsion, Garnet shuddered as the rough hands brushed against her thighs. If she cried out he would kill her, but anything was better than this. His breath foul against her mouth, she tried to push him from her but with a grunt he knocked her hand away.

The basket! Suddenly Garnet's brain was ice cold. Her hand was touching the basket.

Her struggles ceasing she could almost feel the smile spread across that wet flabby mouth. Steeling herself against the touch of it she tilted the basket towards her.

'I could see you was up for it, I could tell...'

Forcing herself to moan softly as his fingers trailed the warm cleft of her stomach she closed her fingers over the thick pottery bowl, crashing it with all her force against his skull.

Chapter Twenty-Three

She would be gone no more than two weeks. Tyler Cadell stared across the bare heath as his thoughts went back to the conversations of the afternoon.

Olivia had returned with nothing after accepting Winifred Benson's invitation to go with her to shop for a trousseau.

'*Birmingham has nothing I would want you to see me in...*' she had pouted as she told him of their fruitless expedition.

'*...the fashions in those shops are not only matronly they are positively archaic. I could not wear any one of them especially not on my wedding night ... our wedding night... I do so want to look beautiful ... to look beautiful for* *you, Tyler.'*

He could have told her it would make no difference what she wore that or any night, that he preferred the woman in his bed to be completely naked.

Riverton had walked in on them then, preventing any such answer and Olivia had crossed to his side, a pale hint of colour whispering to her face as she had kissed his cheek.

Tyler touched a hand to the neck of the horse moving restlessly beneath him. Strange he should think any hint of a blush foreign to Olivia Denton, almost as though any sign of demureness were forced in her.

'These arrived today.'

Settling his niece into a chair Riverton had smiled at her before drawing a small velvet pouch from his pocket and handing it across to him.

Touching his own waistcoat pocket Tyler felt the reassuring bulge of the same small pouch.

He had tipped the contents into his palm, watching the brilliance of the gemstones flash a myriad darts of sparkling colour as the light played over them.

'The diggings have still reached only to the second level so of course the stones are rather small and have a few slight imperfections...'

Riverton had talked on as each stone had been held between thumb and forefinger.

339

'...but already there is a difference to be seen between those and the first ones you saw, don't you agree?'

He had nodded though in reality he could perceive no change.

'May I see them?'

Olivia had held out her hand for the stones, her smile as she fingered each one warmer than any he had seen curve her mouth before.

'Those tiny pieces of rock you are holding are worth several hundred pounds, my dear,' Riverton had smiled at his niece, 'be careful you do not lose them.'

She had handed them back, her fingers touching them to the last second of parting with them; a parting that had appeared more difficult for her than last evening's parting from him.

Perhaps Olivia Denton's feelings towards him were not those of a woman in love... Touching his heels to the animal's side he gave it freedom to trot on across the heath. But then his love was not for her ladyship but for the social prestige her title would lend.

'The truly perfect stones are always to be found in the lowest stratum of a mine...'

A brisk breeze rifling his blond hair Tyler rode on.

'...the pressure of ground building up over the eons of time press out the tiny air bubbles and

340

impurities leaving unblemished, immaculate stones, any one of which will sell for an unbelievable amount in the diamond market.'

The words of Viscount Riverton rang in his brain. But how long before that lower stratum was reached? He was already heavily in debt and creditors were never among the most patient of people.

'A matter of weeks.' Riverton's smile had been confident as he had answered the seemingly casual question. *'It might already have been reached by the time my niece and I are returned from Paris.'*

'Paris!' Olivia had clapped her hands together. *'Two weeks and all of Paris in which to choose my trousseau. Oh Tyler, don't I have just the most marvellous uncle!'*

That had been when the conversation had turn to the gift of alms houses for the poor and a title for himself.

What would it be … a knighthood? He wanted more than that, more than the non-hereditary privilege of using the word 'sir' before his Christian name! The money he donated to the memory of the Queen's late consort had to be enough to ensure a title he could pass to his son and his son after him; enough to make him a peer of the realm.

Baron Cadell? Riverton had smiled as Tyler had voiced the hope, then shook his head saying why reach for the lowers end of the stick when the handle was just as much within his reach. Why not a marquis? Such honours had been bestowed before.

A marquis! Tyler felt his blood surge. That would give his old Guards officer associates something to chew over; Christ, it couldn't come quickly enough! And the Indian pig? He reined in sharply. He would be kept in that costume it had upset him so much to wear to that party, he would be kept as body slave not to an Indian Maharaja ... but to an English peer.

'You think it would be wrong to return, you think perhaps it would be better to find some other place to spend the winter?'

'One valley be like any other to me, wherever you chooses finds no complaint.'

'My mind don't be at one.'

Your heart neither. The thought slipping silently through her mind Hepzibah Kane puffed on her clay pipe. Judah had kept his counsel all the weeks of their travelling and she knew he would keep it still, but that did not prevent her knowing the pain he was suffering, the longing he had for a love denied him.

He could put the question to the Kris but they would wonder at that, wonder why he appeared so hesitant where normally he was resolute. She watched the smoke of the camp cooking fires drift lazily into a reddening sky.

Her son wanted to return to Bentley Heath, wanted to see the woman who filled his thoughts and, she guessed, often kept the sleep from his eyes; but who was to say she was still there in that town, that she had not travelled on? There had been no word from her nor none *of* her. Hepzibah drew on the pipe. Of all the wagons they had met on the road, of all the Romany folk they had passed the time of day with not one had mentioned a red-haired gaujo enquiring after Judah.

Taking a stick she raked the ashes of her own fire, watching tiny new-born flames spurt beneath the steaming kettle.

Had Garnet Cadell fulfilled the vow she had taken on herself, had she found that husband of hers and seen him pay for his crime; or was it the other way round, had he found her and done to his wife what he had done to his child?

There had been no hint, no rumour treading the streets of Darlaston or it would have been heard by the Romany. But that was no guarantee it had not happened; there had been no rumour that first time, Cadell had covered his tracks well after the murder of his child. P'raps he had covered them equally well after the killing of his wife.

Beside her Judah rose to his feet. Tall and broad-shouldered he moved like a shadow against the sunset. Watching him cross to the tethered horse and take it to the brook to drink before settling it against the coming night, she felt the cold touch of worry along her spine.

Should her son hear of harm having befallen the wench then he would take no mind of tracks, his actions would be done for all to see, he would take the life of Tyler Cadell and lay no thought to the consequence.

They had seen her image in the crystal, seen her reach her arms to take a child; and the crystal had never lied, but that same picture had shown another image, behind the woman had stood a man, a man whose hair was pale gold but whose eyes were dark with evil. To believe the crystal was to believe Garnet Cadell yet lived but the vileness that had robbed her of her child followed her still.

'Was he very disappointed?'

'Desperately.'

'But you didn't care. You are heartless.'

'Am I?' Lady Olivia Denton smiled at the man watching her undress. 'Would you have preferred I stay behind with Tyler, maybe show him what his thousands have bought?'

'He will know soon enough what his thousands have bought.' Lifting a languid hand Riverton stroked the soft white flesh. 'Tomorrow I will send him a telegraphed message, it should prove very enlightening for our dear friend Cadell; I find myself almost wishing I could be there to see his face when he reads it.'

'Then why come away so soon, why leave Victoria House before we have to; Tyler had no idea ... had he?'

'No, my dear, Cadell had no idea.'

Stepping back to the dressing table, Olivia picked up a hairbrush and drew it through the heavy folds of hair that dropped like a deep sherry-coloured veil over her naked breasts.

'Then why?' she asked again. 'Wednesbury is a dowdy smoke-ridden, boring little town but it is quite generous in its bounty.'

'Unfortunately good things have the annoying habit of coming to an end and sometimes, my dear, it is beneficial to leave a town sooner rather than later. One can sell a thing just so many times before the business of doing so becomes, shall we say, a trifle risky.'

'Benson ... he didn't...'

'Suspect?' Riverton's well-defined eyebrows rose then fell. 'No, that man is too unintelligent to suspect a smell should you hold a month-old fish beneath his nose. He signed and he paid, and he will keep his mouth shut, at least until the urge to boast of owning a gold mine in the Transvaal becomes too much for him by which time his cheque will be cashed and the money in my pocket. But Austin Rowland was a different kettle of fish, he wanted time to send his man out to Africa to check the validity of the mine I tried to tempt him with. To refuse would have raised doubts in his mind, doubts that would indutiably reach the ears of Arthur Benson and of course your bridegroom-to-be. By the way, my dear, how did you explain away your absence this evening?'

'I told Tyler I would be with you.' Her laugh soft and sultry, Olivia leaned over the figure, touching her nipples to lips open to take them. 'I said there were last-minute arrangements to be gone over before we left for Paris.'

'And did you tell him we would be doing this?' Reaching an arm around her slim waist he drew her down on to him.

Pushing herself up she straddled his naked body, moss-green eyes smiling as she felt the jerk of hard flesh beneath her. Taking his hands she held them against her breasts. 'Somehow I feel he would not have liked hearing that any more than he will like knowing he has paid thousands of pounds for a diamond mine that does not exist; and Arthur Benson, poor generous, foolish Arthur Benson finding his gold mine does not exist either.'

'Some win, some lose.' Riverton groaned

softly as she began to move slowly up and down, teasing the hard column.

'But Tyler Cadell loses more than most,' she smiled more deeply, 'he loses a bride as well as money.'

Fastening both hands on her hips he thrust upwards, pushing deep into her.

'What would you have me do?' He lunged again, her throaty cry adding to the flame shooting through him. 'Give you to Cadell? Sell him my own life along with a non-existent mine?'

She had run from that barn and down the drive of Leam House, running until every breath was gone and every muscle cried out.

Her hand still trembling Garnet lifted the bowl she had struck out with, not loosing it until she fell sobbing on to her bed. She could not remember the return ride on the trolley bus, or running the length of Queen Street, her only memory being that of that man's foul breath on her face, his hands touching her flesh.

She had left her basket where it lay. Panic filling her she had pushed him from her the moment his body had become limp, scrambling to her feet and flying from the barn before he regained consciousness.

She could manage without the basket, manage without the spices it had held. With fingers shaking she checked the contents of her cupboard. She could manage without the spices, but her fee, she could not manage without that ... she had to go back, she had to risk coming face to face with the man who had tried to rape her!

The girl who ran messages, she would go to that house, collect the basket and the fee, her family would be glad of the few pence it would bring! The thought had risen quickly, a mental salve to the wounds of her mind, but even as it came Garnet dismissed it. She would never ask the girl to go there and possibly face the horror she had been subject to. The money was hers, the responsibility of collecting it was hers. Reaching for her coat she slipped it on, fastening each button with trembling fingers.

'Young Seth said as 'ow you'd forgot your basket...'

The woman she had worked beside the evening before set Garnet's basket on the large table in the centre of the kitchen.

'...it be easy done when a body 'as had a bit of a tumble.'

'Tumble?' Shame a red-hot needle to every nerve end, Garnet's fingers tightened on the handle. Had he told this woman what had happened, told her not of an intended rape but a willing tumble in the hay?

'Ar.' The woman nodded. 'He told we about your fall in the yard and how he'd picked you up, 'aving to half carry you to the trolley bus. Said he'd not noticed you'd dropped that basket, not until he found it this morning in the yard. I keep saying as them there setts be needing to be relaid; somebody be like to break their neck one o' these days.'

He had lied, and he would lie again if she attempted to tell the truth. Garnet stood silent watching the other woman count coins from a tin box she unlocked with a key taken from a cord about her neck.

'I said you would be like to thank him when you called today but Seth had to be over to the blacksmith, seems the master's 'orse has throwed a shoe.'

He was not here, she would not have to see him again, to meet the eyes that looked at her breasts rather than her face. Relief threatening her self-control it was an effort to bring herself to smile.

'Might I ask you to thank him for me?'

'I'll do that.' The cook nodded. 'And mebbe we will see you 'ere again some time soon.'

Not if soon were eternity! Scooping the coins into her purse Garnet hid the thought that flashed like a beacon in her eyes.

She would never again set foot in that kitchen! Clutching the basket in her hand she walked quickly, wanting to be far from Leam House, far from the memory of that stable.

But there were other houses, other women wanting her to organise their oriental evenings ... other stables!

I can't ... I can't! The cry silent on her lips she turned towards the market. She couldn't take that risk again ... but it was that or the road; she knew which she had to take.

'Come Christmas you will be a married man, eh Cadell?'

Cocking his shotgun Arthur Benson let fly at a rabbit, swearing softly as the creature bounded away unscathed.

'And to the niece of a peer of the realm no less. You be a lucky chap.' He aimed again. 'Not that her being *Lady* Olivia had any bearing on your choice.' He squeezed the trigger. 'A man falls in love with a woman not a title ... bugger!' He swore again as a rabbit fled for its burrow.

'As you say,' Tyler raised his own gun, 'it is the woman rather than a title.' Cradling the stock against his shoulder he ran his eye along the sights, swinging the barrel in a slow arc across the fields. What would Benson say if he told him it was not Olivia he wanted but what her uncle could do for him; not her title, that was no good to him. He wanted the title that his money and Riverton's influence could win for him. That was more to him than marriage with Olivia

350

Denton, but he could not hope for one without first taking the other.

And when the honour was granted? He swung the barrel slowly. When he became Marquis of Bentley, what then? The barrel halted, focusing on a line of trees edging a field and centring on a dark shape moving across them. A wife would be of no consequence. The forefinger set on the trigger tightened. Bentley House would be of no consequence... The finger pressed harder... And the servant he had planned to use as a rich man's toy, as an object for his amusement? The man who had dared to tell him he would not allow that marriage... A smile on his mouth, he brought the trigger slowly back. That Indian pig was also of no consequence!

'Careful, man!' Arthur Benson's hand struck out, knocking the rifle barrel to one side a hair's breadth before the hammer struck and the gun fired. 'Christ, Cadell! Didn't you see the Indian over there? Half a second more and you might 'ave killed him.'

There would have been no might about it had you kept your interfering hand out of it! The Indian dog would be lying dead and his threat with him!

'Killed ... him?' Years of guile springing immediately into play, Tyler struck just the right perplexed note.

'Your man ... your Indian servant, he's

351

over by the trees,' Benson pointed to the dark shape turned to face their way. 'He was right in your line of fire. Lord, man, you could 'ave killed him!'

So you have already said. The thought acid, Tyler lowered the gun and stared in the direction the other man pointed.

'Raschid!' He gasped. 'I didn't see ... I was following that fox ... thank the Lord, I ... I might have shot him.'

'Could 'ave been a nasty accident.'

'I ... I could have shot him...!'

Fooled by the trembling voice and shaking hand, Arthur Benson laid his rifle aside then drew a hip flask from his pocket, giving it to Tyler while he took the rifle and broke it as Tyler swallowed a mouthful of brandy.

'It be past now and no harm done...'

He took back the flask swallowing a mouthful himself. '...you would 'ave thought the man to 'ave more sense than be out there, surely he heard the guns ... less he be deaf.'

Tyler passed a still-shaking hand across his mouth, the contrived look on his face that of thankful relief.

'No, no Raschid is not deaf. But whatever possessed him to take himself in front of the guns?'

Screwing the top back on the flask, Benson returned it to his pocket.

'You 'as to make allowances, that sort

don't 'ave the sense we've got, they ain't English, but that ain't to mean as you shouldn't give 'im a tongue latherin' when you get 'im back to the house ... bloody fool of a man! I thought these Indian wallahs was used to huntin', what with all them tigers you hears folk who've spent time in that country harp on about.'

Taking back his own gun, Tyler removed the cartridges while watching the figure of his manservant come towards them.

'Raschid was a house servant,' he said, 'he never joined the beaters when we went on a hunt.'

'P'raps that explains it.' Benson nodded. 'Like I says, him bein' a foreigner he don't have the brains, but next time we goes after a fox I suggest you leave him behind.'

I could have left him behind for good had it not been for you! Putting a shot in his head would have proved the best sport I've had since coming to this miserable town. Keeping the chagrin from his face and the thoughts to himself Tyler handed the gun to the man joining them. It would have been the perfect opportunity and so much cheaper and more enjoyable than shipping him back to India. But what fate takes away with one hand she replaces with the other.

Turning back towards the house he smiled inwardly. There would be other chances ... other opportunities to amuse himself.

Chapter Twenty-Four

Setting the freshly brewed tea on the table, Florrie Wilkes beamed at her visitor. It were nice to sit and take a cup while talking with another woman. Since Tyler Cadell had become master of Bentley House times were few and far between of her having the opportunity to talk with anybody; seems the friends who used to call on their days off had no liking for the new master, taking less and less chance of meeting up with him. Yet strange to say they all liked the servant he'd brought with him. Strange that! She filled two cups, handing one across the table. Everybody liked that Indian; but then, even though she wouldn't say as much, she too found him at all times to be polite, always more the gentleman than his master would ever be. That were only one side of him, though, the side the outside world saw; but here in this house she had seen the other side, seen him do Tyler Cadell's bidding as tame as any lap dog. She had seen him snatch that babe and run with it from the bedroom, throwing it to the dogs like so much carrion. Yes, she knew Tyler Cadell, but she also knew his Indian!

'I were talking with Bessie Peake the other day, you remembers Bessie?'

Florrie wiped away the thoughts as her visitor spoke.

'Bessie Coates as was? Come out of Pinfold Street, her mother kept a pie shop … married a fella from out along Wolverhampton way?'

'That be 'er.' The woman spooned sugar into her tea. 'Been cook at a place there for a good number of years now.'

'I remember her mother's bragging when her got the job! You would 'ave thought her 'ad been made cook to the Queen!' Florrie spoke with asperity.

Stirring her tea vigorously the visitor nodded. 'Ar, old mother Coates thought there were none to match her own brood, but then you can't condemn a body for that.'

'It has to be said her did a good job of rearing all six of them lads and two daughters into the bargain.' Florrie's nod of agreement was sympathetic. 'Life in Darlaston ain't never easy at the best of times but with a brood of eight and all less than ten years of age, and no man to help with the raisin'.'

Feathered bonnet nodding, the other woman accepted a slice of cherry cake on to her plate.

'That be true enough, Florrie, it were a

bad day when that pit shaft crowned in along of the Kings Hill Road, it took many a good man with it. I remembers my own mother saying as father would 'ave been among them if the beer in the Frying Pan 'adn't been so good the night before.'

'We all 'ave our reasons to thank the Lord for his bounty.'

Except for Garnet Cadell and her babe. Florrie let her mind slip back as her visitor chewed. What were that wench's bounty?

'Well according to what Bessie Peake were saying it seems her be thankful; that post her has along of Leam House be one many a woman would give her eye teeth for, 'ceptin' one night a two or three weeks since.'

'Oh!' Florrie was once more attentive. 'An' why was that?'

Brushing a crumb of cherry cake from her mouth the woman smiled, a triumphant condescending smile. Florrie Wilkes always claimed to know everything, well here was one thing her didn't know. Deliberately finishing the tea, she relished the vexation that she knew being kept waiting caused the woman watching her.

'Well!' She returned the cup delicately to its saucer, touching her mouth with a handkerchief while watching the frown deepen on her friend's forehead. 'It appears the mistress held a supper, invited just about everybody to Leam House...'

'That!' Florrie snorted disparagingly. 'I knowed of that, the master were given an invite but at the last minute he changed his mind and didn't go, said he would find it all too much of a bore.'

'I suppose it would 'ave been for him, spending as much time as he did out there.'

'Out there?' Florrie's frown deepened.

Taking the cup that had been refilled the other woman stirred it a trifle too long, bringing Florrie's explosive reaction. 'Well ... out where?'

Selecting another slice of cherry cake the woman broke it daintily on her plate before answering.

'India, it were India he served in when he was an Army officer, weren't it?'

'What be that to do wi' the price o' taters?'

Pleased with the ring of irritation in the question, Florrie's visitor looked up innocently.

'India be the Orient, don't it...? Leastways I always thought it were!'

Since being a child, Fanny Siddons had taken pleasure in baiting others and her were taking pleasure now. Florrie met the innocent look with one of total disinterest though the pretence of it was like a stone in her throat. Whatever it were the woman had to tell could be heard elsewhere, Fanny Siddons were not the only tongue in Darlaston liked to wag.

'Be your house taking folk at Christmas or be it closing? I knows the family sometimes spends the Yuletide abroad.'

Turning the conversation Florrie slipped a cherry into her mouth, the frown fading before her own triumphant smile.

'They be spending it at 'ome. Like as not the mistress will be wantin' one o' them do's herself.'

It was a clever stroke. Florrie chewed a mouthful of cake. But then Fanny Siddons had ever been a clever wench.

'Bessie Peake said as 'ow the preparing of it all left 'er worn out for days.' Seeing her strategy failing, Florrie's visitor gave up the game. 'All them fancy dishes and spices her ain't never 'eard tell of ... said her could smell 'em around her kitchen for days after! Says her don't never want to hear of no oriental evening not never no more. It be all right for the folk upstairs dressed up in their fancy Indian costumes, they don't be the ones havin' to cope with cooking Myhee Jogur ... wotsit or that there lobster coff ... summat or other.'

'Lobster cough? Lobsters don't cough.'

'Laugh if you wants to!' Fanny showed her annoyance. 'But while you be laughin' you should also be 'oping the next oriental evenin' don't be given at Bentley House.'

'Ain't no fear of that.' Florrie allowed her satisfaction to show. 'His nibs Mr Tyler

Cadell don't 'ave a lot of liking for remembering his time in India, least he never makes no mention of it. If it weren't for his keeping that manservant of his you might swear he'd never been to the place, so I don't see him throwin' no fancy supper … but who were it did the cooking if not Bessie Peake?'

'Well … ain't every man as likes bein' in foreign parts, not everybody gets something from it!' Fanny Siddons sniffed. 'As for the cook, Bessie Peake said her were called Garnet … Mrs Garnet.'

Still stunned by what she had heard Florrie watched the other woman leave, her boots tapping bossily across the yard. Tyler Cadell got more from India than ever he took into it and if he found one remaining, one he had wanted dead…

Glancing towards the enclosure where the dogs were housed she shivered as a cacophony of barks rent the quiet afternoon.

Yes, that man got more in India than might be thought, and destroyed that which he hadn't wanted known! Garnet … the name was not unknown, there were other women of that name. Closing the door quietly she returned to her chair. That name must never leave her lips again.

Stood on the deck of the ocean liner

Viscount Riverton watched the chalk cliffs of Dover fade into the horizon.

'Are you having regrets?'

Resting a hand over the one touching his arm he smiled. 'No, regrets, my love, but then how could I ever regret being with you?'

'But leaving England?'

'It's a small price to pay.' His fingers twined about the long slender hand, drawing it close against him.

'But it is a price none the less.'

'One I would pay a thousand times over … however it is not a final one. We will be back once the dust has settled.'

'That will take some time seeing the storm that will rise once those men realise they have been duped.'

'Who knows. It might be I have done them a favour.' Riverton smiled at the attractive face. 'The next man may have taken them for more.'

Eyes grey-green as the sea that swelled beneath them shone as the smile was returned. 'And what more could anyone take? You left poor Tyler virtually nothing but the clothes on his back and Arthur Benson with not much more. They will nurse vengeance. No, my dearest, you must not visit that part of England for a very long time.'

'The Black Country.' Riverton laughed

softly. 'It describes the place perfectly, smoke and grime so thick a man could taste it. But that smoke and grime hid more than coal and steel; for you and me, my love, it hid money and it didn't take much digging to extract it.'

'I still can't believe it. Who would dream two such men would part so readily with their money?'

'There are fools in every part of the world, fools with money, and for a man with his wits about him it does not take long to separate them from it.'

'Especially if one is helped by an attractive woman!'

'As you say, my dear.' Riverton looked into eyes that reflected the colour of the sea. 'A woman can be of enormous help diverting the attention.'

'But that was not the case with Benson.'

Turning his glance back towards the faint smudge of hills that seemed as though they floated on the rim of the ocean, Riverton smiled at the ease with which he had divested the portly little industrialist of his money. He had talked of gold literally rising out of itself in the Transvaal, how it glittered in the ground like the paths of heaven, how it brought him so much wealth in a year his only difficulty was finding ways of spending it. Benson had been like a fish swimming around a worm, eager to taste but nervous of taking the first bite. But there had been no push, simply a flash or two of diamonds supposedly bought as a gift for the wife of an old friend, diamonds that also served to hold Cadell's interest. Seeming as though money such as that could be given away without thought it had been a short step to taking twenty thousand pounds from the man. Benson and Cadell, so different yet so alike. Both were greedy men, greedy for money; but with Cadell it had been more than that. He had wanted more than wealth, he had wanted a title: and a title he would be given but not one of baron or marquis. Tyler Cadell would be titled a fool by every man who knew him.

Releasing his arm the elegantly dressed figure beside him whispered into his ear and Riverton followed, acknowledging the smiles and nods of other passengers as they made their way to their first-class cabin.

'I know what you were thinking but you must not do it.' The remonstrance was soft as they entered the cabin.

'But it would be so easy, some of the folk on this boat...'

'May be as clever as you! What you have in mind is too risky. Why endanger what we have when in a year or two we can play the game again in England or even try America? You must not be so greedy or so vain, my darling.'

Vanity and greed. Riverton watched the coat being tossed to a chair.

'We have enough to live comfortably, we will be happy together...' Fingers unfastening buttons the green eyes smiled seductively. '...I will make you happy.'

Forty thousand pounds. Yes, they would live comfortably. Riverton felt the quickening of his flesh as the last stitch of clothing fell from the slender figure. It was worth every risk he had taken.

'We will have a villa in the hills overlooking Tuscany.' He touched a hand to the smooth tight flesh. 'Our own beautiful hideaway in the hills...'

'Not too hidden away, we do not want to live like some poor monks in a monastery.'

The delicately shaped mouth pouted though the eyes held a promise that ripped like fire through Riverton's loins.

'We will not be poor, my dearest,' he answered, his hand tracing the shapely waist, 'nor will we live like monks, our days will be spent with my eyes making love to you and our nights will be one long paradise, holding you in my arms, making love to you with more than just my eyes ... as I intend to do now.'

'Not yet. First we must drink to your success.'

A playful tap knocking his hand away, Riverton snatched at his own clothes, ripping them hurriedly away, spreading himself naked on the bed as a champagne bottle was uncorked and two crystal flutes filled with sparkling golden liquid.

Accepting a glass from an elegant long-fingered hand he smiled at the attractive face looking down at him, at the full-lipped mouth parting suggestively, the tip of a pink tongue sliding slowly over it.

'To us, my love…' The cool glass caressed the bottom lip while above it the eyes smouldered green fire. '…to all our days and to every long love-filled night.'

His naked flesh throbbing with the promise of the toast, Riverton reached a hand to the taut body, following the curve of a rounded hip as he echoed the words.

Catching his hand as it edged towards the mound of glistening gold-brown hair the green eyes gleamed. 'In a moment, but first should we not drink to the Viscount Riverton?'

The question held a hint of laughter and the answer a hint of sarcasm.

'Let us make it to our friend Cadell. May he enjoy yet another surprise. I wonder, how long will it be before he finds that too is a lie, that there is no such person as the Viscount Riverton and that he has been taken not once but twice? No diamond mine and no viscount to aid him in securing an honour from the Queen.'

'And his bride-to-be ... do you not think the loss of her to be a disappointment to Tyler?'

'The Lady Olivia Denton!' The laugh was soft and scornful. 'Tyler Cadell ... another surprise to add to his list, though discovering that to be yet one more dupe will not, I think disappoint as will the other two; but Lady Olivia ... the title suited so well my darling, it will be galling to forgo it. But then actresses have played such roles before and will again, each just as phoney, all a part of the well-planned charades of plain Mr Alfred Rivers.'

'Then you have no regrets?'

'No regrets, only my love for you. You are the one true love of my heart, you, my dearest "Olivia", are all of my desires ... desires I shall satisfy to the full.'

'How?' Explicit in its invitation, the word whispered between enticing moist lips, the lambent eyes gleaming pure temptation.

Releasing his hand from the one holding it free of the glossy mound, the erstwhile Viscount Riverton dipped a finger into his champagne touching a shining golden drop to the column of hard flesh just inches from the bedside.

'Like this.' Smiling he threw the glass aside, pressing his face into the base of the other man's stomach. 'Then like this.' The smile becoming a throaty laugh he caught the figure about the waist, drawing it to the bed, rolling its face down beneath him.

The woman had meant well. Garnet sat before the dead ashes in her grate, her nerves in shreds. The meal she had prepared had been well accepted and the gold-threaded amber sari and jewellery with which she had dressed the hostess had been enthused over by the women, and the looks of the male guests had been admiring. Then some of them had asked to meet the cook. To give their congratulations, they said, and to arrange for a meeting in their own homes with a view to holding such an evening themselves. Unwilling, but realising that to refuse might damage the future of the living she had made for herself, Garnet had complied.

In the drawing room she had answered questions politely, all the time aware of two or three whose smirking faces clearly said she was a paid servant and for them something to provide a passing amusement.

'*What do Indian women wear underneath?*'

The question had raised a gale of giggles from the women who had told the man who asked it not to be so naughty.

But he had asked it again, that time coming to stand close to her. Garnet's fingers twisted in her lap as she remembered the look in his pale eyes, how they had swept over her body as he went on. '*And what of bed-time? Do they sleep in one of those saris, or do they sleep as they were born ... naked?*'

He had laughed off the mild protest. Garnet would know, she had lived out there for some time.

Colour blazing in her cheeks she had excused herself, dropping a quick curtsy, but as she had made to turn away the pale-eyed man had caught her shoulder.

'*You have given us only half of an oriental evening; a superb meal, yes, but what of the rest?*'

'There is nothing more.' She had tried to twist away.

The memory of the look on that vapid face brought the same tremble along her spine that it had brought as he had laughed at her answer.

'*Oh come now!*' He had held on to her like *some prized catch on the hunting field. 'No self-respecting Maharaja would dream of inviting guests to an evening without providing enter-tainment. My grandfather tells the dancing girls are quite something... I say we should see a little of it for ourselves.*'

That had brought a chorus of assent and the man had taken advantage. Calling for the use of an evening shawl he had thrown the silken gauze about her shoulders.

'*But dancing girls do not wear heavy skirts and cotton blouses....!*'

He had said it lightly, as though for the amusement of others, but she had read his eyes, seen the lust darken their pale depths and knew it was not mere titillation which smoked them.

'...*Salome danced in nothing but a veil, a veil and her beautiful hair...*'Darting like a whip-snake his fingers had pulled her hair free of pins so it fell like an additional silken cover across her shoulders and over her breasts.

'...*now,*' he had laughed, '...*you shall dance like Salome!*'

The hand had grasped her skirts, yanking at them in an attempt to snatch them away. And the others had laughed, men and women they had laughed as she had struggled to hold her clothing in place.

She had broken free at last, the filmy cloth falling to the floor as she ran from the room, but the man had raced after her, dragging her into an empty book-lined room.

'*You won't dance!*' he had snarled, hurling her across the dimly lit room. '*Then I'll take my entertainment another way!*'

Grabbing the neck of her blouse he had ripped it to the hem then snatched the straps of her thin chemise, pawing at her breasts as it dropped away.

That had been when the mistress of the house had entered the room. Whether she agreed with her guest that his actions were simply a bit of fun or whether she thought

Garnet to be playing the Salome a little too realistically was not said. The woman's only words had been for her to get out... *'and don't bother coming to collect your fee, it seems you have been paid already!'*

That was all she had been to those people, an object to be used for their own ends. To them she was a woman without value, without feelings; a woman who was less than a woman, less than the ground they walked upon.

Dropping her head into her hands she sobbed into the cold silence.

Chapter Twenty-Five

The sky had already been light when at last she had forced herself to move. She had raked out the dead ash of the fire and re-lit it, leaving the kettle to boil before going to her bedroom and washing her body in cold water. The blouse Flora Redmond had given her had been ruined but she had stitched the straps of the chemise in place; even so, she could not bring herself to wear it, to wear anything that man had touched. Dressed now in the second-hand clothes bought for ninepence at Mrs Blakemore's pawn shop in Thomson Street she reached for her shawl, her hand trembling more with fear than with the cold that seemed to penetrate every brick of the tiny house. She did not want to go out … she never wanted to go outside again.

Fastening the shawl beneath her breasts she looked at the basket standing where she had dropped it last night after locking herself in the house. The chance Flora Redmond had given her had been a godsend, a way of earning her living, but it could not go on. To go alone to those houses was too much of a risk and as yet she could not pay an assistant; even the young girl who had given her the pot could not work without pay.

The pot! Her glance travelled to the small bowl she had set on the mantel above the grate. She had once thought to have more of these, to fill them with her pastes; had that been simply a pipe dream or could she really sell them in the market?

Reaching on the pot she fingered the pretty enamelled lid. Flora Redmond had been almost unbelievable in her help and kindness but she could not ask it again, this was something she must work out for herself. But could she? There was only one way to find out! Packing the basket with all she would need, she left the house.

'Ar, that be my work.'

The basket clutched in her hand, Garnet

watched the thin stoop-shouldered man as he turned the little bowl over in hands dyed almost red with clay. She had walked all the way to the pottery but every step had been an effort of will; with each one she had wanted to turn back, to run to the safety of her kitchen and never come out of it again. But she could not live forever like that, like a mouse in a hole. It was do what she set out to do or carry on with those oriental evenings and continue to face the threat she had faced last evening, a threat that at any one of those suppers could become reality.

'You says you 'ad it given?'

'Yes, a ... a neighbour gave it to me,' Garnet answered nervously as the man continued to inspect the object held in his hands.

'And the lid?'

He looked at her, a sharp look from beneath bushy eyebrows, their true colour lost beneath the dust of clay.

Did he doubt the bowl and its lid were hers, was he thinking she had stolen them? The thought brought a quick resentment edging away the nervousness. Her head lifting, she faced the challenge.

'The bowl and its lid are both my property,' she said calmly. 'As I told you, they were the gift of a friend, but though they were given to me as you see them I believe the two parts were not originally

371

intended for each other. I was told by a woman on the trolley bus the lid was the work of the father of the girl who brought me the gift, the work of Thomas Holden.'

'Which Thomas Holden would that be? There be more'n one man carries that name in Bilston.'

He was still testing her! Drawing a breath that held back the desire to take her pot and walk out she answered coldly.

'He is the Thomas Holden who lives in Queen Street. The woman on the trolley bus said that anyone in the town would recognise his work, that there was not another enameller in Bilston could match it.'

''Er d'ain't tell you no lies theer.' He looked again at the beautiful flower-painted lid, touching each leaf and petal as if clay-stained fingers could feel their velvety softness.

'So what be you 'ere to ask 'cept the potting be my work?'

Still feeling that she was suspected of lying, Garnet stared.

'It were only a question, wench,' the man smiled kindly, 'I meks no charge for it nor for any other your answerin' might call for.'

It had to be said, she had come this far and she must not back out now. Swallowing hard she met the man's eyes. 'I ... I wish to enquire how much bowls such as that would cost.'

'I can answer that in part only.' He turned the bowl again. 'I can give a price for the pot but the lid … you would need consult Thomas Holden on that.'

'Consult Thomas Holden on what?'

Garnet turned towards the figure entering the small room that served the pottery as an office. A cotton bonnet framing a high-cheek-boned face, an ankle-length apron splashed with the stains of clay covering dark skirts, a woman stood watching them with clear russet-brown eyes.

'The lid to this pot. I said her must ask him to the price of buyin' one of them, I can only say to the cost of the pot.'

Going to his side the woman took the bowl, running her fingers over its smooth surface.

'This were made here in Fletcher Street.'

'Ar.' The man nodded. 'And the lid be the 'and of Thomas Holden, together they meks a sight pretty enough for any bedroom table.'

'Be that your reason for askin' the cost? For I tells you there don't be too much of a market for knick-knacks, them as can afford to spend on such already has a plethora of 'em, and them as don't then they needs what money they 'ave to put food in the children's bellies.'

'I was not thinking of ornaments.'

'Oh!' The woman's look settled on Garnet.

'Then what was the use you was thinkin' of?'

'I was thinking of filling them with potted meats such as chawl and ox tongue or maybe meat paste.'

'Meat paste! That be one I ain't heard afore.'

'Meat paste in a pot.' The man smiled. 'I think that be summat you won't find sale for, folk hereabout don't have the coppers to go throwin' about on pots they'll 'ave no use on once the food be gone. I says you should give the idea up afore you starts.'

'What be this meat paste you speaks of?'

'I make it myself.' Taking a package from her basket, Garnet opened it. Scooping a little of the paste on to a knife she spread it on a water biscuit, offering it to the woman. 'The people in and around Queen Street like it and I have sold some in the market.'

Biting gingerly at the biscuit the woman nodded appreciatively, handing the remainder to the man whose face showed his own liking for the paste.

'It be tasty I grant you, and I can see folk buyin' it, but as for puttin' it in pots ... I has me doubts to that!'

Covering the basin with its wrapping of grease-proof paper, Garnet tied it back into its cloth. Then picking up the small widebellied pot she placed them both in her basket.

'Hold on.' The woman spoke as Garnet murmured her thanks for the time they had given listening to her. 'My 'usband be a fine potter but he don't always see what be staring 'im in the face. I think what you 'ave in mind be a fine idea, just be it's run ahead of you. What I advises is this. You said the folk who've tried your meat paste showed a liking for it, same as me and my Enoch likes it. Then instead if puttin' it in fancy pots the pockets of working folk won't run to, why not put it in bigger ones and sell it from them, wrap a wedge of it in grease-proof paper as you would a portion of cheese? That way it won't cost them so much and you'll 'ave your pots to wash and use again. If it should 'appen as it grows to be a paying concern then that be the time to pack it fancy and try selling it to folk wi' money enough to buy knick-knacks.'

She had doubted she had enough money to buy a few small pots, anything larger was out of the question.

Telling them both as much, Garnet apologised for wasting their time but the woman waved the apology aside.

'We 'ave them dishes that was ordered then cancelled.' She looked at her husband. 'They be sitting in the shed across the yard doing nothing to earn the cost of their making.'

'You means the creamware ordered by

Forman afore he went out of business?'

'Ar, them! They be fit for the holding of foodstuff, don't they?'

'Tin glazed first then clear glazed over that...'

Garnet watched him nod.

'...they be more'n fit, you won't get no better nowheres.'

'That's it then!' Russet-brown eyes smiled across at Garnet. 'That be the answer; as my Enoch says, you'll find no better a dish nowheres.'

'I'm sure of it,' Garnet answered. 'But I would need to know the price of them.'

Running a hand through hair rouged with the dust of red clay the man grinned sheepishly. 'Eh wench, I be a right noggy 'ead, me mother always told me that one day I'd be in me box from forgettin' to breathe. Now then, the price of them there dishes be–'

'Be nothing!' his wife cut in firmly. 'Not if the rest of what I has to say be acceptable. This be what I proposes. My Enoch provides them there dishes, you makes what goes in them ... that be a fair division of labour. As for the cost of meat and such we share 'alf an' 'alf. But you 'ave the sellin' to do so you must take the bigger share of what the selling brings. 'Ow do that sound to you ... be you agreeable to sharin' a day's business with Enoch and Mary Parkes?'

'Parkes and Cadell.' Garnet held out her

hand. 'But please, we share equally.'

Walking home, the several large shallow dishes weighing the basket heavy on her arm, Garnet breathed a prayer of thanks. Had it been agreeable? She had almost kissed the woman. To be trusted as that couple had trusted her. Don't let me fail, she prayed silently. Please Lord, don't let me fail their trust.

'It be close.' Widow Korkyck removed the clay pipe from her mouth, emptying ash into the fire. 'Ye knows it, Hepzibah Kane, feels it sure as I feels it meself, there be trouble close at hand.'

Packing a small bowl of her own long-stemmed pipe Hepzibah remained silent.

'Think ye we should tell the others?' Widow Korjyck shaved paper-thin slivers from a block of Shag, pressing them into her pipe before returning the small block of tobacco to the pocket of her wide black skirts.

'Tell them what?' Hepzibah puffed, sending spirals of pearl-grey smoke twisting into the cold air. 'That we feels trouble be about to descend; that would be no surprise, for trouble finds the Romany no matter where he rests his head, he has no need to go meeting it half way.'

'Ar, trouble finds the wagon of the Romany and bides in its shadow no matter where it comes to rest,' Alcina Korjyck agreed. 'But this be different, this be the kind such as one sleeping in the grave might 'ave brought.'

She had the same feeling. Hepzibah stared into the glowing heart of her fire. It had been as if the spirits had walked up the side of this tiny valley to meet the wagons, drawing them into the heart of their own evil.

The customs had been observed. She puffed quietly on her pipe. Once camp had been set up, the first action had been to pay respects to the dead. What they had been or what they had done in life was no longer of consequence; punishment or reward, that was in the hands of the Lord but custom remained with the living. She glanced to where a separate carved flower marked each of the three graves, indistinguishable now from the minute rise and fall of the surrounding heath. Group prayer had been offered for the peaceful rest of the souls of Marisa Lakin, Lorcan Nash and his mother, but as she turned her gaze to the fire Hepzibah felt the stirrings of the younger woman's spirit. That one did not yet lie peaceful in the ground, was she even now reaching out to harm Judah, for it was beside him she felt the shadows of evil to walk.

'Should we not at least see for ourselves what it be waits to strike, even if we tells it to no other?'

Holding the pipe between her teeth Hepzibah thought over the other woman's question. Every man and woman in the camp respected the word of Alcina Korjyck, there would be no refusal to heed her warning though it held no substance. But why warn of that which even now might pass them by, why stir a pot that held naught but air? But was her way the right one, was hers the way of protection or the way of denial?

'Ye be thinking o' the crystal?'

Amid a veil of tobacco smoke the widow Korjyck nodded.

'Think ye to risk the losing of its powers?'

That question took longer in the pondering. Hepzibah's meaning was plain. Consult the crystal on matters not concerned only with one's self and it would ever fail to answer in the future. No Romany did that lightly, none consulted it without true cause. Sat beside a silent Hepzibah the woman questioned her own reasons. Hers would not be the seeking for herself alone, for the self of any Romany was given gladly for his companions.

'I be ready to take that risk.'

Hearing the quiet determination in her friend's answer, Hepzibah smiled to herself. She had expected no other of Alcina Korjyck.

'You give 'er sixpence for the tellin'? Why all of her words put together don't be worth a tinker's cuss! I 'ad you down as havin' more oil in your lamp than to go listening to the bletherings of a gypsy woman, much less the paying for it!'

'Ah well,' the second woman answered acidly, 'we don't all 'ave a razor blade for a father!'

'You can snipe, but I reckoned you sharper than to go paying sixpence to 'ear what anybody in Bilston could tell you for nothing!'

'And that be?'

Making her selection the first woman smiled as Garnet wrapped a portion of pressed chawl.

'It be that for the like of us your fortune be this ... if you don't work then you don't eat! You need to learn, wench, it be too late to save after the coppers 'ave been spent, you 'ave to remember not to buy today what you can't afford to pay tomorrow.'

Her companion's purchase wrapped and payment made, the second woman pointed to a dish of pressed ox tongue.

'That weren't med last week, were it?'

'It was made fresh last evening,' Garnet answered, handing the woman a tiny piece on the end of a knife.

'It be tasty.' The woman nodded her approval. 'I'll tek a four pennyworth and a four pennyworth of that there pig's chawl.'

Keeping a sharp watch on the meats being cut, she resumed the tit for tat with the woman standing waiting for her.

'Well I don't give a kipper's cod for what you thinks, I enjoyed 'aving my fortune told, it ain't often I gets to spending a sixpence on myself.'

'Hmmph!' The first woman snorted. 'You'll be getting to spend a shilling and sixpence on doctor's bills if your old man gets to finding out what you be doin' wi' money he earns sweating like a robber's 'oss a'front of a steel furnace fourteen hours of the day!'

Taking her packages the second woman counted out the exact amount.

'Two threepenny bits ... a penny ... a half-penny and two farthings.' Saying the value of each coin as she fished it from a worn purse she pressed them firmly into Garnet's palm.

'Excuse me ... I thought I heard you speak of a gypsy woman.'

The woman who had spoken first looked sharply at Garnet. 'Ar, so you did, a gypsy who sweet talked her way to tekin' a sixpence off Sally here.'

Glancing at the one carefully placing her purchases in her basket, Garnet smiled.

'I was wondering ... could you tell me where I might find her?'

'You wants to find a gypsy!' The same woman as before answered scathingly. 'Don't tell me you be daft as Sally, wanting your palm read! I think I'll tie a cloth about my 'ead and go knockin' on doors, seems there be more money to be med telling daft women an earful of lies than ever I meks picking coal on the pit banks.'

'You pay no heed to what *her* says.' The second woman smiled understandingly. 'You get yourself a six pennorth, far better spend it on that than let a man drink it, I says. But as for your finding that gypsy well I can't 'elp you there, wench, her told me they was travelling through Bilston but said no word as to where … I can only tell you her followed the road a'leading to Darlaston.'

Darlaston! Having thanked both women, Garnet hugged the word to herself. It might be them, the gypsy those women spoke of might be from Judah's camp.

With the last of her cooked meats sold she quickly packed the empty bowls into her basket. She could buy fresh supplies now and if she hurried she could have the cooking done and the meats pressing in their dishes before nightfall. Then she would go to the place where she had stayed with Hepzibah.

The place she had stayed with Hepzibah! Her fingers clenching stiffly on the handle of her basket, she stared at the chequered cloth. That tiny shallow dip that had housed the wagons was on Bentley Heath … and so was Bentley House!

She should not go there … there was the

possibility of Tyler ... she should not take the chance! Maybe Hepzibah would come to her. But how could she when she did not know where it was to come!

Her thoughts whirling, she lifted the basket on to her arm. It would be safer to forget she had heard those two women talking, safer not to think of seeing Hepzibah and Judah.

That would be safer physically ... but what of her mind? How could she come to terms with not trying to find them ... how would she mask the recrimination that must remain in her heart?

Hepzibah and Judah ... had they quaked at the thought of what Tyler could do to them if he found her in their wagon, had they put her back on to the road when told who she was? They had not turned their back on her and she would not turn hers on them. No matter what the risk she would go to Bentley Heath.

Chapter Twenty-Six

Picking up the letter laid on his desk, Tyler Cadell looked at the address written in a flourishing hand. It had been a long time in coming but then Africa was a long way off.

He had not mentioned the fact of his writing to the manager of the mine either to Riverton or to his niece; that way he might be sure that a reply to his letter would not be influenced by the viscount.

Slitting the envelope with an ivory-handled letter knife he withdrew the one sheet of heavy vellum notepaper. Opening it he frowned at the logo-impressed heading then read rapidly to the refined yet stylish signature at the end.

Teeth clenching hard together, fingers tightening on the paper he read it again then glanced once more at the impressed seal mark of the notepaper.

...De-Voerk Diamond Mines...

Rage cold and searing blinding him to the words, he stared at the sheet of paper. This was the answer he had dreaded. This was the reply he had lain awake at nights thinking of; thinking what would he do if doubt became reality? Now it was reality and he knew exactly what he was going to do ... and not to one but to both, for she must have known what her 'most marvellous uncle' was up to ... she was likely a part of it ... and if she was then by God she would pay, they would both pay ... both would regret the day they decided to play Tyler Cadell for a fool.

Twenty-five thousand pounds! Twenty-five thousand bloody pounds! He smashed a fist hard on the desk. Riverton had taken him for every penny he had in the world. How the swine must be gloating! But the gloats would turn to screams when he met up with that thief, he would suffer a pain not for every pound but for every penny!

Blinking the red film of rage from his vision he looked again at the letter, reading it through slowly, taking care he made no mistake, ensuring each word registered clearly in his brain.

Sir,
I have several times received letters such as the one you write me now and I must answer the same as before. I have to tell you there is no Halloran diamond mine in Kimberley, nor to my knowledge in the surrounding district; the properties contained therein being in the sole ownership of myself. I fear, sir, that you are the victim of some hoax and would refer you to the said Viscount Riverton.
Ian De Voerk
Director: De-Voerk Diamond Mines.

A hoax! Crumpling the letter, Tyler threw it savagely against the wall. A bloody hoax, a swindle ... and it had cost him twenty-five thousand pounds! Oh yes, he had been taken for a ride but Riverton would also take one, in a wooden box decorated with flowers. He would find the bastard and wring every last penny of that money from him and then he would wring his aristocratic bloody neck! And his niece ... the Lady Olivia Denton? Throwing the door of the study back on its hinges, Tyler stormed along the corridor leading to the rear of the house. Olivia Denton would return the baubles he had given and then, like her uncle, she would suffer before dying. Like Garnet before her, Olivia Denton was to him a woman of no consequence ... a peppercorn woman.

He would ride to Victoria House, and if Riverton were not yet returned from Paris he would go there too, but one way or another that swine would give back what he'd stolen.

Following the corridor that led the quickest way to the rear of the house and thus to the stables he caught the sound of voices. Florrie Wilkes was talking with another woman, but it was not that she had company that brought him to an abrupt halt, it was the words they spoke; words that brought the burning tides of anger flowing faster.

Standing stock still he listened.

'...India, it were India he served in when he was an Army officer, weren't it?'

Each word grasped his attention, holding it in a vice-like grip. It was him, they were talking about him!

'...Says 'er don't never want to hear of no oriental evening not never no more ... folk upstairs dressed up in their fancy Indian costumes...'

It was nothing. He breathed more easily. The women were merely gossiping about that supper party given at Leam House. Taking a step forward he halted again as his housekeeper's voice reached into the corridor.

'...his nibs Mr Tyler Cadell don't 'ave a lot of liking for remembering his time in India...'

How dare the woman discuss him with her cronies! Anger bubbled faster, churning and rolling like red-hot lava in his veins. Florrie Wilkes would be sorry for letting her tongue run away with her! His face dark with fury he reached for the door, but as his fingers touched the handle the burning throb in his veins became ice cold.

'...the cook...' The words were loud, reaching clearly to his ears. '...Bessie Peake said her were called Garnet ... Mrs Garnet.'

Garnet! The blow of it rocking him on his feet, Tyler released the door handle, turning back towards the study. Myhee Joguranth ... Lauta Kofta, the dishes that woman could not pronounce ... he had eaten them often in that bungalow overlooking Mari-whal but nowhere in Bentley nor any other town since returning to England, and no house he knew of kept an Asian Indian servant except himself. But Raschid did not leave the house other than in his company so who else ... who else had the knowledge of Indian cooking?

Reaching the study he closed the door behind him.

Why had he not realised ... why had he not put two and two together when he had received that invitation?

Lowering himself into his leather chair he breathed long and slow while the blood in his veins pounded.

Put what he had just realised together with the name that had floated through that kitchen door.

'Garnet!' Hands curled into fists he spat the name. Garnet ... it had to be his wife!

'You be certain it showed true?'

Judah Kane's black eyes gleamed anxiously as he looked at the woman sitting opposite him across the cooking fire.

'The crystal tells no lie.'

It was almost a remonstration but Judah disregarded Hepzibah's reproach.

'I know that but...'

'But old eyes sometimes don't see what they thinks they see!'

'I mean no disrespect, Mother,' Judah answered quickly. 'But I see no reason for what the crystal showed.'

388

'You ain't never showed me disrespect, lad, nor do I think you shows any now.'

Removing the pipe from her mouth Hepzibah looked at her son, her own dark eyes bright as jet beads. 'You don't be the almighty, Judah Kane! Nor should you set yourself up as Him by thinking as you should see the reason for a thing where no other body do. The crystal showed what it showed, no more no less; it be left to them as witnessed its pictures to place on them what meaning they will.'

'And you both felt the same, you and the widow Korjyck felt the crystal warned it was the time?'

'We both felt it and we both feels it now.' Hepzibah stared at the flames licking the base of the smoke-blackened kettle. 'There be a man approaching ... man with death in his heart. He comes for to take that which can testify to his mortal sin.'

'How close ... how close be this man?'

Switching her glance back to the face that meant more than her own soul, Hepzibah felt the powerful surge of love and protection she had felt since the first moment he had left her womb. But she could not protect him from what lay ahead. Her son had chosen his path and he must follow it.

'No more than a mile off on this same heath he sits with evil black in his heart. He has raised his hand twice afore and soon will

389

raise it a third time.'

Staring across the empty heath Judah remembered what he himself had seen in the crystal: Garnet and a man, a man who handed her a child. Perhaps the gift had already been given, perhaps even now she carried a child within her. The thought was a driving hurt inside him but he could not allow his own pain to cloud his judgement or affect a promise he had made.

'Let none but us two share what I have told you ... swear it will remain secret...'

The words of the man who had caught up with the wagons as they had crossed over Bentley Mill bridge seemed to sound again in his ears. Was the danger his mother spoke of something to do with that promise?

'You reckon it be the time?'

Meeting the glance Judah turned to her, Hepzibah nodded.

'Before the rising of the moon he will come.'

'That be a fair day's trading...'

Mary Parkes smiled as Garnet placed the money from selling her meat products on the table in the office of the small pottery works.

'...so now you knows you can sell what you cooks, so you be able to manage wi'out the help of the Parkes.'

This was what Garnet had half expected

and now it was said it was no surprise. She had thought over her response many times since setting out for the market that morning and as many times had imagined a different answer; but there could be no answer unless the question were first asked.

'It is not so much a case of managing without your help.' She paused, feeling inside herself for the courage to go on, to say what it was she wanted to say.

'Then what be it a case of?' The other woman's smile widened as if only now remembering something she had forgotten. 'If it be the paying for them there dishes then you needs worry over it no more, Enoch and me meks you a present of 'em.'

'No.' Garnet shook her head as the woman watching her let the wide smile become a frown. 'I appreciate your kindness but it is not the dishes...'

'Then what? Out with it, wench, there be neither of we 'ave the time to behavin' like mawkins! Say what be botherin' you ... Mary Parkes don't bite lessen her has to.'

'Mrs Parkes,' Garnet swallowed hard, 'when I came here yesterday you asked was I agreeable to sharing a day's business with yourself and your husband. As you have pointed out, my cooking has found a market—'

'And will go on finding 'em.' Mary Parkes interrupted.

Glancing through the window Garnet watched the stoop-shouldered potter cross the yard to the brick-built cone that dominated the huddle of tiny blackened buildings. Would these two people agree to her request, or were they too busy?

'That is what I hope, certainly, but not what I wish to ask.' She returned her look to the other woman. 'My ... my question is this, would you consider making the arrangement of yesterday again?'

'You means share the takings for another day?'

Pale December sunlight danced scarlet rhythms in deep auburn curls as Garnet again shook her head.

'No, I do not mean sharing the takings for another day I mean sharing them every day, I am asking if the arrangement agreed on yesterday might become a permanent one... If my cooked meats should become a business, will you share that also?'

'Eh, wench!' Mary blew a short breath. 'Me and my Enoch knows you be grateful but you don't 'ave to go givin' we a share of every penny you makes.'

'It would not be giving ... if things go as it appears they might then Mr Parkes will be having to make a lot more dishes, so you see it would be a partnership.'

'I ain't sayin' we couldn't do with it.' Mary Parkes glanced across the yard to where her husband was stacking pots in the kiln prior to firing. 'The potting business 'ave been going downhill this twelve month; Enoch still throws every day and fires that kiln once a week yet more'n half what he meks lies wi'out customers. But the misfortunes of one can't become the misfortunes of another so I thanks you kindly, wench, but tells you to look to yourself.'

Their own business was failing yet these two people were offering to give her those dishes for no payment at all! Garnet felt a tightness pull at her throat.

'I am looking to myself, and I know…'

'You don't be meking enough to support a what you said … a partner … you 'as to learn to walk afore you runs, wench.'

'Then teach me.' Garnet reached across the table, taking the older woman's hand in her own. 'Help me to walk.'

'You means it?' Mary Parkes's tired eyes filmed with tears. 'You really means it, you wants me and Enoch to be partners wi' you?'

'Yes.' Garnet smiled. 'Yes, I really mean it.'

She had suggested a formal written agreement signed by both parties but Enoch had refused. He would not bind her to any contract, he had said; she had made the offer freely and must be just as free to end it if she so wished. But she would not end it. Garnet packed her purchase of meats into her basket. So long as she made one half-penny from her cooking then one farthing of it would belong to the Parkes.

A straw boater on his head, blue and white striped apron tied about his middle, the butcher rested both hands on a chopping block that dipped in the centre from years of wear, his glance sweeping over the slender figure. She was dressed in plain russet-coloured skirts and high-buttoned white cotton blouse, which instinct told him had come from some unredeemed pledge made at the pawnshop, but the meat she bought were always of the finest quality. He had wondered at that each time she had come to the shop. The clothes she wore, though near enough worn through, were always spotless as were her face and hands, and her way of speech ... he watched her now casting a keen eye over his counter ... hers were no clipped words and dropped aitches, the wench were educated and more than likely had a background that didn't belong in Bilston back streets.

'Would you weigh that ox tongue, please?'

How many times a year did he hear the word please? It was to be hoped he had more hot dinners! His ironic smile tucked away, he lifted the chosen piece on to the scales.

'That be 'eavier than it looks.' He added weights one at a time until both pans balanced. 'It be two shillin' an' ninepence.'

Wrapping it in brown paper he handed it across the counter, taking pleasure in the smile that received it. The wench were pretty as a picture.

'I will take half of that please.'

Every order were ended with a please ... that were as rare in Bilston as tits on a fish.

Resetting weights to the scales he balanced the meat.

'That be eleven pence and a nice bit of beef cheek it be an' all, pressed in a basin it meks a tasty potted meat.'

'I'm sure of it.' Garnet smiled as she calculated whether the money she had left would stretch to purchasing half of the pig's head sitting in the window. The brawn that would make would be equally tasty.

'Ninepence the 'ole 'ead and that be with the brains as well.'

He had seen where her glance rested. Satisfied, Garnet nodded.

'You're goin' to be busy, wench' the butcher said, meat cleaver slicing the head in half. 'I envies the man sitting at your table.'

There was no need of envy, there was no man shared her table ... nor any child either. She could have answered but didn't, giving her attention instead to counting money from her purse, hiding the pain suddenly clouding her eyes. She had no family to care for, no husband to love her and no child to hold in her arms, all of that had been snatched away almost three years ago.

'Will there be anything more?'

There were many dishes shc could cook but, her money stretched to the limit, Garnet shook her head reluctantly.

'Then that be four shillings and fivepence ... and this be a bit to thank you for your custom.'

Garnet watched the fry, liver, lights and heart ... together with the lacy kell that was the pig's stomach lining being deftly wrapped in a parcel.

'You cook them along with an onion, a pinch of sage an' a leaf or two of bay and it'll mek a supper fit for the Queen 'erself. That man of yourn will enjoy a dish of faggots, especially with a few grey peas alongside of 'em. It fair sets me mouth a'waterin' to talk of it!'

Lifting his boater as Garnet smiled her thanks the butcher watched her from the shop. That young woman were not usual. Hers were not the brusque ways of a miner's or a steel worker's wife hard-pressed to feed the mouths of her young ones; true, her careful use of money and her poor clothes showed she was little if any better off than the women he was used to serving in his shop, but her speech and manner showed a wide difference. That wench were not of the working classes so what was her doing in Bilston?

They had not returned to Victoria House. Furious at what he had been told, Tyler rode towards Bentley.

'I assure you I have no knowledge of the Viscount Riverton ... whoever that might be ... or of his whereabouts.'

Dressed in Merton cloth breeches, tweed jacket and leather gaiters the man had stared coldly as he spoke. Irritated by the offhand attitude Tyler's own reply had held much of the anger boiling inside him.

'Well you work for him, don't you?'

'No, sir, I do not. I work for no man other than myself.'

'Then what are you doing in this house?'

Cold as before, the man had answered. 'That, sir, I see as entirely my own business, however I will tell you. I am trying to ascertain exactly what has been going on in my own house.'

'Your house?' Tyler had answered incredulously.

'That is correct. Victoria House is my property.'

'But the Viscount...'

'Riverton, you say?' Tyler remembered the sharp accusing looks on the other man's face. 'I would like to know more about what he was doing in this house, claiming it as his own, and what, for that matter, are you doing in it?'

They had talked for some time after that, every word adding to the fury stinging Tyler's nerves. William Pinner, owner of Pinner's Bank, had closed the house for six months while accompanying his wife to Egypt, the doctor assuring him the equable climate there would benefit her recovery from an illness of the chest. He had returned to find several horses not belonging to him in the stables and two gardeners each with a tale to tell of a man and a woman claiming to have stayed in the house as his guests.

'I made no such invitation ... damn the man, I've never heard of him! But I will find him and when I do he is going to wish he had never heard of William Pinner!'

That is one more thing you will be cheated of, Pinner, Tyler had thought. By the time I've finished with Riverton there will be nothing left for you! But despite the anger bristling beneath the surface, his brain had worked quickly. His reply calmer and laced with the apologetic charm and slight embarrassment so concentratedly practised, he had claimed the horses as his and offered to pay again for their feed and care, saying they were brought here to be covered by Riverton's stallion. Those at least he would have today and then he would leave for Paris.

But not yet! He touched the riding crop to the horse's flank. First there was other business he must settle; the business of his wife!

Chapter Twenty-Seven

Having banked the fire with a bucketful of coal sleck, Garnet looked around the tiny room that was both kitchen and living room. She had prepared as much for selling at the market tomorrow as she could, the rest she could do on her return.

Through the narrow window the sun was pale in the winter sky. Another hour or so and the long night would begin. She would have to hurry to reach that place before the last trace of sunset left the world in darkness.

Running up the bare wooden stairs to the bedroom she removed her blouse, washing with as much care as if she were going to meet the Queen. Pulling the brush through the wealth of her long, deeply auburn hair she smiled at her reflection in the damp-speckled mirror hung over the wash stand. To see Hepzibah again meant more to her than any meeting with royalty.

And Judah? She slipped the blouse over her shoulders, fastening the front row of tiny buttons. Yes, she had missed Judah too, missed his kind smile and gentle touch. They had both been so kind to her, so patient and understanding, so very like Raschid.

Raschid. Her fingers halted in the pinning up of her hair. He and Judah, they were both in her thoughts at night, in her prayers along with her child. Neither of them had the wealth or position of Tyler Cadell but somehow she knew both of them would give what he would not; each would risk his own life to help her. Reaching for her shawl she draped it about her shoulders before going downstairs and out into the street. Raschid had been the one to bring her from that prison, but who had provided the money that had secured her release? And knowing she was no longer to be deported had Raschid tried to find her again or, like Tyler, did he want her gone for ever from his life?

No! The whisper was in her mind but the sudden jolt of pain was in her heart. Not that, not Raschid too! But why did the thought of him never wanting to see her again matter so much, why did it cause so much pain? He had been kind, more thoughtful and loving than Tyler had ever been…

Loving! Garnet almost stopped in her

tracks. Was that the root of her own feelings, was the desolation she felt after every night-time prayer caused by more than the loss of her baby ... were her feelings for Raschid more than she had ever admitted? But that was impossible!

Pulling the shawl tight about her she tried to shut the thought from her mind. She could have no feeling other than gratitude; Raschid was her husband's manservant!

Twisting the corners of the shawl in her fingers Garnet didn't know if she wanted to laugh or to cry. Being in love with her husband's servant should be impossible ... but it wasn't!

'Get me a change of clothes!'

Flinging his coat at the turbanned man watching him throw himself up the stairs, Tyler stormed into his bedroom.

'That lying swine ... I'll rip his bloody heart out...!'

Listening in silence to the storm of abuse tearing from the throat of the man who ordered his life, Raschid fetched fresh riding jacket and breeches from the dressing room.

'Not them, you fool ... out of my way!'

Fetching the servant a sharp blow across the mouth, Tyler strode into the room that held a row of wardrobes. Snatching a pair of pale-grey pin-striped trousers he pulled them on, roaring for Raschid to 'get a bloody coat!'

Ignoring the servant's bleeding mouth, Tyler grabbed the charcoal-coloured coat and fastened the three central buttons over a crisp white shirt before seating a pearl silk cravat snugly between the coat's short revers. He was in a hurry but it wouldn't do to be seen visiting looking like something from the ragman's cart.

'Harness the carriage, and be quick about it!'

Placing suede gloves and black silk top hat on the foot of the bed, Raschid left for the stables.

What had given rise to that storm of temper? Could his visit to Victoria House have furnished him with more than word of the absent Viscount Riverton?

That lying swine ... but I'll settle him and then I'll settle her!'

The words had struck like stones. Did they refer to Riverton and his niece, or had Tyler found out about Garnet, had he somehow found out she had not been dispatched to the colonies ... had he seen her, was that where he was going now ... to fetch her back to this house?

And what then? Securing the last of the traces that attached horse to carriage Raschid glanced at the tall figure striding from the house, pale-gold hair all but hidden beneath the silk hat. Would he do that which he had wanted to do years ago, would he kill Garnet in order to hide his crimes of the past ... in order to achieve his plans for the future?

Climbing into the carriage Tyler snatched the reins into one hand, the other raising a plaited leather driving whip.

'There are horses stabled over at Victoria House,' he glared at the waiting servant, 'they belong to me, fetch them!'

Throwing himself backwards Raschid felt the rush of air as the whip whistled less than an inch from his face. Rising to his feet he watched the carriage hurtling down the drive. Tyler was not returning to Victoria House or he would have taken him along to collect those horses. Staring after the carriage fast becoming a dot amid the broad expanse of fields he felt his heart grow cold. Tyler had not taken the road to Wednesbury, he had followed the one that led towards Wolverhampton.

Wolverhampton. Turning, Raschid ran for the house. That was the town which held that prison, the town where he had last seen Garnet.

'Before the rising of the moon he will come...'

His mother's words echoing in his mind, Judah cast an eye towards the sky. An hour more of daylight, maybe less, then he would see the truth of those words.

He did not doubt his mother, she less than any Romany would twist what she saw in the crystal, she less than any other would desecrate its powers. They had consulted it, she and the widow Korjyck, they had asked and been answered and that answer had been told true. Tonight a man would cross the heath, a man with death in his heart.

'It be a fair enough filly I grant you, but twenty pounds is more than I had wanted to pay.'

'But if the pony be a present for your daughter as you said then I would have thought you would want the best.'

'True … true.' The lean bewhiskered man nodded. 'The best be all that's good enough for my girl … but twenty pounds for a horse…'

'Not for any horse.' Judah ran a hand over the sleek, arched chestnut neck. 'This one be out of a fine dam with an Arab for a sire.'

'An Arab?' His heavy grey eyebrows coming together, the man glanced at Judah. 'Such lineage, I'm surprised to find her sold to a … to you.'

To a gypsy was what he meant to say. Judah's hand tightened on the rope halter fastened about the young animal's head.

'The dam were covered when the sire broke stable,' he explained, 'the owner didn't want his future bloodlines mixed so he sent the filly for sale to Brough horse fair

404

where I bought her.'

'So, little one, your father left his calling card where it were not wanted.' The man laughed, touching a hand along the silken hind quarters.

'The man was a little too concerned for his blood stock to see the prize on his doorstep. Let her grow then get her covered with a good stallion and this little lady will throw young that will not disgrace any man's stable.'

'You may be right at that.'

'I am right,' Judah answered. 'But if you buy this filly then feel you might not have had your money's worth or she has not lived up to all I claim for her then say as much to the first Romany you come across. He will pay you back your twenty pounds plus anything more you might have spent on her. I will know of it soon enough to take the filly back. That is the word of Judah Kane.'

Taking another close look at the horse the man pursed his lips. 'I suppose I'll have to trust you.'

Judah forced down the anger rising in him. It was the old story, never place any store on the word of a gypsy, they were all thieves ready to rob a man of the very air he breathed.

'No.' He gathered the lead rope in his hands, his answer filled with a quiet dignity. 'You do not have to trust me, there has been no bargain struck between us nor will there be. Judah Kane sells to no man who fears he is being robbed.'

A quick leap carrying him on to the bare back of the dappled mare he had rode in on, Judah turned her head the way he had come.

'Wait!' The other man's call followed after him. 'I never said I wouldn't buy that filly.'

Nor did you say you would! Judah rode on in silence, the young animal trotting beside the mare. But from now on you will remember the Romany is an honest man, as honest as are many of those who name him a rogue.

'Before the rising of the moon...'

The words had hovered on the brink of his mind the whole of the afternoon, they had plagued it while he was riding to that house giving him no respite while he was conducting the business of selling the filly. Was that the true reason he had turned his back on the buyer? No ... the real reason was as he had stated. He wanted no man to feel he had been cheated, he would rather do no trade than strike a bargain that left a party dissatisfied. Honesty had been the policy taught by his father and it was one he would live by all of his life.

Running on the heels of the mare the lurcher dog that accompanied him everywhere growled low in its throat, but its warning was unnecessary for Judah had already heard the beat of footsteps on the heath.

'Before the rising of the moon he will come.'

On the rim of the sky the horizon reached dark arms, drawing the dying sun down into itself. Squinting against the gathering dusk Judah watched the figure approach. The tall figure of a man.

'...he will come...'

The words of his mother had come true, it had happened as the crystal foretold.

Dismounting, quieting the rumble of the dog, he waited.

In the shadowed distance the man came on. This was the trouble that was expected.

Teeth clenched, every nerve tense, every fibre of his body alert, Judah stepped forward to meet the turbanned man.

She could not be in love with Raschid! Shawl drawn tight against the ingathering of the day, Garnet hurried towards Bentley. He had always been the perfect servant, aware of her comfort, thoughtful of her well-being, she had never thought it any more than that. But those had been Raschid's actions not hers, he had simply been fulfilling his duties ... they were nothing to do with love, that feeling was hers alone.

Had she shown it? A frisson of alarm rippled along her nerves. Had Raschid known what she had only now discovered … had she somehow conveyed to him what had been so deeply hidden in her heart she was innocent of its existence?

Head drawn to her chest she hurried on, misery tainting the happiness of the afternoon.

Please don't let me have embarrassed Raschid, she prayed silently. I wouldn't want his life made more difficult on my account.

But if Raschid had known, if in some inadvertent way she had shown that unrealised love, might not Tyler have seen it too?

The thought, so sudden in its attack, struck her like a blow to the face, halting her in her tracks.

Tyler had accused her of a liaison, of bearing the child of his own manservant, he had killed the child because of it … because of her! What she had not realised, not dreamed of, must have been apparent to her husband and as a result…

'Noooo, please God, nooooo!' Agony carrying the words from her lips she pressed both hands to her mouth, but could not press the thought from her mind. She had been the true underlying cause of Tyler's blind rage, it was not he who had murdered the child, it was she!

Sick with the knowledge, blind and deaf

with the pain of it she stumbled on, oblivious of the shouts of carters warning her clear of horse and cart, hearing only the drum of pain tearing her apart.

Ebony ... the child she had loved like nothing else in the whole world, the child whose heartbeat was her own, whose every tiny smile haunted her soul, Ebony her baby was dead, murdered by the mother who adored her.

''Ere, watch where you be goin', there be other folk on the streets ... pushin' an' a' shovin' ... ain't got no manners, some folk!'

Loud in its indignation the voice rang after her but Garnet did not hear. Caught in her own searing pain she ran towards the gathering shadows, ran towards the all-hiding darkness of the heath.

'I was disappointed too...'

Hiding his irritation behind the so often rehearsed smile of regret, Tyler kissed the hand of the woman he had come to see. He would rather demand flatly the information he wanted but boorishness was not the way. Charm had always been his unfailing ally, it had always brought him what he wanted and it would not fail him now.

'...you must have thought it so discourteous of me declining your invitation at the last moment but fever does not always give warning of its coming.'

'Fever!' The mistress of Leam House looked alarmed.

'Nothing to worry about.' Tyler's smile lit his eyes like soft-blue torches. 'Just a touch of malaria, it goes in a day or so though it leaves a person feeling weak.'

'But should you have come here so soon?'

Ensuring the movement had all the aspects of a man not yet fully recovered from illness, Tyler lowered himself to a chair.

'I could leave it no longer before coming to apologise ... a note would have been too impersonal.'

The woman had swallowed it! Behind the smile Tyler congratulated his perfect performance. A man leaving his sick-bed in order to deliver his apology personally ... how could it not succeed?

'But, my dear Mr Cadell, a note would have at least explained a delay in your calling, I would have understood the reason for your not attending my supper party.'

'And would have forgiven, I know.' Tyler let the smile fade tiredly. 'But I could not have given myself forgiveness ... not until I had begged yours.'

Across from him the woman's face beamed. 'You have nothing to beg for, Mr Cadell, we were both disappointed but you can in no way blame yourself. As you say, illness is not always preceded by a visiting card.'

'Indeed.' He touched a hand to his brow watching beneath the half-lowered lids for a reaction, smiling to himself at the concern he saw cloud the woman's face.

'You are still far too unwell to he paying social visits.' She stood up, maroon taffeta rustling as she rang for a servant. 'I advise you to return to your bed.'

Swaying a little as he stood, the affected gesture of touching his brow repeated, it was an effort to hide the laugh bubbling in his chest. It was always so easy ... always so damned easy!

'Yes ... yes, you are right of course,' he answered in short breathy gasps. 'But first I have to ask will you furnish me with the recipes your cook used in preparing the food for the evening?' He smiled weakly, carrying the charade to its conclusion. 'Having been denied the pleasure of attending your supper party I thought if I repeat it then I might have the pleasure of your attending mine at Bentley House a little later in the year.'

'I would be delighted to attend your supper,' the woman answered as her maid entered the room. 'But those dishes were not prepared by my cook, they were far more exotic than she is used to ... so many spices. The whole buffet was catered by a woman recommended to me, a Mrs Garnet ... now let me see, where was it she lives...'

411

Remember, you stupid cow ... remember! Watching the woman it was all Tyler could do to stop himself slapping her, slapping the rest of the words from her silly smiling mouth.

'Perhaps I should not have asked, it is rude of me to bother you.' He turned to follow the frilly aproned maid.

'Nonsense, it is no bother, no bother at all. The woman lives in Bilston, a place called Queen Street.'

Queen Street! Tyler guided the carriage along the roughly surfaced road. That should not be difficult to find and once he did there would be no more Mrs Garnet ... no more wife to threaten his future. But that future had to be grabbed back. If he were to continue to live a life of comfort he had more to take care of than one woman, he must find the man who had robbed him, the man who had claimed to own Victoria House, one who claimed to be Viscount Riverton ... who would soon be a very dead viscount!

Laying the whip to the horse's flank he glanced at the darkening heath bordering each side of the road for as far as he could see. This land held many gin pits, holes sunk for coal so long ago no one remembered how many or where they lay. Dark and deep, the bowels of the earth, a fitting grave for Riverton ... and for Garnet.

His attention swallowed by the bitter-sweet pleasure of the thought he paid little attention to the road, barely saving himself from being hurled from the carriage as the horse reared violently.

Wrestling with the frightened animal it was several moments before he looked at the huddled bundle lying at the edge of the road. Some drunken fool not watching where he was going ... well let whoever it was lie there, he had no time for charity.

Gathering the reins that had been snatched from his hand he heard the soft moan as the bundle moved.

The man was not dead. He hesitated, his mind racing.

Alive he could possibly identify who it was had run him down, identify the carriage. But that would be nigh on impossible, one carriage was very like another and in the semi-darkness, with no markings to define it, this one could be any of a hundred others. He was safe on that count. But what if the man had seen his face, what if he had had sight of him?

In this light? Tyler glanced along the road now wreathed in shadow. No magistrate would believe the claim. But believe it or not he could not afford to be tied up in a court of law, every minute was another in which Riverton could get further away.

There was no other carriage on the road,

no cart as far as he could see and his own carriage would be virtually invisible in the gloom. Thank God he had not taken the time to light the driving lamps. What had to be done was best done under cover of darkness.

Grasping the whip he climbed down to the road. A few heavy blows of the handle would finish the job completely.

One more quick glance telling him there was no other person in sight, he raised the whip high above his head.

Chapter Twenty-Eight

Luck had been on his side, luck of heaven or the luck of the devil, he couldn't care less which.

Tyler watched the cart roll on down the road. How the hell could he not have heard that thing approach! The rumble of its iron-rimmed wheels was like distant thunder. But he had not heard it and it had almost been upon him when that bundle at his feet had moved. The whip raised he had bent to grasp the figure by the collar, the better to get a blow to its head, when it had turned over.

It must have been the shock that had

prevented him delivering the blow; but shock or surprise, whichever, the fact was that as he drew the figure upwards the lamps on that cart had registered in his brain. He had barely had the time to lift the figure and bundle it into the carriage before the cart drew alongside.

'Is anything wrong?' the carter had asked. Wrong? Tyler smiled to himself. Things couldn't be more right.

He had thought to have to ask in the streets, possibly to knock on doors and both ways would arouse suspicion. Gentlemen in expensive dress and driving a carriage did not ask around back streets for a woman without setting tongues wagging, and if word of him had reached Garnet before he did she would be gone where he might never find her again.

But word had not found her first ... he had. He had bent to grasp what he thought to be a man's jacket, to haul the figure wearing it into a position to make the blows from the whip tell, but the jacket had turned out to be a shawl and the figure was not a man but a woman ... the figure that turned to look up at him was Garnet!

But even though the carter had been satisfied with the explanation given about stopping to light the carriage lamps and had moved on, giving every opportunity of killing Garnet there and then, Tyler had hesitated. The pitfalls were too many, in every sense of the word. To carry a dead weight across the heath at any time was foolhardy, but with darkness almost complete it was downright dangerous. Pit shafts, he knew, dotted the place in abundance, as currants in a fruit cake, one wrong step and they would both be lost. He could kill her and leave the body lying at the side of the road, it would not be the first pauper to be found that way.

Fine ... except Garnet was no pauper. She had been organising fancy supper parties which meant she was paid a fee. Besides that, how could he be sure she had not told anyone of her husband, there could be several people who knew of the man living at Bentley House and whether they believed her or not people relished gossip; and if that carter added his piece, how he had seen a gentleman with a carriage in the same spot as the body was found...!

The hazard had been too great, he would have to do it somewhere else, a place with fewer risks attached. It had to be Bentley House. There would be no one to see what he did, the Indian he had dispatched to Victoria House and Florrie Wilkes? Florrie Wilkes would most likely be asleep in the kitchen but if she wasn't then it didn't matter, she knew better than to open her mouth!

Lying the whip to the already sweating animal he sent the carriage hurtling up to the front of the house then dragged Garnet up the steps, leaving the horse quivering and trembling in the shafts.

'How the hell did you get out of that prison?'

It was a snarl as he threw her to the floor of the bedroom he had never shared with her.

'Who got you off?' he snarled as Garnet blinked, not yet fully conscious. 'Who paid that hundred pounds ... who was it prevented your deportation? Tell me, Garnet, I want to know who it was took you from that prison!'

Prison ... who took you from that prison...? The words floating hazily in her brain Garnet tried to focus her mind. She was on her way to see Hepzibah and Judah, she had kept to the road that ran across the heath, she had been going to Bentley...

'Answer me, damn you! I want to know ... who was it?'

The slap hard and savage across her face brought Garnet's senses to sharp reality.

'Tyler!' she gasped. 'Tyler!'

'Yes, Tyler!' he snapped. 'Now tell me what I asked, who was it paid that one hundred pounds that bought your freedom?'

How had he found her ... how had he

known where to look?

'I could always beat it out of you.' Crashing a fist into his open palm he smiled venomously. 'Don't think your being a woman will save you, it won't. In fact I would rather enjoy it.'

'As you enjoyed murdering our daughter?' The effect was startling, the smiling mouth tightened like a trap, the eyes becoming smouldering volcanoes spitting blue fire.

'That thing!' he snarled. 'The child of an Indian pig!'

She had thought to have a different revenge, to see him pay in a different way for the death of her baby, to see him brought to justice. Garnet stared at the face she once thought so handsome, at the man she had once loved. There would be no justice for Tyler Cadell, she would not be given revenge that way. Yes, he meant to kill her but that would be her relief, she would be once again with the daughter she yearned for, but first Tyler Cadell would hear the truth.

'No, Tyler.' She scrambled to her knees. 'Not the child of your manservant. You know that well enough, you took that for the excuse you needed to be rid of me; my father's property was not enough for you, was it? Our marriage was only the first stage in your grand design, but as long as I was alive you could take it no further. But I was young and in perfect health...'

'Quiet!'

It was like the hiss of a snake but Garnet was not to be deterred. This was the only retribution that would be visited on Tyler Cadell and to end it he would have to kill her now.

'....in perfect health,' she went on, 'poison was not the answer. To use an instant one would bring immediate suspicion but to use a slower one would take too long ... you were never a patient man were you, Tyler?'

'No, I was never a patient man...'

The words slithered over her, creeping along her spine like some living thing bringing a new, even more terrible coldness to her heart.

'...that was why your parents had to be helped in their departure from this earth.'

'My parents...?'

'Yes!' A vicious laugh erupted from his throat. 'As with yourself, my dear, I could not wait for nature to take its course, allowing them to live into old age did not suit me at all, that is why I sent barrels of infected water to their home in Mariwhal. So thoughtful of a son-in-law, don't you think, to send drinking water all that way ... what a pity it appeared to have arrived too late!'

'You killed my mother and father!' Garnet

reeled under the shock of his words.

'Oh come now, my dear,' he laughed again, a contemptuous despising laugh, 'there is no reason to look so distressed … it was a painful way for them to go, I admit…'

'You killed my parents!' Garnet fought against the sickness rolling up from her stomach.

As he stood over her his handsome face lost its smile, but the blue eyes spat darts of brilliant ice. 'Let us say I just helped them on their way.'

'As you did a helpless child,' Garnet breathed, 'as you helped your own daughter on her way?'

'I admit it!' He shrugged nonchalantly. 'Why not, since there is no one to hear? The child was my daughter, I never had any doubt of it. Raschid, the oh so honourable Raschid, he would suffer death before touching you in such a way, before laying you open to scandal, not you, not the wife of his master, not Garnet Cadell the woman he is in love with! But you had to go and what better way than dying along with the fruits of your illicit love affair? Oh of course, that is not the story folk heard, but your devoted Raschid knew they would unless he went along with what I did.'

He had killed them all, her parents and her child!

Stunned, Garnet could only stare. She had

thought to sting him with her words to see, if only faintly, some trace of repentance in that cold serpent gaze but he had turned the tables. Covering her face with her hands she shrank down to the floor, folding in on herself, trying to shut out the horror, but it remained, hurting, torturing every tiny part of her.

'I ask you again, who was it secured your release from that prison?'

The words seemed a world away, existing in a dimension she did not know, one she was no part of.

'Answer me!' The blow to her temple sent her reeling, but still she floated in a vast silence, heedless of the kick that followed.

'Who paid the money?'

Stood on the landing Florrie Wilkes listened. She had heard Tyler come into the house, caught a glimpse of him as he had dragged a figure into that bedroom, a figure with its head huddled beneath a shawl. But the skirts had been testimony that it was a woman Cadell had brought with him, a woman he was now screeching at. But who was she? Not some prostitute, some woman of the streets, one who would spread her legs as wide on the heath as she would on a bed supposing she was first shown a shilling; surely he had not fetch a common whore into his house!

Florrie stepped cautiously nearer the open

door, it wouldn't do to be caught listening but she could always say she thought it were a burglar he was shouting at.

'Tell me...'

The words burst from the bedroom, the anger of them echoing from every wall.

'I will know, Garnet, I will know before I let you die!'

'Garnet!' Florrie winced at the sound of hand slapping against flesh. That was no whore he had found for himself, that was his wife. Raschid ... she half turned towards the stairs before remembering, the Indian had not returned, he had rushed off saying something about horses and hadn't come back.

'I ... I thought it was you.'

That did not sound like the Garnet she knew. Florrie pressed a hand to her mouth, holding back her cry at the sound of yet another blow. But not sounding like her didn't means as it wasn't her. Who was to say he hadn't beaten her half senseless? Would any wench sound like herself were that the case?

'Me!'

The laugh rang out following the echo of anger along the walls of the corridor, the viciousness of it curdling Florrie's blood.

'Me pay to have you freed? It was me had you arrested, me paid that woman to accuse you, me bribed the magistrate to sentence

422

you to the colonies. Me, Garnet, the husband who killed your parents and your daughter and is now going to kill you. What does it matter who it was parted with a hundred pounds, it was money wasted!'

With breath trembling from her lungs Florrie listened to the sound of a drawer being opened then slammed shut. Garnet … he had said the name again.

'No one will even know you are dead, Garnet … no one will ever know I killed you. I last saw you three years ago, dead in your bed in this very room, so you see even should your body be discovered in some mine shaft no one will know who you are…'

'I'll know, you murderin' swine!'

The vase she had picked up from a small table half-way along the landing lifted above her shoulders Florrie smashed it down on the blond head, sending a pistol tumbling from Tyler's hand.

Scrambling for it as he staggered against the bed she grabbed the fallen gun, holding it in both hands and pointing the barrel straight at him.

'I 'eard what you said.' Florrie's breath trembled. 'I 'eard what it was you done to that wench's folk and what you intends doin' to 'er. It be the same thing you done to 'er babby; but not again, this time you be goin' to answer for your wickedness.'

The blow had landed more to his shoulder

than his head, the surprise of it helping to send him stumbling to the bed, but almost at once his senses had cleared. Looking at Florrie he smiled.

'I don't know what you think you heard…'

'I ain't thinking nothing!' Florrie snapped. 'I knows what I 'eard and I knows what you was bent on doin'; well you won't do it no more, when the Indian comes back I'll send him for the constable.'

'That would be foolish, the word of a paid servant against that of a gentleman! As for Garnet–' he looked to where Garnet watched with wide anxious eyes '–you should know a wife cannot testify against her husband. Now,' he stood up reaching out a hand, 'give me the pistol and we will say no more of your striking me, you are far too good a housekeeper…'

'Don't go gammitin' with me, I ain't so mutton headed as to believe your foolin', everybody knows a crooked stick throws a crooked shadow and there ain't a one more crooked than you.'

'I am not trying to fool you, Florrie…'

Florrie's hands trembled. She had never so much as seen a gun before and now she had one pointed at Tyler Cadell's head. What if it went off? What if the Indian didn't come home?

'…give me the pistol.' Tyler moved slowly, one step after another. A little closer and he could grab the gun, snatch it out of her stupid hands and have her dead before she realised what was happening. 'Give it to me,' he smiled again.

'You sit yourself back on that bed!' Florrie waved the gun. 'My mother d'ain't get me on no onion boat, I knows your ways and I knows the only action you be like to forget be them you does yourself.'

'Give it to me, you–!'

Hurling himself forwards, Tyler grunted as the gun went off, a bullet scraping his shoulders.

'I told you,' Florrie sobbed, the gun still in her hands. 'I told you to sit down.'

'You'll regret this!' His eyes gleaming with rage, Tyler steadied himself, a hand to his bleeding shoulder.

'Get out … get out now afore I blows your bloody 'ead off.'

Florrie's voice rose on a tide of fear, the hands that held the gun trembling as she stared at the wound.

The woman had gone crazy. Tyler gasped with the screaming sting of the wound. Or was it simply that she saw the chance she must have waited these three years for? A chance she might well take again if he attempted to seize that gun from her.

'I'll go.' He met the woman's wild stare with a growl. 'But I will come back and when I do you will die, you may count on that.' Glancing behind him to where Garnet crouched, her tumbled hair an auburn cloud about her shoulders, his lips drew back in a feline snarl. 'You may both count on it!'

'He said the same thing you said, the time were now.'

Judah looked at his mother sat on the steps of her wagon. He had watched the turbanned man draw level then had listened to all he had to say.

'He asked the woman who is servant along of him in that house, asked her to tell where it was the killer of Garnet's child were hurrying to but the woman didn't know any more than he did.'

'So where be the owner of that going?' Hepzibah watched the strong face of her son as he looked at the turban in his hand. It had been worn for the last time, was her feeling, its time was ended as was the time for so many more things. But she kept the thoughts silent. Let happen in one day what would and leave the rest to a new one.

'But the woman spoke of a visitor to her kitchen,' Judah went on, 'her told of their conversation, of hearing of a woman by the name of Garnet cooking for what was called an oriental supper, seems they was foods they hadn't heard of before.'

'And the man that spoke with you on the

heath thinks as the one cooking them oriental foods be Garnet?'

'He does.'

'And that tells where he'll find her?'

Judah shook his head. 'I told him only where that supper were given, Leam House. He is going there himself to ask after Garnet.'

Chewing the stem of her clay pipe, Hepzibah switched her glance to the flames leaping beneath the blackened kettle. He could go to that house but he would not find her there.

'It be no guess the mistress of that place would answer the question of a gentleman,' she said, 'her would give the name of the one who cooked them dishes for 'er, but to tell the same to one who be obviously a servant, ye can be certain 'er will not, so what will 'e do then?'

'He didn't say. He said only that he was going to Leam House.'

Was that all that man had said or was there more, more yet for her son to bind in his soul? Removing the pipe from her mouth she tapped out the ash on a stone before putting it in the pocket of her dark skirts.

'Then I will say what 'e failed to. The time be now for secrets to be told … it be time for the past to be revealed, and in the doing of it for many hurts to be soothed. Ye 'ave kept your peace, my son, kept it as ye were bid, but time 'as come when ye must tell it to another. No, that other don't be me.' Hepzibah shook her head as Judah turned to her. 'I already knows as I knows many things. Now I tells ye as I 'ave always told ye, do what is bid in yer heart.'

He had been bidden to go to Bentley House. To watch there against the return of Tyler Cadell, but he would be watching for Garnet.

'Strike no man wi'out fair cause...'

Despite the growing shadows Hepzibah had seen the nuance of emotion sweep across her son's face and understood its cause. Judah was suffering and the end of pain was not yet in sight.

'...But take care, be wary of the serpent that lies among the bracken.' Soft though the words were spoken they reached to the figure striding from the camp.

What had his mother meant? Keeping to the narrow track worn across the heath by men walking to and from their work, Judah ran towards Bentley House. He had not wanted to ask but he knew Hepzibah was not given to warnings unless they were needed. She was telling him of danger, but was that danger for himself or for another? *'Be wary of the serpent that lies among the bracken!'*

Was it waiting for Garnet? His mother knew the love he felt for the woman he had found beneath a hedge; was it to protect those feelings she had not put name to who it was that danger lay in wait for?

As for her other words, 'Strike no man wi'out fair cause...'

That word he would heed, but should it be that the husband of Garnet ever lifted his hand against her again then the hand of Judah Kane would reach for him and would not leave him until he were dead.

Chapter Twenty-Nine

She had not returned to Leam House.

His fears mounting, Raschid turned the horse in the direction he had come.

He had not gone to the front of the house; even with the turmoil that reeled in his mind he had realised that dressed as he was he would not be received there. He had thrown off the hated turban but the rest of his clothes proclaimed him a servant and as such he must make his request at the rear of the house.

'Ar, there be a gentleman.' The cook had eyed him with suspicion, a heavy wooden rolling pin resting beneath her hand. 'Why be you askin'?'

He had heard the caution in the woman's

voice and could not blame her for lifting the rolling pin. With his dark hair plastered to his head, beads of perspiration running down his face he must have proved a frightening sight.

'If the gentleman is a visitor by the name of Mr Tyler Cadell then he is my master. I have an urgent message for him, if you would be good enough to have it taken to him...' The lie had been spoken with a politeness that was seemingly assuring. Shaking her head the cook had let the rolling pin rest once more on the table.

'It were who you asked, but he be gone 'alf an hour an' more.'

She had shaken her head again when he had asked where his master might be found, but the young maid stood at the further side of the table had smiled.

'I thinks I might know...'

She had hesitated as the cook's sharp eyes had fallen on her.

'I... I weren't earholin', honest I weren't, they was talkin' when I went into the sitting room, that be the truth, cross me heart an' hopes to die!'

'You knows what 'appens to them as listens where they oughtn't, and what 'appens to liars, they goes to 'ell, my wench!'

The woman's voice was stern and the girl had trembled visibly but affirmed what she had said.

'My master will be most grateful if you could assist in my finding him, ma'am.' Raschid had intervened but made no attempt to step further inside the kitchen.

'Ma'am!' The older woman had smiled her pleasure at being addressed so graciously. 'Then we must 'elp if we can. Tell 'im then, wench,' she had ordered her underling. 'If it be you thinks you knows where it is he might find 'is master then say what it were you 'eard upstairs.'

The girl had smiled at him, her glance admiring. 'The mistress were saying as the woman who organised 'er oriental evening, Mrs Garnet, her lives in Bilston, a house in Queen Street. Seems your master were enquiring after her.'

He had thanked them both, the girl smiling as she had seen him into the yard, saying pointedly that the first Sunday of the month was her free afternoon and that she usually walked in the park.

But concerned that Tyler was so far ahead he had jumped back on to the horse Judah had lent and ridden away, giving no reply.

Had he found her there? Raschid's heart pounded as loud as the stallion's hooves. Tyler was capable of anything, once before he had tried to take Garnet's life, searching for her everywhere he could think to look; if he had found her now there was no doubting he would kill her.

For almost three years, since Tyler Cadell's return to England, Raschid had taken his blows, suffered that intolerable insolence and abuse as he had suffered it all those years in India; been the hated manservant, the butt of the other man's feelings of anger and betrayal, of a deep-down inferiority.

Raschid urged the horse to greater effort, keeping it to the edge of the road that led him towards Bilston. But he would suffer it no more, that had all ended. From this night on he would be his own man.

'Oh, Garnet wench, I shot him ... I shot him...'

Trembling all over, Florrie Wilkes dropped the revolver.

'...I wanted only to stop him hurting you, I never meant to do no more, as God be my witness I meant to do no more.'

Her own limbs quivering, Garnet got to her feet. 'Shh,' she soothed, taking the sobbing woman into her arms. 'It is all over, Tyler is gone now.'

But for how long? Helping Florrie downstairs to the kitchen, she sat her in the chair drawn to the glowing range. He had said he would come back and Tyler did not make empty threats.

Would he keep that threat tonight, return to this house to do what he so obviously intended? She glanced at the woman sat

432

sobbing into her apron. It was not only herself he had threatened, Florrie Wilkes too was in danger.

She should go back to Queen Street, take the woman with her; they would be safe there, Tyler did not know of the house in Bilston.

'There be nothin' that man don't know,' Florrie sobbed as Garnet told her what they should do.

'I am sure he will not know of that.' Garnet tried to reassure the woman she had known since childhood. 'Please, Mrs Wilkes, we will be safe there.'

Lowering the apron Florrie sniffed, regarding Garnet through red puffy eyes. 'Where was it 'e found you?'

'I...' Garnet frowned trying to recall the event. 'It was a carriage, it ... it seemed to be on top of me before I had chance to move, the driver ... he did not shout any warning. Perhaps like myself he was so deep in thought he did not see me... I don't know any more until I found myself here with Tyler.'

'More like 'e did see you and recognised you. I bets the carriage that knocked you down was driven by your husband, that 'e hoped to 'ave killed you. P'raps 'e were disturbed afore 'e could finish you off and so 'e brought you 'ere to do his dirty work.'

'It could not have been him...'

'Why not?' Florrie's trembling gave way before contempt. 'That swine be smarter than a cartload of monkeys. Tell me, wench, which way was you 'eaded when you was run down?'

Which way? Garnet's frown deepened. She had not waited for the tram that would take her from Bilston to Darlaston Bull Stake. Excited at the thought of seeing Hepzibah and Judah she had walked into Moxley. She had passed the church on her right and was walking down Woods Bank, she had thought how beautiful the sky looked with scarlet ribbons of sunset fading into purple grey covering the heath. That was when it had happened, the carriage was travelling towards Bilston!

'I can see the answer for meself,' Florrie said. 'He were travelling the same road you 'ad took from Bilston.'

'But we can't take that as proof he knew where I live,' Garnet protested.

'I would take it as proof!' Florrie was adamant. 'My reckoning be the same as Raschid's was when I told him of what me and Fanny Siddons had talked of here in this very kitchen, that he put two and two together and come up with the answer it were you as had cooked that there oriental supper at Leam House and it would be there he would get the answer to where you lived; but when he found you weren't where

434

he was sent he took the road home and come upon you as you started across that 'eath. I say that Tyler Cadell knows full well where you lives, and take it from me, wench, you'll be no safer from his wickedness there as you be 'ere.'

'Did Raschid go with him?'

She had asked the question but dreaded the answer. Had Raschid been in that coach, had he helped Tyler bring her here?

'No.' Florrie wiped her tears on her apron. 'Tyler sent 'im off to Wednesbury to collect some horses from Victoria House.'

Thank God! Garnet felt the warmth of relief ride into her cheeks, mixing with a flush of guilt. How could she have thought such a thing of the man who had been so protective of her?

'You go put the bolt across that.' Florrie nodded towards the door that gave on to the stable yard. 'Me ... I'm going upstairs to fetch that there pistol, I feels this night's business be far from over.'

As safe here as in Queen Street! That meant she was safe nowhere. Slipping home the bolts at the top and the foot of the door Garnet froze as the sound of a scream and a second shot reverberated through the house.

Tyler! Garnet's limbs seemed turned to stone but her brain raced like a merry-go-round. Tyler was in the house ... he had returned ... Mrs Wilkes ... that shot, he must have shot Mrs Wilkes! Now he would be coming for her!

With her breath caught tight in her lungs she listened, nerves jangling with every slight sound. He might search upstairs, look for her in those rooms before coming here, there might be time to escape, to release the bolts on the door and run from the house, perhaps find help.

Her fingers scrabbled with the bolt above her head, then stopped. What was she doing? Had Florrie Wilkes run away that night all those months ago ... had she left a frightened girl alone with a killer? Her hand slid slowly down the heavy door to hang against her skirts. The woman had not left her, she had risked her own life in getting her away from this house. Releasing her breath in a rush, Garnet turned around. She could not run away, she could not desert the woman who had once helped her.

'I seen it were 'im...' the woman's terrified sob greeted Garnet as she rushed into the bedroom, '...I 'eard 'im coming up the stairs... Oh God, I've killed 'im! God help me, I've killed him!'

'You are not to blame, Mrs Wilkes.' Garnet ran to the woman, easing the pistol from her hands and letting it drop to the floor as she tried to comfort the frightened house-

436

keeper. 'He threatened to kill you, we both heard him say he would come back, that he would kill the two of us ... you had to shoot or he would have done what he promised.'

'I be going to 'ang ... I be going to 'ang.'

It was a cry of pure fear. That same fear she had felt when standing in the dock at the magistrate's court. A cold all-encompassing fear. Suddenly Garnet's mind was quite clear.

Holding the older woman close she took a deep breath. 'You will not hang,' she said calmly, 'you have done nothing you might hang for.'

Her face pressed against Garnet's shoulder, the woman's answer was muffled. 'I killed 'im, Miss Garnet, that be murder and a body be 'anged for murder.'

Touching a hand to the head enveloped in its starched cotton cap, Garnet answered quietly.

'That will not happen to you for it was not you murdered my husband ... it was me.'

'No!' Pushing free, Florrie stared at the girl she had thought so long dead. 'No, that be untrue!'

'But I will swear it is the truth and after hearing what was done to me and my child no one will disbelieve it was my hand held the pistol, my finger pressed the trigger.'

'You can't go expectin' me to let you take the blame, to let you go to the gallows in

437

place of me … to give your life–'

'I don't doubt you will try to prevent it,' Garnet cut her short. 'But I have no life, Mrs Wilkes, it ended the night my baby's life ended. I eat, I breathe but I do not live; I will be giving nothing.' I prayed for vengeance, she thought silently, prayed that in some way Tyler Cadell would pay for the murder of our child, I did not think it to be this way, but fate does not always play as we might have it.

Retrieving the fallen pistol she turned towards the figure slumped on the bedroom floor. Stepping closer she looked at it for the first time.

Standing over it she gasped, pressing her knuckles against her mouth to hold back the scream which followed. Fate did not always play as we would have it!

It was not Tyler lay dead … it was Raschid.

Bentley House was just ahead, it stood among the fields and pasture that bordered the other side of the heath. He could leave the track, cut across the rough ground and be there minutes quicker. But doing that might also mean he never got there, Bentley Heath like so many parts of the Black Country was honeycombed with disused mine shafts, their black mouths half hidden by bracken and shadows. Judah glanced at the path worn bare by clogged feet; winding like a silvered worm it stretched away from him.

Take the secret to Bentley House, his mother had said, only then can the healing of your own heart begin.

The healing of his heart! Judah ran on. She had meant he would begin to forget but the love he felt for Garnet would never be forgotten. The crystal had shown another man, one who gave her a child, a man who was not Judah Kane; she would never be his wife but she would always be his love.

Rounding a curve in the track he stopped as he saw outlined against the grey night a carriage tipped on its side, one wheel turning slowly in the air.

An accident, was anyone hurt! The soft whimper of an animal in pain drawing him on he raced to the carriage, searching it for a driver. Finding none he moved to where the horse lay. Running a hand over its front leg he knew he could do nothing for it, a horse with a broken leg could not be saved. But the fact there was no driver, that at least was a good sign; whoever had been in that carriage could not be seriously injured, most likely had walked to the house lying a little further on. He would get someone from there to deal with the horse, put it out of its pain. Turning to continue on his way he heard another cry, soft as before but it was no animal, the cry had come from a

439

human throat.

Standing on the edge of a small incline where the ground sloped gently downwards from the path, Judah stared into deeper shadows cast by a clump of ancient trees.

He *had* heard a cry, senses alerted to the slightest sounds since he had first walked did not deceive him now. There was someone there in the darkness, someone who could be in pain. Judah knew he could not pass by.

A few strides bringing him to the trees, he saw a figure stood against a trunk. It was a man, thrown from the carriage and no doubt rolled down that slope, but he was on his feet. A helping hand and he would be able to walk.

Reaching a hand to his arm Judah withdrew it as the figure screamed. Then he saw it, the man was not standing of his own volition, he was being held on his feet ... held by a jagged split branch embedded in his back!

He could not leave him there, leave the man to die like some animal caught in a trap.

A sound once more catching his ear, Judah called loudly and was answered by a man who came running to where he stood.

'You be lucky.' The man glanced at Judah then at the figure that seemed to be resting against the tree. 'I was tempted to go 'ome

440

by way of the canal, if I had I would 'ave missed you. What 'appened, take the bend too fast?'

Ignoring the question Judah took hold of one arm and shoulder of the injured man.

'Take the other side,' he said, 'we have to get him free.'

'Get him free ... wot you mean? Oh Christ! Oh Christ Almighty!' Turning his face away the man vomited into the grass.

'Take him!' Judah's bark rang among the shadowed trees. 'Help me lift him down.'

Gagging with every movement the workman did as instructed, lifting the unconscious figure into Judah's arms.

'Go for a doctor.' Judah was already moving up the slope. 'Send him to Bentley House.'

Dropping to her knees Garnet bent over the fallen man, one hand touching the still head. This couldn't be happening ... not this, it couldn't be Raschid ... it couldn't!

'We, we should cover 'im up ... put a sheet over 'im...'

Above her head the voice of Florrie Wilkes trembled. '...it ... it be better ... I'll go get one.'

She had lost him. Garnet stroked the glossy black hair. She had lost a man who had been her friend, a man she had not known she loved. Gathering the still figure in her arms she touched her cheek to his.

'Raschid,' she sobbed. 'You will never know I loved you, never know how much I will miss you.'

'There be somebody in the 'ouse!' Florrie Wilkes let the sheet she had fetched drop from nerveless fingers. 'There be somebody down in the hall, I 'eard a shout.'

Taking the sheet Garnet draped it quickly over the unmoving body. Florrie Wilkes was in a high state of nerves, another shock following so quickly on the two she had already suffered might throw her into a state of collapse.

Hearing a shout herself she stood up, brushing the tears from her face before the older woman saw them.

'You go rest in your room,' she said gently, 'I will see who it is.'

But she knew who it must be, who it could only be: Tyler Cadell!

'This man be injured bad.'

'Judah!' Come to the head of the stairs Garnet stared at the man stood below. 'Judah, oh thank heaven.'

'This man is badly hurt,' Judah's answer was curt, 'he needs help.'

'Up here.' Her mind clearing, Garnet beckoned then led the way along the corridor to the open door of a bedroom. 'Put him on the bed.'

'I've sent for a doctor, he should be here

soon. I thought as the master wouldn't mind, seeing as this man be hurt so bad.'

Looking at the white face and closed eyes of her husband Garnet paled. 'No,' she murmured, 'the master will not mind.'

'I found him just a ways down the road, seems he had been driving too fast and turned the carriage over. The horse has a broken leg and has to be put down, is there a groom?'

Still staring at the figure, his blood staining dark red into the white sheets. Garnet shook her head. 'No, there is no groom, there is no one save myself and the housekeeper.'

She could tell him that minutes ago there had been someone, someone who now lay dead.

'A shotgun then, the animal has to be put out of pain.'

'In the study.' She had to force the answer. 'Tyler … Tyler always kept a shotgun in the study.'

'What you be wantin' wi' a shotgun?'

She had thought the woman to be resting in her room. Stepping quickly to the foot of the bed, Garnet placed herself in the housekeeper's line of vision. She must not see who lay there, not yet.

'There has been an accident, Mrs Wilkes, would you please fetch hot water and towels, and would you show Mr Kane where to find the shotgun, a horse needs to be put to sleep.'

Having something to do providing a temporary opiate for her frayed nerves the woman bustled from the room.

'Tyler,' Garnet returned to the side of the bed, her voice soft with pity. 'Tyler, I would not have had it happen this way.'

'Have what happen ... my death?' A laugh mixed with pain broke from a mouth tinged with blue. 'I always thought vengeance held a sweet taste.'

'The doctor be 'ere.'

Florrie set bowl and steaming jug on a wash stand as the man with her crossed quickly to the bed.

Opening the black medical bag he had placed on the bedside table he looked at Garnet.

'How did this happen?'

'The carriage ... it tipped over.'

Placing a stethoscope to Tyler's chest the doctor listened a moment before straightening. 'Do you know who this man is?'

Glancing at Florrie she drew a short tight breath. 'Yes,' she answered quietly, 'he is Tyler Cadell ... my husband.'

'There is nothing you can do.' Tyler's eyes flickered open. 'Doctor or priest, neither can help me now.'

Taking Garnet aside the doctor spoke

quietly. 'I cannot speak for a priest, Mrs Cadell, but I have certainly done all that a doctor can do. His injuries are too severe for there to be a recovery. I am afraid you must prepare yourself for the worst. As for your housekeeper,' he looked to where Florrie Wilkes sat white-faced and trembling, 'this has proved a great shock for her but a sedative and a night's sleep should prove beneficial. As for yourself, you too have received a great shock, if you will allow I will send a nurse...'

'No, no thank you.' Garnet shook her head. 'That will not be necessary.'

'I will fetch my mother, she will nurse them both.'

'As you wish.' The doctor glanced at Judah standing just inside the room.

'Send for no nurse.' Tyler's voice was weak bur firm. 'Raschid ... Raschid, where the hell are you?'

Moving to the bedside, Garnet looked at the man who had hurt her so deeply but for whom she no longer felt any hate.

'Try to rest,' she took his hand, folding the fingers between her own. 'Raschid is not here, you sent him to Victoria House.'

'But I'm back now.'

Looking across the room to the tall figure standing in the doorway, a trickle of blood oozing from a temple wound that had knocked him unconscious, Garnet felt the world lurch wildly, her senses whirling in a sickening spiral. 'Raschid!' she gasped. 'Raschid!'

Chapter Thirty

'I always thought I would see you off, either dead or sent back to India.' Tyler laughed, flecks of blood bubbling on his lips, shrugging off the doctor who came to him. 'But I was wrong, wasn't I? I am the one to go.'

'He really should rest.' The doctor opened his bag.

'What do you think I'll be doing the remainder of eternity?' Tyler pushed away the spoon the man held to his mouth, his eyes resting on the pale coffee-coloured face of his manservant.

Recovered from the threatened faint yet still afraid that what she had seen was a figment of her own shock, that she only imagined it was Raschid had held her, Garnet kept her own glance on Tyler.

'Please,' she said softly, 'do as the doctor says and rest, you can talk with Raschid later.'

Coming now on short breathy gasps, Tyler's words spilled into the quiet room.

'No... not later, and not with Raschid but

with Richard.'

Taking the limp hand once more into her own, Garnet looked pityingly at the man whose life was bleeding away despite the doctor's ministrations. 'You are confused,' she murmured. 'There is no one of that name.'

'Not confused...' He coughed, a stream of blood trickling from the side of his mouth as he reached towards the man he had so often mistreated. '...not Raschid but Richard, he is my brother!'

His brother! That was impossible, they were master and servant! The loss of blood had weakened Tyler's mind, he was rambling, he did not know what he was saying; but meeting those eyes, still so bright and alert, she knew that he did. Tyler and Raschid were brothers!

Somehow finding the strength to lift himself from the pillow, Tyler's glance found his housekeeper.

'Florrie Wilkes...'

He was dying. Florrie clutched nervously at Judah's sleeve. Who could tell what a dying man might say, especially a man as vindictive as Tyler Cadell; did he intend to carry out the threat he had held over her head for so long, was he going to accuse her of killing his child here, in front of witnesses?

Holding tightly to Judah she stared at the

blood-soaked figure calling her to the bed.

Freeing her hand gently, Garnet went to the woman's side, her glance at Judah thanking him for being there.

'Florrie Wilkes...' Tyler gasped as Garnet urged the housekeeper forward, '...you know what I am guilty of...'

Clutching now at Garnet, Florrie Wilkes's whole body trembled. Tongue tied with apprehension of what was to come next, she nodded.

'...you can testify to the truth and you, sir,' he glanced at the doctor, 'I ... I call you as my witness ... before God and before you all I own this man my brother, Richard Cadell, we are born of the same parents ... we are of the same blood.'

Drained by the effort he fell back on to the pillow, his breathing fast and shallow, the stream of blood oozing from his lips a bright scarlet against the chalky white pallor of his face, but still the eyes held the will to speak.

'Garnet, I ... I married you for your father's property, I thought you of no real value...' Tiny bubbles of blood spewed from his throat as he smiled. '...a peppercorn woman! How... how wrong I was.'

The frightened housekeeper sobbing against her shoulder, Garnet's own tears streamed silently.

'Richard!' It was only a whisper now but as Tyler's eyes sought his brother's they held a new urgency. 'Richard,' he breathed, '...the child ... I ... I'm sorry, tell them...'

Dropping swiftly to his knees, one arm going gently across the injured man's chest, Richard Cadell touched his cheek to his brother's. For a moment Tyler smiled, then with one last glance at Garnet his eyelids closed and he lay still.

'So many years, Rasch ... Richard.' Garnet smiled at her own slip of the tongue. 'So many years yet you never complained, why? Why allow yourself to be treated that way?'

The funeral attended only by herself and Tyler's brother over at last, Garnet sat in the quiet little room in Queen Street.

'It was a promise I made to our mother.'

He was so like Tyler and yet so different. Garnet watched her visitor dressed now in dark grey morning suit and three-quarter-length black Chesterfield coat, a silk top hat balanced on his knee. He was handsome as his brother had been handsome, but where one had had fair hair and blue eyes the other had black hair and brown eyes. But that had not been the only differences. Garnet watched the sensitive mouth tighten with memories, the eyes fill with sudden pain. Tyler Cadell had been a heartless man mindful only of himself and the things he felt life owed him, but his brother was perceptive of the needs of other people, alive

449

to their comfort and well-being, putting them before himself.

'Our mother knew Tyler's shortcomings,' the rich deep voice went on, 'she knew the fear in his heart, a fear that might one day prove to be his downfall.'

'Fear?'

Meeting that moss-green gaze, Richard Cadell felt his heart tilt. Like her husband, she would be repulsed by what he had to tell, like Tyler, she too would be ashamed.

'Tyler was afraid of his ancestry.' He answered steadily though his heart thumped. 'It seems our paternal grand-father was Asian Indian, a fact that had not shown itself before my birth. When Tyler discovered the reason for the difference between us he never spoke to our father again. He virtually disowned them both. It broke our mother's heart. Father bought him a commission in the Army and he never visited the house in Simla until after both of our parents were dead. I told him of the promise I had given that I would take care of him, stay with him no matter what; but the only way he would accept that was for me to become his Indian manservant.'

'And I treated you like a servant too. Oh Richard, I'm so sorry.'

'No, you treated me like a friend.' Once more he caught the tenderness of her eyes and again his heart twisted but this time it was with the thought that she would never be other than just a friend.

'I hope we will always be that.'

It had been harder to say than she could ever have imagined. Garnet rose from her chair, moving restlessly to the rickety dresser that held the dishes for her potted meats. She had said she wanted him for a friend but the ache inside her said she wanted more than that.

'I'm sorry, I'm keeping you from your work.'

'No, no,' Garnet answered quickly. 'A neighbour and her daughter are cooking for me until ... until affairs are settled, but perhaps you have business elsewhere.'

He nodded. In a moment he would be gone and there would be no reason for their meeting again. Hiding the sting of pain she asked, 'Before you go, there is one thing I would ask.' Waiting for his nod she went on. 'Tyler did not pay the hundred pounds that released me from prison, was it Judah ... was it the money belonging to Lorcan and Marisa, money none of the others would take?'

A slight frown settling between his fine brows, Richard Cadell flicked an imagine speck from the silk hat. 'Does it matter? It's paid now.'

Garnet's reply held a note of demand. 'Tell me, Richard, I want to know. I must

451

repay it. Hepzibah and Judah were kind enough to me and it was kindness that led to their giving that money, but like them I will not take it!'

'It was not their money.' He flicked the hat again before looking across to her. 'It was mine.'

'Yours!'

He heard the surprise and smiled. How could he have a hundred pounds when Tyler rarely gave him a penny?

'My paternal grandfather was an Indian Princeling. Quite wealthy in his own right he showered my grandmother with gifts, one of which was a necklace of perfectly matched Burmese rubies. Knowing Tyler would claim everything in the event of the death of our father she gave the necklace to me, making me vow never to let my brother know of its existence. In the end it turned out to be all that was left apart from the bungalow in Simla, which by that time was too run down to be worth more than a few hundred rupees; my father, you see, married without telling the secret of his mother's lover and when my mother died he was overcome by guilt. He spent every penny keeping her memory alive.'

'And you sold the necklace, sold your grandmother's last gift to you? Oh Richard, you should not have, not for me!'

Only for you! He was across the room, his

452

arms about her almost as the tears spilled on to her cheeks. Only ever for you. The thoughts tore at him. What is a necklace without you there to wear it ... what would life be worth without you!

Her face pressed to his shoulder, the pressure of his arms about her, Garnet closed her eyes to the wonderful sweetness of the moment, but beneath the rapture of it her soul cried in answer. It will be empty, my love ... empty as it was before!

Any second she would break free, push him away from her but until then he would hold her as he held her in his dreams. Touching his lips to her hair soft and red-gold as an autumn sunset, Richard Cadell felt his heart would break. He loved this woman, loved her with all his heart but that too was a secret never to be told.

Releasing herself with a pain almost too bitter to bear, Garnet looked at the man who was her dead husband's brother, the man she would love to her life's end.

'I will pay you back, Richard,' she said chokingly. 'I will repay every penny but that will not repay your kindness, that is something I can never do sufficiently.'

Afraid his yearning must show he picked up the hat he had thrown aside, giving himself a moment to hide the emotions tearing through him.

'Just be my friend.'

Just his friend! The tenderness she had felt in his touch had been no more than comfort for a friend.

'I will always be that.' She smiled, her heart breaking as he turned away.

He could so easily have written to her. Richard Cadell guided the carriage through the crowded smoke-palled streets of Bilston. He could have left it to the manager of that bank to tell her, but after today he would have no further excuse for visiting Queen Street.

Promising a penny to the snub-nosed, ragged-trousered boy who grabbed the reins the moment the carriage halted he knocked on the door of the tiny house joined to the long string of identical buildings.

'Mrs Garnet don't be in.' Her brown skirts patched with blue peeping beneath an apron as spotless as her hands and face, a young girl smiled at him. ''Er be at the market but if you waits a minute I'll go change places with 'er. Shall I tell 'er who it be wants to talk?'

Giving the girl his name he entered the small room, warm and welcoming with its aroma of cooking meat.

'Is anything wrong, Richard?'

He turned as Garnet entered the room, her breathing rapid from running, several strands of auburn hair loosened by the

454

breeze caressing her flushed face.

'I'm sorry if I have worried you.' Richard apologised, watching her remove her shawl and hang it behind the door. 'It was thoughtless, I should have written.'

That way I would have been denied the pleasure of seeing you. Keeping the thought just a thought she reached for the teapot.

'Have you time for tea?'

'No, thank you, no tea.'

He did not want to be with her any longer than he had to. Unhappiness that was a constant weight on her heart pressed heavier.

'I came to tell you I have taken over the mortgage Tyler took out on Bentley House, I want you to live there, I will live here.'

'But how! I mean how on earth can you pay...?'

'Judah and I have gone into business.' He smiled at the look of utter disbelief. 'I first met Judah Kane the day of your release from prison. I asked him to keep secret the papers I gave him, the ones he returned to you the night my brother died.'

'Certificates of my birth and marriage, the registration of my baby's birth...'

'I had to get them out of the house.' Richard heard the anguish in that softly spoken reply. 'I knew Tyler was unstable, that given the first opportunity he intended to kill me. I knew also he would destroy all papers relating to his marriage, his wife and his child, that without those records no one would ever be able to prove a word of what he had done almost three years ago. I had often heard that the word of a Romany once given was never broken and I reasoned that could I get one of them to take those papers and have his word that when the time came he would get them to you, then Tyler would never be able to get hold of them. I did not misjudge Judah.'

'A wonderful man, as honest as the day.'

Seeing the smile that accompanied her answer, Richard swallowed the ache it brought to his throat. She had lived among the gypsies, had she fallen in love with one of them?

'That is the reason I have asked him to join me in the business I spoke of,' he went on. 'Tyler had possession of some fine horses, and everyone knows the best judge of horse flesh is a Romany ...so Judah agreed. He buys in the best we can afford, I raise their offspring and between us we sell and share the profits ... that is, of course, if the mistress of Bentley House will allow the use of her stables. It will be a successful venture, one that will repay the mortgage and return the house to you.'

'No, Richard, I can't.' Garnet shook her head. 'I cannot let you do that. You worked for Tyler, I will not have you work just as hard to give Bentley House back to me.'

'Then share it with me...'

Across the space between them Garnet saw the tenderness in his eyes.

'I love you, Garnet ... I have always loved you. Stay with me in Bentley House, I swear I will never touch you.'

'That would be too unbearable, to see you every day yet have you never touch me, to be unable to show you the love I hold for you.'

'Garnet ... Garnet, my love.'

One stride bringing them together he gathered her in his arms, his mouth claiming hers time after time.

'I love you so much.' He released her at last. 'But there is one thing I have long deceived you in. I am afraid it is going to hurt.'

How could Richard possibly hurt her? Sat beside him in the carriage Garnet smiled to herself. Only one thing marred her happiness but perhaps with time that pain would fade.

'We must walk from here.'

Calling the horse to a halt he threw the reins over a gorse bush close to the track overlooking a hollow in the gently rising ground.

Why had he not said they would call at the gypsy camp before going on? He must know she welcomed any chance of spending a

457

little time with Hepzibah.

Engrossed in the pleasure of hugging her friend, Garnet did not notice Richard walk towards where Judah stood at the base of the steps of the caravan.

'Garnet.' She turned as Richard spoke. 'It was not only those papers I entrusted to Judah.'

'Richard!' Her face pale as death, Garnet stared, her whisper barely audible. 'Richard … is it…?'

'Ebony.' He held out a dark-haired child, her pretty face flushed with sleep. 'Your daughter.'

'But I don't understand.' Driving on to Bentley House, Garnet looked at the face of the child held so tight in her arms. 'Why didn't you tell me?'

Richard shook his head. 'Before Tyler's death it was too dangerous; he found you, it was equally possible he could find the child… With Judah and his mother she was safe; and in the day immediately following that accident I could see that one more shock would be too much for you. Forgive me… I did only what I thought best for you and the child.'

'But that night … the dogs?' She clutched the child instinctively close, the memory of that terrible night alive and vivid in her mind.

Feeling the shivers of fear tremble through the woman at his side Richard wanted only to halt the carriage, to take her and her child in his arms, to tell her that never again while he lived would anyone or anything harm her. He had seen the look in the eyes of Judah Kane, seen the pain in them as Garnet had reached for the tiny figure; Judah too knew the agony of a love he could not speak of.

'The dogs were fed a large leg of pork,' he answered her question. 'I hid Ebony in the pantry then wrapped her shawl about the pork and topped it with a ball of black wool snatched from Mrs Wilkes's work basket, hoping from a distance it would look like dark hair, then I threw the whole lot into the compound. Tyler ranted and raved but luckily by the time he reached the yard only a few scraps of the shawl and bits of black wool remained. Then the same night I took the child to the Convent of our Lady of Grace and told them what had taken place. They agreed to care for Ebony sooner than have her taken to the workhouse. I visited as often as I could but always I had to wait until Tyler was not at home.'

'And Mrs Wilkes?'

Richard shook his head. 'She never knew anything about it. I couldn't take any risk. Tyler had the woman terrified, the least notion of her knowing what had really happened and he would have got it out of her if only with a whip.'

Glancing at the dark shape of the house as the carriage rolled into the stable yard, Garnet thought of that figure lying bleeding on the bed. What her husband had done was unforgivable yet now with her daughter safe in her arms she felt she could forgive. She had wanted vengeance, thought during those black empty days of revenge, but now...

'I wish I could have told Tyler,' she whispered, 'told him he had not caused his child to die ... I wouldn't have him go to his grave with such a weight on his soul.'

Coming around the carriage, Richard held his hands for the child. His smile understanding her reluctance to let the tiny bundle leave her arms even for a moment he lifted Garnet gently to the ground.

'I told Tyler,' he said quietly, 'when I knelt beside him and put my cheek to his, I told him. For all his wickedness I could not, for our mother's sake, let him die with so terrible a sin on his heart. Forgive me, I should have told you.'

'There is nothing to forgive.' Garnet smiled at the child cradled against her breast. 'We both thank you with all our hearts, the crescent moon and her mother.'

Later, with Florrie Wilkes's tears of joy dried and explanation given for the umpteenth time, Garnet touched her lips to the tiny forehead of her sleeping child before turning to the man stood at her side.

'Do you think what Hepzibah said can possibly come true?'

Richard Cadell looked at his brother's child, a child he had come to love as his own. 'I can't answer with any truth,' he said, 'but it seems all else the crystal foretold has come to pass and Ebony does have a birthmark of the predicted shape and in the place Romany folklore puts it.'

'Before the new century be reached its half way the crescent moon will bring freedom to the Romany...'

In the quiet of the nursery bedroom the words of Hepzibah Kane echoed in Garnet's mind. Would Ebony in some way be responsible for helping bring about that freedom?

Looking up into those clear brown eyes she whispered, 'You have done so much for me, Richard, you have given me back my life.'

Standing close to her, the rays of the night lamp sparkling like tiny rubies in her lovely hair, her eyes soft and tender as spring moss, Richard felt the love he had hidden for so long well up inside him. He had to hold her again, to take her in his arms just once more, to feel the beat of her heart against his own ... just once more...

'It was you,' the urge to touch her too strong he drew her to him, 'it is the love I

461

have for you which made my life worth the living.'

Her voice soft as his, each word filled with the same tenderness, Garnet smiled. 'I will try to go on doing so as long as I live.'

'Garnet!' It trembled on his lips. 'Garnet, I love you, I love you so very much.'

Lifting her mouth to his, she whispered her reply, 'I love you too, Richard, I think I always have.'

Wrapped in each other's arms, the rapture of love revealed itself in the touch of their mouths as kiss followed kiss.

'I love you,' Richard said again as she smiled up at him. 'More than anything I have ever known I love you, and I want you for my wife but the law dictates a wife may not marry her husband's brother even though that husband be dead.'

Love a glowing beacon in her eyes, Garnet kissed his mouth. 'In my heart I will always be Mrs Richard Cadell, and in my soul I will trust to the mercy of God. His love overrides the dictates of the law and His compassion is greater than that of the Church, He will not condemn what He in His clemency has brought about. In the eyes of God and in our own eyes we will be man and wife. We have our love, Richard, can we let that be enough?'

Lifting her mouth to his kiss, Garnet knew that it would.

The publishers hope that this book has given you enjoyable reading. Large Print Books are especially designed to be as easy to see and hold as possible. If you wish a complete list of our books please ask at your local library or write directly to:

Magna Large Print Books
Magna House, Long Preston,
Skipton, North Yorkshire.
BD23 4ND

This Large Print Book, for people
who cannot read normal print,
is published under the auspices of

THE ULVERSCROFT FOUNDATION